Anita Burgh was born in Gillingham, Kent, but spent her early years at Lanhydrock House in Cornwall. Returning to the Medway Towns, she attended Chatham Gramar School, and became a student nurse at UCH in London. She gave up nursing upon marrying into the aristocracy. Subsequently divorced, she pursued various careers – secretarial work, as a laboratory technician in cancer research and as a hotelier. She has a flat in Cambridge and a house in France, where she shares her life with her partner, Billy, a Cairn terrier, three mixed-breed dogs and three cats. The visits of a constantly changing mix of her four children, two stepchildren, six grandchildren, four stepgrandchildren and her noble ex-husband keep her busy, entertained and poor! Anita Burgh is the author of many bestsellers, including *Distinctions of Class*, which was short-listed for the Romantic Novel of the Year Award.

By Anita Burgh

Daughters of a Granite Land 1: The Azure Bowl
Daughters of a Granite Land 2: The Golden Butterfly
Daughters of a Granite Land 3: The Stone Mistress

Distinctions of Class
Love the Bright Foreigner
Advances
Overtures
Avarice
Lottery
Breeders
The Cult
On Call
The Family
Clare's War
Exiles

Tales from Sarson Magna: Molly's Flashings
Tales from Sarson Magna: Hector's Hobbies

ANITA BURGH

EXILES

ORION

An Orion paperback

First published in Great Britain in 2001
by Orion,
This paperback edition published in 2001
by Orion Books Ltd,
Orion House, 5 Upper St Martin's Lane
London WC2H 9EA

A CIP catalogue record for this book
is available from the British Library.

Typeset by Deltatype Ltd, Birkenhead, Merseyside
Printed and bound in Great Britain by
Clays Ltd, St Ives plc

For Billy who makes everything possible.

Chapter One

April

1

Just as she was about to push open the shutters, Kate Howard paused momentarily, her hand wavering. It was the same every morning, the same indecision as if she feared what lay outside. She didn't understand her action; she was the first to acknowledge how illogical it was. Why should she be afraid? She was happy, she had an idyllic life, she wanted for nothing – and yet. . . ! She told herself to pull herself together.

'Do you realise you do that every day? It's as if you're afraid to open them.' Smiling affectionately at her, Stewart stood in the doorway carrying a tray with a mug of tea, which he laid down on her bedside table.

'Silly, isn't it? I've this stupid idea that once the shutters are opened I'll find the view has disappeared overnight. That living here and you are just a dream.' She thought, but didn't add, that she was afraid to find herself back in England with her ex-husband, in the same old house with the same old problems. She didn't explain because Stewart always hated her speaking of her past. 'I'm a stupid old fool.' She was not sure if she had said that or merely thought it, for Kate had an intrusive inner voice that often

1

handed out advice when it was least expected. She smiled at how odd she sometimes found herself, and turned back to the window.

The shutters clattered open. The dense creeper, which covered the front of the house rustled as the birds she had disturbed flapped free into a complex aerial display above the terrace, screeching angrily at her as they swooped and pivoted back and forth. 'Sorry,' she apologised. She took a deep breath of the clear, unpolluted air. It had to be the best tonic in the world.

There had been a violent storm in the night, which was common in these mountainous parts. Consequently the earth smelt warm, almost musty. There was a sparkle in the air as if nature had had a spring-clean. 'Isn't that the loveliest valley in the world?' She sensed Stewart standing behind her and leant back. With his arm about her she immediately felt safe – she always did. Of course the view was there, just as it had been yesterday and would be tomorrow. If only she could rid herself of her illogical fears, which only exacerbated her real worries.

Their house stood high on a hill – a *suc*, the locals called it, a safety valve for the volcano of which this valley was part. The extinct volcanoes made the area the intriguingly beautiful place that it was. She leant out of the window and looked towards them: snow was still topping their summits even though it was spring. They were not jagged like the Alps but soft and benevolent-looking, like huge, comforting breasts. Although they were a good twenty miles from this particular valley, she felt they protected her, preventing the hordes from invading them. There she was again – allowing those unspecified fears to appear.

'Are you cold? You shivered.' Stewart held her tighter.
'No, I'm fine. Someone must have walked over my grave.'
'Ghoul!'

2

Fears and worries, worries and fears. Like the background needlework in a tapestry they were always with her, the backdrop to her life, affecting everything she did, marring her happiness, her joy. What dominated her worries, and diminished the others by its enormity, was the mystery of where her daughter Lucy was.

Nearly five years ago, clever, confident, selfish Lucy had simply dropped out of their lives. Kate was luckier than many others in a similar position, whom she had met in her days of searching for Lucy – she knew her daughter was alive. An occasional postcard would arrive to say she was fine, but there had never been a phone call.

One friend had even met her by chance but had sworn never to divulge where. Kate presumed she was in a squat or had become one of the street people. For a year she had gone searching in London. But now she had given up. If this was how Lucy wanted it, then that was how it had to be. But the constant nagging worry, like a canker inside her, never diminished, was constantly with her.

'Try not to think about her,' Stewart whispered in her ear.

'How did you know I was?'

'Because I'm part of you.'

'What would I do without you?' Her gratitude to him for his understanding, his patience, was enormous. He could never feel as she did, and she did not expect him to: Lucy wasn't his daughter. But she doubted if anyone else could have been a greater support.

He leant forward. 'Just look at that river. One hell of a lot of water must have come down from the Ardèche last night – it looks like Brown Windsor soup.'

This morning the Loire was tearing helter-skelter through the valley instead of meandering smoothly, like a sluggish ribbon of mercury, which was what it normally did. Across from their house the steep hills, similar to the one this

3

house stood on, were covered densely with forest and among the teeming animal life it was the wild boar who held sway. Strangely, the idea of them roaming so close didn't bother her at all; it was the shadowy dread that troubled her.

From the terrace immediately below their bedroom window, steps led to the garden. She was wrestling it from the wilderness about them – a task she was convinced would take her the rest of her life. The garden never failed to give her a sense of satisfaction. Of the sadly neglected plants she had inherited from the previous owner, and which she had pruned and mulched back to health, the forsythia was spent, the lilac finishing but the wisteria was about to open its buds. Soon the white blooms of the Boule de Neige would follow, then the roses, clematis and lavenders, which she had planted in abundance. The beauty of gardening was that there was always so much to look forward to. She sighed with contentment. 'You know, Stew, I still can't get over the idea that this isn't a holiday and we'll have to leave in a couple of days.' She turned round in his arms to face him.

'Heavens, woman, we've been here nearly four years. How long does it take you to settle?'

'Oh, I'm settled. It's just I can't believe my luck.' They turned back into the room.

'It's got nothing to do with luck. You've worked bloody hard to earn all of this.' Stewart crouched to see himself in her dressing-table mirror. He borrowed her brush to smooth his thick silver hair. She loved to watch him as he tidied himself up: he concentrated so hard he was not aware of her watching him. He pursed his lips, practised his smile, arched his eyebrows – he always did that, and she found his vanity oddly touching. 'The other day someone said how lucky you were to be published. I told them that the harder you worked, the luckier you became.'

'That was gallant of you. Who was it?'

'Some snooty woman – I can't remember who or where.'

More likely he'd made it up to make her feel good about herself – she'd caught him out once or twice saying things he couldn't back up. It was a rather endearing quality.

'Shall we fill the pool this week?' The winters were long here and by April she found herself desperate to be swimming. It was the only exercise she enjoyed.

'I thought next – it's still cold. Do you realise we had it up and running at this time the year before last? I don't know what's happening to the weather. No, I thought I'd ask Henri to tidy up the flower-beds and plant the last of those shrubs you bought. I forgot to tell you, I've ordered some fabulous pots from Gamme Vert for the steps.'

The worn, lichen-covered stone steps led to the swimming-pool. It was the only thing she had insisted on having when Stewart had been persuading her that it was in her interests to move to France. 'More likely in *his* interests,' Joy Trenchard, her literary agent, had commented acidly, as she tried to convince Kate that it was a bad idea. But Joy had a jaundiced view of most men and Kate hadn't listened to her. But it was odd, when she loved Stewart so much, that many of her friends hadn't taken to him. Still, that was their problem, not hers.

'You're shivering again. What's worrying you now?'

'Nothing. I was thinking about Joy, that's all.'

'That woman is cause for worry.' He laughed, but not sincerely.

'Stewart!' She pushed at him playfully. 'I don't understand why you don't like Joy. She's been good to me.'

'I don't dislike her personally. I just don't respect her as a professional. With a husband as rich as Barty Silver she's no

5

need to graft. You need a hungry agent, not one who's playing at it.'

'She isn't.'

'When was she last in London? She's forever swanning around the world. What good is that?'

'She's always e-mailing me. These days it doesn't matter where she is – instant contact, that's what the web has given us.'

'How can she keep her pulse on what's going on in publishing if she's never there?'

'She's got her partner. Faith Cooper's very good at her job.'

'But you're not one of her authors, are you? Half of the year you're one of Joy's orphans. It stands to reason that Faith'll put the interests of her own writers first.'

'I like to think she puts the interests of the agency at the top of her list.'

'You reckon?' This time his laugh emerged as a snort. 'And didn't Joy try to persuade you not to come here to live?'

'She didn't try to put me off in as many words.'

'Oh, come on.'

'She was concerned that I might be too cut off from the publishing world. You know, out of sight . . .'

'Yet she's never in London, so it's OK for her and not for you?'

'Darling, please, don't let's argue about Joy. It's such a lovely day, don't spoil it.' She stood on tiptoe and kissed him full on the lips. But his frown persisted.

'Fair enough. It's your career, not mine.' He turned towards the door. 'I'm going into Le Puy, anything you want?'

'A new printer ribbon. I think the one I have is about to run out. That and a diamond ring – can't think of anything else.'

'Solitaire or cluster?'

'Oh, cluster, I think, for a change.' It was a game they often played. In an odd, roundabout way, it made Stewart feel better about having no money. Two ex-wives and three children had seen to that.

She picked up her mug, which was emblazoned with the legend 'The Boss'. She insisted on using mugs. Tony, her ex-husband, would have had apoplexy at drinking out of such a thing – 'workmen's cups' the pompous fool called them. She hid a shudder as she looked at the tea. She had known Stewart for five years, and he still hadn't learnt that she hated milky tea. Before she tasted it she knew it would have sugar in it and she disliked that even more. She took a tentative sip so as not to hurt his feelings, then asked, 'Going into town for anything specific?'

'I've some wine to pick up.'

'Well, there's a surprise!'

'You needn't get uppity with me. You'll help me drink it,' he said sharply.

'Keep your hair on.' She forced a laugh. 'I didn't mean to sound critical. I don't mind how much you buy.' She was sure she had sounded flippant not cross, but then men, she had discovered, were always sensitive about the amount they drank – or, at least, Stewart was. 'It's going to be a lovely day.' It seemed safer to change the subject.

'You've already said that.' He was smiling again as he hugged her goodbye. 'Sorry – I guess I get a bit too sensitive that it's your money I'm spending.'

'*Our* money, Stew.'

Once she had heard the front door slam she crossed to her bathroom and sloshed the tea down the basin. She stripped, steeled herself to get on the scales – nothing lost but nothing gained either – and then stepped into her latest toy, a power shower. She'd only had it a month and already she couldn't imagine how she had managed without it.

Once, the height of luxury for Kate would have been to spend hours soaking in a bath – when she had time. She had always regarded her bathroom as her refuge, the one place she was guaranteed to be alone, away from her family. That's where she'd done most of her thinking; wifely thinking to be sure, the what-to-have-for-supper, the shall-I-redecorate-the-spare-room class of thinking. But there had been other thoughts too. It was in her bath that she'd allowed herself to acknowledge the shortfalls in a life that everyone else had thought perfect – everyone but her.

Now, with the shower jets coming at her from all directions, thinking was the last thing she did: she was far too busy with soap, shampoo and lotions. Invigorated, that's how the shower made her feel, she decided, as she wrapped herself in a bath sheet. She switched on the lights around the mirror – just like a film star's, she had thought when she had them installed.

Baths! She remembered how Gloria Catchpole, her first editor at Westall's, had queried, 'Kate, does this heroine of yours have a problem? She lives in the bath! She has a skin complaint? BO?' Gloria had laughed as she had pointed out the repetition in Kate's first novel. She had such a light editing touch, always disguising any criticism, always thinking of her writer's feelings.

'No, it's just that's where I like to do all my thinking. It seemed logical she should too,' she'd explained.

'Could she possibly do some of it somewhere else? Why not change the venue occasionally? Have her thinking on the bus or in the kitchen.'

'On the loo?'

'Exactly!' And, with a laugh, the lesson had been learnt – perhaps too well, for now Kate had ended up with a mental block: in the five books she had written subsequently – four safely published, the fifth just delivered – not one contained a heroine having a bath. Still, Kate wasn't one of the characters she created so she was free to think wherever she wanted.

If only Stewart and Joy could get on. Each year they were invited to stay at Joy and Barty's house in the Bahamas and each year she had to come up with an excuse not to go. The two of them together would have made it a holiday from hell.

She was pretty sure that nothing would stop his campaign against Joy. She was also almost certain that he was angling to become her agent instead. She also knew she would not listen. To Kate, loyalty was one of the most important virtues. If it hadn't been for Joy and her belief in Kate, they wouldn't be living here; if it hadn't been for Joy's expertise in negotiating her contracts Stewart would be working at a job below his capabilities and he'd be hating every moment of it, instead of having taken early retirement.

She began to blow-dry her short hair. She had thought she would never master it but she had, and doing it herself was preferable to going each week to the hairdresser's in the nearest small town. It was a meeting-place for the local women, so much like a club that on the few occasions she had been there she had felt an outsider. She had never managed to get the stylist, Martine, to understand how she wanted her hair done. And one day, if she wasn't careful, she might well emerge with that rich mahogany tint that was almost a badge for French women of a certain age. 'No colour!' the hairdresser had declared, with disbelief, on Kate's first visit. It was why she had it highlighted in London, where she felt more in control of the situation.

Not going to the salon also saved her from the agony of trying to speak French. She had resurrected her schoolgirl French, dusted it down and ventured to speak it, only to make a fool of herself. She always felt she must try to breaking-point the patience of the French with her emasculation of their beautiful language. She seemed to get worse rather than better, and now she spoke it as little as possible. If it wasn't for Stewart and his excellent command of the language they would be in a real mess.

As she applied her makeup she thought how odd it was that this was now part of her morning routine, yet when she had been with Tony she had not bothered. She went out of her way to look nice for Stewart and hadn't for him. That had been wrong of her. However, knowing Tony, she doubted he would even have noticed if she had worn mascara or not.

It was rare for her to think much about the past, these days – hers was not a particularly happy land to revisit, even before Lucy had disappeared – but when she did she was amazed at how fortunate she was now. Not that she and Tony had had a hard life together: compared with some, it had been a privileged existence. But somehow she had always felt guilty about it, as if she should have managed to do more than she did.

Now she was in control, and here, one man tended the garden and another the swimming-pool. A woman came in to clean the house, do the laundry and, most importantly, the ironing. Tony had always balked at the expense of employing anyone. Having acquired a wife he had decided that all household duties were hers alone – why should he pay when he had her? Her best friend of those days . . . She frowned as she remembered Pam. *Don't go down that road*, she told herself firmly. Pam had said Kate only had herself to blame. If she hadn't been such a good homemaker, Tony would have been only too happy to pay someone else. Perhaps Pam had been right, but Kate knew herself: whatever she did, she always had to do it in the best way she could.

Now there were no such problems. Now *she* paid, and gratefully, with no guilt, and was relieved of the monotony of housework. Yet it was only now when she had help that she could acknowledge she had often been bored with keeping house. But she had seen it as her duty and had got on with it, careful not to moan since her own mother had been a fully-fledged martyr to domesticity.

These days, apart from writing which took up most of her time, her only main task was preparing the evening meal. Cooking for two, she'd found, was much easier than cooking for a family, with their different likes and dislikes.

She studied her image in the mirror. Never vain, she allowed herself to think that she looked younger. At least, she hoped she did. Her inner voice kicked in: *What did you expect, woman, with the wonderful life you lead?* Once she would have felt guilty about that, but no more. 'You've earned it, girl,' she said aloud, and laughed with joy.

2

Each morning as Kate entered her workroom she felt like pinching herself that she was here, she was a success and that this room was her domain, her sanctuary. Of all the things that had happened to her perhaps this was the greatest luxury of all: a room dedicated to her work. Before, she had made do with the spare bedroom.

It was a delightful room and she had picked it out as soon

as they had seen the house. At the eastern end French windows opened on to a small enclosed terrace. In winter she would watch the birds she fed pecking away in the snow. In summer the windows were open and she could hear the sound of the fountain she had had installed, and the sun would pour into the room. On the south side another pair of windows opened on to the main terrace. Here she had her pot garden, another fountain was planned and, if they had guests, she could see them taking the sun as she worked and need not feel too shut off.

Yellow had seemed the right colour, echoing the sun but also because she had once been told it was the colour of inspiration. So why not? she had thought, as she chose a lovely primrose. The curtains were a yellow, white and blue plaid, and the *chaise-longue* was upholstered in the same fabric.

'All writers should have a *chaise-longue* for thinking on,' Stewart had said, when he gave it to her as a birthday present. She'd had her doubts, but she enjoyed lying on it even if she often nodded off rather than doing any constructive thinking.

She had her fax machine, answering machine, e-mail. She had four computers: one to work on, one as back-up, a lap-top for when she travelled, and the fourth for sentimental reasons – she had written her first novel on it.

In the corner was a large cabinet, with the filing piled on top, waiting its turn for her attention, which rarely came. She had a rack for her eclectic collection of CDs – she never knew what mood she would be in and which music she would want to play on her state-of-the-art Bang and Olufsen.

One wall was devoted to bookshelves. Here were all her dictionaries, reference works, and the many books she was sent but rarely had time to read. In pride of place were copies of the books she had written in every edition that had been published – hardback, paperback, large print, audio, in English and in the many foreign languages into which she had been translated. *Winter Interlude*, *Spring Moment*, *Summer Space*, *Autumn Fever*. She was often asked which was her favourite but, as if referring to children, she always answered that she loved them all although it wasn't strictly true.

Over her desk and beside her computer work-station was an oil painting of her old house in Graintry. Even if her marriage had failed, her affection for the house hadn't. She still missed it, and thought she always would. There were large photos of her children Steve and Lucy. The one of Lucy was a recent addition. There had been a time when a photograph of her daughter made Kate's heart shatter all over again. Putting it up had been a positive step forward.

On the remaining wall hung the covers of each of her books. As they were published, Stewart had them framed and presented them to her with a bottle of champagne – it had become quite a ritual.

Her day was filled. She began work early: in summer it was six or seven in the morning while it was still cool and also so that she could spend the afternoon by the pool; in winter she began at ten and didn't finish until five or six. One of her problems – which, as a published author, she had hoped would disappear – was that no one but other writers seemed to regard what she did as work. 'Earning a bit of pin money, are we?' an insufferably smug man had once asked her.

'No. Keeping all the financial balls in the air, actually,' she had snapped back, which had offended him, Stewart and their hostess so she had ended up apologising to all of them. Now when she was patronised she gritted her teeth and smiled as graciously as she could while longing to kick the offender in the balls. It was invariably a man.

Male authors didn't seem to have this problem – no one patronised them. Pehaps, she thought, because they might just kick. The men were given space and time, and what they did was treated seriously, as work.

She had female friends who wrote while juggling home and family, squeezing it into odd moments of freedom during the day. One wrote at night when everyone else was in bed, while another set the alarm for five and also scribbled on the bus going to the office. Compared with most, she was fortunate in that she had more time and space – but even then, though he too wrote, Stewart thought nothing of interrupting her, without a by-your-leave, to ask her all manner of trivial things.

'It's the lot of women,' she said to her computer, as she plugged it in. When last night's fierce storm had been forecast she'd thought it safer to disconnect it. 'Morning, Alice, did you sleep well?' she greeted it. She had called it Alice after a character in her first novel, who had been the reliable sort of friend she missed here. Stewart thought she was barmy to personalise it. She didn't know what he'd say if he knew she talked to it too.

She waited while Alice searched herself for any viruses that might have visited in the night – though who would want to contaminate Kate's computer she'd no idea, but Steve had drummed it into her that she must do this to be on the safe side when 'booting up'. The new language and phrases she used as a matter of course was amazing – her mother hadn't even been able to record on the video machine without phoning Kate first. If anyone had told her five years ago that one day, in her middle

14

years, she would be mildly computer literate she'd have thought them mad.

Dear Steve, how she missed him. One of the worst things about the move to France was not seeing her son as often as she would like. Accustomed to the long school holidays, she had not taken into account what would happen once he was working, with limited holidays. Now she knew. She had seen him once since the move, when she'd been in Harrogate to lecture to the Red Rose Society. 'You're not a mum any more, are you?' he'd said, as they grabbed a quick drink together. She remembered looking up sharply, afraid he was criticising her, but he was smiling broadly. 'You're a career woman now. I can't tell you how proud I am of you, Mum.'

'Sometimes what I've managed to achieve takes me by surprise – as if it's happening to someone else. However, I still feel like a mum – guilt-ridden that I'm not seeing enough of you.'

'Don't be daft. I'm old enough and ugly enough to look after myself. Of course I wish I saw more of you, but even if you were still at Graintry, it's one hell of a long drive up to here from the Chilterns.'

'Ugly you are not,' she'd chided him playfully. 'Fishing for compliments!' But she marvelled at how quickly he'd become a man. It seemed such a short time ago that he had been gauche and clumsy, his big feet forever tripping him up. His arms had been long and constantly moving, as if he never knew what to do with them and his oversized hands. Now he was a tall, well-muscled, tanned and handsome young man, and she was even more proud of him.

'You're happy, Mum?'

'Very.'

'You'd tell me if you weren't?'

15

'Of course.'

'You didn't when you and Dad were breaking up. Of course I knew, but you never said.'

'You were a child then, it wouldn't have been fair. But there's nothing for you to worry about. In the circumstances I'm extraordinarily happy.' They never spoke of Lucy – it upset him too much, though she knew he was angry rather than regretful. 'And what about you?'

'I get by.' It wasn't the answer she wanted to hear, but she knew her son: he wouldn't elaborate – not wanting to worry her, no doubt.

That conversation had taken place nearly two years ago. As each book was published she had expected that her publishers would summon her to London to publicise it, but they hadn't. And she and Stewart never seemed to get back to England as often as they had originally planned.

Her computer roared at her that it was ready. She had chosen jungle noises for it, a lioness roaring, an insect buzzing. Stewart didn't like them.

She clicked on the folder marked *Bitter Memories*. She was none too sure of that as a title – it might put readers off because it sounded a fairly miserable subject – but it would do for the time being. Come to think of it, she was none too sure of the book either: it wasn't going the way she had intended, a story of a broken marriage.

Kate was suffering through the time she dreaded most: she had delivered her latest manuscript, *The Lost Troubadour*, and she was waiting to hear if they liked it. Or not. It had been a new venture for her, an historical time-travel theme set in the years of the Crusades. Living close to Le Puy, whose bishop, as the Pope's legate, had launched the First Crusade, had made the research more interesting. However, Joy had had the devil's own job persuading Kate's

16

new editor at Westall's, Julie Forbes, that it was a good idea. 'You see, Kate, it's dangerous to change genres.'

'It's still fiction.'

'Yes, but Westall's have spent money building you up as a writer of contemporary novels for women. This is a completely new venture.'

'But I can't go on writing the same book.'

'I think they'd be a lot happier if you did. They like to be able to categorise authors.'

'I can only write what's in my head.'

She had ignored the advice and had ploughed on for the simple reason that she *had* to write it: it just wouldn't go away. Normally, when she had finished a book, she liked it for a couple of days but then she began to loathe it and was sure it was the worst thing she had ever written, and she couldn't sleep for thinking of all the things she should have put in and hadn't. But this time that hadn't happened. This time she still loved it, and was proud of it, and was sure it was the best thing she had done.

However, at night she couldn't sleep for worrying what her publishers thought of it and what she would do if they didn't like it. Would they demand their advance back? She'd probably spent most of it by now, not that she'd know – Stewart saw to the money side, leaving her free to write.

To occupy her during this hiatus, she had dug out *Bitter Memories*, mainly to keep herself occupied while decisions were made. It was a novel she had started some time back and had given up on. She now thought, or rather hoped, that she could resurrect it, rewrite parts and patch it up. She had decided yesterday, though, that she had been right the first time, it was crap. To make matters worse she was midway into it, the danger area for any writer; the plot was sagging, perhaps terminally. Someone had said a novel was a beginning, a muddle and an end – he or she had been right! Nothing she had intended was taking shape. She didn't like anyone she was writing about and, worse, couldn't care less what happened to them, so if she didn't, why should her readers? Since it was set in Cornwall, she fantasised about having them all fall down a mineshaft so that it ended prematurely – and to hell with everyone!

This thought cheered her as she imagined her editor's reaction. Julie Forbes was not her favourite person at the best of times. No doubt she'd have the vapours – Julie was the sort of woman who would go in for them. She was fussy, pedantic, lacking in imagination and, worse, humour. God, how she longed for Gloria and the fun they'd had – working with her had never seemed like work – but marriage and a baby had made her do what everyone in the publishing world said she never would: she'd given up. 'I'll be back in three months,' she had announced when she'd gone to have the baby, but that had been three years ago and they were still waiting, Kate more than most.

She reread what she had written yesterday, grimaced, highlighted it and deleted it. She looked at the calendar hanging over her desk, though Steve called it her work-station: two months hence was ringed in red. It was the deadline she had set herself, and she knew there wasn't a hope in hell of her making it. She was restless, couldn't concentrate and didn't know why. Last time she'd been like this she could blame the menopause and her deteriorating relationship with Tony. What was there to blame this time?

She accessed her *Pretty Good Solitaire*. She should never have downloaded this set of games from the web – there were over three hundred and she was wading through them all. They were serious time-wasters. She was addicted to them, she knew, but . . . what the hell? What else was she addicted to?

When he had been doing the accounts Stewart had queried her credit-card payment for them. 'What's this? It's in dollars.'

'Oh, that'll be for my *Solitaire*.'

'Well, you can't claim tax on rubbish.'

'I realise that. And it's not rubbish, I enjoy the games.'

And she did. She played them incessantly, and felt so guilty when she did. But she was annoyed that she had let Stewart get to her over it. When she had been married to Tony she had felt guilty about a multitude of things – in fact, there were times when she thought there was nothing to her but guilt. She had presumed that, with the divorce and his mean spirit just a memory, it would disappear, but it hadn't. Maybe she had been born with a guilt gene which had nothing to do with the men in her life and everything to do with her.

The phone rang. She looked at it in horror. If speaking French was hard for her, answering the phone in it was a nightmare. If she was lucky she would grasp one word in ten. Normally she let it ring until Stewart answered it. 'Ignore it,' a voice inside her said. Easier said than done. She picked it up gingerly as if it would sting her.

'Hello?'

'Kate, it's Sybil. Fancy a bite of lunch, just you, me and Netta?'

'When?'

'Today. Sorry it's such short notice but, well, Sim-Sim's away for the day and, on the spur of the moment, Netta and I thought it would be nice to have a girls' lunch. I've booked a table for one o'clock at Vidal's in St Juliene Chapteuil. Come if you can. My treat.'

Kate began to say she couldn't, she'd too much work, but

in mid-sentence she changed her mind. 'Why not? I'd love to.'

She had not met Netta Rawlinson but had heard a lot about her and she did not sound the sort of woman who would enjoy a 'girls' lunch'. Stewart wouldn't be back until early evening, and she was not enjoying the most productive of days where work was concerned. She patted Alice as she put her on standby. Maybe she'd do better tomorrow.

3

Stewart had met Sybil Chesterton in the local DIY store – or what passed for one in this part of the world. How Kate longed for a well-stocked B&Q! He had invited her and her husband for a drink but Kate hadn't been sure that she wanted to meet them. She and Stewart knew nothing about them, and perhaps they wouldn't have anything in common. But the invitation had been given and accepted, and she was going to have to meet them whether she wanted to or not.

However, on meeting Sybil, Kate discovered just how much she had missed chatting to a woman in her own language without the rigmarole of trying to explain what she meant; someone who understood her humour; someone she could categorise with ease as only the English can.

Sybil, she discovered, was a sweet woman, and over the months since they first met, she'd never heard her say a bad word about anyone. She was always pursuing a new enthusiasm, which she liked to share. While not especially close friends, they respected and had begun to see each other quite regularly.

Unfortunately Sybil's husband, Sim, was another matter: he was a pipe-smoking, pedantic individual, far too pleased with himself and the sound of his own voice. He also took it upon himself to offer advice to everyone about everything, even when they didn't want to hear it.

It soon became apparent that there were two Sybils. There was the smiling one who never stopped chatting – but only when her husband was not there. When he was, there was a dramatic change in her. Then she said little but when she did she appeared nervous; frequently she had to take one or two runs at a sentence, as if summoning the courage to say what she was thinking. And, oddly, she rarely made eye-contact.

Once or twice Kate had tried to broach the subject of what was wrong, but it was an impossible task. How could she ask baldly, 'Does your husband beat you?' Which was what Kate thought must be happening.

The doors of Vidal's swished open automatically for her and she entered the cool of the air-conditioned interior. With its white walls and marble flooring, it always made Kate feel as if she was in Italy rather than the Auvergne. Madame Vidal swept over to meet her. She was a bright-eyed, impeccably groomed, intensely intelligent-looking Frenchwoman who had intimidated Kate, at first, but she had now learnt that such women were more likely to have a smattering of English to ease communication.

'Cooee! We're over here.' Sybil was on her feet and racing across the restaurant towards her, arms expansively held wide open – one of the nicest things about Sybil was the exuberant way she always welcomed her friends . . . if Sim wasn't about. Her faded blonde hair was always tightly curled and reminded Kate of the results of the home perms she and her friends had indulged in in their teens. If she wore makeup, it was not discernible. Her pale grey eyes seemed always full of tears as if she had just stopped crying or was about to begin. She never wore bright colours, but

21

opted for greys and mauves, which always made her look far older than she really was. Not that Kate could have put an age to her with any confidence, she looked young-middle-aged or old thirties – impossible to differentiate since she was so ingrained with modesty that she rarely spoke about herself.

'Madame Chesterton, telephone.' Madame Vidal waved the receiver in their direction.

'Oh!' Sybil skidded to a halt, and looked concerned, glancing from the telephone to Kate.

'You get the phone,' Kate said, and made her way towards their table where a slim, beautifully groomed woman, in a peach silk dress with a perfectly toned deeper peach wrap around her shoulders, sat smiling indulgently at Sybil.

'Poor Sybil. Decisions, decisions – they drive her mad with anxiety. I'm Netta Rawlinson and you must be Kate Howard.' The woman's voice was deep and husky; she was blanketed in self-confidence. She held out a well-manicured hand with improbably long scarlet-painted nails.

So this was the Netta that Sybil talked about constantly, thought Kate, as she took her seat. From what she had been told, Netta had to be in her sixties yet had the style and skin of a much younger woman. And that confidence! How Kate envied women like that.

'I have to tell you, at risk of boring you rigid, that I've read *all* your books and gobbled them up with relish.' At which she smiled.

Kate sat transfixed. She had always thought a smile was a smile, but not so. She felt embraced by this one, as if Netta had smiled just for her. Kate had read about charm and realised now that she was meeting it face on. 'It doesn't bore me a bit. In fact I love praise, my ego needs it.' She smiled too but not with such success, and concentrated on unfolding her napkin on her lap. That had been a complete fabrication. Kate hated talking about her books since she had convinced herself that anyone heaping praise on her was fibbing to save her feelings. Since *The Lost Troubadour* was the only book she continued to like, she couldn't believe that anyone else would like the others, which she loathed.

'You're so fortunate. I would love to write.'

'There's nothing to stop you,' Kate replied, almost on automatic pilot, quite expecting her to trot out the usual excuse that she would write but she didn't have the time. This always enraged Kate: the person who said it had to believe that writers lived in a different world with a different time scale.

'Oh, but there is. I've time a-plenty but I'm too idle, or perhaps I'm using that as an excuse for being too dense. I hope you like Kir Royale? We've ordered a whole bucket of the stuff.'

'That's nice.'

'I've told Sybil she's to get drunk since the unspeakable Simon isn't with her, thanks be to God.' She opened her eyes wide then winked slowly.

She had the most amazing blue eyes, which she used to great effect. Kate found herself staring at Netta far too intently. 'Who's Simon?' she asked, flustered by her rudeness.

'You mean you've been fortunate enough not to meet her husband? Lucky you.'

'Oh, you mean Sim. I've met him several times.'

'Ludicrous name. I call him Simon on principle. Sim! And there *have* been occasions when I've heard Sybil call him Sim-Sim.' Netta shuddered dramatically. '"Sim" smacks of the nursery and makes it sound as if the man is still sucking a dummy. But, then, come to think of it, he is, isn't he,

23

constantly sucking on that revolting pipe of his? No doubt he was weaned too early. Why Sybil bothers with the unspeakable toad is an ongoing mystery. I've *begged* her to ditch him, but will she listen? No. But I'll have my way one day – I always do.'

Kate was aware that she was gawping again but she couldn't help herself. Was Netta being presumptuous or was it a joke?

'Sybil – nothing untoward, I hope?' Netta asked, as Sybil, in her customary rush, returned to them.

'I feel such an idiot. It was Sim. I left him a note to say where I was going only I forgot to finish it! The poor darling's been phoning every restaurant he can think of to track me down.'

'What's he want?'

'Oh, nothing.'

'Then why bother you?'

'It was no bother.'

'It most certainly was. We're nearly one glass of Kir ahead of you.'

'He likes to know where I am.'

'Nosy sod.'

At this, Kate looked at Sybil with concern, afraid that an argument might ensue.

To her surprise, Sybil was laughing. 'Oh, Netta, you are a one! You don't understand. He worries about me when I'm not with him.'

'He's a control freak, more like. Does your husband know where you are, Kate?'

'I said in my note I was meeting you but not where.'

'See? The man is too claustrophobic for words. Does he let you go to the loo unattended?'

'Silly, of course he does. Sim-Sim loves me and he cares –

24

that's why he has to know where I am. I like it. Now, let's see what there is to eat. I'm starving.'

When Madam Vidal returned with the wine list it was Netta who put out her hand for it, ignoring Sybil. There was silence for a short time as they all studied their menus. 'Divine! Stuffed pigs' trotters ... Oh, no, they've sweetbreads too. See, Sybil, my dearest? You're not alone in having problems with decisions,' Netta said.

When Madam Vidal appeared to take their order, Netta proceeded to talk to her in fluent and beautiful French, which made Kate squirm with envy. They talked in depth and with great knowledge about food, the quality of this and that, then had an even more intense discussion about the wine, which was most suited to which course.

'Netta's an expert on food and wine. Leaves me standing,' Sybil confided.

'Her French is wonderful.'

'Isn't it? I can't string one sentence together.'

Kate took this with a pinch of salt. She'd been out once too often with people who said they were hopeless then launched into an impressive flow of French.

'Sybil, for us I've ordered the *timbale* of langoustine, then the *sandre*. Madame has assured me it doesn't taste muddy – you have to be so careful with that particular fish. Then the fillet of beef with marrow and *morilles*. And you, Kate?'

'Oh, I'll have the same.' She hadn't intended to, she'd decided on the lamb, but she knew herself: she was incapable of ordering one dish without lusting after her companions' when it arrived. On the other hand, she wasn't too sure that she liked the way Netta had taken control. It wasn't her party, after all. Maybe she wasn't as nice as Kate had first thought. 'You speak the language beautifully. Were you born here?'

'No, but I learnt by far the best way. On the pillow.' And Netta laughed at Kate's expression.

'She says things like that to embarrass people, Kate. Don't let her get to you.'

'I'm not even trying to. It's the truth and if you can think of a better and more pleasant way to pick up a lingo I'd be most interested to hear it. Ah, the *amuse-bouche*. So delightful, so French.'

'You get these little tasters back home now.' Kate found that, suddenly and mysteriously, she felt quite protective of English restaurants.

'One never used to get them here in quite the same abundance, truth be told. I went to one restaurant and we had six! Can you imagine? We hardly had room for anything else.'

'Bet *you* did. Netta likes to say she eats like a bird, and I always say, yes, a vulture!' Sybil enjoyed her joke.

'I noticed you said "back home". Are we to infer that this isn't your home or, at least, you don't feel it is?'

'Did I? Force of habit, I suppose. I wasn't thinking.'

'Isn't it fascinating that when we're not thinking the truth has a habit of popping out?' Netta bestowed one of her wondrous smiles on Kate. But this time she was not so transfixed. This time she had decided she didn't go much on Netta after all.

The meal was a delight, and Kate was the first to admit that Netta had chosen well. Each course complemented the next, and the wines she had selected enhanced the food.

Despite her reservations about the woman, she was entertained as Netta held forth on a wide range of subjects. Once or twice she thought that Sybil looked at Netta like a mesmerised acolyte. Kate hoped she was safe with this best friend.

'Tell Kate about the day your mother disowned you. Go

on, I love that one,' Sybil urged her.

'Kate doesn't want to hear my boring old history.'

'You will, Kate. Go on, Netta, tell her.'

'I'd love to hear.' Which was half true.

'Very well. You have to understand that my mother was a loathsome old cow.' She paused as the wine-glasses were refilled. Kate hadn't particularly liked her own mother but she could never have imagined talking about her like this to a stranger.

'My problem was that Bernard, my husband, wanted children, and I didn't. I'm sure that was because of Mother. She quite put me off having children in case I turned out like her. Probably for the best, anyway. I'd have made a ghastly mother. So he divorced me.'

'Wouldn't it have been a good idea to have sorted this out before you married?' Kate asked.

'Probably, but I was young and foolish and thought I could change his mind.' She stopped to sip her wine. Kate was sure she could hear a tightening in Netta's voice as if she was having to control it. 'You see, his longing for offspring was greater than his love for me. And my fear of motherhood was greater than my love for him. Still, it all worked out for the best. He has four sons – his second wife is particularly fecund if somewhat large in the beam.'

'If you'd had a son with him, would you still be with him?' Sybil asked.

'How the hell do I know?' Netta paused for what seemed a long time, as if mulling over the question. 'I'm not sure that I would still love him . . . Or would I just imagine I did. Or perhaps . . .'

'Familiarity breeds contempt?'

'Something like that, Sybil. Who could tell?'

'Perhaps it's hard for you because the relationship ended prematurely – like unfinished business?' Kate suggested.

27

'Good heavens, forgive me. What an impudent thing to say to someone I've just met.'

'It could be,' Netta said, as if she was not in the least put out, or hadn't even noticed Kate's apology. '"You were born a fool and you will die a fool." That was my mother's reaction when I told her. "I can't imagine how the poor man has put up with you this long." Such a sensitive soul, my mother.' She laughed gaily enough, but to Kate it sounded hollow. Netta's voice had changed as she repeated her mother's words, taking on the unmistakable tone of an elderly upper-class woman. Not only that but she sat like one, *became* one in front of their eyes. Kate wondered if she had ever been an actress. 'She assured me that no one else would be foolish enough to marry me. "Second-hand goods" is how she described me.'

'Charming!' Sybil said, affronted for her friend. 'Still, she was wrong there, wasn't she? Netta's had loads of husbands – well, four, haven't you?'

'Too many!' Again the laugh that wasn't a laugh. 'Anyhow, that day I left home vowing never to return. But when I heard my mother was dying I was stupidly drawn back – I can't imagine what I hoped to achieve.

'"Netta? Is that you?" The room was dark and fusty, already it smelt of death. "What are you here for? Sniffing around, hoping to be remembered in the will?" Terminally ill the old bitch might have been, but there was nothing wrong with her spite, which was still in good heart. "You can choose one item from this room, that's all." I was about to tell her what she could do with her possessions when I saw the birds she kept in cages against one wall. "I'll have these," I said, and grabbed them while she was screeching that I couldn't take them. Then I let them all fly free in Hyde Park.'

'Wouldn't they have died?'

'No, Kate, they were song-birds, nothing exotic. Her having them had always offended me. Now, where was I?' Netta continued. 'At the time, my lover worked in the City. I lied to him about the family firm – concocted a story about a vast law-suit in the United States that was pending and which the company could never win. Shares were sold in a matter of hours. So my cousin to whom mother had left her millions got far less.' She laughed again and this time it sounded genuine.

'For all that, he still got more than you, Netta. I'm always telling her she should write to her cousin and explain her circumstances. He owes you something. After all, blood is thicker than water,' Sybil counselled.

'Darling Sybil, how predictable you are.' Netta patted her friend's hand.

'Isn't that such a dramatic story, Kate? I said to Netta she should tell you and then you could write a book about her. She'd love that, wouldn't you, Netta?'

'Why do you tell it when it obviously pains you to do so?' Kate asked.

'Perhaps if I tell it as a story then I can begin to believe that that is all it is.' She was suddenly serious and looked at Kate with a penetrating stare, as if realising that she, too, knew about pain.

'I think it's one of the saddest stories I ever heard.'

'Nonsense. You'd be amazed the number of women I meet who actively loathe their mothers.'

'I didn't mean that. I meant that it was sad you still loved Bernard.'

'Piffle! I never said I did.'

'You didn't have to,' Kate found herself saying.

Netta paused as if unsure how to continue. 'I'd have no doubt divorced him years ago,' she laughed in an abrupt way. 'But if you can use it, be my guest.'

29

'I think *you* should write it.'

'Me? I wouldn't know where to begin.'

'I'll help you.'

'I couldn't.'

'You won't know until you try, will you?' Suddenly Kate felt protective towards this woman, which was odd when she had decided that she didn't like her.

4

'So how was your girlie lunch?' Stewart was waiting for her when she got home.

'It was fun . . . Well, fun isn't quite the right word.' She took the gin and tonic he had poured for her at the sound of her car on the gravel. 'In fact, it was rather sad. Sybil's friend Netta Rawlinson was there. She's had such an unhappy life. I'd almost decided I didn't like her, that she was too bossy for words and could be quite sharp, and then, it was strange, I felt an almost overwhelming pity for her.'

'I wouldn't worry about that one. From what I hear she's quite capable of looking after herself. I gather she's a right old sponger and has covered a fair bit of carpet in her time.'

'Stewart! I hate that expression. How could you possibly know that about her? You haven't even met the woman.'

'I was told. She's not averse to snatching a husband if she takes a fancy to one. You should beware. I gather that despite her age she's still an attractive woman.'

'God, and they say women are the gossips.' She took a large sip of the drink she hadn't really wanted but now found she needed. 'What did you do today?'

'I bought the wine that so bothered you.'

'Stewart, it didn't. That's not fair.'

'I had *moules* and *frites*, met up with Sim and had a beer with him at the English pub. We discussed the cricket club I want to set up. Then moseyed home. Stunningly exciting day.' He was pouring himself another drink.

'I thought Sim was away on business.'

'He'd been to the bank. Another gin?'

'No, thanks.' She looked at him anxiously. He was in a mood. She'd noticed before that if he drank beer during the day he was likely to get grumpy. It was something to do with drinking in the sun, a friend had once told her.

She stood up. 'I think I'll check my e-mails.' If he was going to be argumentative, she'd make herself scarce.

'But I've bought some *foie gras* for supper.'

'Not for me, thanks. I couldn't eat another thing.'

As she let herself into her workroom, she was pretty sure that there would be no e-mails for her. She'd just wanted to get away from Stewart, not just because he was in a bad mood but because he had annoyed her with his chauvinist talk. *Girlie lunch!* How patronising. He was a fine one to talk; he'd never been averse to a night out with *the boys*.

She switched Alice on and clicked on to her *Solitaire* program. She was so rarely annoyed by Stewart that when she was it made her uncomfortable. She felt restless and itchy, as if she was being disloyal. Was it her imagination or were they snapping at each other more than they usually did? Correction: was Stewart getting irritated with her more easily? And, if so, why? She was the same as usual, she was sure she was. So what was wrong with him? She must try to find out without causing more exasperation on his part.

All her life Kate had avoided rows. Friends said she'd crawl a hundred miles rather than be involved in one. She knew the reason why: her parents had been in a constant state of armed warfare and she'd witnessed enough rows in her childhood to last her a lifetime. She often wondered if when she and Tony were together she'd been more assert-ive, argued more, things would have been different. But then, if that was so, she wouldn't be with Stewart and she loved him far more than she had ever loved Tony.

She ignored the ringing of the telephone. Stewart would answer it. 'It's for you,' she heard him call, and only then picked up the receiver.

'Mum, it's Steve.'

'Darling, are you all right?'

'Mum, you are funny. This is the twenty-first century and people make phone calls all the time, not just when there's a drama.' He chortled at her customary anxiety. 'What's with Stewart? He was bloody short with me.'

'Was he? You must have imagined it. He's fine.'

'He sounded drunk.'

'Well, he isn't.'

'Trouble with him is, he doesn't have enough to do. He needs a job.'

She let that pass. It wasn't her style to agree or disagree with her children about her lover. 'To what do I owe this lovely surprise?'

'I'm having to go to Paris next month. I might be able to wangle a day off and get down to see you.'

'How wonderful! What will you be over for?'

'A garden I've been asked to look at.'

'In Paris? Good gracious, doesn't your boss want to go?'

'No.' There was something about the way he said it that made her frown. Had he been sacked by the large firm of landscape gardeners he worked for? She had been edgy when he had given up his job as an under-gardener at a stately home in Yorkshire. He'd said the new job had better prospects, and she hadn't known enough about the subject to argue with him. Best not ask – he'd tell her when he wanted to.

'When?'

'I don't know the dates for certain yet, but I'll call you when I'm there.'

They talked a short while longer but when he said he was rushed she had reluctantly to replace the receiver. When wasn't he rushed? she wondered. It was ironic: Steve had always been the slow one compared to his smart, bright sister. At sixteen he had known exactly what he wanted to be: a gardener. She smiled at the memory of his father's fury: it was not the sort of job he regarded as proper for his son – stupid snob. She clicked on yet another game – *Rainbow Fan* for a change. Who could have foretold that he would knuckle down and prove himself a natural gardener? Whereas Lucy . . . poor Lucy . . . The misery wrapped its tentacles around her.

'What did Steve want?' Stewart was standing in the doorway.

'He's coming for a visit. Isn't that lovely?'

'For you it might be. He was bloody short with me.'

'Surely not. You must have imagined it. He was on fine form.'

'You could have fooled me. Sure you don't want any supper?'

'Positive, thanks.'

How curious that they had said the same about each other. Perhaps Steve had been right about Stewart, though. She always told friends that he'd taken early retirement but in truth he'd been given the push. His speciality as a journalist had been heavy in-depth political interviews and he'd been good at it. Then one day he'd been summoned by his editor to be informed that, with the advent of spin-doctors, articles like his were no longer in demand. She had thought it odd so had not been surprised when a colleague of his had confided that Stewart and the editor had had an almighty row, something to do with his expense accounts and not turning up once too often. As this acquaintance had said, with marked glee, he'd cooked his goose and been sacked.

Several times she had wondered if she should have reported this conversation to Stewart, discussed it with him and sorted it out once and for all, but Kate believed that people should be allowed to confide things when they wanted to.

Stewart seemed resigned to not working – certainly he hadn't bothered to look for another job – but in any case Kate had suggested that he could now concentrate on the novel he'd always wanted to write but, with his professional obligations, had never been able to. She was earning enough to keep them both. He had been reluctant to take her up on this offer and it had taken her months to persuade him to make a start.

'How would you feel about moving to France?' he had asked one night, out of the blue. 'You'd be better off there, fewer distractions, less call on your time. And we could scribble away together, have two desks side by side like Victoria and Albert.'

'Oh, I'm not sure. I mean, what would it cost?' At which he had taken from his briefcase some brochures he had picked up at a French property fair in London.

She glanced at one or two. 'But I like England.'

'You'd save a mint – just look at some of these prices.'

'But what if I sold this cottage then changed my mind? You know how volatile the housing market is in England. I might find I couldn't afford to come back.'

'You'd never want to, once you were there. And why sell up? Property is so much cheaper in France that you could let this and still afford to buy.'

'I'm not so sure. I need to be here – it's the English I write

34

about. I can't risk losing touch.'

'Ah, but therein lies the beauty of it. If you were away from here you would be able to see the country and its inhabitants far more clearly. It would make writing easier.'

'But I've only just moved here. I'm hardly settled.'

'Then it won't be such a wrench to let it go, will it?'

She was not convinced and it had shown on her face.

'You should live a little, Kate. Honestly, you'd love it. Just look at these brochures. You don't have to do anything you don't want to do.'

Now, nearly four years on, she could see how it had all come about. She had been in that phase of their relationship when all she wanted to do was make him happy and, against her better judgement, she had agreed to look. But also seeping into her mind had been the thought that if she could get right away it would be easier to deal with the misery of not seeing Lucy.

They had come to France on a recce – 'Just to see,' as Stewart kept repeating. She had not been keen on the various places they'd been to until – she remembered it as if it had happened only yesterday – one morning, two weeks into their holiday, they descended a steep hill and there, laid out before them, protected by a huge red statue of the Madonna, was the most lovely town she had ever seen. She promptly fell in love with it. The red-roofed houses cascaded down the steep hills on which the town was built. From the wide main boulevard, with the ubiquitous plane trees, led a tangle of myriad narrow streets and appealing squares. Stewart had mocked the statue, calling it ugly and creepy, but Kate loved it from the beginning.

Of course, there had been problems – any move threw them up – but now they were settled, and despite her inability to speak the language, she felt totally at home and could not imagine moving ever again. Unused as she was to

35

having a man about the house all day every day, she had wondered that Stewart's constant presence might strain their relationship; instead she found she liked it. It was nice to have him around and as a consequence she was never lonely.

There wasn't space in her workroom for two desks and two computers, so Stewart had his own study further along the corridor, decorated to his taste, with his books and knick-knacks. The first year he had worked diligently, but each subsequent year he had done less and less. She hadn't heard him typing for ages and she had given up asking how it was going since he invariably said he couldn't find time to write. She'd let that pass, and carried on working.

Remarkably, although this had all been Stewart's idea she appeared to be more contented than him. Maybe Steve was right, she thought again. Perhaps he was bored and needed a job. But what? He had one at his fingertips – he could write, and if not the novel perhaps he could get some journalistic work; she would have to suggest it to him.

She packed away *Solitaire* and clicked the mouse on the Outlook icon. There was an e-mail. As she read it she thought she would be sick.

> Darling, we've a problem. We must talk. Any chance of you coming over? I'm afraid it's thumbs down for *The Lost Troubadour*. Love you, Joy.

5

'So, what did you think of her?' Sybil asked, as she manoeuvred her car adroitly through the rush-hour traffic.

'I liked her.' Netta hung on to the strap for grim death as, with a blasting of the horn, Sybil overtook a truck and yelled at the driver. 'For someone who claims they can't speak French you surpass yourself at times, Sybil,' Netta said, with as much of a laugh as she could muster in the circumstances. Sybil, normally so quiet and docile, became a raving lunatic behind the wheel of her car. Netta had decided long ago that it must be her way of releasing the tension and frustration of living with the unspeakable Simon.

'She's no side to her at all, has she?'

'Why should she have?'

'You know, being so successful. It hasn't gone to her head, made her grand or difficult. She's quite the most easy-going of people.'

'She's probably a bit long in the tooth for fame to have spoilt her – if she's famous, that is.'

'I'm sure she is, perhaps not like Jilly Cooper but people who read know all about her.'

'Then perhaps with success coming later in her life it's easier for her to handle.' Netta closed her eyes as Sybil's Mercedes nearly swiped the side of an inoffensive Peugeot that wasn't moving fast enough for her. 'I don't think she liked me.'

'Netta! How can you say such a thing?'

'Because it's true – and I wish you'd keep your eyes on the road and not on me, darling.'

'But everybody likes you, you know that.'

'Don't be silly, of course they don't. None of my ex-husbands for a start.'

'That *was* a bit presumptuous of her to say those things about Bernard, you know. I wouldn't dream of saying things like that. It's rude.'

'Rubbish. She was just saying what she thought. After all, it was I who broached the subject. I think that automatic-ally confers a right on the listener to say what they think. And, darling Sybil, please do me a favour, stop telling me what I know when half the time I don't.' The minute she had said it she glanced at Sybil, saw that she was biting her lower lip and regretted it. Why was it that when someone could be hurt so easily a demon inside her always made Netta want to do just that? She patted Sybil's arm. 'That was uncalled-for. I'm sorry. Lunch-time drinking always makes me grumpy.'

'Don't give it another thought.'

'Care to come up for a glass of wine?' she asked, as they pulled up outside the tall, narrow house where she lived.

'I'd love to, Netta, but I've got to get back. Poor Sim will be wondering where I've got to.' She looked genuinely concerned as she said this. She really was the sweetest person Netta knew.

'Next time,' she replied, in a jaunty manner as if it didn't matter, when it did.

'I nearly forgot.' Sybil turned and took a carrier-bag off the back seat. 'Some books and magazines for you.'

Gratefully Netta took the bag and held it to her as she stood on the uneven pavement and waved as, far too fast and noisily, Sybil drove off.

In the stone-flagged entrance hall she wound her way around the collection of prams, bicycles and boxes which always littered it. To anyone unfamiliar with the clutter, entering this building at night was a dangerous proposition. She pressed the light switch, and the dim bulb did its best to illuminate the steep flight of stairs; well acquainted with the steps, Netta did not stumble in the gloom since she knew where the worn ones were and where one was split. A couple of years ago she would have raced the light on its timer switch, but not any more: it always beat her. Now she would be plunged into darkness before she reached the first landing and every landing thereafter, until she reached her flat on the fifth floor.

'You're getting old,' she said aloud. The time would come, she supposed, when she would have to think of moving to an apartment on the ground floor. Not that she wanted to, she loved her little eyrie with its lovely view of the roofscape of Le Puy, with the cathedral and the Red Lady majestically protecting them. If she leant out of her bedroom window she could just see the statue, which she loved best of all.

'Hello, Tam, my darling,' she said to her Siamese cat who, at the sound of her key in the door, had come running, only to sidle away as if regretting his first enthusiasm. 'Sulking, are we? Did I leave you? Poor sweetheart. Will some food put things right?' She delved into her handbag and brought out the scraps from her plate, which she had asked Madame Vidal to pack for her, although Sybil had made a fuss and said it was embarrassing to ask, that she'd be happy to buy a tin of cat food. What was wrong in asking for the titbits for her pet? Sybil knew her circumstances yet, sweet as she was, she could sometimes be quite insensitive. In the last few years she had discovered that those with money had little comprehension of what it was like to be without.

Tam's scowl became a mighty purr at the sight of the meat in his bowl, which she placed on his feeding mat for him. She smiled indulgently as she watched him tuck in. She would have liked a dog – she'd always had dogs in the past, salukis, wolfhounds, real dogs, not the yapping lap breeds. Now any sort of dog would do, yappy or not. But she couldn't afford one, not with the vet's bills and the cost of their food. Cats were cheaper to maintain. She had rescued Tam from some English people who were returning home when animal quarantine regulations were still in place. They said they didn't want to inflict kennels on him, but Netta thought it was more likely that the cost had put them off. She didn't understand some people. Why get an animal if they might have to leave it? They wouldn't do that to their children. 'Come to think of it, had I had children I would have found it a lot easier to abandon them than you, Tam.' The cat twined around her leg, purring mightily at the compliment.

'Now what to do?' That was the trouble with lunch, how to fill the rest of the day. Odd that it was only a problem when she went out. Well, that wasn't strictly true, she told herself. An appointment or not, the days were long and the loneliness which was now her constant but unwelcome companion never left her.

'Come back to England,' her godchild had suggested, when she last came over to visit Netta.

'I don't know anyone there any more. They're all dead.'

'Oh, come on. That can't be true. You're not *that* old.'

'No, but *they* are. I've always preferred older people to those of my own age group.'

This wasn't strictly true, but she did not want to burden the child with her problems. There were times when she would like to go back, usually when she counted up how many years of life she had left – if she was lucky. She'd been reading in the newspaper only yesterday of an *elderly* woman being attacked, only to discover that she was sixty, which meant in the eyes of the world, if not her own, that she would be labelled old too. That was a sobering thought.

No, she stayed here because this was the only place she could afford. While the utilities were much as they would be in England, food was cheaper and rents most certainly were. Where in England would she find three rooms plus kitchen and bathroom with the heating included at such a modest rent, and with such a wonderful view? Nowhere.

She poured herself an Ambassadeur – not that she liked it: it reminded her of the malt extract her nanny had made her have each winter. As with so many things, it was all she could afford. She kicked off her vertiginously high heels and sank into her battered but comfortable wing chair – another thing she'd adopted from returning Brits and it was just as well she had: no French chair could compete with it.

Having started on this line of thought she couldn't stop. What would become of her when she was really old, if she became ill? She had no permit to live here, and she was not in receipt of the minimum income the French insisted on before they would give her one. She didn't blame them: it was to prevent her becoming a burden on their state. Why should they take responsibility for her? She'd never given them anything, except the taxes on her meagre shopping. When Mike was alive and they were living here they had never got round to applying for a permit, just as Mike hadn't got round to changing his will. Such a disorganised couple they'd been.

Dear Mike. How she missed him. What fun those few short years together had been. She'd never thought about the future and what might happen. Why should she? She'd always assumed that she'd die first. Not because she'd been ill but because he was fifteen years younger.

Their life together had been simple. Mike sometimes sold a painting, more often he didn't. They'd tried various ways to make money. None had worked. Mike had bought their house near Vorey for peanuts, and they had a small income from his trust fund and an even smaller one from hers. But they'd not wanted much. Their heady love had been a banquet to them.

Now all she had left of him were his books, a couple of his paintings and his name. She'd never counted how many times he'd asked her to marry him and she'd always said she would . . . but next year. Then suddenly there were no more years, and she was alone, and his unchanged will had left everything to his sister, who had never liked Netta from the beginning so she hadn't bothered to ask her for help. But, then, she knew herself: even if the woman had liked her she wouldn't have asked. Pride was a most uncomfortable companion – the twin of loneliness.

Mike's sister hadn't liked her and now this new woman, Kate – Netta just knew she had taken against her. She couldn't blame the woman, it was Netta's own fault. Her problem was, and always had been, that when she wanted someone to like her she often went overboard and ended up alienating them. It had always been so. 'Showing off' was what her mother had called it, when really all she was doing was trying to amuse. What on earth had induced her to tell that stupid story about herself and her mother? Neither of them came out of it well. And she could be so bossy, and that was so unattractive, and she didn't know why she was but she could never seem to stop herself – especially when she was with Sybil.

The thought of meeting Kate had excited her: she'd always had a secret yearning to write – not that she had ever told anyone. Maybe Kate would have helped her – fat chance now. Perhaps if she asked her to lunch? It would have to be next month, though – no pennies in the coffers at the moment.

It never failed to astound her that no one knew how she felt about herself. She knew the world saw her as a confident woman, frightened of nothing. That was a laugh. She was a seething mass of insecurities, she always had been. Why she bothered to pretend otherwise was a mystery to her.

She looked at her empty glass. Could she face another? No, not really – she longed for a decent bottle of wine or a whisky. She'd make a cup of tea, better for her. She went back to her tiny but immaculate kitchen. It never failed to surprise her how tidy she managed to keep everything. When she'd had space she'd been the messiest person in the world but living in such a small confined flat the only way to keep sane was to be neat and orderly. She'd love her dear old nanny to see her now.

It was early but she might as well go to bed. She took her tea and one of the magazines Sybil had given her. She lay on the bed, but she didn't read. She couldn't concentrate. Loneliness kept intruding on the words.

She shouldn't have sat thinking of Mike. It always had this effect on her. Would the grieving never end? Would a time come when she could think of him and not be sad? How she longed for him, *ached* for him. Was it wrong of her to want someone in her life to care for her? Was that disloyal of her? Someone who'd say, 'Don't worry, it'll be all right.' Someone who'd tell her, 'Leave it to me.' Someone to love her, to cuddle up to, to lie here with her and hold her. Take away this infernal loneliness. A tear slid from her eye, but only Tam was there to lick it away.

6

The next day Kate flew from St Etienne; she didn't feel up to dealing with the Lyon traffic, which was bad at the best of times. Now settled in the plane she gazed out of the window at the lovely patchwork of the vast French country-side beneath the wings and didn't see a thing.

No drinks were offered on this flight, and the sandwiches were overpriced. Not that it mattered, she couldn't face a thing. She supposed she would have to get used to flying in this economical way in the future, if money was going to be tight. Her stomach lurched at the thought.

To say she felt battered was no exaggeration. The memory of last night was still too clear in her mind. She wished she could obliterate it, but it wouldn't stop replaying in her head.

She had been crying when she went through to the sitting room.

'Kate, what on earth's the matter?' Stewart jumped up, looking concerned.

'They don't like *Troubadour*.'

'They what? Nonsense!'

'There was an e-mail from Joy . . . I've just phoned her. They don't want me—' She burst into tears again. She knew crying wasn't helping her but she seemed unable to control herself. She was vaguely aware of Stewart pouring drinks.

'Love, sit down. Drink this – it'll help.'

'Thanks.' The smile she tried to give him failed, emerging lopsided as if she had had a minor stroke. He had poured her a large brandy, which she loathed but she sipped it dutifully as if it were medicine. 'I felt something was wrong. I feared this would happen.'

'You never said.'

'I didn't want to worry you and . . .' She didn't finish the sentence. She had been about to say that she'd been trying to get hold of Joy for ages but she knew that, even at a time like this, Stewart wouldn't let slip a chance to moan about her.

'And what?'

'I don't know, I've lost my drift.'

He sat down opposite her. 'Now, tell me right from the beginning what has happened.'

'It seems that Joy has been trying to negotiate with Westall's for weeks. It was why I hadn't heard anything. She didn't want to distress me until she was sure. She was very sweet . . .' At the memory of Joy's voice, commiserating, cajoling her, the tears threatened again. She dug in her pocket for a tissue and blew her nose.

'I'm just amazed she found the time,' Stewart said bitterly.

'Not now, Stew, please.'

He had finished his drink already and he held out his hand for her glass to refill it, but she declined.

'They said it was pedestrian writing, that my characterisation was weak and that they were disappointed in it.'

'That's the best book you've ever written.'

'That's what Joy said to them. And she said that's what I thought too. And they said the problem was that when an author thought *that*, it was invariably their worst . . .' The word 'worst' came out as a muffled little wail.

'Bloody cheek. Typical of editors who can't write to try to destroy those who can.'

'I can't believe that. Admittedly Julie Forbes isn't my favourite person, but she's fair and she loves her books and her work.'

'You were always too soft with them. But they won't get away with this. Oh dear me, no!' It was at this point that Kate stopped concentrating on herself to realise that Stewart was verging on fury. It gave her comfort of sorts. 'That manuscript is a bloody good romping yarn. It's publishable. They *can't* just refuse it. We'll sue them.'

'What would be the point?'

'Your reputation, for starters.'

'Reputation for what? I feel so demoralised I doubt I'll ever write another word.'

'Of course you will. Don't let them walk all over you. Fight them! You know the score. If they don't publish, the advance they paid on signature of contract is yours, although you won't get the other tranches for delivery of manuscript and the publication of hardback and paperback. If they're refusing on the grounds that its unpublishable they're on a sticky wicket. Remember Joan Collins and her publishers?' He stabbed at the air with his forefinger.

'Stewart, you've forgotten. There was no advance. You – or rather we,' she corrected herself hurriedly, 'decided that I would probably be able to get more money if I waited until the manuscript was finished before I sold it to them. You felt they were beginning to take me for granted and that the payment I got for *Summer Space* wasn't nearly enough.'

'Nor was it.'

'I felt it was fair.'

'Trying to blame me, are you?'

'No, Stewart, what on earth made you say that?'

'Because it's what you're thinking.'

'I'm not. It was your idea but I went along with it. I'm not blaming anyone.' She felt as if her head was about to burst with pressure. 'They told Joy my sales were slipping and they couldn't possibly justify the same advance.'

'What the hell are you supposed to do? Set up a stall in Victoria station? Flog the bloody things yourself? That's their job, not yours. You write them, they market and sell them.' He marched to the drinks tray and poured himself another hefty whisky.

'Getting drunk isn't going to help us.'

'Don't get pious with me.'

'I'm not. I just think we should both keep steady heads.'

'Mine is.'

'Yes, I realise,' she said wearily, too tired to argue. 'I should have taken Joy's advice. She was against the venture all along – she warned me that changing genres was a dangerous game.'

'That's rubbish. Lots of authors write different books. Look at Iain Banks.'

'But not in women's mass-market fiction. She pointed out that my readers expect a book from me to be set in modern times.'

'Ken Follett changes, does the occasional historical.'

'Yes, but I'm not in his league. He sells so many books for his publisher he can do what he wants.'

'And you will too, one day.'

At last she smiled, in gratitude at his faith in her.

'And what does your brilliant agent suggest you do now?'

'That I take the offer. She says—'

'What offer?'

'Didn't I say? They offered but it's only a third of what I've been getting. Joy says times are hard, everyone's advances are being slashed to the bone, that I'm not alone.'

'Stupid, useless woman.' He banged one large fist into the other. Kate was none too sure who he meant. She hoped it wasn't her. 'What's the point in telling you all this now? You should have known, you should have been fore-warned. This comes of having an amateur for an agent. Why does she do it? She doesn't need the money, as I've said so many times to you but you won't listen. She's playing at it, and your bloody career suffers because she is.'

'That's not fair. Joy can hardly be held responsible for the state of British publishing.'

'Oh, no? You're a fool, Kate, a bloody fool. You're so pig-headed you won't listen to any other opinion. You know it all, don't you?'

'Hurling insults at each other isn't going to help, is it? What's the point of getting aggressive with me? It's my book, my failure. You know how I feel about them, as if they were my children—'

'Oh, for Christ's sake, don't give me that crap. Why, you

47

say you hate them eventually. They're books, that's all. You tell stories, Kate, you're no genius. They're read one day and forgotten the next.'

She felt as if he had slapped her. She stood up and sat down again, then got up, shouted at him and, for good measure, hurled her glass at him. It shattered, tiny shards of glass showering the room.

'Temper, temper!' he goaded her, in a singsong voice, and that was when she pitched the ashtray at him . . .

Now, high in the sky, she shuddered at the shameful memory. She had never done anything like that in her life. She hadn't known she was capable of such an ugly action. Where had all that violence come from – and towards Stewart, of all people? She loved him – how could she possibly want to hurt him?

He shouldn't have said that about her books, though. He knew how important they were to her, how they had taken over her life, how she worried about them. That had been spiteful in the extreme. Why on earth should he want to attack her when her morale was at its lowest and she needed reassurance not insults?

It was the first full-blown row they had ever had. She had apologised, and he had grudgingly accepted, but they had driven to the airport in silence.

'Now, Kate, you mustn't let this get you down.' She was sitting opposite Joy, whose large, modern desk dominated the sleek, beautifully presented and obsessively neat office. 'You're not alone, you know. I've several authors who've taken huge cuts just to keep being published.'

'Knowing that doesn't help me much.'

'I know it's hard. One of the problems is that you've had it so easy. First book accepted before you'd even finished

48

writing it. TV rights sold the same week. Now, I'm afraid, you're seeing the harsh reality of publishing.'

'I can understand that. If there are financial problems, they could have told me, I'm not an idiot. But why did they have to attack the integrity of my writing? That was uncalled-for. I'm not the most confident of people where that's concerned, and they know it. It was cruel of them.'

'I'm sure that was an excuse. I was honest with you, I did have doubts at the beginning. I worried about trying to sell them an historical, but the buzz is that they're back, everyone's doing them. And it's a lovely book, I adored it.'

'Then why?'

'God knows. There's a rumour Westall's are about to be sold. They may be tidying up the accounts to make the books look better than they are. Not having to pay your normal huge advance will make them look even better. No doubt they hoped we'd panic and accept the lower offer.'

'Westall and Trim being sold? Surely not. Look at the fight that Peter Holt and Gloria put up to keep the company independent and away from the big conglomerates. Peter wouldn't let that happen.'

'Peter has moved on to other things. Didn't I tell you? You really should take the *Bookseller*, you know. That way you can learn who's going where and when.'

'What's he doing?'

'He's setting up another imprint with plans for the US too – vertical, lateral publishing. Peter has never been able to stay in one place long. I can't work out if that is his strength or his weakness.'

'When did all this happen?'

'A few months back now. One of the family decided to sell her shares, which meant that the employees' trust, which had kept it safe, lost its majority. Peter saw the writing on the wall and hightailed it.'

'But he loved that firm.'

'Yes, but Dulcett – remember the nutty sculptress? She died and unfortunately left her shares to a donkey sanctuary. They need cash, and . . . I'm sure I told you all this, all the fuss about the Lepanto trust . . .'

Kate could remember none of it and switched off as Joy rambled on. She couldn't care less who owned what. It was her book she feared for. But if Peter . . .

'That's the solution, then.' Kate interrupted Joy in full flow. 'Peter likes my work, he'll take me on.'

'I'm afraid not. He's not in mainstream publishing any more. He's set up a small specialist house – history and fine art mainly. It gives him more time with his garden and Gloria, he says.'

'Peter, gardening? Doesn't sound like him.' For a moment there she had felt relaxed and confident. No more.

'We all change with age.'

'You haven't, Joy. You're still working with books, still as lovely as that day we first met at Barty's party.'

'God, that seems like a lifetime away, doesn't it?'

'How *is* Barty?' Suddenly Kate realised she had been so obsessed with her own problems that she had forgotten to ask after Joy's husband.

A slight shadow flickered across Joy's face. 'He's fine. Not quite as busy as he used to be, thank God. I try to get him to slow down even more but he won't.'

'Is he not well? I don't want to be impertinent but when I asked, you . . .'

'His ticker isn't too good, but he's having treatment. He's fine. Really he is.' But she was too reassuring. 'Still, to business. We have to make some decisions.'

'I'm amazed Gloria hasn't come back to publishing.'

'She's besotted with her child and there's another on the way. Still . . .' She shuffled some papers on her desk. All at

50

once Kate was aware that Joy didn't want to gossip, that she really wanted to get on with their business. 'I showed your book to a couple of other editors. Jane Wood at Orion loved it, and would have bought it, but they've just taken on a new author who's written one too similar to yours. Portia Ringwood at Pewter's has offered – a two-book contract. World rights, unfortunately, but she wouldn't countenance it without.'

'Joy, that's wonderful news.'

'I'm sorry to have to tell you she's offering more than Westall's but it's still only half what you've been getting. She's offered a sweetener. She'll pay another tranche of advance *if* you sell more than a hundred thousand in paperback.'

'But if Westall's say my sales are slipping, how the hell will Pewter's improve on them?'

'Kate, I'm sorry, but it's the best I could do. Times are hard . . .'

Abruptly Kate stood up. If she heard that expression once more from Joy she would hit her or scream, God help her. There it was again – that unacceptable violence.

7

The next day, having accepted Pewter's offer, she met Portia Ringwood. Her office was large and air-conditioned. Kate felt sorry for those working in such an atmosphere; she hated the chilly air, which always made her sneeze. They all sat hunched over their VDUs – so like the first publishing house from which she had fled. Westall's had been different, chaotic offices tucked away up steep staircases, a happy buzz as people popped in and out of each other's rooms – not the cubicles in which these poor souls worked.

But the chaos remained: there were books and manuscripts, Styrofoam cups, coats and carrier-bags everywhere.

Portia was pleasant and welcoming, but Kate had a problem: however nice her editors were, they could never replace Gloria Catchpole. Sometimes she wondered if she didn't exaggerate Gloria's importance to her. Through knowing her Kate had learnt a sharp lesson. She had thought she and Gloria were friends, but once Gloria had left to have her baby Kate had never heard from her again – not even a Christmas card. She was forced to the sad conclusion that it had been just a working relationship. It was another reason she refused to listen to Stewart when he suggested getting rid of Joy. Of all the people she had met in publishing, Joy was the only one she would bank on being a friend.

It seemed to her that people in publishing were inter-changeable. They wore the same earnest expressions – she was sure they used to smile more. The younger women dressed in what amounted to a uniform, as if they were back at school: short black skirts, opaque black tights and loose jumpers. She had long ago decided that their shoes would have looked good on a squaddie. At Pewter's the only one with any individuality was the girl in the design department. The hotchpotch of oranges, blues and reds she was wearing, not to mention the pinkish-looking hair, boded ill for any cover she might design. When they got down to discussing her book and its possible packaging, Portia was coy about any publicity budget and Kate guessed there wasn't one or that it was so infinitesimally small that it might just as well not exist. She filled in the author-profile form and tried to make herself sound interesting – she knew now of the problems publicity departments experienced in getting journalists interested in their writers; all they wanted was to interview the mega-sellers, the new *wunderkinder*. Put simply, there were too many writers with too-ordinary profiles, and too many books so that the gravy of exposure was spread thinner and thinner each year.

When she had first been published she had been fêted. She'd met all the directors, and had drunk enough champagne to last her a lifetime. In those days she had complained and said it was all too much, the demands were too onerous, there was too much bubbly. She had to smile to herself at what a spoilt little author she had been as now she accepted a polystyrene mug of milky coffee.

Oh, how are the mighty fallen, she thought, as she packed away her notes of what Portia had suggested might be good ideas to improve the book. That was another change: once she had changed publishers rather than alter her book; today she had gratefully scribbled down any crumb of wisdom that Portia had given her.

As she left the smart, modern building, she felt that, at a stroke, she had become unimportant, invisible almost, just as she had been with Tony. A nondescript nonentity, that was how she had felt, and as she walked towards Trafalgar Square she felt herself donning that mantle once again.

The Dolphin Club was busy. Members of the Red Rose Society, of which she was one, were granted associate membership of this old and distinguished club too. The rooms were cheaper to stay in than a hotel's, as were the drinks and food. In the past she had enjoyed coming here, knowing there was a good chance that other writers would be around to talk to and gossip with. But this afternoon she looked purposefully at the floor as she scurried across the hall towards the lift and the solitude of her room. She needed to think.

'Kate! It's Kate Howard surely.'

'Bella, how lovely to see you.' Hypocrite, she told herself.

If there was one woman she couldn't stand it was Bella Ford. Years ago the woman had tittle-tattled about Kate to an editor and got her into serious trouble. But, as in so many professions, it was simpler not to make enemies. A time might come when she would need Bella, so she beamed at her.

In truth Bella didn't look her usual fragrant lilac-chiffon-dressed self. In fact, she looked bedraggled and her eyes were suspiciously pink, as if she had been crying.

'Fancy a drink or some tea? The beauty of this club is that one knows one will always find a kindred spirit here,' Bella gushed, and Kate became guarded. No doubt the woman wanted something.

'And how's France?' Bella asked, once they were settled with glasses of wine in the large comfy chairs in the club drawing room.

'Wonderful. Best thing I ever did.'

'Not career-wise, though, was it?'

'I'm sorry?' Kate looked puzzled.

'Out of sight, out of mind. I often think the media and the world of publishing are far more fickle than any flighty lover, don't you?'

'I hadn't thought about it.' But, like an express train, the idea that Bella was right and she should never have left England rushed towards her.

'Oh, I'm sure.'

'My agent wasn't too keen but my publisher thought it was a great idea.'

'Well, they would, wouldn't they? They wouldn't want to antagonise you.'

'I thought they meant it.'

'Have you not noticed with publishing people that they invariably hold the opinion of the last person they spoke to? They remind me of lemmings.'

'I can't say I have. In fact, I think the business is full of one-off originals.' For a start Kate could hardly think of Gloria as a lemming: she was the most unique and confident woman she'd ever met.

'I hear you've been given the boot.'

'News travels fast.' She smiled. Watch her, she told herself.

'They've been having a purge. Any writer – female, I hasten to add – over the age of forty-five is getting the chop. They only want thirty-somethings now. Our day is over, Kate, my friend. We're too long in the tooth.'

'We?'

To her horror Bella burst into tears. 'Twenty years I've been with my publishers and now—' Frantically she made a chopping motion across her throat.

'Oh, Bella, I *am* sorry. But you'll get picked up again, I'm sure.'

'You think so? I fear not. Were you at the Red Rose winter party? It was like the aftermath of a battle – walking wounded everywhere. Every other writer looking for a publisher. They say times are hard . . .'

'They'll pick up.' Don't react, her alter ego ordered.

'Have you had any luck? We're all pooling any knowledge, to see if we can help each other.'

'No, I haven't.' To her shame she lied, and pretended to herself that she hadn't the foggiest idea why. But she knew damn well why: she was protecting her own vulnerable position. Worse, she despised herself for doing so. She stood up. 'Thanks for the wine, Bella. I'd love to stay and natter but unfortunately I've an appointment.' She looked pointedly at her watch. She had, but not for another two hours. However, although she felt sorry for Bella, she was finding the tone of the other woman's voice and her negativity draining. As she left she turned round. 'It might

55

be of no use, but I did hear Portia Ringwood say she's commissioning regional sagas.' What the hell had made her say that, she wondered, as Bella gushed her thanks.

In her room she took stock. She had come here feeling sorry for herself. Now, perhaps, she should be thinking how lucky she was. Poor Bella.

Thinking that she might as well get all the unpleasantness out of the way at once, she had phoned Tony upon her arrival and had arranged to meet him for a drink that evening. He had written to her recently that it was imperative they discuss certain things. She doubted it: it was probably an excuse just to get at her.

He was waiting for her in the Palm Court of the Adelphi. He didn't see her at first, and as she crossed the large hall she stared at him and found it odd, yet again, that she could look at him so dispassionately. She couldn't even remember what it was like to be married to him now, and certainly she couldn't recall what he looked like with no clothes on – not that she wanted to.

'Hello, Tony.'

'Kate.' He was on his feet. It didn't mean he respected her, just that he had been well trained.

'That's nice.' She nodded towards the gin and tonic he'd ordered for her.

'You always liked one at the end of the day, didn't you, back in the good old days?'

Oh, God, she thought, I do hope he's not going to get maudlin. 'It's more likely to be wine these days.'

He harrumphed. He hadn't liked her going to France – in fact, he had thrown quite a little paddy when she had told him of her intentions.

'How's what's-his-name?'

'Stewart's fine. And how's . . . Stephanie? Wasn't that the

last one's name?' She referred to the third woman he'd been involved with since their split. There might have been more but she did not keep tabs on him.

'She's fine. Fine.' He handed her a bowl of olives, looking shifty. Did that mean Stephanie was no more? Was he alone? Hard cheese, she thought.

'Seen anything of Pam?' She smiled sweetly. If she was honest Pamela, who had once been her best friend, had done her a great favour in choosing Tony for an affair. She had thus set in motion the ending of Kate's marriage and ensured that Kate enjoyed more happiness than she'd ever imagined possible.

'I never see her these days.'

'Oh, I'm sorry.' Now, that was odd too. She found she was genuinely sorry. Why? 'Is she still with Doug?'

'As far as I know. The house is looking good.' He perked up as he said this. 'The couple we sold to look after it well. But it's still known as "the Howards' place" by all and sundry. We left our mark.' He looked wistful.

Don't fall for it, she heard herself think. 'Have you seen Steve?' she enquired.

'Not for several months.'

'He's hoping to visit me. Something to do with a garden in Paris.'

'Gardens!' He spat the word.

'I don't understand your resistance to his work. He's proved himself a natural gardener. He'll be a big success one day, no doubt with his own TV show.' She smiled at the idea.

'You *would* regard that as success,' he sneered.

She chose to ignore it. 'He's happy, and that's all I've ever wanted for the children.'

'How can you sit there and say that when your other child is far from happy?'

'I know, I know. Poor Lucy . . . I know it's hard for you, Tony. She's such a clever little thing and I know you had such dreams for her. Why, she might easily have become your partner.' She could remember so clearly his pleasure when Lucy had announced she was going to read law. There had been no warning when something, neither of them knew what, had happened, and the dream had become a nightmare. In her first year at Cambridge Lucy had simply dropped out. Last heard of she was in a squat, she'd become an anarchist and a vegetarian and, of course, there were the drugs, but that was a subject on which Kate preferred not to dwell. She shuddered at the very thought.

'It's all your fault,' Tony remarked.

'And how do you make that out?' she asked, with studied patience, sipping slowly at her drink while tensing her body, knowing full well how bitter and twisted this conversation was likely to become.

'Swanning off, giving up on your real job of being a wife and mother to follow your own selfish way.'

'My selfish way helped support Steve when you refused, I'd like to remind you.'

'You always spoilt him rather than Lucy and she, poor child, knew. That's what damaged her.'

'Rubbish, I never did. I found Steve easier, that's all. I loved them equally and she knew that. And you're a right one to talk about swanning off. You're a hypocrite, Tony Howard.' How the hell had this started, she asked herself. She knew she was saying things she hadn't intended to say and that her voice was too loud, that other people in the hotel lounge could probably hear, but she couldn't seem to stop. 'Maybe your adultery had something to do with it.'

'She went off the rails long after that.' At least he had the grace to look uncomfortable, she registered. 'When you'd taken up with that parasite Dorchester. Then that stupid

58

plan of moving to France. What do you think that did to her?'

'You've seen her? How is she? Is she eating?' She leant forward, eager for news of her daughter, all irritation with her ex-husband momentarily forgotten.

'No, I haven't.'

'She probably doesn't even know I've moved to France. Steve hasn't heard from her.' Kate slumped back in her seat. 'If she doesn't contact us, what are we supposed to do? Her rebellion has nothing to do with me. She couldn't give a damn where I go or what I do – she's demonstrated that she doesn't care about either of us.' That was below the belt, she realised, but he was making her angry, blaming her, just as he always had. 'Tony, she's twenty-three, she has to lead her own life. I don't approve, as you don't, but there's nothing we can do about it.' She bent down to pick up her handbag. This conversation was getting them nowhere. 'And Stewart is not a parasite. That was an unforgivable thing to say.'

'Only a fool would deny it.'

'If anyone's a parasite how about you? When we got divorced you laid claim to my earnings because they were higher than yours. You said you'd helped me in my writing career. Help? You only know about self-help.'

His thin lips tightened. 'Writing career? Scribbling for morons who have nothing better to do than read your drivel.'

She would have liked to hit him for that. Instead she took a deep breath. He wasn't worth it. 'I don't blame either of us for what has happened. If Lucy wishes to live in the way she does, that's her business not ours. She's a grown woman.'

'Abnegating your responsibilities . . . again.'

It was the slight pause before he said 'again' that had made her intention not to lose her temper desert her.

59

'Right, you asked for this,' she shouted, and stood up. People were staring and she didn't give a toss. 'If Lucy has reacted to anything I think it is far more likely to have been the oppressive manner in which you preferred to bring them up, the smug, self-satisfied, intolerant, bigoted atmosphere you created while you held your Bible and trotted off to church on Sunday. You're a hypocrite, Tony, of the first water. No doubt our daughter, bright girl that she is, twigged it far faster than I did. You are so anally retentive, Tony, I am amazed that you haven't exploded since you're so full of shit!'

'I see you're learning vulgarity from that excrescence you choose to live with.'

'Yes, and I've learnt a lot more too.'

'Such as?'

'You really want to know? Fun, with a capital F. How to relax and, best of all—' She stopped. Decent sex was what she had wanted to say, but she grasped at a shred of decorum and didn't. 'After all, my dear friend Pam tired of your lack of . . . You know what I mean.'

With that parting shot she swept out of the lounge, leaving the people at the next table gaping with shock, Tony about to erupt with fury, and the feeling she had gone too far, that she should never have said all those things, and close to tears. But it was too late now. She had said what she had been thinking for too long. Perhaps if she'd said things sooner . . .

She hailed a cab. Back in the sanctuary of her room she punched in the numbers of her home telephone. 'Stewart. I'm sorry. I love you . . .' Then she wept as if she would never stop.

Chapter Two

April–May

1

'A party, you say?' Netta Rawlinson's voice lifted at this information. There was nothing she liked more. 'What sort of party?' She was virtually purring down the telephone. Immediately she was mentally riffling through her wardrobe, discarding and setting aside possible clothes to wear.

'Lunch,' Sybil Chesterton, equally excited, replied.

'Oh.' The small word dripped with Netta's disappointment. 'I hate lunch parties. One gets a bad head, ratty, the man in your life is incapable and the rest of the day is lost. It's like weddings – there's only one solution, keep on drinking until you pass out.'

'Netta, you *are* awful!' Sybil giggled.

Netta wished that Sybil would stop her irritating habit of trotting out catchphrases and clichés. It was almost a nervous tic with her. 'Who's giving it?'

'New people, the Bollands. They arrived a few months ago. She spends more time here than he does. They're not residents, you see.' There was a smidgen of dismissiveness in Sybil's voice, which made Netta smile. Those with holiday homes were not regarded as belonging as were those who lived here all the year and did battle with French bureaucracy.

'Where?'

'Near Retournac. We'll give you a lift.'

'But I don't know anyone called Bolland, we've never been introduced.'

At this Sybil's laugh was so shrill that Netta had to hold the instrument away from her ear. 'Dear Netta, for such a racy creature you can sometimes sound like a dowager duchess. Wendy, that's our hostess, asked me to bring anyone I knew who might enjoy a party. And I suggested you. They don't know anyone.'

'So how do you know her?'

'I met her in Bricolage.'

'Do you meet all your social acquaintances in the DIY store?'

'Oh, Netta, you are a—'

'I know, I know.' Netta forced the note of irritation from her voice. 'I'm not sure. Admittedly a party would be welcome, even a luncheon party, but I hate committing myself when I don't know the people. I might not like them. It's a bit like going on a blind date, isn't it?'

'Well, nothing ventured nothing gained, as they say. I bet you enjoy it when we get there. Wendy said it was the sort of party that would go on until it ran out of time and everyone had keeled over.'

'I'm not sure if I could ever like anyone called *Wendy*.'

'You said that about me, remember?'

'I never did.'

'Joan Oxford said you did – the exact words.'

'Well, then, if I did I was wrong. I love you.'

'Ah,' Sybil murmured down the line, followed by a self-conscious little giggle. 'So you could be wrong about a

Wendy. And they're opening their pool and we're to take swimming costumes.'

'Now? They must be mad. It's arctic for April.'

'The party's in May, and in any case it's heated.'

'You don't say?' Things were looking up. A heated pool, with the cost of electricity in France, meant money. And money was what Netta missed, dreamt about and sorely lacked. 'I suppose that miserable sod of a husband of yours is coming?'

'What do you suggest I do with him to keep him at home?' Sybil tittered.

'Poison his food.'

'Oh, Netta, you—'

'I know, I know – *I'm awful*!'

The call over, Netta, now reassured that Wendy had really asked Sybil to invite her and that this wasn't one of Sybil's thoughtful ideas, presented herself at her wardrobe which, given the size of her bedroom, was situated in the minuscule hall. It was such a large piece of furniture that everyone had to breathe in deeply to get past it and was the reason why Netta never invited anyone fat to her flat.

Wendy – what a God-awful name, she thought, as she swung open the door of the cupboard, which was bursting with clothes. She'd have to be in her seventies to have such a name, she'd put money on it. As Netta searched her wardrobe for something suitable to wear to a pool party, she searched her memory for why she so disliked the name. There, lurking in her memory, was a school prefect who had once unjustly put her on detention. She was glad to resolve it, for Netta liked to have a reason even for her most illogical actions.

Still, she thought, what manners, getting someone else to invite her rather than doing it herself. That implied someone much younger. Women of her generation and older maintained some level of courtesy in this crazy world, even rebels like herself.

The wardrobe was one of the few good pieces of furniture she had left. It was made of cherrywood and the doors had large carved lozenges on them – the Le Puy lacemakers' mark, she'd been told. Although it was well over a hundred years old, the wood still scented the contents. One of the doors was a bit wobbly and needed a good polish, but she loved it and had hung on to it.

'Cupboards like that cost a pretty penny. I've seen them in the "antiquitie" shops,' Simon, Sybil's awful husband, had informed her on one visit, while sucking deeply at his pipe. Fortunately for Netta his visits were rare. She loathed him, and everything about him. She hated his haircut – short back and sides – and his voice, nasal and whining: it declared to all what a let-down life had been to him. She despised his socks with sandals, but most of all she loathed his pipe, which she'd never seen him without. When he began the long, tedious, disgusting process of cleaning it she wanted to hurl it out of the window or ram it down his throat. Sybil was either a saint or a fool to put up with such a bore. Sadly, Netta had concluded, it was the latter.

'I know its value,' she had said, through gritted teeth, hoping he would notice. As always, he had seemed oblivious to her dislike.

'Then why don't you sell it? What do you want an old thing like that cluttering up the landing for?'

'Because it gives me pleasure. But I doubt you would understand that.' This time, as she spoke, she had beamed at him with the smile that had broken a sackful of hearts, and then, just when he had reacted to it, smiling back in an inane way that he must have thought attractive, she had deliberately turned her back on him. 'Looky, no touchy,' she sang to herself.

These days, Netta rarely went out but when she did, and the cupboard containing her treasures was opened, it always took her a month of Sundays to decide what to wear. She had never thrown anything away – hence its overcrowded state – and going through it, picking out a dress or a suit, she would find herself remembering when she had worn it in the past or why she had bought it. Hence, the pale blue chiffon she pulled out was not a dress by Balenciaga but the afternoon at Longchamp when she had met Duc Henri. She had also worn a wonderful huge hat set at a sharp angle on her head. It had a wide brim, ideal for flirting under, but sadly one of her dogs had eaten it. And where was it? Yes, here, the dark blue Lanvin she had worn that night to dinner with him at Maxim's and he'd given her a gardenia. She could never smell that particular flower without thinking of him. Which inevitably led her to remember the night when she had discovered what lovemaking was meant to be. What a man! What a sensitive lover! What finesse! 'Ah, happy days.' She sighed.

Reluctantly she hung the blue dress back in the wardrobe. A pool party in the Auvergne was not quite the same as Longchamp. Pucci! Somewhere in here hung the silk pyjama suit with the palazzo pants she had worn to a party given by that delicious Italian count in his villa on the Via Appia Antica. That one had got away. She laughed to herself. No one had seen fit to tell her he was homosexual and consequently she had made a total fool of herself that night. Despite this inauspicious start, she and the count had made friends and remained so until he had died of Aids back in the eighties, not that anyone discussed it then but everyone had known. She had never quite forgotten the humiliation of that night in Italy and had quite taken against the suit, but now . . . well, a lot of water had flowed under the bridge since then. Heavens above, she was sounding like Sybil! 'That won't do at all, will it, Tam?' Sometimes she thought that if she didn't have the cat to talk to she'd go mad on those long days when the phone didn't ring and the food cupboard was bare.

Carefully she inspected the Pucci suit for any repairs it might need. It was cream silk with a wonderful psychedelic pattern in turquoise, red and blue – sensational design. She sniffed it but was relieved to find that it smelt only of the Calèche that she had once worn as her signature smell, so no dry-cleaning bill. Here, they never failed to shock her. No wonder the French had a reputation for not cleaning their clothes – one had to be well heeled to do that.

Signature smell. She liked the sound of that. She had read it in a recent *Vogue* that Sybil had given her. It was a good way to describe one's own special scent. She had discovered that one in the late fifties and had stayed true to it ever since. She kept old bottles in her knickers drawer, the delicious summery smell lingering still, even though she could not remember when she had last been given any. Netta had never bought herself a bottle of scent: that would have been tantamount to failure.

So the Pucci it was, with the gold Ferragamo sandals and matching bag. She'd have to paint her nails – oh, for a pedicure. 'Shut up, you silly old cow, stop feeling sorry for yourself,' she said aloud. Now, what about a hat? Would she need a hat? Wouldn't that be overdoing it a bit in this day and age? 'Yes, it would. So, Tam, no hat. What would Mother say to that?' She shivered. Thankfully the woman had been dead for over twenty-five years but just thinking of her made her daughter quail.

Best to try it on. She laid the suit on the bed and stripped. She loved the feel of the silk as it slithered over her body. She shut the door so that she could see herself in the mirror that hung on the back.

'Not bad, not bad at all.' She might be poor and a pensioner – even if she wasn't entitled to draw one – but she still looked good and could easily pass for late forties. She made sure she stayed that way: plenty of exercise – walking was free; plenty of water – that was almost free; little food – she wished that was free; and a beauty routine she had never given up on even though the creams and lotions were from the supermarket, these days, and not the perfumery.

'You were born a fool and you will die a fool.'

She looked over her shoulder half expecting to find her mother in the room with her. Would the old bitch never leave her alone? Was she going to be remembering her until the day she herself curled up her toes? Doleful thought.

Netta had tried to be happy, she'd tried to be a good wife. But she often wondered if her mother's loathing of her had marked her so that she never could be either. And, over the years, as relationship after relationship had foundered and she had begun to acknowledge that perhaps she was at fault, she also found herself wondering if she was incapable of really loving since she had been unloved herself.

Had she been an American she was sure she could have kept an army of psychiatrists busy with her upbringing, her insecurities. The odd thing was it had become a matter of pride to her that no one should know. Strong Netta, sensible Netta – but that woman Kate Howard had seen through her. How many others had?

Still, she thought, with the Pucci suit airing on a hanger, it hadn't always been her fault. Bernard, yes, she could see she had failed him with no children, but what about husband number two, Freddie? Even Sybil could not have endured him. He was an alcoholic and had whopped her once too often, and she had had no intention of putting up with that. Then there had been Humph: silent, dependable, he had bored her rigid and she'd bolted with number four. That certainly was her fault: she shouldn't have allowed herself to be seduced by his money. Then there was Carlo – not that she'd married him but she had thought about it. He had been Spanish, dark and passionate – and addicted to sex, which was probably what had attracted her. But she had her pride and she had balked at sharing him with a harem of mistresses.

She poured the last of the Ambassadeur and sank into her chair. Tam jumped up on her lap and she stroked him as she thought of the last one, amusing, reliable Mike, a gentle man, and a kind one, but a failure by profession. If Mike went into a venture his friends had learnt to avoid it like the plague because it would fail – it always did when Mike was involved.

If it hadn't have been for Mike, would she have been here? They had eventually ended up in France, where property was cheap. Fifteen years ago they had come. They had been good years, if lean ones, until he had died five years ago. 'Oh, the silly man.' She wiped a tear from her cheek. The subsequent years had been even leaner.

2

Mo had been christened Maureen but long ago she had changed it to Mo, which, she thought, had more style. She sat on the window-seat, a book on her lap that she was pretending to read: Tristram was keen that they should like the same things. She didn't see why, and sometimes it was a real pain. She liked magazines – but why read about life when you should be living it?

To circumvent this problem she read the reviews in the Sunday papers and the last few pages of the book in case it had a surprise ending. Consequently she was renowned for being well read. It worked with theatre and art reviews too. There was no need to cheat on films because she loved the cinema.

People were so easy to fool, so easy to con, she'd found. She had learnt that if someone wanted something to be just so it was the easiest thing in the world to make them think it was.

Mo looked out of the window on to the small farmyard opposite and watched the rain sheeting across, stirring the droppings deposited by the cows that morning into a fine old slurry. The dog, chained to its kennel, looked dismally back at her. She pulled a face at it. She did not like dogs and that one looked a particularly vicious specimen.

'What a day!' Tristram said, entering the small sitting room, his bulk making it seem even smaller.

'We might just as well be back in England.' She sighed.

'It could be worse. They tell me they often have blizzards in April, this high up.'

'But we make up for it with the views,' she said, while thinking what a fool he was not to have checked the prevalent weather before moving here.

'Poor Mo, you're far too exotic for this, aren't you? By rights you should be sunning yourself on a white beach in the Seychelles.'

'I wouldn't be anywhere else but here,' she lied, smiling up at him, pouring all the love for him that she should be feeling into her eyes.

'Enjoying the book?'

'Marvellous. It's so innovative. Such a clever use of space and time.'

'I just knew you'd love it too.' He struggled into his stiff, crackling Barbour.

'You're not going out in *this*?'

'I want to check that the hay isn't getting wet.'

'Don't be long, will you?' she called after him, as he went through the door in a flurry of wind and rain that flung itself gleefully into her sitting room. Hell! They hadn't even got a hall.

In one fluid, sinuous movement she stood up. The woodburner needed stoking – again! She stirred the ashes in a desultory way, and hurled a log on. Then she collected the mop and cleared up the rainwater – if there was one thing Mo couldn't abide it was mess.

From the window she could see Tristram, his head bent against the wind and rain, struggle across the yard. He stopped to pat the dog, which wagged its tail and looked up at him eagerly, begging for more. That's what she didn't like about dogs – too subservient.

Preparing to make the coffee she found that, yet again, the electricity had cut out. She yanked the *disjoncteur* switch and the kettle began to make a noise.

What a God-awful country! The tiniest storm and everything went off. That didn't happen in Peckham. She allowed herself to think longingly of the tiny house she had rented there. It might have been shabby but she had loved it and felt secure there, until . . .

She shook herself as if icy water was trickling down her back. She made herself think of other things . . . One of these days the electricity wouldn't go back on and then what would she do? If she lost her TV and video she'd top herself, she knew she would. As it was, at the first hint of a storm they had to rush around unplugging everything. The insurance wouldn't pay out if they were damaged. What was the point of having insurance that didn't cough up?

She returned to her perch by the window. Sunny France!

Hell, she'd seen more rain here than she ever had at home. Or was it just easier not to notice it in the city? Here, with nothing else to distract her, she was more conscious of it. She had only herself to blame; no one had made her come here. It had been convenient, that was the point. Still – she picked up a cushion, and plumped it up vigorously – she didn't want to think about any of *that*, not now. Bury it, forget it, she told herself determinedly. Switch on the TV.

Thank God she'd demanded they have Sky TV. But how she longed for *EastEnders* and *Corrie*! She flicked to the news channel. This particular news-reader irritated Mo, with her false bright air and flashing teeth. She always looked so infernally pleased with herself. Would she be so self-satisfied if she knew her roots were showing? Which reminded her.

She jumped up and crossed to the mirror she'd hung by the door. She could do with a visit to the hairdresser herself. If Tristram would give her the money. Christ! What a state to have let herself get into, dependent for every penny, stuck in the back of beyond, in a foreign country, no money and no prospect of any.

The girls at work had envied her this move. If only they could see her now. There was nowhere to go. The food was foul at the local restaurant, about all they could afford without going into Le Puy – so much for French food! She hated the local bar, which was dim and dirty with men eyeing her in a less than respectful way, as if they had some God-given right. The only French she met she could barely understand, so impenetrable was their accent. And in any case why should she want to speak to them? They'd nothing in common. 'That's a pretty sheep,' they might say. 'What a lovely stone!'

There was no bath, only a sodding shower – if you could

call it that. There wasn't even a cubicle, just a hole in the floor where the water drained away.

'Brilliant, isn't it? The heat will dry the tiles,' Tristram had said, with that infuriating enthusiasm he went in for.

'What heat?'

'Just you wait till the summer comes.'

Although she liked the heat she wasn't too sure that she was going to enjoy it here. That farmyard was a little too close for comfort – it spoke of flies, when the summer came. They'd arrived in February, which, Tristram had agreed, was not the best time to begin their life here. Still, London with no money was no place to be, and in some ways she supposed it would be worse than here – seeing and not being able to touch, so to speak.

Tristram liked the country. He was fond of saying that he'd always wanted to be a farmer. But he hadn't achieved that: he was a smallholder – not that she'd let on. She had made it sound as if he was buying hundreds of rolling French acres – she hadn't actually said he was buying a château, just hinted at it, and they had all gobbled up her fantasy, just as she had expected them to.

Tristram pottered about happily with his chickens, rabbits and the two sheep they'd bought to raise for meat. She sighed. She felt cheated, yet it wasn't Tristram who had done the cheating.

'How do you fancy living in France?' he'd asked one day last year, as they sat at the Mitre and Feathers, sharing a bottle of champagne with Caroline and Chris after work.

'France? Me?' She had perked up at this. In her mind France equalled sophistication.

'I want to buy some land, raise a few animals. Be self-sufficient. Another of my great-aunts has coughed it. She's left me enough to set myself up, get away from the rat-race.

Good old Auntie Freda, bless her.' Solemnly he'd raised his glass, and they all toasted the late aunt Freda.

Mo's mind had raced. If he was thinking of buying a farm, even in France, his aunt's legacy couldn't be peanuts. But why not here? She'd humour him, go along with his plans while advocating Berkshire, or maybe the Cotswolds.

'Sounds dreamy,' sighed Caroline. How Mo hated the way Caroline often sounded like a reincarnated hippie. 'I'd love to get away from all this.' She swung her hand, indicating the unsuspecting drinkers in the pub. 'Now, that would be a good life. Grow the vine and drink the wine.' She giggled. Honestly, that woman sounded stoned all the time. Mo despised her.

'We could all go! How about that?' Chris, normally so lethargic, suggested suddenly.

'What? Pool our resources, get a decent spread? Are you serious?' Tristram looked animated.

'Too right.'

'Like a commune? Count me in. My mother lived in one when she was young. She said it was paradise.'

'Free love – all that sort of thing?' Chris asked, intrigued.

'Knowing my mum, probably.' Caroline grinned.

Caroline irritated Mo all the time. She had everything that Mo wanted but it was wasted on her. She had extremely rich parents, yet shopped at Next and Gap. Worse, she had her own trust fund, but didn't even boast about it. She had a glamorous mother, who'd been a minor film star in the fifties. Her father was still dishy enough for Mo to flirt with. And, stupidest of all, Caroline worked when she didn't have to, silly cow.

Mo had met her at the modelling agency. She let people think she was a model, rather than a lowly secretary: it seemed to excite them and she had the looks but had never had the luck. Everyone was at lunch the day Caroline had called, needing to book some models. Mo wasn't particularly interested until Caroline mentioned she was organising a charity ball at the Grosvenor. Mo smelt contacts, networking, and went out of her way to be helpful.

Caroline took her out to lunch and there Mo learnt all about the love of her life: Tristram. They'd been friends ever since. Or, rather, Caroline thought they were. Mo knew she had no real friends but, then, she didn't want any.

She was astonished that the friendship had survived.

'Caroline, you'll never want to speak to me again ever but I've done the most dreadful thing.' She had looked suitably tearful for the confession.

'Darling Mo, what on earth are you going on about?'

'Tristram and I have fallen in love. I'm sorry, but we couldn't help ourselves.'

Momentarily Caroline looked shattered, but the genes of the long line of generals and diplomats from which she sprang came to her rescue. 'You can't help love. I hope you'll be very happy,' she had said. Despite herself Mo had to admire her control and dignity.

Caroline remained a friend, which was why Mo was not too pleased with this French plan. Tristram might always fall in love again with Caroline, and where would that leave Mo? The project had to be scotched.

'Caroline, I don't know quite how to say this . . .' She had begun then demurred and kept it up for so long that, in the end, Caroline was begging her to tell her whatever it was. 'Well, you asked but don't ever say I told you. The bottom line is that neither Tristram nor Chris wants you to go with them.' She had been so sympathetic, mopping up the tears, agreeing what bastards the others were. Then, by the simple expedient of telling each of the others the same story – just changing the names – the whole scheme foundered, and their friendships with it.

She wasn't sure why she did such things. She didn't want to share Tristram, she supposed, though why not remained a mystery to her. She didn't love him, nothing like.

Tristram, however, wouldn't be diverted from his plan. He was adamant that he was going. It was up to her if she came or not. And when it came to it, she'd had no choice. She persuaded herself that it wouldn't be too bad. There was the wine, the food. 'Just for a couple of years, then,' she'd said.

The France she had imagined bore no relation to the one they ended up in. She had dreamt of a quaint farmhouse just outside somewhere like St Tropez. Not this God-for-saken hole, miles from anywhere, high in the hills – hence the bloody rain – in the bloody Haute Loire. Peasants, peasants wherever one looked. It was green, very green, but now she knew why – because it never stopped bloody raining.

It was a trap. Her problem was that she couldn't go back. Involuntarily her hand moved across her face as if removing a cobweb.

The telephone rang. In her haste to get to it she almost tripped. 'Hi, Mo Hargreaves,' she said breathlessly, using her best telephone-answering voice. She wasn't really Hargreaves but it had pleased Tristram that she had changed her name to his. She hoped he never found out why.

'My name's Wendy Bolland. We haven't met but I got your number from Stewart Dorchester – you know, the famous journalist. He said he had met you and you were new here, as we are.'

'A Stewart Dorchester, you say?' She hoped she sounded sufficiently vague.

'He said he'd met you in Bricolage. I reckon that's where all we ex-pats meet up. It's the manager – he's convinced

75

that we're all dying to know each other.' Whoever it was had a delightful laugh.

'I can't say I remember.' She did, though. Stewart Dorchester was a good-looking, confident fifty-year-old, rather full of himself but with a certain style, who might be useful one day. A journalist, Wendy had said, now that was interesting. But Mo wasn't about to admit that her life was so devoid of excitement that an encounter in the local DIY store had been memorable.

'Anyhow, we're having a party and wondered if you would like to come.'

'We should love to.'

'The first Saturday in May. Bring your cossie – the pool should be opened by then.'

The pool. Things were looking up, Mo thought, as she replaced the receiver.

Tristram battled against the wind and the rain that was being funnelled down the steep lane. It had been a worthwhile trip for the water was seeping in at one end of the shed. He clambered up a ladder, hauled the tarpaulin back into place where it had blown off, and hammered it on.

The job completed, he looked about him. To the east were the mountains, still topped with their winter snow. Living with the mountains was a bit like living by the sea: he never tired of looking at them, and found that they constantly changed colour and shape. They were comforting, in a strange way, as if they were guarding them. He wished Mo could see them like that.

Next he checked the rabbits. He changed their water, stroked them, spoke to them. They were pathetically pleased to see him. He was raising them for food, but each day he knew them made the prospect seem less and less likely. Maybe he should stick to growing vegetables.

He'd confessed how he felt to Martin, their squat, square-shaped neighbour with his matching short wife. 'I'll see to them for you, when the day comes,' Martin had said, and to Tristram's surprise, he realised that the man understood. Mind you, he might think differently when he learnt that Tristram was thinking of pensioning off the sheep too.

He began to slip and slide his way down the rutted lane, watching every footstep he took. It was a lane that you couldn't just walk down: large basalt rocks had a habit of working their way to the surface overnight. He'd probably fallen over more often since they had been here than in his entire childhood. At least it made Mo laugh when she saw him returning covered in mud. It was great to hear her laugh – she hadn't done much of that since their arrival.

Poor Mo. He wished there was some way he could make her happy. He should never have brought her here. He wasn't normally a selfish person, but he had been over this venture. Truth was, when he had decided to come, he'd thought she'd back off, but she hadn't.

He stopped to look at a plant he didn't recognise, bright green foliage with heavy green petals. It looked too exotic to be a weed. He wondered if he could replant some in the garden he was planning. He stroked its cool leaves. It would die if he tried to – you shouldn't transplant wild things. The same could be said about Mo.

Mo needed the city and champagne, mindless chatter, a social life and pretty clothes. He was the opposite: his years in London had been sheer hell. What was more, he'd wanted her all to himself if he was honest – which was always uncomfortable, he'd learnt. But you couldn't pin down butterflies – except when they were dead. At the image he pulled his coat closer.

The odd thing was, they both played this charade: Mo pretending that all was well, and him pretending he didn't know she was bored and unhappy. He did it because he respected her trying to like it for him. He did it because he knew he had used her.

He did not love her and he never would, but he had wanted her – and that had been wrong of him. He told her virtually every day that he loved her to try to make her feel secure. At least she had never said she loved him in return, which was a mercy. How much worse that would have been. Once he had asked her if she did, but she had laughed and accused him of being *soppy*. Weak and ineffectual – wasn't that what his own father had called him? One step away from being soppy.

Chris had had a go at him. 'Don't you realise she's going round saying you don't like us, don't want us with you? Poor Caroline was so hurt.'

Why did people always tell him what he already knew? He hated Caroline's pain, hated Mo for causing it, but he needed her, and he couldn't stop her. *Weak and ineffectual!*

'You've broken Caroline's heart.'

'That's her problem.' He sounded hard when he wasn't. He had hated distancing himself from his old friends but, looking back, it was as if he had been in the throes of some dreadful fever, a destructive obsession that for a time had taken control of his life.

He regretted bitterly the ensuing row with Chris, which had ended a friendship that had begun at prep school, continued through Harrow, and later as undergraduates together.

He paused at the barn opposite their own small house and patted the dog again – Max, he was called. Poor bloody animal. He liked Martin, but he wished he was kinder to his mutt. He didn't much like the way he treated his sheep either. They were penned up in a barn, and Tristram heard them bleating all day long and at night too. They never seemed to go out, and when once they had, he wished he hadn't seen them for some had such foot rot that they could hardly walk. Only Max snapping at their heels had made them. Still, when in Rome . . . he told himself, for the umpteenth time.

He saw the yellow van of the postman approaching and leant against the fence waiting for him to deliver the mail. Some days he allowed himself to dream there was a letter from Caroline, forgiving him, begging him to come back to her. But what if there was? Would he go? Like as not he wouldn't.

He missed Caroline, her sweetness, her love for him. If he hadn't met Mo they would be engaged by now, planning the wedding, children. Instead? He shook his head. What was the point in trying to change things in his mind? He'd only himself to blame.

He took the mail. No letters, just bills as always.

'Tristram! Guess what!' Mo hurled herself at him the moment he stepped in the door.

'I can't.' He smiled in the face of Mo's bright-eyed excitement.

'We've been invited to a party. What about that?'

'Lovely. When? Where?' His heart sank. The last thing he wanted was to go to a party full of ex-pats, but she wanted to, and he couldn't deny her this. Her life was hardly a bed of roses now – but had it ever been? She was so lovely she should be truly loved. He hoped to God *they* never found her here, he thought, as he changed from his boots into soft shoes.

'How was it?'

There were moments in life that were sheer bliss, and without doubt this was one of them, Kate thought, as she felt Stewart's arms envelop her and hold her safe. She felt herself putting on the security that being with him gave her, like an old familiar coat.

'Oh, not so bad.'

The wind whipped them as they walked across the car park at Bouthéon airport. 'Heavens, what's happened to the weather? It's even worse.' She pulled her pink pashmina closer to her.

'Airports are always the same. It's the flatness, I suppose.'

'Any chance of stopping at the garden centre?'

'None whatsoever.' He grinned. 'You need to get home and put your feet up.'

'I'm not that old!' She laughed, as she slid into the passenger seat of the Alfa Spider she'd given him for his last birthday. Having enough money to give presents, big ones, was one of the best things to have happened to her from her writing – a bit like winning the lottery. She snuggled down into the leather seat while Stewart stowed her case in the boot. Would she have lavished such things on Tony if they had still been together? Probably not. She smiled to herself.

'Something funny?' Stewart asked, as he got in beside her and slid the key into the ignition. She loved all of Stewart but she particularly liked his hands, big, brown, capable – not soft namby-pamby ones like Tony's. He had always fussed over his nails in a way that she found distinctly unmanly – well, there was a sexist thought if ever she'd met one.

'I saw Tony.'

'I'm glad it's cause for amusement for a change.'

'He blamed me for Lucy going off the rails.'

'Typical.' They passed through the car-park ticket barrier. 'It made me wonder . . .'

'Well, don't. You know as well as I do that in parenting you can't win, that you'll cop the blame for everything, no matter what. She's an adult, she chose to do what she did, no one forced her, it's her life.'

'That's what I said to him. But all the same . . . Perhaps if I didn't live here . . .'

'She'd have done the same. And think of Steve – at least you've been fifty per cent successful.'

'I lost my temper with Tony.'

'Good. About time.'

'I made an exhibition of myself yelling at him in the Palm Court of the Adelphi.'

'He deserved it, no doubt.'

'He said I never gave Lucy a thought, that I was selfish.'

'Bastard.'

'I don't think there's a day when I don't think of her a hundred times and wonder and worry. It was so unfair of him.' She fumbled for a tissue and blew her nose. 'He said you were a parasite.'

'Coming from him I take that as a compliment.' Stewart laughed. 'And what about the book?'

'They seem all right at Pewter's – I'm telling myself that one publishing house is very much like another, just to console myself.'

'And does it work?'

'A bit. The trouble is, the office is so big and impersonal, not at all like Westall's. I met Mike Pewter – he's a mountain of a man. But my editor is nice. Young, which is a shame – there always seems to be such an age-gap

81

problem in publishing. I mean, what she likes isn't necessarily what my readers like.'

'Such as?'

'She doesn't like Abigail getting angry when her husband confesses he's come back from the Crusade a homosexual. She said it would offend my readers. I said in Islington, if I had any, perhaps, but in middle England, never. They seem to think that what London thinks is true for the rest of the country.'

'So you kept it in?'

'It's under negotiation. I thought it best to wait until the contracts were safely signed. Then I'll make a fuss.'

'Oh, yeah? Who says? The trouble with you, Kate, is that you don't make nearly enough fuss.'

'I don't want to be regarded as a *difficult author*.'

'Popularity never won anyone success. Look at Bella Ford.'

'She's been sacked too. Joy wasn't making it up – publishing is really odd at the moment.'

'When hasn't it been?'

They were on the motorway now and the sun finally emerged. Kate opened the glove box for the spare sunglasses she always kept there. 'That's odd. Where are my glasses?'

'Which ones?'

'You know, the spare ones I always leave here – I lost my Ray-Bans in London.'

'Typical. I lent them.'

'Well, thank you! To whom? I'd like them back, they were expensive. And whose is this?' She held up the chiffon scarf she had found at the back of the glove compartment. Suddenly she felt sick – first her glasses, now this scarf. What was going on?

'That's Netta's. I gave her a lift the other day and she left

82

it behind so I stuffed it in there. Moron!' he shouted, and gave the finger to a careless driver.

'You've met Netta?'

'Yes. Where else but at—'

'Bricolage!' She laughed. 'And my glasses?'

'I lent your glasses to another woman I met in Bricolage – she was crying. Apparently she wore contact lenses and the dust was hurting her so, being the good Samaritan, I gave her your sunglasses.'

'And will I get them back?'

'Of course. She and her husband are giving a party – we've been invited.'

'Oh, Stewart, no. I hate parties.'

'You don't get out nearly enough. You're becoming a virtual recluse.'

'You know the problem I have with my French.'

'They're English.'

'I thought you said you never wanted to get involved with an ex-pat community.'

'We're going and that's that. By the way, I've booked us a table at L'Air du Temps.'

'Lovely.' Perhaps a party in her own language wouldn't be too bad.

It might be a cliché but, like so many of them, it was true. One of the best things about going away was coming home. The first thing Kate did was a tour of her garden. She was still at the stage where she was finding out what would and wouldn't grow there. It was a challenge, for not only were the summers hot but the winters were bitterly cold and finding plants that would flourish, given these two extremes, was hard.

Since there was already a well-established, flourishing wisteria she had planted two more. Lavender was happy so the hedge she had planted was growing apace. She'd proved the owner of the garden centre wrong by managing to establish several rosemary bushes – he'd told her that her garden was too high and too cold, but she had mulched their roots and wrapped them up for the winter like babies in swaddling clothes and they were doing well. She still needed to fill the spaces round the pool, and the big flower bed outside the sitting room had gaps that made it look as if it had had teeth extracted. When Steve came she'd get him to advise her.

If she had the money – if she did, say, a big film deal . . . She smiled. It was a game they played: when she longed for something she would say, 'When my friend Mr Spielberg rings . . .' Only he never would, she knew that. But *if* the miracle happened she'd try to persuade Steve to open a nursery and garden centre here – the one they had was so predictable, full of the ubiquitous geraniums and little else. Yes, she would willingly finance that. But as she walked back up the steps her smile melted. There was little chance of it now, not with the advance she'd been paid, which was half of what she had become accustomed to.

Then she had remembered some advice given to her right at the beginning of her career. At a Red Rose Society meeting, a well-established author, congratulating her on her success which had been mentioned in all the trade papers, had advised her to squirrel most of it away. 'Publishing is a funny old world, Kate. You're flavour of the month one minute and *passé* the next. I've been labelled too eighties to publish, the next will be too nineties. Publishers chase the latest fad.' At the time she had thought it was the moaning of a bitter woman past her sell-by date. Now she, too, had experienced rejection and she didn't even know how much she had saved. She must ask Stewart.

'You look solemn.' Stewart was standing on the terrace

holding a tray with a jug of Pimm's on it. 'I think it's clearing up and warm enough to have it out here, don't you?'

They sat at the pretty wrought-iron table she had bought and placed beneath the large walnut tree for shade. She wondered now if they were right for here: perhaps they smacked too much of patios in bijou residences in London. Perhaps she should have gone for wooden furniture . . .

'So, why the long face?'

'I was thinking about money.'

He laughed. 'Oh dear. No wonder you looked so grave.'

'It was something someone said to me. It made me think. We are all right, aren't we, Stewart? I mean, with this cut in my advance. We can manage.'

He leant forward and took her hand. 'Now, for goodness' sake, my darling, don't worry. That's my job, isn't it? In any case, there's nothing to worry about. I've made sure that the future is secure.' He poured the Pimm's into the tall crystal goblets she had found especially for it. 'It's a lovely evening, you're back, I've some wonderful steak for supper. Let's enjoy, not talk about boring old money.'

'You're right.' He was such a reassuring man to be with. If there was ever another war she was glad she would have Stewart to rely on: he'd be steadfast, sensible and brave. Since she was a child, she had divided people into two categories: those she would want to be with in a catastrophe and those she'd avoid. Odd, then, that she had married Tony: he'd panic, she was sure. 'I love you, Stewart.'

'I love the way you say that apropos of nothing. It makes me feel truly loved. I'm a lucky old bugger . . .'

'We both are.'

They sat contentedly watching the swallows, who had returned from their southerly migration only the week before. She loved it when they came – it meant that summer was coming fast.

They both peered towards the gate at the sound of a car halting.

'Who can that be?'

'I'd better go and see.' Stewart was on his feet.

The gate, badly in need of oiling, whined as it opened.

'Good God!' She heard Stewart say.

'Hello, Mum.'

'Lucy! Oh, Lucy, my darling.'

4

Kate didn't mean to, and had promised herself that if this day ever came she wouldn't, but she did. She fussed.

'Lucy, Lucy!' She was stroking her daughter's face as if unsure she was really there. 'Lucy!'

'Can't you think of something else to say?' Stewart laughed at her and Lucy giggled. In reply Kate burst into tears.

'Mum, I'm so sorry.' Lucy put her arms round her, patted her shoulder, mussed her hair and whispered that everything was all right.

'We're role-reversing.' Kate smiled through her tears.

'I should have phoned.'

'It might have been a good idea,' Stewart said, as he poured Lucy a glass of Pimm's.

'I was in such a hurry to get here.'

'You took long enough.'

'Stewart, please. She's here now. Are you hungry? Can I get you something? You're so thin . . . When did you last eat?' Already she was on her feet about to head for the kitchen.

'Mum, I'm fine, honestly. I'll eat when you do – that's if you want me to stay.'

'What a silly thing to say. There's a room here for you. It's been waiting ever since we got here.'

'For me?' This information made Lucy look close to tears.

'I decorated it in your favourite colours. Peach and red. I knew you'd come one day, you see. When you were ready.'

At this the tears flooded down Lucy's cheeks, and Kate, who didn't want to cry again and spoil the moment, couldn't help herself either. Between sobs, Lucy apologised not once, not twice but continually, like a mantra: 'I'm so sorry, Mum . . . Will you ever forgive me?'

Kate patted her and kissed her and reassured her.

'I thought you'd show me the door.' At this image the sobbing intensified.

'As if I would!'

Times without number Kate had wondered what this moment would be like. Would she be angry? Would she slap her daughter, as she had that day when she was four and had wandered off in Woolworth's? Not a smack of anger but of relief, which Lucy had never quite understood. Would she shout at her, punish her? None of these. She just wanted to hold her, love her and try to forget it had ever happened.

'Deep down I knew you'd be like this, Mum.'

Stewart muttered, but Kate didn't catch what he said. As she was asking him the phone rang in the house and he bolted for it, as if relieved to be away from their emotion.

'He doesn't like me.'

'He hardly knows you.'

'He was angry with me.'

'Probably for me. It will pass. He's a kind man, and he knows how much I've longed to see you. And now, at last, you're here!' She hugged herself from sheer joy. 'I want to

87

ask you so many things but don't worry, I won't. You'll tell me in your own time.' She was trying to reassure her daughter, who looked so tired and beaten.

Lucy took a tin of Old Holborn tobacco from a string bag she was carrying and began slowly but with practised ease to roll herself a cigarette. To Kate, the simple action seemed to emphasise how far from her her daughter had travelled.

She was going to need clothes, thought Kate – far better to be practical than to dwell on imponderables. She looked so drab. Everything she wore was faded and worn and dirty – she'd been such a smart little thing too. She'd need feeding up to get some flesh back on her. And sleep, she looked hollow-eyed and grey with fatigue . . .

'Mum, I'm married.'

For a few seconds, there was complete silence in Kate's head. There was no song from the birds, the water of the fountain fell silent, she was deaf to the sound of the pool pump, the tractor passing, the dogs barking in the valley. 'What did you say?'

'I'm married. His name's Dominique. I call him Dom. I . . .' Her voice trailed away as she saw the expression on her mother's face.

Shards of ice were pricking at Kate's heart. She felt as if she had fallen and all the air had been expelled violently from her lungs. She perceived her skin tauten as if it were made of parchment and was aware of her hand at her mouth, as if she was stifling a cry.

'How nice. Congratulations,' she said, though she felt bereft.

'I knew you'd understand.'

'I don't, but it doesn't mean I can't be happy for you.'

'At least you were spared the expense.'

'I had looked forward to that one for years.' She wished she hadn't said that, but she felt so hurt, so deeply hurt.

88

'Mum, I'm sorry.'

'It's done now.' She was finding it difficult to speak, as if there was a stone of unhappiness lodged in her throat. She'd lived with the pain of no Lucy for so long, and she'd stupidly thought that when she came back it would go. Foolishly she hadn't anticipated further anguish. She wanted to cry; she wanted to lash out; she longed to shake her daughter. She needed to dissipate her distress. But what good would any of that do? Stewart, reappearing, distracted her. 'Who was on the phone?' She made her voice sound almost normal.

'Sybil. I told her you were busy with your prodigal daughter – she said to tell you she was happy for you.'

'Lucy's got herself married.'

'Are you pregnant?'

'Only a man would ask a question like that.' A frown flickered over Lucy's face. 'As a matter of fact I'm not.'

'Then why not let your mother know?'

'Stewart! It doesn't matter.'

'Of course it bloody well matters!' he said. Then, to Lucy, 'How could you do that to her? Not only do you swan off for all those years, but then you return with this shock. Or did you think your mother would be amused by your little surprise? You're a selfish, thoughtless little bitch.'

'Then I'll go.' Lucy was standing.

'No!' The word emerged in a wail from Kate. 'Please, you can't go, I couldn't bear it – not again. Leave us, Stewart. This is nothing to do with you.'

'Great! *I'd* have said it had everything to do with me. Who's listened to you wittering on about Lucy interminably? How can you say it's not my business?'

'I didn't mean it that way.'

'Then why say it?'

'I meant leave us to sort through this. You being cross with Lucy isn't going to help any of us.'

'Well, sod the lot of you, then.' Grabbing his keys, Stewart marched briskly to the gate, swung it open roughly, which made it screech more than usual, and slammed it shut. Soon they heard his car being driven angrily down the hill.

'I hope he hadn't been drinking,' Lucy said.

'He had.'

'Christ, what a mess I've made of things. The last thing I want is for you and Stewart to fall out over me.'

'We won't. He flies off the handle but he'll calm down. He's worried for me, not so much cross with you. I'm fine now – it was a shock, that's all. First the surprise of you appearing out of the blue and then such momentous news. It's your life, Lucy, and you can do what you want.' Kate spoke calmly, even if it wasn't how she was feeling. She knew she would always feel a sadness that she hadn't seen her only daughter married; a silly thing, but she'd never be the mother of the bride. And already, in these first moments, she knew she would always be puzzled that Lucy had done this. 'Now, tell me everything. Where and when did you get married?' she asked, in as upbeat a tone as she could muster.

'Nearly a year ago. In London. Chelsea Register Office – posh or what?'

'Very. And what did you wear?'

'This. I'd no dosh to buy anything new.'

How often Kate had planned the shopping trip when they would set out to find a bridal dress. 'And flowers?' Even as she asked it she realised it was a stupid question.

'We didn't think about flowers, but a friend rushed out and bought me a peach-coloured gladioli – hardly my favourite flower and I must have looked a prat holding that.'

'You've photographs?'

'No. We didn't think about that either.'

'And did you have a reception.'

'A curry on the Fulham Road!' She was laughing, then stopped abruptly. 'Mum, how can I make amends? I didn't mean to hurt you, but I see now that it was inevitable I would. I was thoughtless. I hadn't been home for so long. And, you see, the longer I was away the harder it became to come back. And I guess that I just got used to doing my own thing and not letting anyone know what that was.'

'So what changed? Why did you suddenly want to see us?'

'I was pregnant. Stewart was wrong in so far as I wasn't when I got married. But once I was pregnant, the enormity of what I'd done to you hit me. And I knew I had to come as soon as possible. And then . . . Then I had a miscarriage. As if I was being punished . . . And I had to see you. I had to make it right again . . .'

'Lucy, my poor child . . . Don't even begin to think that way. Please don't . . .' And she held her child and rocked her and comforted her. But it was an odd feeling. Once, her daughter's body would have felt so familiar, yet now it was as if she were holding a stranger.

'And Dominique?' she asked, once the tears had ceased.

'He's wonderful. He's so thoughtful and kind, and he understands me. It's like he knows what I want even before I know myself. When I'm with him I feel as if we're one person.' Now Lucy's eyes shone with happy excitement instead of tears.

'That's good. And what does this paragon do?' She regretted that word: it sounded snide and unkind and she didn't mean to be either – but then she knew that that was exactly what she had meant to be. What she had thought just minutes ago was not how she felt: she acknowledged that while she was pleased to have her daughter safe and with her, she also wanted to punish her for all the pain she had caused.

'He's trained as a chef.'

'Then he's come to the right country.'

'Oh, no, you don't understand. How could you? He's French.'

It was nearly midnight before Kate could persuade Lucy to go to bed. It seemed that she couldn't stop talking, as if now she was here she wanted to make up to her mother in some way and tell her of everything that had happened to her. There was much that Kate would have preferred not to know – about the drugs, the sleeping rough, the miscarriage, the stealing, the cold and the hunger. 'But you're here now, and a comfortable bed is waiting for you. I really am pleased to have you safe and with me but—'

'But what?'

'Oh, nothing. So pleased!' She had hugged her then but now, alone, she could think of that *but* and what it had meant. She knew that while she *was* pleased she could never forgive Lucy, not completely.

'Tony, it's Kate.'

'Do you know what time it is?'

'Your time? It's only eleven.'

'Some of us have to work for a living.'

She smiled at his words. How typical. 'I'm sorry if I woke you but I thought you should know that Lucy has turned up here safe, sound and married. That's all.' She replaced the receiver sharply, aware that it was a malicious act on her part not to explain further but rather pleased with herself that she hadn't. The phone rang again.

'Kate.'

'Do you know what time it is, Tony? Not now, I'll call you in the morning.' Now she had the double satisfaction of having annoyed him twice in the space of minutes.

It was three before Stewart returned, somewhat the worse for wear.

'You shouldn't have driven in that state.'

'Spare me the lecture, Kate.'

'It wasn't meant to be a lecture, I was concerned for your safety, that was all.'

The harrumph he made showed he did not believe her. 'Is the blushing bride asleep?'

'Soundly.'

'And I suppose you forgave her?'

'I doubt if I ever will entirely, but I couldn't see any point in playing the heavy parent. What's done is done.'

'You sound like Sybil,' he said, as he climbed into bed beside her.

'Her husband is French. He went to see his mother to tell her he was married so I'm not alone.'

'It's different with boys.'

'Is it? I don't think so. I would be just as devastated if Steve did this to me.'

'Let's hope he doesn't. Now, if you don't mind, Kate, I'm knackered.'

'Where did you go?'

'Does it matter?'

'To me it does.'

'The English bar in Le Puy.'

'I'm sorry I snapped.'

'That's OK. I guess I was being heavy-handed, and you were right, it was none of my business.' Thirstily he drank a whole glass of Perrier.

'That's not exactly what I said.'

'Does it matter?' he said sleepily.

'I've said they can live in the barn.'

'You *what*?' He was awake now, sitting up and looking thunderous.

'Don't flap, just temporarily until they get themselves straight.'

'And that's an offer I bet you live to regret!'

5

When she awoke the next morning Kate knew something was different. Still drowsy from sleep, it was several seconds before she remembered what it was. Then she lay looking at the ceiling with a grin on her face. Lucy was back! . . . She was married. At this Kate's happiness drained away. She sat upright. She was going to have a fight on her hands against her own bitterness.

Stewart rolled over in the bed and made an angry-sounding snort, then waved his hand at his nose, missing it, as if something in it was annoying him.

Kate propped herself up on one elbow and looked down at him. For the first time she noticed a fine web of broken veins on his cheeks. Had they always been there and she had never noticed them? How unobservant of her. Come to think of it, his nose looked a bit red too, as if he was starting a cold. Perhaps that was it. *You reckon?* enquired her inner voice, which she wished sometimes would stay mum. Just recently there had been occasions when he had been a bit tiddly. *Tiddly! Drunk more like.* No, that was not fair, she told herself. Drunk meant falling down, aggression or silliness. *There you go – he gets aggressive.* Not really. Had she

94

thought that or said it? The words seemed to hang in the air.

Certainly Stewart liked his wine but a Frenchman would have thought he drank quite modestly. Perhaps he was knocking it back when she wasn't around. Well, hardly, she told herself. There would be no need for him to do so. *How would you know?* She was not censorious about drink – at least, she didn't think she was. But when a person said they weren't, they too often were. She'd one friend who claimed she felt no jealousy when she was riddled with it, and another who always said she kept her mouth shut when that was the last thing she did. Was she like them?

More likely it was her own edginess that was making dramas where none existed. Not only had she had the disappointment of her book being rejected, but there had been her concern for Lucy. Now she had returned, loaded, no doubt, with another bundle of problems for Kate to take on board. There you go again, presuming problems where perhaps none exist – *you reckon?* This was getting her nowhere.

As quietly as she could she got up. She wrapped her dressing-gown around her and padded down the stairs. In the kitchen she made herself a cup of tea, which she took out on to the terrace. It was only seven but the sun was up, and from the mist in the valley it promised to be a good day. The way the weather could change here was astounding: it could be freezing one day, blistering the next, pouring with rain in the morning and sunny in the afternoon. It was because they were so close to the mountains, she'd been told.

The swallows were dive-bombing the newly filled swimming-pool, noisily demanding that the cover be taken off so that they could have their early-morning dip. Kate sat up, placed her mug on the flagstones, ran down the steps to the pool, and wound it back. Then, clutching her tea, she sat down under the pergola to watch them. As if aware that they had an audience the birds put on an amazing aerial display, dipping into the water, shooting across the pool to miss each other by millimetres, just like fighter planes at an air-show. They shook their feathers, soaring back up into the sky, the sun glinting on the ultramarine of their under wings.

For the umpteenth time she told herself just how lucky they were to live in such a paradise. But then uninvited came the nasty question: if her book didn't sell well, and the next advance was even less than this one, how long could they afford this life style?

From this worry another sprang, like a many-headed hydra. Before she disappeared Lucy had only met Stewart a couple of times, not enough to get to know each other. Now, from last night's scene, it was obvious that they had got off to a bad start. Still, perhaps it was as Stewart had said, that he was angry for Kate. Lucy certainly seemed to have changed – but for the better. In that case maybe it had been just an unfortunate blip that would be remedied when they finally got to know each other better. This was an optimistic thought but the next wasn't. *They are going to loathe each other and you're going to end up piggy in the middle!*

'Kate, stop talking to yourself! You are a fool,' she said, quite firmly. *But an intuitive one.* 'Oh, shut up, do!'

This was nothing new. Worry was part of her life and always had been. Steve used to tease her that if she wasn't worrying about something then she'd worry about why she wasn't. It was part and parcel of her adulthood, but in the last few weeks it had been getting out of hand again; like a mental eczema that made her soul itch. It was something she must watch and try to rein in or . . .

'Here you are! You were up early.' She hadn't heard Stewart, bare-footed, approaching.

'I couldn't get back to sleep and it was such a lovely day I decided to get up.' She smiled up at him, blanking out the morning's thoughts. 'Perhaps summer has arrived at last.'

'You've got tea.'

'I'm happy to drink another one.' She took the mug from him. 'Those birds are amazing, aren't they?' It would be better, she decided, if they talked of things other than Lucy for the time being.

'Has Lucy told you why she got married without the courtesy of telling you?' he asked, and she wished he hadn't.

'Not yet, but she will.' Her tone was stalwart.

'Bloody odd thing to do. Maybe she doesn't like you.'

'What a thing to say.' She managed to laugh while wanting to cry out.

'What other reason could there be?'

'Maybe she didn't think it was that big a deal. I don't know.' God, how she wished he would change the subject.

'Did you really say last night that Lucy was to stay in the barn?'

'Yes.'

'I hoped you hadn't, that in my fuddled state I'd made it up.'

'Were you fuddled?' she asked, all innocent.

'You know I was. I just said it to forestall any wifely inquisition.' He guffawed. '*Did* you mean it about the barn?' he repeated, catching her momentarily unawares.

'Yes.'

'It's very inconvenient.'

'Why? No one uses it.'

'I thought we could rent it out as a *gîte*.'

'Whatever for? I don't fancy that. I don't want to share my pool with anyone.'

'Kate, sweetheart, you've had a financial setback. I was just hoping to recoup some money.'

'But renting the barn as a holiday cottage is hardly likely to save our bacon, is it?'

'Will Lucy contribute to the electricity, the oil, the taxes?'

'Hardly. She *is* my daughter.' Her heart was thudding. She'd been right all along – trouble was most certainly a-brewing.

'I think you should have discussed it with me first.'

'You weren't here to talk to. You'd pi– you'd gone—'

'Pissed off. Was that what you were about to say?'

'Something like, yes.'

'It could have waited until morning.'

'I didn't think it could.'

'This is our home.'

'Yes, I know, and Lucy is my daughter. I'm fully aware she isn't yours, but if she was I hope I would act in the same way.' She sat upright, as if her posture reflected the formality of her speaking tone.

'How long is she staying?'

'I haven't the foggiest. We didn't get that far. They've had a rough time in England so they've come here to lick their wounds, recover and then set up in some way.'

'What way?'

'She didn't say.'

'She wants something.'

'Maybe she was tired and wanted to be home again.'

'She'll be on the cadge, you mark my words.'

'I've no intention of doing so.'

'How can you be all over her when she's left you worried sick all these years? How does she have the audacity to just turn up, begging-bowl out?'

98

'You don't know that and how dare you say it! She is welcome to stay here for as long as she likes. And if there's something she wants, as her mother I shall be happy to help her. Thank you for my tea.' Kate stood up and walked, stiff as a soldier, up the steps to the terrace, through the morning-cool house, to her room.

Once safely inside she slammed the door and retreated into her bathroom. She was seething with anger. This morning there would be no shower: his words called for a bath and some serious thinking.

'How do you like your coffee?' Kate asked Lucy, as she fussed about her. She had returned from the *boulangerie* to find Lucy up and on the terrace, watching the birds as she had done. She laid the plate of croissants and *pain au chocolat* on the wrought-iron table on the terrace.

'Have you forgotten, Mum?'

Were those tears in Lucy's eyes? 'Good gracious, no,' she said hurriedly, placing the pot of apricot jam on the table. 'I remember you prefer to drink instant, but this is the real McCoy – one of the many joys of living in France. Do you like it black or milky is what I meant.'

'Black and strong as it comes.'

'That's bad for your pancreas.'

'Some things never change, do they, Mum? You're still a worrier.'

'I'm not any more. I've stopped. Oh, not on the big things like were you safe and well, but the little things don't bother me at all.'

'And do pigs fly in this neck of the woods?' Lucy laughed.

It was a wonderful sound to hear, rare too. As a teenager she hadn't been particularly light-hearted and had taken life too seriously, like her father, no doubt. When Lucy laughed Kate had always grabbed it, held it to her and cherished it, which was unfair to Steve. He laughed often so she did not appreciate it as much.

'So, when's your husband coming? Heavens, that does sound a strange thing to say to you.'

'I hope tomorrow. We don't like being apart. But his mum isn't well and he might get delayed. He's that sort of fellow.'

'And have you met his family?'

'No. He said I was to come here immediately.'

'Then I already like him.'

'He was shocked with what I'd done. He says that to the French the family is very important. He said what I had done to you was unforgivable and I was to come and make amends.'

'Then I already *love* him.' Kate grinned. 'Look, if you don't want to tell me I'll understand, but for all that I'd like to know. Last night you didn't really explain why you did what you did.' She couldn't quite bring herself to say 'run away'.

Lucy looked all ways but at her.

Should she have asked so soon? Kate wondered. But she had. There was no going back, she'd have to press on.

'You see, Lucy, I'm not just being nosy. I need to know for my own peace of mind. Was it something I'd done?'

'You? No, of course not. And yet it's hard to tell because half the time I don't know myself. I guess I was, probably still am, too self-centred for everyone's good. There was you and Dad, separated. Steve was in the north. Dad had found a girlfriend – evil old hag. You'd got Stewart. There just didn't seem any place for me.'

'There's always a place for you. You should know that instinctively.' So it was our fault, she thought, and felt bleak at the prospect.

'Well, I didn't. Or I thought there wasn't. And then, to

compound everything, I suddenly didn't have a mum any more. There was this career woman with other obligations, deadlines – no time for me.'

'Lucy, that's just not true. I always made the time. You know that.' Kate couldn't believe what she was hearing. 'No, I won't accept that as an explanation since it simply isn't true.' She spoke in such an emphatic tone that Lucy looked at her with surprise. Had she expected Kate to apologise for something she hadn't done? If so, they had all moved on and they were different, even if she hadn't realised quite how different. She waited for Lucy to react but she sipped her coffee and said nothing. She wondered if her daughter, consciously or not – it didn't matter which – was trying to divert the blame away from herself. That she wasn't as grown-up as Kate had hoped.

'Then Cambridge was the biggest let-down of all, a load of pseuds floating around. I hated my tutor, and it was like a club I didn't belong to. It wasn't my scene at all so I decided to split.'

'And you couldn't explain this to us?'

'I sent you the odd postcard so you'd know I wasn't dead in a ditch.'

Hold it, Kate told herself, don't lose it now and risk her bolting again. 'I appreciated that.' She was aware that she sounded sarcastic but it just wouldn't come out any other way. 'And the getting-married?'

'I didn't think it was that important and, in any case, I'd rather cooked my goose, hadn't I?' She smiled at her mother and the smile said more than her words: it begged her to forgive, to understand.

Kate put out her hand and squeezed her daughter's. 'We'll never discuss this again, I promise. Now . . .' she stood up '. . . let's go and look at this barn we've converted and decide which room you want to use for what.'

101

6

'I didn't expect you.' She held the heavy oak door wide open. She could not see his face since the sun was blinding her, but she knew his silhouette. The marvellous hugeness of him. 'Come in, quick, before that nosy old bastard of a gardener sees you.'

'I thought you'd told him I was your cousin.'

'I did, but from his leer I don't think he believed me.' Her laugh was light, almost girlish. 'So, to what do I owe the pleasure?'

'Another little domestic squall.'

'Why do you put up with it?' Her spindly heels click-clacked across the highly polished red tiles of her hallway. 'Don't get me wrong, I'm not complaining. The more rows you have the happier I am.'

'The same could be said of you. I reckon you beat me hands down in the turbulence of your marriage. I take it the coast is clear? Where's his nibs?'

'London.'

'Thank the Lord for big business.' He scooped her into his arms.

'Don't you want a drink first?'

'Later, not now. I want you, and then again and again and again!' For a man of his age he carried her lightly as he ran up the long stone staircase. From habit he knew which room to go to – not her marital bed, even they drew the line at that, but the bed of the guest room was as wide as her own, its bathroom as well appointed.

He kicked at the door, threw her on to the bed and ripped off his own clothes while she slipped out of hers. For an hour they made wild and abandoned love in a way that neither did with their partner. Not until they were satiated

102

did she get the champagne that she always had cooling on ice – just in case he came.

'You know, I still can't believe we've managed to pull it off.' She was uncorking the bottle with practised ease.

'It certainly took longer and more planning than I imagined.'

'I thought we'd never find a house close to you yet distant enough not to arouse suspicion.'

'And one he approved of. Mustn't forget his need for status and standing.'

'That's not kind.'

'But it's true.'

'He's worked hard for it, he's earned it.'

'And his trophy wife.'

'I'm a bit old to be described as that.'

'But beautiful and sexy enough.' He slapped her rump playfully. She squealed with delight, and rubbed her body close to him as if she was trying to get into his skin.

A little later they lay again in each other's arms. 'Do you think you'll ever leave him?'

'And all this?' She waved her arm at the beautifully furnished room. 'I'm not mad.'

'But what if he found out?'

'He won't, if no one tells him. And who knows about us?'

'Your gardener.'

'No problem. I'm the only one here who can speak French.' She laughed again.

'But what if I asked you to?'

'But you won't. That's why we get on so well. No demands, just sex.'

'Sometimes I think I might be falling in love with you.'

'Don't spoil it all, Stewart, there's a love.'

103

Chapter Three

May

1

Sybil, being a ditherer most of the time, was at her worst when shopping for clothes for herself. This was the third dress shop they had been in, searching for something for Sybil to wear to the party. Already she had tried on around a dozen outfits.

'I really don't know why you want me to tag along. Whatever I suggest you reject out of hand.'

'Netta, I don't mean to offend, honestly. But, well, our taste is so different, isn't it?' Sybil's face was screwed up with anxiety and the stress of shopping.

'But *I* know what suits you.'

'I sometimes think you choose things that would be perfect for you but hardly for me.' From anyone else this might have been construed as a sharp comment, but Sybil was merely saying what she thought, which was devoid of rancour.

Used to her, and accepting it as such, Netta laughed. 'What a trial you are, my dear Sybil. I agree. What I like isn't necessarily what you are looking for. But what about some colour? You always choose dull pastels. Why not try something brighter, jazzier? You know, give yourself a bit more oomph!' Netta offered, from her position of confidante, adviser and critic. She was draped elegantly on a small gilt chair in one of the exclusive dress shops tucked away in the narrow back streets of the old part of Le Puy.

'Gracious, if I did that poor Sim would run a mile. He's terrified of sex.' Sybil giggled as she twirled in front of the full-length mirror in a grey silk dress that did nothing for her.

'Well, there's a surprise!' Netta drawled. 'Madame . . .' She turned to the proprietor of the shop, who was anxiously smoothing and draping the dress on Sybil. 'I suggest something with more colour.'

The shopkeeper ignored her and continued to flutter about Sybil. She had noticed Netta before: her flat was only one street away. She had registered that she was always well turned-out but that nothing was new and that this was likely to remain so. Instead she smarmed fulsomely over Sybil, telling her how chic she looked in this particular creation. This was the first time she had met her but with one professional sweep she had noted the expensive patent-leather shoes, the good handbag and the distinctive smell of Joy perfume. So she concentrated on where the money obviously was. The snub to Netta was blatant.

'Madame, did you not hear me? I asked for something rather brighter for Madame Chesterton.'

'But she looks perfectly charming in this grey.'

'And I think, and you know, that she looks like a moth.' She stood up, gathering her bag. 'Come on, Sybil, we can do better than this. Get changed, we're leaving.'

'Really?' Sybil stopped twirling. 'I thought this one was rather nice.'

'*Nice* being the operative word. It's not good enough for you. It's time you changed your image. Come on, chop-chop.' She clapped her hands and Sybil skipped off to the dressing room. Netta swung round and faced the shop-owner. 'You, Madame, ignored me.' She smiled her astonishing smile, while speaking in an icy tone. 'It is very ill-advised of you to foist a garment on someone so lacking in confidence simply because it is the most expensive you have.'

'Am I supposed to know what problems your friend has?' The woman smirked in a superior manner.

'If you are to succeed you should have all your antennae acutely attuned. You should be able to read your customers. And it would be wise of you not to presume that just because someone is a foreigner they are a tourist and you can palm off any old thing on them, simply because you think you will never see them again. It's such a pity you are as you are – you have some nice things here. I would so like to have recommended you to my other friends.' With a dramatic gesture, Netta threw the end of her long scarf over her shoulder.

'Madame, I am desolated. I did not mean . . .'

'Oh, yes, you did. You see, Madame, being ignored is deeply distressing to me – egotist that I am.' As she spoke Netta was fingering the fabric of a particularly pretty crêpe blouse in reds and blues.

'Perhaps Madame would like to try this blouse. Unless I am mistaken it is in your size.'

'That won't be necessary.' She waved her hand dismissively, as if she was not in the least interested in the garment. She began to study another. The proprietor watched her but evidently, Netta decided, did not understand what was expected of her. 'I have a dear friend whose granddaughter is to marry later this year . . .' She arched her eyebrows. 'Perhaps you would like an introduction?'

'Why, Madame, how very kind of you.' In a trice the blouse was off its hanger and being wafted this way and that, demonstrating the excellence of the fabric, the beauty of the cut.

'Perhaps, Madam, you would accept this small gift as a token of my devastation at our little misunderstanding?'

'Well, of course, if you insist. It would be churlish to refuse.'

'Would you like it gift-wrapped?'

'No, one of your excellent bags will do.' Again she concentrated her smile on the woman. Netta watched as the woman folded the blouse. She had much to learn if she was going to succeed. If she introduced people she had every right to expect a 'present' without going through this rigmarole. It was how things were done. How else was she to survive? It was a nice blouse – she could sell it and buy food for a month for her and Tam. 'I am so happy that now we understand each other.' She smiled as she accepted the bag.

In her usual flustered state, Sybil appeared from the dressing room. 'You're buying something, Netta. Let me pay for it.'

'No, dear friend, that won't be necessary.' She turned to the shopkeeper. 'I trust we shall have better luck in your establishment next time we visit.'

'Oh, you've made friends, I am pleased,' Sybil gushed.

There was much bowing and scraping as Netta and Sybil sallied forth. Netta held herself more proudly than ever since she felt her status had been restored to her.

'By the time we left that shop where you didn't like the woman she was a different person. What happened?' Sybil asked as they entered the Palais Brasserie.

'We came to an understanding,' Netta said, enigmatically.

'The blouse!' Sybil, leading the way, stopped dead in her

tracks so that Netta cannoned into her. 'It's a bribe!' She pointed at Netta's carrier bag.

'Not at all. It's a gesture of appreciation.'

'But we didn't buy anything.'

'But we shall in the future.'

'Did you ask for it?' They were taking their seats at a table by the window.

Netta slid along the banquette. 'Really, Sybil! As if I'd do anything so crass.' But, uncharacteristically, she felt herself colour.

'Netta, you did! You are a caution. What a thing to do!' Sybil laughed.

'Nonsense, I implied, that is all.' They ordered omelettes and salad, with a carafe of white wine. 'But even if I did, why shouldn't I? It's a new shop, not yet established. If I choose, I can help her. She knew that.'

'You do this often?' Sybil was wide-eyed with astonishment.

'But of course. I regard it as an introduction fee. Madame and I finally understood each other. A woman in my position, what else can I do?'

'My poor friend. I didn't think.'

Netta laughed. '*Poor*, yes, you could say that. She was in the wrong. I couldn't let her sell you something that was not right for you.'

'But I liked it.'

'You looked like a faded wren. You could look so much more stunning if only you'd let me really advise you. Your hair, it's a pretty colour but who can see it with all those tight curls? And you've a lovely figure but you hide it under such baggy clothes.'

'You know me. I'm not interested in how I look.'

'But why aren't you?'

'How would I know?' She laughed. 'I never have been.'

Her laugh was hollow, Netta decided, and she had seen the tiniest of frowns flicker across Sybil's face as if she had been fibbing. 'Pull the other one,' she said, and topped up their glasses with wine.

'Look, I compromised today. I bought the green trouser suit you liked so much in the next shop. Though why I did when I hate green I'll never know. And what Sim will have to say – well! He doesn't like women in trousers. He says our *derrières* are the wrong shape for them.'

'Has he looked at his own behind recently?' Netta enquired.

'I like his bottom.'

'Then you need specs as well.'

'Why do you dislike Sim so?'

'Because he pulls you down and dominates you, and I don't like to see it.'

'He doesn't. He's looking after me.'

'Some looking after! He dictates to you.'

'Then maybe if he does it's my fault. You don't know everything.'

'S-y-b-i-l! Women like you make me wonder why others bothered to chain themselves to railings, starve, fling themselves in front of horses! I despair.'

'Still you know what they say. "I'm an old-fashioned girl" and I have to "stand by my man"!' Sybil giggled, but stopped abruptly when she saw just a whisper of annoyance speed across Netta's face.

'That's another thing. Why do you speak in clichés all the time? Why?' There! She had said it even though she had never intended to, and now the words hung between them. Sybil sat silent for a moment, as if unsure how to proceed. 'I shouldn't have said that, it was rude, I'm sorry.'

'Don't be, it's true. I realise it must be irritating to you, and I try not to do it but they keep popping out.' Sybil looked upset but spoke with a dignity that made Netta feel ashamed. 'I think I do it because I'm nervous all the time. I think it's because I want people to like me. And, in any case, I've nothing original to say.' Her normally watery eyes were even fuller of tears than usual. Her bottom lip quivered. 'There are times when I think I no longer exist, that I'm just a cipher. And I don't know why it happened or when. I wasn't always, you know. Only when . . .' Her voice trailed off.

'My sweetheart, you're no such thing. Don't you even think it for one moment.' Netta's hand shot out to take her friend's. But even as she held it she found herself thinking that Sybil had hit the nail on the head, that that was exactly what she was – insignificant – and she shouldn't be. 'That bastard husband of yours has made you like this. Leave him, make a new start. Come and live with me,' she said urgently. Christ, she thought, what on earth had made her say that? She'd end up killing Sybil in no time at all. 'There, there,' she added, quite inadequately she knew.

'I know you mean well, Netta, but I could never leave Sim. I don't expect you to understand. It's not his fault that I am as I am.' She blew into a tissue, dabbed at her eyes, opened her handbag, shut it again, and then repeated the blowing and mopping-up procedure all over again.

There was much that Netta wanted to say but for once sense prevailed and she managed to keep quiet.

Across the other side of the brasserie, Mo watched the scene with interest as she waited for Tristram, who had gone to the bank. 'See those two women over there? One's crying. I wonder what the other one said or did to make her?' she said, as Tristram joined her.

'Perhaps they've had a lovers' tiff.'

'Hell, you sound like my old man.' She looked at him with a horrified expression. 'If he saw two women having

110

coffee together he said they were dykes. Don't tell me you're the same.'

'No, I meant maybe one of them was nursing a broken heart or some such.' Tristram had noticed that whenever Mo mentioned her father a bleak look came into her eyes. He was sure the old bastard had done something awful to her before he died. But it was a subject he did not want to pursue for fear of what she might tell him. It was no wonder she had problems: a father she hated, an alcoholic mother, and a grinding poverty that he could only imagine. Whenever she told him of her past he felt such anger for her.

'That's more like it.' She smiled, the tense moment dissipated. 'Mind you, I've often wondered what it would be like to do it with a woman.'

'You were in the right place to try. Aren't loads of models bi or lezzos?'

'Some are. I often thought it was because they were lonely. Poor souls. All that beauty and men too scared to approach them.'

Tristram looked at her with surprise. She didn't often make such sensitive remarks – and certainly not about other women.

'I'd bet anything that those two women are English. You can always tell.'

'How?'

'The body language, the way they're dressed. They're friends but not close friends. The older, beautiful one—'

'Beautiful? That? She's old!'

Tristram smiled at her. That was more like the Mo he knew. '*I* think she is. You see, she's concerned but reticent with it. The one with the dreadful hair is embarrassed that she's on the verge of tears. I think you're wrong, I don't think she cried – almost but not quite.'

111

'Quite the psychoanalyst, aren't you?' Mo was laughing – he loved it when she did. 'What did the bank want?'

'Oh, nothing important. There was a query about a cheque I'd signed.'

'It didn't bounce?' Mo didn't look horrified as Tristram might have expected: bounced cheques were too common an occurrence.

'No, nothing like,' he lied. She might be nonchalant about the subject but he didn't want to worry her unduly. In fact, three cheques had bounced and the bank had said it was illegal in France to issue cheques without funds to cover them, and that normally his account would be closed and no other bank would take him on. He felt weak and sweaty from the fast talking he had done. He'd promised them money within the week – somehow.

Once they had finished their coffee they got up to go. Mo led the way past the table where Netta and Sybil sat.

'Hurry up, Tris, I'm dying for a shag,' she said loudly, as she passed.

'Well, really!' said an affronted Sybil.

Now why would a lovely creature like that go out of her way to shock? thought Netta. She must be bored. A beautiful, bored woman could be dangerous – she should know.

2

Kate should have been working, but for once didn't feel guilty that she wasn't. She put the answerphone on in case her editor, Portia, phoned about the book. She just wasn't in the mood to write – settling Lucy into the barn was a far more exciting thing to be doing.

The barn was situated on the far side of the garden, just visible from the house but with its own entrance and parking area.

'You see, although you're near you're completely independent.'

'Mum, this is fabulous,' Lucy exclaimed. 'How many bedrooms are there?'

'Only two, with this sitting room and the kitchen and bathroom. I do hope it will be big enough for you.'

'Big enough? You should have seen the squat we've been living in – every rodent known to man as our neighbours.'

'Please, spare me the details.' Kate shuddered. 'We need more cushions in here and a mirror. I assumed I'd thought of everything but there are sure to be things I've overlooked. See? You have your own little garden.' She slid open the large patio doors, which opened on to the small walled garden she'd had constructed.

'You can see where Steve gets his talent for gardening from. This is lovely. And you meant to use this for guests? But it looks as if no one has stayed here.'

'They haven't. We've always had room enough in the main house. You see, the first couple of years we were here, people descended in droves – curious, no doubt, to see where we'd ended up. There were so many we had to use the local B-and-B. So we decided to convert this into a little house for them. Then they stopped coming.'

'They'll be back. They're probably waiting for a decent interval until they invite themselves again.'

'I hope so. Visitors are important and I look forward to them. Not all of them, mind you. There were people we barely knew who phoned and asked if they could drop in for a couple of nights *en route* to the south.'

'It happens if you live in Cornwall too.'

That was interesting – another little snippet of information about Lucy's life to file away, but she'd better not pursue it now. Patience, that's what she needed.

'People have astonished me,' Kate continued instead. 'We'd get some who, when there was still duty-free on the ferries, would plonk down a bottle of gin as if giving us riches, and then proceed to drink us out of house and home.'

'But I thought booze here was cheaper than duty-free anyway.'

'It was. That just added insult to injury.' She laughed. 'And then Flo Bateman from Graintry came – do you remember her? And she was quite affronted that I worked while *she* was here. Just because they're on holiday they expect us to be too.'

'I remember her. She was always a pain.'

Kate was opening the windows to air the rooms. 'Stewart was talking about using it for holiday lets.'

'You couldn't do that, strangers on your doorstep – what if you loathed them on sight?'

'Exactly. You came in the nick of time. He'll drop the idea now.' She said this with more conviction than she felt. 'What about we go into Le Puy and buy a mirror, cushions, anything that takes our fancy? There are some excellent antique shops and who knows what we'll find?'

Over lunch at La Tournayre Kate reflected that this was how she had always wanted it to be with her daughter – shopping together, sharing ideas, chatting, gossiping, rather than the irritated armed truce that had tended to be their normal relationship.

'Seen Dad recently?' Lucy asked, as she speared an early stalk of asparagus, dripping with butter. Kate managed not to say, 'Don't drop it down your front.'

'Last month. We had a drink and a few words.' She

114

smiled a secret smile at this understatement. She still had flashes of guilt at how appallingly she had behaved. 'He's angry with me.'

'Why? Because you're happy and he isn't?'

'Probably.'

'You *are* happy, aren't you?'

'Very. Funny you should ask, Steve posed the self-same question the last time I saw him. Why?'

'Neither of us likes Stewart. We don't trust him.'

'What a thing to say!' Kate began to laugh but stopped abruptly when she realised that Lucy was serious. 'In what way exactly?' Her voice was very controlled.

'Nothing specific. It's just something about him.'

'Well, to take what you say seriously I would have to have something more than that. I think you're both being stupid. You don't know him, either of you.'

'Do you?'

'Of course. He's been good to me, and kind, and without him I don't know how I would manage. You know my head for business.'

'Quite.' Lucy looked into the far distance over the rim of her wine-glass in the way of one who is making a point.

'And what does that mean?' Kate could feel herself getting rattled.

'Nothing.'

'Then you shouldn't have said it.'

'I'm sorry. I should have kept my big mouth shut.'

Suddenly Kate saw that Lucy was looking at her almost pleadingly. Perhaps she had spoken without thinking. Perhaps this was a consequence of the new relationships that she and Tony had inflicted on their children when they split. Writing about complicated relationships, as Kate did, was far easier than living with them. But on the other hand, in the book she was writing at the moment, maybe she could utilise such a situation . . .

'Mum, you're miles away. What are you thinking?'

'Nothing,' she replied, taking a leaf out of her daughter's book. She was not about to confess that she was doing what all writers did, squirrelling away an idea – Lucy mght take it the wrong way and regard her as cold and calculating. But she supposed she was when it came to her books.

'Don't be cross with me. I don't want to spoil my homecoming.'

But the day was marred, as if a black cloud had passed over Kate's happiness. They finished their lunch and picked up their purchases, but the old barrier was once more between them, which Kate had so hoped had disappeared.

A couple of days later, the noise of a Deux Chevaux climbing the hill would have woken the dead. As it was, every dog in the village began to bark or howl. It even drowned the tractor.

'It's Dom!' Lucy was excitedly on her feet and racing out of the house, across the terrace and to the gate. Kate checked her appearance in the mirror, patting her hair, moistening her lips, and realised that she felt ridiculously nervous.

'*Chéri*, this is my mother.'

'Madame, I am enchanted to make your acquaintance,' Dominique said, in excellent English, as he bowed formally over her hand.

Kate had to hide a smile. When translated into English French greetings always sounded so poncy. But at least he spoke her language. 'Welcome,' she said. And, not sure what was the right thing to do, she put up her arms, hugged him and kissed him on both cheeks.

Dominique was short and of a slight build. He had dark

116

hair with what looked suspiciously like Brylcreem on it. His brown eyes, with long lashes – to which no man had a right – were his best feature. His complexion was sallow, as if he'd once been brown but the colour had faded from a life spent unhealthily indoors. He had stubble on his chin – still fashionable here if *passé* in England. He was neatly dressed in black slacks and jumper, with polished slip-on shoes and a gold bracelet. He was carrying a packet of cigarettes with a gold lighter in one hand. He was not at all the drop-out Kate had expected to see.

Stewart was introduced and the two men eyed each other with suspicion. But, then, if Lucy had said the same odd things to Dominique about Stewart that she had to Kate, it was hardly surprising. Meanwhile, Stewart was probably just being protective of his honorary stepdaughter, she reassured herself.

'Well, this is nice,' said Kate, knowing that such a sentence was inadequate, and compounded it by asking everyone if they would like tea.

They sat in the garden drinking the champagne that Stewart suggested instead. Kate wanted to know everything about Dominique, but no question she asked seemed to warrant a straight answer. While not impolite, he was not at all forthcoming.

'How is your mother?'

'She is well.'

'Lucy said she had been ill.'

'It has passed.'

Silences kept descending on the little group. Kate found herself constantly studying her plants, the distant view, her hands. Stewart was of no help whatsoever, sitting silently glum, and Lucy just looked at her husband with speechless adoration.

'You are from Paris?'

'Yes.' She was not encouraged to ask from what part. He toyed with his cigarettes. He flicked the packet and tapped one out. What should have been a fairly simple action, in his hands became complicated. The lighter was twirled and flicked and twirled again, as if to ensure that everyone saw it. Only then was the cigarette lit and deeply inhaled, and smoke exhaled through his nose. Perhaps he considered it sophisticated to smoke, Kate thought.

'Lucy says you're a chef?'

'That is correct.'

'Where have you worked?'

'Many places.'

And so the first meeting dragged on. There was a highlight, though, when Dominique produced the largest box of chocolates Kate had ever seen. It was as well he didn't know she never touched chocolate because it gave her a headache. This was followed by a big bottle of Chanel No. 5 – the one perfume that reacted adversely with her. Stewart received a bottle of malt whisky. The triumph was an exquisite orchid, its thick white petals looking almost artificial in their perfection. 'A beautiful flower for a beautiful woman,' he said, as he presented it to her. And Kate knew for certain there and then that she didn't like him and never would.

'What do you think?' Stewart asked, as they prepared for bed.

'I thought the presents were a bit OTT. But he isn't English, so we must make allowances. He seemed pleasant enough. And Lucy is obviously in love with him.' She was brushing her hair. She could have been honest with him but something held her back – family loyalty, she supposed. After all, for better or worse, Dominique was her son-in-law.

118

And then bleakness filled her as she was reminded that she hadn't been there when the vows were made.

'I thought he was too obvious.'

'What's that mean?' She paused in her brushing.

'He's a gold-digger.'

'How on earth can you deduce that?'

'He looks like one. My mother would have called him a lounge lizard.'

'What a hoot!'

'I don't think it's anything to laugh about.'

'But it's a silly theory. Lucy hasn't got two halfpennies to rub together.'

'No, but you have.'

'He doesn't know me.'

'But he could know *of* you.'

'Hardly.'

'You've never grasped that you've become well known, have you?'

'I don't feel I am. I hardly get mobbed in the street.' She smiled at the very idea.

'What would be more natural than that Lucy took him into a bookshop to see your books? And he's put two and two together.'

'He might love her. Simple as that.'

'He might.' But Stewart sounded remarkably doubtful. 'How long are they staying?'

'You keep asking that. I've no idea – until he gets work, I suppose.'

'There's something odd about him. I don't trust him.'

She could have said, 'Others say the same of you,' but, of course, she didn't. And then she wondered why she resented him saying these things about Dominique when he was only saying what she was thinking. It was almost as if she was marginalising him. 'You reading? I think I'll go straight to sleep,' she said, not wanting to pursue this line of questioning.

The following morning Steve phoned: he'd be arriving the following day and he was sorry it was such short notice. 'If that's all right, Mum?'

'*If?* What a silly question! Of course it's fine. Your room's ready for you. And guess what?' She hugged herself with glee. 'Lucy's here and has moved into the barn and . . .' she paused for dramatic effect '. . . she's married!'

'Good God! What's he like?'

'French and very nice.' She crossed her fingers as she spoke – she'd lied but she wanted her first impression to have been wrong.

Later, for the umpteenth time, she checked Steve's room. It was decorated in blue and yellow – his favourite colours, he'd once told her, though now he denied he had ever said any such thing. She'd put in a CD player for him, and a TV. She placed an ashtray by the bed, just in case he was still smoking. She didn't want him to think that just because she had given up she expected him to as well. Though she hoped he had. But if he was smoking, she mustn't comment . . . She sighed deeply. It was so hard to stop being motherly. Had the cleaning woman put in the big towels for him?

'You know what you remind me of? A mother hen.'

'So? I suppose I am. Once a mother always one. How long have you been there?' she asked Stewart, who was standing in the doorway.

'Long enough to see you fussing about. It's rather endearing. I wish I'd had a mum like you. I hope he appreciates you.'

'Steve? Oh yes, he always has.'

'Does that mean Lucy didn't?'

120

'I think she did deep down – or, rather, I hope she did. Mother-and-daughter relationships are often a bit fraught until the child grows up, aren't they? We're fine now, how I always hoped it would be.'

'And Madame reckons she's grown up?'

'Yes, I think she has.' She was smoothing the perfectly smooth counterpane, a pretty Provençal print in blue.

'I didn't mean Lucy, I meant you.' Playfully he ruffled her hair. 'You're the last person I'd call an adult. Who gives her computers names and talks to them? Who names the cars?'

'Lots of people do that.'

'Then who else do you know who believes in fairies?' He laughed. 'I remember when you saw that mushroom ring last year at the bottom of the garden. "Oh, look, France has fairies too," you said. I thought to myself, I've found a right one here.' He kissed the top of her head.

Kate laughed. 'I'd *like* to believe in them, that's different.'

'It's not a criticism, Kate. I love your funny ways. I wouldn't alter one thing about you.'

'You'd like me to spend less.' She rearranged the cushions on the bed, wondering if they were too fussy for a young man. Yes, they were, and with one swift movement she scooped them up and put them on the top shelf of the cupboard. Stewart hadn't answered her. 'Wouldn't you?'

'Ah, well, yes, but that's just being practical. So, to what do we owe the honour of this visit?'

'He's in Paris looking at a garden. He can only stay two nights. I wondered if you'd telephone that woman who's giving the party and ask her if we could take him too?'

'She's called Wendy. Why don't you? She won't bite.'

'Someone French might answer.'

'Kate, you've got to get over this.'

'I've ordered a new CD Rom – a teach-yourself-French program. I got nowhere with the other one.'

121

'About time too. There's a parcel at the post office, maybe it's that. I'll go and pick it up and have a beer while I'm about it. Anything you need?'

'No, nothing, thanks.'

Once the inspection of Steve's room was complete she returned to the safety of her workroom. It was odd how she always thought of it as a sanctuary – perhaps because it was exclusively hers. Stewart tended to call it the library, but she felt that sounded a bit pretentious. For her, libraries were where you went to borrow books, or were glorious rooms in stately homes, preferably furnished by Chippendale. Nor did she like it described as a study since that implied something different from what she did, which was work.

At her desk Kate looked out of the window at her garden and wondered what Steve, the professional, would have to say about it. If he criticised it she was certain it would be in the nicest possible way. Not like Stewart.

It annoyed Kate how critical he was about her inability to speak French. She had tried, but apart from her lack of skill in learning languages, she had found that when she was working and immersed in English, she found it virtually impossible to understand or speak French. It was as if her own language had put up the barricades to prevent any other words breaching it and muddling her.

Before beginning work she checked her e-mails. There were two, both from fellow writers who were having a moan. Writers moaned a lot, including Kate. It seemed to be par for the course in this profession. She was sure it had to do with the isolation and insecurity they all felt, for, one of the first things she had learnt was that you were only as good as your last book.

The web had changed things dramatically for her. She didn't feel so marooned now. She had joined a Cyber Chapter of writers. Lucy had shrieked at that, claiming it made her sound like a witch, and it was certainly a coven of sorts. Each week a long e-mail came with their thoughts and ideas. She found herself looking forward to Sunday evenings when it arrived and felt quite stupidly bereft when, for some reason, it didn't. They exchanged advice, gossip, hints – and, of course, the inevitable complaints. There were several mighty egos among the group, out in cyber-space. But there were others who had their feet planted modestly on the ground. At the click of a button she could be in touch with a number of them. One or two had become friends, though she had never met them. She often wondered if they would like each other in the flesh and, if they did, would they be so open with each other?

While still connected she accessed Amazon, then the websites of Smith's, Blackwell's, Heffer's, Waterstone's and did a quick check of her books, looking to see if they were in stock. However, she had learnt not to complain to her publishers if they weren't. That was a sure way of being made to feel she was a *difficult author*. She scanned for any readers' reviews. For the most part they were nice to read – although they couldn't take the place of fan letters – but there was the occasional nasty one. Once she'd had a particularly bad one but her cyber-friend Christina Jones had posted a glowing one for her afterwards. She wondered if the customers were aware of how easy it was to manipulate the site.

It was all so easy, these days, and ordering books too, though when she did that she always felt a pang of guilt that she no longer patronised the small bookshop in Graintry that had been her mainstay for so many years. How could it survive against these e-commerce giants?

She glanced at her watch. It was lunchtime already. Where on earth had Stewart got to? She could guarantee with that man that if he went to get one small parcel it would take him at least two hours, but she was surprised at three.

3

Armed with his French Telecom card, Tristram drove into the village. He had told Mo he was meeting Martin for a drink. Just in case their neighbour should say anything to his wife, which got back to Mo, he popped into the local bar and had a Ricard with him. Not that he could concentrate on what Martin was talking about because all the time he was planning what he was about to say. After one drink he made his excuses and left.

He drove another ten miles before he found a phone. He hadn't wanted to use the box in the village since he was sure to be seen and someone would ask Mo what was wrong with their phone – it was that sort of community.

He sat for a good five minutes in his car, steeling himself to make the call. Looked at dispassionately, he'd one hell of a nerve to be calling her. What if she told him to get lost and slammed the phone down on him? He couldn't blame her if she did, not after the way he'd treated her.

'Caroline, it's Tristram.'

'What a lovely surprise,' she said. There was no hint of rancour or bitterness in her voice. He felt ashamed that he had thought less of her. 'Nothing wrong, is there?'

He blustered a bit at that, assuring her that there wasn't and then confessing that there was. 'I've been a prat, Caroline. I overspent on some equipment. A couple of cheques bounced – my funds from England haven't arrived.'

'Is that all?' Caroline laughed with relief.

'It's a major offence here. They guillotine you, if you're

not careful.' God, he thought, he was even managing a laugh while wondering how to form the words to ask her for a loan.

'I'll help you. How much do you need?'

'A thousand, if you could run to that.' He winced as he said it, and was aware that he was holding his breath as he waited for her reply.

'No problem. Give me your bank details and I'll send it straight away.'

'Caroline, you are the proverbial angel.' He wondered now if he should have asked for double and was shocked at his unworthy thoughts. 'I'll pay you back.'

'Whenever. I'll get a pen.'

He heard her rootling among papers, cursing softly when she couldn't find one – or at least what amounted to a curse for her. She dropped the phone, then something fell on the floor.

'You OK, Caroline?'

'Sorry about that. I'm in such chaos here – I've got the builders in. And I'm so flustered at you calling and so happy that you have.' The words bubbled out of her. 'Right, I'm ready.' He could picture her, pen poised, a serious expression on her face as she helped her friend.

He gave her his account number. 'What are the builders up to?'

'You remember my poky little bedroom and bathroom? Well, I'm knocking down the wall of the room next to mine, making it huge with an *en suite* – don't you hate that expression? – and a dressing room. Quite grand, actually.'

'That'll be nice.' Of course he remembered, and the times they had slept and bathed there and had such fun, only at the time he hadn't realised quite how much fun they were having. He didn't seem to have had much since.

'And I've had the sitting room redecorated. I decided I

had to change everything.' There was a slight pause here, and he could sense her embarrassment at this hint that all was not well with her.

'Remove all trace of me? I can't say I blame you.'

'No, of course not. Nothing like that.' She laughed, but he knew that was why. 'No, just a sort of mega spring-clean. And I've changed the colour of my hair. You wouldn't recognise me any more.' She was still laughing but he was sure it was to cover up the hurt which still lingered.

'Caroline, I'm sorry.'

'What on earth for?'

'You know . . . I shouldn't have . . . I don't know what got into me.'

'It's all right, sweetie. You fell in love and not with me. You couldn't help it. All gone. All forgotten.'

He wanted to explain to her that he wasn't in love with Mo, that it had been, and still was, lust. But how could he expect her to understand that? And if he did, how much would she despise him that he had allowed his hormones to take control, make her life misery and lose command of his? Women weren't like that, he was sure – certainly she wasn't. He couldn't think what else to say.

'Tris, I don't want to make problems or anything but I think I should tell you – actually I wanted to write but I didn't have your address, not that I expected you to give it to me, of course I didn't,' she said breathlessly. 'But, basically, there have been some odd coves asking about Mo. Where they could find her.'

Tristram suddenly felt icy cold. 'What sort of odd?' He forced himself to sound light-hearted.

'Like bouncers – you know the sort. Big and gruff and looking as if they've been in a fight or two. Quite menacing, actually, not at all the sort you'd want to take home to Mother.' Her laugh was brittle, indicative of her

126

nervousness. 'At least in all honesty I could say I hadn't the foggiest where she was. But they've been to see her mum.'

'And she told?'

'That's what's so odd, Tris. Her mum told them she was in Spain, and I think she thinks that's where she is.'

'Mo always said she was a bit dotty.'

'Really? She didn't seem so when I last saw her.'

'You know her?'

'Yes, charming people.'

'People?' That was puzzling.

'Fortunately the agency were wonderful. They refused to divulge anything – because, of course, they know she's in France. I should think it's only a matter of time and they'll find out – they didn't look exactly patient. I don't like to pry, Tris, but is it something serious?'

'You know Mo. Scatterbrained as always. She probably thinks she is in Spain.' It was his turn to laugh falsely.

'You didn't answer me Tris. Why do those men want to see her?'

'It's nothing to worry about. She owes them a bit of money, that's all.'

'That's a relief. I thought it might be something serious. I'll pay them off, if you like.'

'No!' he exclaimed, too loudly, the little word rebounding round the telephone box. 'It's very sweet of you,' he added hurriedly, 'but Mo wouldn't like that. You know how proud she is.'

'How thoughtless of me. And I suppose I'm the last person in the world she would want to help her. But I will, if you ever need me to.'

'Bless you.'

He felt sad when they were disconnected – his card had run out of money. Caroline was something else, especially after the way he had behaved to her. Yet somehow he

127

thought she had seen through Mo long before he had. If only he could be honest with Mo and tell her how he felt, how simple everything would be. He could clear the decks, Caroline would forgive him and then . . . 'Bloody fool,' he said, to the night sky. 'As if she would want you back. *I'll pay . . .*' Caroline was too generous; once, long ago, he had wondered if she used her money to bribe friends, like the lonely child in the playground who buys friendship with his sweets. It had been a despicable thought on his part, but it had never quite gone away.

The car would not start. 'What now?' He kicked the tyres in fury. He lifted the bonnet, but mechanics had never been his strong point. There was nothing for it, he'd have to walk. He plodded rather than strode along the country road. Not one car passed to give him a lift. When he arrived at their village the garage was shut, as was the bar, so he had to press on the further five miles to his home.

Fortunately when he returned Mo was fast asleep. There was a plate of dried-up supper on the table which, in his tired state, seemed to be accusing him. He undressed in the sitting room, crept up the stairs in stockinged feet and slid into bed beside Mo. She didn't stir, and he wondered if she was just pretending to be asleep.

'What time did you eventually get home?' Mo was standing in the kitchen, arms akimbo, looking daggers at him.

'Late. God, my head.' He stumbled to the sink and poured himself a glass of water and downed it in one. He had decided that the best strategy was to pretend to be mightily hung over.

'Well, it wasn't with Martin you got into this state. He was back by nine, I heard his car.'

'No.' He sluiced his face so he didn't have to look at her. 'Who, then?'

'I can't remember.'

'Don't give me that crap.'

'I mean I don't know where I went. I met these blokes and they suggested we went on somewhere else and we did.'

'And where's the car?'

'It broke down. I left it beside the road somewhere and had to hike it. God, I'm knackered!'

It was odd that she should react in this way – possessive, wifely. Was she simply putting on an act, playing games, or was she genuinely cross?

He cycled into the village. At the garage he told the mechanic where he'd left his car. He need not have bothered since the man already knew.

'Who told you?'

'If you fart the whole village knows. Something wrong with your telephone?' He smiled slyly.

'But I saw no cars. How the hell . . . ?'

'As I said, you can't do anything around here but someone knows. That's country living for you.'

'I'd appreciate it if you kept it quiet.' It was Tristram's turn to look sly.

'No problem, my friend.' And he tapped one black, oily finger on the side of his nose.

In fact there was little point in asking any of the men in the village not to let on that he had been using the public call-box. Undoubtedly it had already been mentioned to one of the wives – that was all it would take.

'So, what's wrong with the phone?' Mo was standing in the doorway of their house as if barring him entry. He took some time to put his bike in the shed, trying to collect his thoughts. 'Tell me, you sneaky bastard.'

'You going to let me in?'

'Not until you tell me what you were doing using another

phone when, as far as I'm concerned, there's nothing wrong with ours.'

'Who told you?'

'It's no matter.'

'But you hardly speak French.'

'Evidently I speak enough.' She looked furious with him. She'd a nerve, he thought.

'I was phoning Caroline.' Why should he lie, he asked himself.

'You were what?' she shrieked, and Martin, passing in the lane, heard. He grinned in sympathy with Tristram.

'I didn't want to worry you.'

'I'm not worried, I'm plain furious that you should be speaking to that mealy-mouthed bitch after all the crap she said about you.'

'Mo, just for once let's be honest with each other. She never said anything. You know that and I know that. It was your subterfuge.' He leant against the porch. Why, when he'd gone along with this deception all these months, should he suddenly decide to have everything out in the open? Was it because he'd been speaking to Caroline, heard her voice, her sweetness?

Mo looked flustered as if his words had caught her off-balance. 'I heard her, you didn't. She's a mean cow and I hate her and I feel betrayed that you should be speaking to her.'

'Mo, you can say many things, and I'll let you, but never call Caroline mean in my hearing ever again, nor bitch, nor cow. Do you understand?' He was shouting in his turn. 'I should never have listened to you in the first place. I still don't understand your game in turning me and my friends against each other.'

'Because I wanted you all to myself. And she's in love with you and I didn't want her near you.' She was pouting, she was widening her eyes, tears forming in them. He knew what she was doing, what she was about, but his nether regions hadn't got the message and he felt an ache in his crotch that he didn't want. 'Now, excuse me.' He pushed her to one side and entered the house.

'Tristram, you have to understand.'

'I'll never fathom you, ever. I'm sick to death of your games.'

'But I love you!'

'Do you? Oh, come on. You only say it when it suits you.'

'But I make you happier than she ever could.'

'Do you know what Caroline's doing? Despite what you've done, despite my despicable behaviour, she's sending me a cheque to get out of the mess I'm in. And that's not all. To show what a true friend is about, she's offered to pay off the debts that have got you into so much trouble – since the goons are sniffing around.'

This time Mo was taken completely by surprise and sat down on the kitchen stool with a bump. 'You know?'

'Of course I bloody well know.'

'How long?'

'Ages.'

'Then why didn't you say?'

'I had this stupid idea that you would eventually tell me.'

'I don't see how you could possibly have known. You're making it up.'

'I was always suspicious. You had too much money for the job you did. So where did it come from? You told me your mother was poor. You might have been on the game but I couldn't see when you'd have the time. It had to be something that brought in large amounts of money fast – it had to be drugs. Working where you did, I guessed cocaine. Proud of yourself, are you?'

'Tristram, don't be mean to me.' The lovely puppy-brown

131

eyes refilled with tears. He knew it was a trick, that she could cry at will. When it didn't work she changed tack. She leant forward, her blouse falling open so that he could see the swell of her breast. She had an earnest expression on her face that was as false, he knew, as the tears had been. 'I didn't mean any harm. One of the girls asked me if I could get her some snow one day and I did, and then another and another asked. It was their fault I got sucked in. I didn't want to do it.'

'Oh, come on, Mo. You liked the money. What happened? Did the temptation become too much? Did you steal from the dealers? That's a dangerous thing to do, Mo.'

'I always intended to pay them back.'

'When? How? From here? That's why you came, wasn't it? You never wanted to come to France or be with me, but it was handy for you when you had to run away. And how long before the heavies come banging at our door? Changing your name to mine, trying to hide. God, Mo, you've been so stupid!'

'But you just said Caroline will pay. Will she give me the whole thirty thousand?'

'Jesus! That much?' It was his turn to sit down from shock.

'Oh, Tris, my darling, I was so afraid when you didn't come home last night. I thought you'd found someone else. I thought you were leaving me. I couldn't live without you.'

'Don't change the subject, Mo.'

In one fluid movement she was across the room and in his arms and she was clinging to him like a limpet and she was crying – this time he could feel the dampness of her tears on his cheek. 'I love you, Tristram. Honest, I really do.'

'She's not paying it. I wouldn't let her.'

In a trice she was out of his arms and the weeping

stopped as if a tap was turned off. 'You what? How could you do that to me?'

'Caroline is not to be embroiled in the mess you have made of your life and mine. Is that understood?'

'Tris . . .' The anger in her face disappeared. Again she sidled up to him and once more he felt his body stir.

'No, not this time.' He pushed her away from him, stood up and rushed for the door. He almost ran up the lane and at the top of the hill he stood for a while, breathing deeply. What a fool he was. What a mess.

4

'Steve!' Kate raced across the terrace, tripped over the garden hose, knocked into the wheelbarrow and fell into her son's arms. 'I'm *so* excited!' she exclaimed.

'I can see that.' Steve lifted her up and twirled her around, with Kate shrieking that he'd get a hernia. He planted a smacking kiss on her cheek.

'Dear Steve, I can't believe you're here!' she said, when her son had put her back on the ground.

'It's so great to see you at last. You look wonderful.'

'So do you.' They stood grinning at each other.

'Can one interrupt this mutual admiration society for just one sec?'

'Lucy! Long time no see.' Steve leant forward to kiss his sister, but Kate noticed a restraint in the way he did so, as if he didn't really want to but thought he should.

'Isn't this nice?' she said, unable to think of anything else to say but wary of the mood between them, which was impossible to ignore.

'I hear you're a married woman. When do I meet my brother-in-law?'

'He's out on business.'

'What might that be?' Steve had his arm around Kate's shoulders as they walked back across the terrace towards the open front door.

'My, you do ask a lot of questions.' Lucy was wary too, Kate realised.

'Just interested. I won't ask any more, then you can't complain.'

'I wasn't.'

'You could have fooled me.'

'How was your train journey, Steve? The TGV trains are wonderful, aren't they? I'd rather go on them than fly these days. You know it only takes seven hours from our little station in Vorey to get to Waterloo?'

'Mum, it's all right, you needn't prattle. Lucy and I aren't going to fight, are we, Lucy? We're adults now.'

'Of course not. I'm *really* pleased to see you, brother.' And she flung her arms around him. But to Kate's keen eye it still seemed cautious.

They entered the house, which, after the heat outside, was wonderfully cool.

'The French certainly know how to build houses, don't they? I hadn't expected it to be this hot in May.' Steve plonked his bag on the quarry-tiled floor of the hall.

'It's been a dreadful spring with storms. The March before last we had decent tans, but not this year,' Kate remarked.

Steve began to laugh.

'What did I say?' She looked puzzled.

'Nothing. It was just that we haven't seen each other for nearly two years and we talk about the weather. That's so English.'

'And French too. They're just like us, obsessed with the weather. It was quite a shock to learn that. Right, Steve, do you want to take your bag up and have a quick wash after

134

that long drive? I've got some champagne on ice and I thought we'd have it down by the pool. We won't wait for Stewart.'

'Where is he?'

'He went into Le Puy for a meeting about a cricket club he's trying to get started, and those meetings tend to go on a long time.'

'Cricket here? Who'll play?'

'The English. I'm sure the French are far too sensible to bother. There's a league – they travel around for matches.'

'How bizarre.' Steve picked up his bag.

While Lucy arranged the chairs by the pool and put up the parasol, Kate collected glasses, the champagne, and some nuts. She carried them carefully down the steps into the garden.

'What a shame the water in the pool isn't balanced yet. I tried to get hold of the man but with this weather everyone wants theirs done immediately.'

'You phoned the pool man? In French? Heavens above!' Lucy teased.

'Don't you start.'

'Why couldn't Stewart do it?'

'I didn't think to ask him.' That was a fib. She had hinted, in her roundabout way, but he hadn't got round to doing it. Come to think of it, there was a whole list of things he hadn't done. Still, he would eventually.

'He's never here. Is he avoiding us?'

'I teased him the other day. I said that at this rate I'd start thinking he's got a mistress.' She uncorked the bottle expertly.

'Chance'd be a fine thing.'

'Lucy! What on earth do you mean?'

'Nothing.'

'Nothing always means something in my experience.'

135

'It was a joke.'

'Not a very funny one.'

'What's funny?' Steve had returned.

'Nothing,' Lucy and Kate said, almost in unison.

'This is the life, isn't it?' He flopped down on one of the garden chairs. 'This garden is ace, Mum. Who'd ever have thought it? It was virtually a field when you bought this place, wasn't it?'

'I've one or two ideas I want to discuss with you.'

'No, not gardening, please!' Lucy clapped her hands over her ears. 'It's all she talks about, that and her books.'

'Because those are the two things I enjoy most.'

'And food, I sincerely hope?'

'Yes, Steve, and food. I've planned all the things you like.'

Steve stood up. 'I fancy a swim.'

'Darling, I was just saying to Lucy – I don't know if the pH and chlorine levels are balanced. You mustn't risk getting an ear infection. I keep meaning to learn how to do it but I always forget to ask.'

'I'll do it.'

'Could you?'

'You don't have to be an Einstein, Mum. If you've got the kit it's the easiest thing in the world to do. I plan to swim every day of the week that I'm here.'

'The week, did you say?'

'Great, isn't it? I need a break, and where better? And I'll show you how to do the pool, Lucy, so that you can keep an eye on it for Mum when I've left.'

'Do I have to?'

'Yes. Hell, don't say you're getting as lazy as Stewart.' He pulled his complaining sister to her feet.

Kate frowned. What did they mean? And, come to that, why hadn't she defended him?

*

136

When Stewart eventually came home, it was almost six and he was drunk. Kate felt mortified while the others laughed.

'Stewart, really!' She made it sound as though she were amused, to cover up the annoyance she was feeling. 'What will the neighbours think?' she said, with mock seriousness.

'It was the neighbours I was with. God, but can't they drink? Steve, what a pleasant surprise. How long have you been here?' He shook Steve's hand, slapped him on the back and then hugged him for good measure.

'Since early this afternoon.' Kate spoke slowly and deliberately, as if to a child, trying to control her anger.

'I'd quite forgotten you were coming.'

'Well, that's let me know where I stand.' Steve smiled good-naturedly.

'I said I was sorry, what do you expect, grovelling apologies?' He swayed, as he looked belligerently at Steve.

'No, I—'

'Don't be so contentious, Stewart. Steve's amused.'

'No, he's not. He's all offended, aren't you, Steve?'

'No. I think it's funny.'

'Oh, yes? What's so funny?'

'Well, you,' Steve said, half apologetically.

'Cheeky sod.'

'As a matter of fact, you didn't apologise,' Kate interrupted.

'Oh, what a transgression!' Stewart bowed stupidly and nearly toppled over. He had to hang on to the side table to steady himself.

Lucy dived for the crystal-bottomed lamp, which wobbled precariously. 'I'm loath to leave the cabaret but we're going out.' She moved towards the door.

'Lucy, no! I'd planned a reunion dinner.'

'Dominique's phoned – he's so excited. He's found just

137

the business he's been looking for and he wants to go out to celebrate.'

'What business?' Stewart asked, while glaring at Kate as if to say, 'See? I told you so.'

'He doesn't want to talk about it until he knows for sure we can get it.'

'Then why celebrate if you haven't?'

'Can't you celebrate here?' Kate hoped she could get them to change their minds and also shut Stewart up.

'I'm sorry, Mum, he wants to take me out. And in any case, as he said, he'd feel in the way. That this evening is a family thing.'

'Isn't he family, then?' Steve asked.

'Where is he taking you?' Kate felt tension rising, and that was the last thing she wanted this evening.

'To the Auberge des Cimes.'

'It's a long drive to St Bonnet le Froid. You'd better borrow my car instead of that rattling tin can. You can't turn up at a two-star restaurant in that thing of yours.'

'Who's being impolite now? Pissing off the moment your brother gets here.' Stewart slurred.

'Steve doesn't mind, do you? And we had a lovely long chat this afternoon when you were out on the razzmatazz.'

'I'm glad you can afford such a restaurant.'

'Stew!' Kate hissed.

'I'm not paying.' To her relief, Lucy was laughing at Stewart.

'Good heavens! You don't mean you've married someone who's got money? Wonders will never cease!'

'And when have I ever asked for anything from Mum?' Lucy looked defensive.

'Oh, come on, folks. I'm here for a week. I don't mind if Lucy goes out with her hubby. There's a laugh – I never imagined I'd be saying that! Ignore the wrinklies, Lucy, have fun.'

'You will be back?' As soon as the words were out Kate regretted them. She must stop treating Lucy like a child. But even in the fortnight she'd been here Kate had felt so insecure about her daughter that she half expected at any moment to find she'd run away again.

'As if! See you!' Lucy waved gaily, gave Kate a quick kiss, hugged her brother and ignored Stewart. ''Bye,' she called from the door.

'They were out all last night.' Stewart was pouring himself a whisky of monumental proportions, Kate noticed.

'Don't tell tales, Stewart,' she said. 'It's not attractive. I'll get the supper while you two talk. It's all ready. Shan't be a mo.'

In the kitchen Kate, too, poured herself a large drink. It was going to be one of those evenings, she thought, with a sinking feeling.

5

Kate sliced the stick of bread, spread the butter and mustard mixture on it, then layered the pieces over the beef in the casserole and popped it back into the very hot oven. She hoped Stewart had remembered they were having this dish – it needed a fairly robust wine to go with it. She felt horribly nervous. She took a gulp of her drink. Everything was going wrong. She'd so often imagined them all here together and what a happy occasion it would be. *Ha! And who's the optimist?*

Kate shook her head, she didn't want to think. The bread should take half an hour to brown so if she got them to the table, they should be through the first course when it was ready. What was happening in her life? She was happy, she was lucky. *You think? Only because you keep telling yourself you are!* 'That's not true!' She looked over her shoulder and was relieved Steve hadn't found her talking to herself.

She felt afraid. Those unspecified fears were closing in.

She dried the crudités, which she had had soaking in iced water, and arranged them on the platter with a mound of aïoli in the centre – one of Steve's all-time favourites. She placed the flaked salt cod in another dish and put everything on the tray. When had this problem with Stewart started? *Which one? There are so many . . .*

'Need a hand, Mum?' Steve appeared in the kitchen doorway.

'No, you talk to Stewart. I can manage fine.'

'I would if I could, but he's flat out and snoring like a walrus.'

'Oh, no. And I so wanted your first night here to be perfect. What a bore.'

'I'd much rather it was just you and me.'

'You say the nicest things.'

'I never say anything I don't mean.'

'If only one could. The trouble is, sometimes it's best to tell a white lie – far less kerfuffle. Here, take these plates, will you? I'll put the veg on at the last minute.' She picked up the tray and followed her son through to the dining room they had built at the back of the house, taking half of the enormous cellar to create it. She had laid the table much earlier, but there was no bottle of wine on the coaster. 'Damn! Stewart forgot.' In the kitchen she picked a bottle at random from the small collection he kept there in the rack. He liked to bring them out of the cool cellar a couple of days before he planned to drink them. 'If you could open the wine, Steve, I'll light the candles.'

'Pushing the boat out, aren't you? I am honoured,' Steve said, having looked at the *etiquette* on the bottle. The corkscrew went in before she could ask him what he thought it might have cost. Oh, to hell with it. If she'd picked a very expensive one by mistake it was hardly her fault – Stewart should have seen to the wine before he went out.

'I never know what bottle to take – I just drink it and know nothing about it. Stewart's in love with his collection of wine.'

'I took a peek. There's thousands of them.'

'It's a hobby with him. He knows a lot about the subject.'

'But you hardly drink.'

'I wouldn't say that!' She laughed. 'I've drunk more since we've lived here than in the rest of my life. It's an occupational hazard of being in France.'

'But you don't get drunk.'

'I try to keep off the spirits. I like a bit of wine and I've become very partial to a glass or two of champagne, especially when I'm sitting by the pool. Imagine what your father would have to say about that!' As soon as she said this she regretted it. She had vowed never to say anything negative about their father to them, but it was so hard not to when all she had was negative thoughts about him. 'It gives Stewart something to do, doesn't it?' she added hurriedly.

'Does he get drunk a lot?'

'Gracious, no. It's just that if he has a drink at lunchtime it goes straight to his head. Odd when he's such a big man, isn't it?' She wasn't going to say anything of her niggling doubts about Stewart's drinking. But she knew the time was coming when she'd have to talk to him about it. 'Isn't it strange how when some people are drunk they're happy and others become morose and difficult?'

141

'Are you talking about him?'

'No, just generalising.' What on earth had got into her to say that? 'I just get more giggly with each glass of wine, which is why I watch what I drink. I hate to lose control.'

They settled at the table, which was oak and matched the rustic chairs she had had made to go with it. The candlelight played shadows on the vaulted ceiling of the windowless room. 'Are you warm enough?'

'I'm fine, don't fuss.'

'Only it gets very cold in here. It's built right into the hillside, you see. And if we have the radiators on full we risk altering the temperature of the wine cellar next door.' She nodded to the wrought-iron gates that bisected the room, behind which was Stewart's collection of wine. 'He hates us using this dining room.'

'It's your house, why can't you?'

'No, Steve, darling, it's *our* house. The problem with these old farmhouses is that the French always lived in the one large room, but I like to eat separately.'

'Mind you, just you and me, we could have had supper in the kitchen just like old times. That was a lovely kitchen at Graintry, wasn't it?'

'I miss my Aga, I must say.'

'Why not get one here?'

'It gets too hot in summer. We'd melt. Is the aïoli all right?'

'Need you ask? Scrummy as always.' As if to make the point he helped himself to another scoop of the pungent sauce. 'Lucy says she thinks he's bored.'

The statement caught her off-guard. 'Stew? Never! He has too many interests.'

'She says she thinks he regrets being here.'

'No. He loves it. It was his idea to come here, you know. I was the one who had doubts about moving to France.'

'And now?'

'I wish I'd done it years and years ago. I love it, even though I have such trouble communicating, but everyone is patient with me.' She began to laugh. 'I told the cleaning woman I had curtains on my face when I meant wrinkles! Last autumn I pointed out to a neighbour that the armchairs were falling from the trees! And I asked Madame Blanc how her father's tyres were when I meant his lungs!'

'How the hell did you manage that?' Steve was grinning.

'It's the words, they're all so similar and I get in a muddle. I can start a sentence, almost confident, then half-way through I run out of steam and it all trails off. Or when I'm with people I sit working out what to say and by the time I have the conversation has moved on to a different topic. But I'm getting better in the shops.'

'Poor Mum.'

'I'm surprised how little I miss – just sausages, bacon, baked beans.'

'Not Marmite?'

'Don't mention it. Everyone thinks we do so they always bring a pot as a present. I've a cupboard stuffed with it. You can't give it to the neighbours, they think it's disgusting.'

'Anything else?'

'The Sunday papers on the right day – they don't seem the same on Monday. *And* we don't get the colour supps yet we pay the same amount as when we did – and I don't think that's fair. Mind you I don't know half the people in the magazines – they became famous after we left.' She stood up. 'Pour some more of that delicious wine, will you? I'll get the next course.'

Years of practice had made Kate a whirlwind in the kitchen. It was why she invariably rejected offers of help at this stage. She knew where everything was and what needed doing when, so helpers tended to get in her way. The tray was heavy with the casserole and the dishes of vegetables; she had cooked three, as well as the potatoes. Steve probably didn't eat properly in his bed-sit. 'I miss the BBC, of course. And English bread,' she said, putting the plates on the table, picking up the thread of the conversation where they had left off.

'I thought French bread was the best in the world.'

'It won't make toast, though, will it? And it goes stale the same day. And you can't make sandwiches. When I told my dentist that, he was deeply offended, and defended the honour of French bread while waving his drill at me most alarmingly.'

'Not the best person to make a comment like that to.'

'Probably not. I do find they take the honour of all things French a mite too seriously.'

'Anything else get you down?'

'Not a lot. I think if I hear one more joke about British beef – you know *vache folle* – I shall strangle the whole nation single-handed. And I do get a bit fed up with never being consulted. They always defer to Stewart as if, as the wife, I don't have a worthwhile opinion.'

'Even though you're paying.'

'Yes.'

'Then Stewart should point that out to them.'

'Oh, he invariably does,' she said hurriedly. 'He says things like, "you should ask Madame La Contrôle, she writes the cheques," but half the time I think they think he's joking. Women have a long way to go here to get equality. I think it's a hangover from the last war when they were told that a woman's place was in the home, having babies and cooking for her man. Did you know they weren't allowed to work? Staggering. Someone like me, emancipated, a wage-earner, is hard for them to under-stand. It's still very backward here – a bit like England in the fifties I always think.'

'Emancipated? You? Oh, come off it, Mum.'

'I am.'

'All you've done is exchange Dad for Stewart. Dad was a male chauvinist, and so is Stewart. Dad was a bully and so is—'

'Don't be silly. Of course he isn't, and your father wasn't that bad.' She'd been talking about lying and here was a prime example of when it was politic to do so. But what else could she say? *Yes, Steve, I agree, your father was a mean bastard and liked to keep me on a tight rein.* But she couldn't. She changed the subject. 'Do you like the beef?'

'You know I do. You served it last time I was here. More wine?'

'Why not?' She held out her glass.

'What's Lucy's husband like?'

'He's very nice.'

'*Nice*, Mum? That doesn't sound very enthusiastic.'

'He's very French.'

'He would be, wouldn't he? What exactly does that mean?'

'Well, I shouldn't be saying this but he is a bit full of himself. A lot of young Frenchmen are like that.'

'You don't like him.'

'Don't be silly, of course I do. But, well, he's a bit over-confident and I'm not sure on what grounds. Probably, of course, because he has that dingly-dangly bit between his legs, which makes him think he's one of the rulers of the universe.'

'Oh dear, you really aren't keen, are you?'

'Yes, I am – keen, I mean. I'm just generalising – always a

145

stupid thing to do. All I want is for Lucy to be happy.' And I don't think she'll stay that way, she thought.

During the night Kate was aware of Stewart stumbling to bed, mainly because he had trouble finding the bathroom door and ended up in a cupboard. She turned over but didn't let him know that she was awake. He'd have reached the maudlin stage by now and she couldn't be bothered with that, not after such a pleasant evening with her son.

They had talked half the night away. She had felt he wanted to ask her something – he hadn't said anything, but she sensed that he was biding his time. At about two she had insisted they went to bed, especially when Steve suggested that a third bottle of wine would go down a treat.

'No more. I shall have a sore head in the morning as it is, and so will you.'

Before going up to her room she had checked on Stewart, who was in the same position as he had been when she had last seen him – sprawled on his back on the sofa, his legs, like felled tree-trunks, spreadeagled on the rug, a hazard to the unwary. His mouth was wide open and he was snoring noisily. She closed his mouth, since it made him look so unattractive, but it immediately flopped open again.

'What a sight!' Steve had joined her.

'It's such a shame. He was really looking forward to your coming, you know.'

'You needn't fib, Mum.'

'I'm not. He looks forward to visitors so much.' But, if she was honest, she supposed it was a half-lie since he hadn't actually said he was looking forward to Steve coming – but, then, he hadn't said he wasn't.

'Are you happy, Mum?'

'Every time I see you, you ask me that. Of course I am.'

'There's no *of course* about it. Are you? Because if you

146

want to know the truth, I don't think you are. You don't seem to be. You're jumpy and defensive.'

'I've a lot of worry about work at the moment. If I appear troubled it's that. Stew and I are fine. You just arrived on a bad evening. I don't know what got into him.'

'I do! Too much booze, that's what.' They had both laughed.

Now, lying in her bed, listening to Stewart blundering about, she thought once more how nice it would be, on nights like this, to have separate rooms. And then she found herself wondering what on earth had made her think that, and that of course it was the last thing she wanted.

'I don't believe it!'

Kate woke with a start as the door burst open and Stewart crashed into the room. To her astonishment it was morning, and she felt as if she had only just gone to bed. He had no mug of tea in his hand for her.

'What the hell—'

'Well, you might ask. What on earth got into you last night, drinking my only two bottles of Lafite-Rothschild?'

'Were they important?'

'Important!' Stewart slapped one hand against his forehead in mock-despair – or was it? 'I was saving them for my birthday. I told you. I said I thought it would be great if we had the Château Lafite. Now you and that wimpish son of yours have sodding well drunk them.'

She pushed back her hair and sat up in the bed. 'Now, hang on a minute. Don't speak of my son in that way. And if anyone drank your wine it's your fault – you shouldn't have put it in the kitchen.'

'I was bringing it up to room temperature. But a fool like you wouldn't understand that, would you?'

'Need you be so offensive? Steve asked me yesterday if I

was happy. I said I was, but I lied. How can I be when you are behaving in this way? You've been a right bastard the last week or two.'

'Is it any wonder?'

'Why? Explain to me. Tell me what's wrong.'

'Nothing.'

'And what do you say when I say that?'

He looked sulky as he stood beside the bed. 'I get pissed off, that's what.'

'With me?'

'Of course not with you,' she heard him say, and felt relieved. She couldn't face being on her own: she might pretend to be strong but she wasn't.

'Then what?'

'I don't know.'

'Male menopause?' She smiled at him.

'Perhaps.' He grinned back sheepishly.

'Stew, I'm sorry about the wine. 'I'll get you some more.'

'You won't get *them*, that's the point. They were the last two at the wine merchant's.'

'Then I'll get you another wine. Simple.'

She had thought that he had calmed down, but she was wrong for now he was stomping about the room in what she could only describe as a tantrum of enormous proportions.

'I think you did it on purpose to annoy me.'

'Stewart, don't be so childish.'

'I'm not. You're so small-minded, Kate, it's just the sort of thing you'd do to upset me.'

Kate sat on the side of the bed and pulled on her dressing-gown. 'Whatever reason would I have to do that? Grow up, man. If it's anyone's fault it's yours. You got drunk, you hadn't organised the wine, that's all there is to say. Now, please, if all you're going to do is shout and stamp about I'd prefer it if you left.' With which she stood up, crossed to her bathroom and purposefully turned on the bath taps.

Chapter Four

May–June

1

Netta, who was never late, had to hide the irritation she felt when Sybil and Sim Chesterton were – very. She had been ready for over half an hour. Her annoyance was compounded when Sim announced their arrival by hooting noisily – as if she were the tardy one. As she tripped down the stairs she played with the idea of quoting to them that punctuality *was the politeness of princes* but decided against it: she feared it might make her sound like Sybil.

'Sorry, Netta, blame the memsahib.' With a courtly flourish, Sim held open the door of his immaculately polished Rover for her.

'Thank you, *Simon*.' She emphasised his full name purposefully, knowing how much it bothered him when she did. And she smiled brilliantly, for it was against her code of manners to let him know how provoked she was.

Sybil mouthed that she was sorry, but from her somewhat pinkish eyes – so like a ferret's – Netta presumed she had been crying *again*. And she looked sheepish. The reason why became apparent when Netta got into the car and saw that she was wearing the grey silk dress.

'*What* a pretty dress, Sybil!'

'Sim didn't like the trouser suit. I did say.'

'What didn't Sim like? Tell me all,' Sim asked, as he slid behind the driver's seat.

'The green suit.'

'Made her look like Jiminy Cricket.'

Instead of an anaemic mole. But Netta managed to keep this thought to herself. Sim, with much ado, put on his driving gloves, soft brown kid leather with air holes in the back, as if they were about to do a twirl round Brands Hatch. Netta hadn't seen anyone wear those since the fifties. But that was Sim, really, if she thought about it, stuck back where presumably even he had once been happy.

In the back seat she offered up a silent prayer to the God she only spoke to in emergencies as, with scant regard for other road-users, Sim drove at a slow, sedate speed along the twisting, narrow gorge road, as the Loire slithered along beside them. Honestly, she thought, she could row the length of the whole bloody river faster than he would drive it. She turned to look out of the back window to see a long line of cars stuck behind them. No doubt each contained a frustrated driver and she knew from experience that there was nothing more dangerous than a thwarted Frenchman.

Sybil and her husband bickered, or rather Sim criticised endlessly and Sybil twittered a defence of sorts. Netta wondered if she should open a book on who was likely to murder whom first. Of course, if *she* were married to him he would have been long dead, but she would never have married such a creep in the first place – even with her track record.

'What's the joke, Netta, old girl?' Sim looked at her in the driving mirror.

'Just a silly thought I was having.' She hadn't even been aware that she had been smiling.

151

'Give us a treat.'

'I couldn't possibly, Simon, since it was about you.' She turned on the megawattage of her charm. 'And, by the way, I'm not, never have been and won't in the future be your *old girl*, so do me a favour, Simon, do desist, there's a sweetie.'

'Sharp this morning, aren't we?'

'As a box of tools.' Sybil simpered.

Dear God, thought Netta, what have I come to? She closed her eyes, hoping he would think she had gone to sleep. He was certainly a mystery. Nothing about Sim was quite right. He wanted everyone to think him a gentleman, except he wasn't. His trousers were a mite too pressed, his cravat too exact, and his shoes and car too polished. His moustache, the pipe, the initialled signet ring – incidentally on the wrong finger – the clothes he wore, the old school tie he sported, the way he spoke, his blimpish opinions, everything pointed to someone trying too hard to be what he wasn't. She had once asked Sybil if Simon was everything he said he was.

'I'm sure I don't know what you mean.'

'Doll, don't be dim. You know. Marlborough, Cambridge, the Army, big business.'

'But of course he is. What a silly-billy you can be, Netta.'

But Netta would have put all she didn't possess on his being a con-man. He knew a lot about India, Ceylon and Singapore, all places he claimed to have been posted. He knew them so well that Netta was forced to the conclusion that he *had* been there but, she suspected, more likely as a batman than the major he claimed he was.

Then there was the money. Sybil, she knew, had been left well provided for by her first husband, Bob – something to do with manufacturing paint, she'd once told her. Netta feared that when Sybil talked of Sim buying this and that he was doing so with Sybil's money – not that she could ever have said anything to her, but it didn't stop her worrying about Sybil, who was such a gullible woman. They'd only been married for five years. His first, her second.

'Why did you marry him?' Netta had asked one day, camouflaging the blunt question with a voice that sounded light-hearted with interest. In reality she would have liked to say, 'What on earth induced you to marry him?'

'I'm not very good on my own. And after Bob died, well, I was lonely. I know you don't like him, Netta, but he does me fine. You see, he's very kind to me and he understands me.'

At which Netta had felt a right bitch and she had given herself a stern lecture – it was none of her business and she mustn't intrude. All of which she had forgotten within the hour, for it seemed that nothing could stop her being rude about him when the mood took her.

The drive was lovely. There was nothing quite like the scenery of the Auvergne. But given Sim's adherence to every speed restriction, and those he made up himself as they went along, it was a tedious journey. By the time they had found the gates to the Bollands' house, Netta was feeling both hot and grumpy.

However, when she saw their destination, her spirits lifted. The house was an ancient fortified farm, with the customary tower in such houses for a look-out. Built in the local mixture of stones – black, grey, brown and beige – it seemed to Netta to have sprung, like the trees, from the surrounding earth. There was such a sense of permanence about it.

'It looks as if it has stood there since time began,' she said.

'Hope they've got decent mod cons,' Sim replied.

The house was on a hill at a point where an ancient bridge crossed the river and two roads met – with its tower, it was at an ideal vantage-point. The land swirled around its base, making it look as if it was settled on a green sea. She was glad to see it so, for too many of the English, once settled here, created flower gardens more suited to suburbia than to the wildness of this countryside. The Bollands had not fallen into that trap.

'What an awful place. Looks dark and too sombre for my taste.'

'What taste, Simon?' Netta smiled sweetly.

'Bit scary, though isn't it? I wouldn't want to live here.' Sybil looked up at the high walls, with their small windows which protected the interior against the ravages of the hard winters.

The car ground to a halt on the gravel forecourt among a motley collection of other vehicles from a Ferrari, two Porsches, an ancient Bentley and numerous people-carriers to a sadly neglected Mini and a battered Deux Chevaux.

'You must be Mrs Rawlinson and the Chestertons.' Wendy Bolland was small, slim, blonde, pretty. She was exquisitely dressed in Chanel – easily identified since the familiar trademark initials were scattered about her person. She launched herself down the dangerously moss-covered steps in dizzyingly high-heeled sandals. In one hand she held a long glass with what looked like a vegetable garden growing out of it, and in the other a cigarette. Netta had been wrong about her age: Wendy was younger than she had guessed, with her theory about her name, but although she dressed as if in her thirties, Netta estimated that she was in her mid-forties.

'At your service.' Sim did one of his courtly bows, which always made Netta want to kick him up the arse. 'Charmed to be sure, Mrs Bolland.'

'Please, call me Wendy.'

'And I'm Sim, though some of my best friends call me Sim-Sim.'

Wendy tittered as he took her hand and planted a kiss firmly on the back. 'I've always wanted a gentleman to do that.'

Long ago, Netta had been on the point of telling him that no gentleman actually kissed the flesh, but had decided to let him continue to make a fool of himself.

'And I'm Sybil.'

Netta said nothing. At the sight of Wendy, fear for the house had taken root within her. This was not a woman who would leave well alone, she was sure. Inside, it would be all ruched curtains, onyx and gilt.

'Do come this way. I hope you've brought your cossies with you, the pool is divine today. Just in case the weather turns nasty we've laid up for lunch in two places – one out, one in – so no need to worry on that score . . .' Wendy prattled away as she steamed back up the steps and into the wonderfully cool hall. They had to hurry to keep up with her.

'For a peasant he's actually quite intelligent, but some of them are, you know.'

The voice, dripping with self-satisfied confidence and a shrill conviction of its own rightness, cut through the blistering heat as a hot knife slices through butter. Kate, sitting by the pool under a large, white, palladio umbrella, heard the ringing tones and felt sorry for Netta, who was on the receiving end. She was glad to see her here.

'The trouble with France is you can't get any decent cream. And as for the milk! It's disgusting, never fresh.'

The voice belonged to a face that might once have been

attractive but which age, or maybe life, had made dissatis-
fied. She was too tanned for the Titian-coloured hair to be
natural. The fabric of a Liberty print dress was straining
over a somewhat rotund stomach. At the sight of it Kate
found herself pulling hers in sharply. The complaining tone
persisted, like a verbal pneumatic drill.

In her time here she had met English people who
moaned so much that she often wondered why they had
bothered to come in the first place since nothing was ever
right. At any minute now the voice would be saying how
much she loathed the French.

'As for the French, well, I could write a book on what
devious characters they are. And do they wash?'

Kate smothered a grin.

Faced with this diatribe Netta wore an amused expression
as if she, too, was used to the litany. A fey creature wafted
up to them with a tray of glasses. She, too, had red-tinted
hair – neither she nor the first woman had been firm
enough with their hairdressers, Kate noted. Everything
about the new arrival floated. Her hair was abundantly
curly and long – she'd been looking at the pre-Raphaelites,
no doubt about it – and she appeared to be inordinately
proud of it since she kept swishing it from side to side, as if
making sure it was noticed. She was dressed in a pink
chiffon dress that moved prettily with her as she walked.
About her neck was a long purple scarf that trailed behind
her like a train and round her large straw hat was yet
another chiffon scarf, this time in fuchsia, which matched
exactly the varnish on her toe nails. Kate was reminded of a
child's kaleidoscope for she did not stand still for a moment
and the various parts of her dress were in constant motion
about her. A Tarot-card reader, thought Kate.

'Hello, I'm Petronella Storm . . .' Kate heard her say. At
this the girl paused, deliberately Kate was sure, as if waiting

for a reaction. Kate found herself wondering if that was really her name. The large woman had already introduced herself as Joan Oxford. Yes, thought Kate, Joan was a name that suited her.

'Isn't this just blissful?' continued Petronella, in honeyed tones. 'Wendy's put me in charge of drinks out here. Would you like some Earl Grey? Wine? Champagne?' She had a pretty voice but Kate was unsure why she found it necessary to make the offering of drinks sound as if she was offering her body as well.

'May I be a pig? Champagne, please, but then I'd die for a cup of tea too. Have you any tea bags? I hate Earl Grey,' said Netta.

'Tea bags?' Petronella exclaimed.

'I hate it if tea leaves get stuck in my teeth.'

'Really? How quaint!' Petronella laughed, but with a slight edge that implied how sorry she was for someone with such plebeian tastes.

'I don't like real coffee either – gives me wind.'

'Really?' She sounded on less sure ground this time. But in Petronella's world no one would have had anything as common as flatulence, Kate decided.

'But the coffee here is so wonderful.' Joan's tone was admonishing.

'Good heavens! Don't tell me there's something about this country you approve of?' Netta leapt on this morsel of information.

'I beg your pardon?'

'All you've done in the five minutes of our acquaintance is to run down your host country. It's a mystery to me, Mrs Oxford, why you have chosen to live here.'

'I say, Netta, I didn't mean—'

'But I think you did. I love this country and feel it is a privilege to live here. I find ex-pats who whine as you are doing quite contemptible. If you don't like it, why don't you scarper back to England?'

'Well, really!'

Netta accepted a glass of champagne, 'And, by the way, it's Mrs Rawlinson to you – I like neither the false camaraderie nor the presumption of using Christian names on scant acquaintance . . . It looks nice and cool under that tree.' Netta smiled at Kate. 'Mind if I join you?'

'Be my guest.' Kate shuffled along the ornate garden seat – from Past Times, she'd seen it in their catalogue.

'Was I too abominably rude?'

'A bit, but she deserved it.'

'I always mean to be restrained and sweet and, God help me, civilised. But I never am. I always do that – shoot my mouth off and regret it the next moment. Like I did with you the first time we met.'

'I can't say I noticed.'

'You didn't like me – and I so wanted you to – but I was in bossy mode. Sybil, the sweet creature, does that to me.'

'I liked you come the end.'

'Did you really? Honestly? Oh, how wonderful!'

'Honest Injun.' Kate grinned. How odd that Netta should want her so much to like her. 'You were right to have a go at that Joan woman, though. It gets my goat the way some people bleat on. I wouldn't go as far as to say that everything is perfect here – it never is anywhere, is it? But I like it. I didn't think I would, but I can't imagine going home now.'

'Odd, isn't it, though, how you still refer to *home*? You did that last time we met. I don't. This is my home now. England is just another country.'

'And how long did that take you?'

'It was instant. But, then, I don't think I ever fitted in at *home*. The Gallic life suits me so much better.'

'I didn't want to come here one little bit, but my partner did, and he persuaded me. Sometimes I think I'm more settled than he is. Not that he ever says so.' Now what on earth had made her say that? She hadn't admitted it to herself before.

'Partner, you say? I'd no idea you and Stewart weren't married. How exciting, how modern, how sensible. I've been married too many times. It was only with the last man in my life that I saw sense – we lived together and it seemed to be working out far better, but then he died. Still, who knows? We might have hated each other by now if he hadn't.' She smiled. 'What is it about you, Kate, that I keep telling you about my past? Do I want you to put me into one of your books, do you think?'

'I told you, write your own.'

'Maybe, one day. Tell me, do you know these Bolland people?'

'Stewart met Wendy in the DIY store and they invited us here.'

'Sybil meets everyone in Bricolage too. I feel rather uncomfortable, not knowing them yet accepting their hospitality.'

'You're a fascinating mix, Netta. On the one hand you like to shock but on the other you're so conventional, aren't you?'

'I suppose so. I think it's because there's order in convention. It makes me feel that little bit more secure. But I had to come. I was so excited about the party I couldn't sleep last night.'

'You? Heavens, I'd have thought—'

'That my life is one big social round? No, sadly, I'm too poor for that. Sodding poor.' She laughed, as if it was really of no importance to her, but Kate wasn't fooled.

Across the grass tripped Petronella, this time with a silver tray that bore a silver tea-set and a bone china cup and saucer. 'Here we are. The cook is like you and only uses tea bags.'

Kate wondered how Netta would react to the put-down but she thanked the girl fulsomely and said that a mug would have done. At that Kate laughed. 'My husband – ex – called them workmen's cups.'

'Oh, one of those! Then you're well shot of him, my dear.'

Petronella looked puzzled but neither woman explained so she sank gracefully on to the grass, arranging her dress becomingly around her.

'Isn't this the most divine spot? It's mystical, don't you think? One can imagine the knights and their ladies riding up the hill. The swish of arrows in the air. Sublime!' Kate hadn't seen it like that exactly. If she thought of medieval times, which was easy in this area and especially in Le Puy, she invariably found herself wondering how bad they smelt and how they did their washing.

'I'm setting my next book here. I've decided. I asked Wendy if I might and she's thrilled.'

'As anyone would be. Have you written many books?' Netta asked politely.

'Loads.'

'Who's your publisher?' Kate asked, with interest.

Petronella looked into the far distance, played with the grass and did not answer the question. 'It's a hard and lonely life being a writer, but I live for my words and the worlds I can build with them. The escape it gives me from the fearsomeness of reality.' Petronella's hair was whooshing from side to side.

'Yes, dear,' said Netta, with a smile.

2

'I've never heard such bombastic crap in my life!' Stewart's voice bellowed across the lawn.

'Oh, dear.' Kate jumped to her feet. 'Will you excuse me?'

'Bless him, he's yelling at Simon! I like him already! This I have to witness.' With an agility which belied her years, Netta followed in hot pursuit.

'He tends to get a bit over-excited at times,' Kate explained.

'Drunk, you mean.'

'Well . . . yes, sort of. You just said . . . You know Stewart, don't you?'

'No, my dear. I've heard of him but I've never met him. I do love a good row, don't you?'

Kate didn't answer that since there was nothing she liked less. 'But I have your scarf, you left it in his car.'

'Did I? How odd.' Netta smiled while thinking what an idiotic mistake for Stewart to make. Kate hoped Netta was not becoming a mite senile.

The two men were standing, feet wide apart, leaning towards each other as if blown by a stiff wind. They were grasping their glasses like weapons, with whitened knuckles. Their eyes were bulging and since both were now shouting at the same time it was impossible to understand what the source of the argument might have been.

'It's the heat.' Sybil flapped her white handkerchief ineffectually, like a peace-keeper under fire. Stewart was turning an alarming puce colour as if he had sucked Sim dry of blood since Sim was becoming alarmingly ashen.

'He called me a subversive.' Sim pointed his glass in a shaking hand at Stewart.

'I do apologise, Sim.' Kate was aware that she, too, was waving her hankie, just as ineptly as Sybil.

'If there's any apologising to be done I shall do my own without your assistance, Kate.'

'I was only trying to help.'

'Then don't!' Stewart glared at her, as if she was an adversary too.

'I won't accept your apology,' Sim spluttered.

'You're mistaken, Sim. I have no intention of apologising to you, you cretin.'

'Gentlemen, gentlemen! Order, please. What appears to be the trouble?' A grey-haired man, deeply tanned, immaculately dressed in casual style, had joined them, an agitated Wendy at his side.

'Watch what you're saying, Peter. This bastard's a government snoop.' Stewart turned to face him.

'Which government? In what capacity?'

'Taxes. English, French, I don't know, but I assure you he's a plant, a spy.'

At this Netta could not retain a snort of amused derision. 'Don't be so ridiculous.'

'And how would you know?'

'I know Simon Chesterton, that's how. He isn't capable of being a spy for the Boy Scouts, let alone a government.'

'Thank you, Netta.' Sim flashed a grateful smile at her and as quickly wiped it from his face, as if unsure whether he should be pleased or not by her defence. 'All I said was that if you haven't got a *carte de séjour* and don't pay your taxes it's only a matter of time before the authorities will catch up with you.'

'See? What did I say? He's a snitch.'

'Hardly, Stewart. He's just telling the truth. You mean you haven't applied for your *carte*? You must be mad – obey

162

whatever pettifogging laws they want, then you can sleep at nights.'

'What's a *carte de séjour*?' asked Wendy, close to tears at this interruption to her party.

'It's what gives you permission to live here, Wendy. Without it you're in dead shtuck,' Sim explained.

'But we're all members of the EU, aren't we? We can live and work where we want.'

'You try telling that to the officials here!' This was Joan who, attracted by the noise, had ambled up and was now putting in her two-pennyworth.

'Exactly, Joan. Once you get into the hands of the bureaucrats you're sunk. And it's all right for you to pontificate, Peter, you don't live here all year.'

'I do think you should calm down. Your colour is most alarming,' Netta counselled, concerned at the deep magenta of Stewart's face. She was ignored.

'No, but if I did, I'd willingly pay.'

'And pigs might fly!' Stewart snorted.

'Please, everyone, let's all be friends. Don't spoil my party.'

'I'd no intention of ruining it. I can't help it if Stewart's half mad,' Sim explained.

'You bastard!' Stewart lunged at Sim, who stepped back nimbly.

'Please!' Wendy burst into tears.

This brought Stewart to his senses. 'Wendy, my love, forgive me. To you a million apologies.' And Stewart bent down, lifted her up high, twirled her around and made her giggle fulsomely.

Netta saw a frown flicker across Kate's face. 'She's a natural flirt. No doubt she can't help herself.'

'So's Stewart.' Kate chuckled to show that she wasn't

bothered, but she was. It wasn't the flirting, it was the question of taxes that was preoccupying her.

'Look, Sim's still simmering.' Netta, an hour later, pointed to where he sat by himself, puffing on his empty pipe, obviously still fuming.

'Is he all right, Sybil?'

'I tried to placate him, Kate, but he wouldn't listen so I said I'd seek out more congenial company.'

'My dear Sybil. At last! The worm has turned. Good for you.'

'I wish I hadn't now. He looks so forlorn.'

'They both behaved disgustingly, didn't they, Kate?'

'It must have been a combination of the heat and too much booze. I've told Stewart before.'

'Men don't listen where drink is concerned. They know it all.'

'I feel so embarrassed.'

'Kate! Really! It was hardly your fault. I've heard that particular argument about the *cartes* so often – but that's the first time I've heard someone being called a spy over it. Bit of over-excitement there, if you ask me. The ex-pat community is divided into two: those who live by the rules and those who don't.'

'This has got me worried now. What about you, Netta? Do you have one?'

'No. But I'd get one if I were you. Just listen to me! Do as I say not as I do. You see, I've never had one, never felt the need.' Netta spoke blithely enough but there were nights when she could not sleep for worrying about her lack of the little laminated card that would make her sojourn here official. Without it, she could claim no benefit, she could not work, she could not even be ill. That was her greatest fear – illness, helplessness. When she was too ill or infirm to care for herself she would have to kill herself. What other alternative did she have?

'Cheered up?' Netta asked Wendy, who by now, her makeup repaired, had returned to the party. 'A remarkably swift recovery.' Her sarcasm was masked by one of her smiles.

'Aren't men so silly? Here, Sybil, since you didn't bring a costume.' She handed over a wispy bikini.

Sybil held it in the air. 'Thanks, but I doubt if it will fit.'

'Of course it will. You've a lovely slim figure.'

'Do you think so?'

'Her husband says she's getting fat – that, coming from such an Adonis.' Netta nodded towards the disgruntled Sim, who was still sitting under the tree looking more and more like an angry toad.

'That's a sign of male insecurity. I'll show you where the changing rooms are.'

Like whopping your wife is another sign, thought Netta.

'Are you coming, Kate?'

'I don't really feel like it.' The truth was, Kate would have loved to jump in the pool but she had the problem common to many women who had once been overweight: while she was now reasonably slim, she did not see herself as others did and felt her body was too ugly for the eyes of strangers. Not that she had, or ever would, confessed this to a living soul. She watched the others walk slowly towards the house. It was too hot even for Wendy to hurry. Since she'd arrived here she had been trying to think who Wendy reminded her of and suddenly she realised. It was Pam. She was as petite. Her features were as delicate. Just like Pam, Wendy reminded Kate of a delicate piece of porcelain.

Wendy led the way down a winding stone staircase and into the basement of the house.

'Wendy, what you just said, is it true?' Sybil trotted along behind her.

'About men making women feel insecure? Oh, yes. They make the woman feel she's so ugly that no other man will ever want her. It's a classic.'

'You tell her, Wendy. She won't listen to me.' Netta brought up the rear.

'But surely no one has done that to *you*?' Sybil asked.

'Haven't they? You'd be surprised.'

'But not your Peter. He's lovely.'

'Is he?' She said this so coldly that Netta shivered.

At a pair of tall pine doors, Wendy stopped and pushed them open. 'Wow', said Netta and Sybil in unison. Before them was a large vaulted cellar hewn from rock in which a mosaic-lined pool had been sunk. Half-way across its length was a plate-glass window which, at the touch of a button, slid back into the walls to reveal the other half of the pool stretching out into the walled garden, where Kate was sitting.

'This has to be the most beautiful pool I've ever seen,' Netta said truthfully.

'We didn't want it too obvious so we built the walled garden. Otherwise Peter said it would look out of place.'

'He's so right.'

'Do you like the house?'

'I think it's perfect,' Netta said. Her fears had been groundless: not only was it decorated and furnished in a style compatible with its age and original use, there wasn't a ruched curtain to be seen, and if there was any gilt it was well hidden.

'That's Peter again. He just knows instinctively what to do. I'd have ruined it, I'm the first to admit. I've no taste, you see.'

'You mustn't say that,' Sybil reassured her.

'But it's the truth.'

'Well, at least you consider that your husband has one redeeming quality,' Netta said sharply.

'I don't know what you mean.'

'Don't you?' Netta replied enigmatically.

'Netta! Don't upset poor Wendy, you've flustered her.'

'Me? I'm not.' But she was. 'Right, the changing rooms are over there.' Wendy pointed to a row of doors with *trompe l'oeil* panels. She had evidently decided not to challenge Netta.

In the area where the showers stood there were vanity units, loaded with perfumes and makeup. How wonderful, thought Netta, as she explored the contents. She wished she was a bit less honest – she would have pinched the lot.

She began to change into her costume – a sleek black number she had had since the fifties and which, fortunately, like so much of her wardrobe, was once more back in vogue. Why was it that when women had good men they always hankered after others?

Netta would have loved to have a man like Peter, urbane, successful, rich. All these were important to her, she would be the first to admit, but there was something else she had seen in the man and which she envied Wendy most of all – in his eyes she had seen a kind man. How she longed for that above all else.

Kate was forcing herself to calm down after the spat between Stewart and Sim. What on earth had made him create a scene like that, embarrass her and make a complete fool of himself?

'Don't worry, Kate. No one minded, least of all me.'

She looked up, shielding her eyes from the sun, and saw her host, Peter, standing over her and smiling sympathetically. 'I minded,' she said, thinking what a charming, equable man he was. She bet he didn't have tantrums like Stewart – tantrums, there was an odd word to choose.

'And what work does your husband do now to occupy himself?'

'He's retired,' she replied, which was the answer she usually gave. It was simpler than having to explain. 'He was a journalist.'

'Yes, Wendy said. And famous too. Does he miss it?'

'He might but he never says so. He's busy writing a novel, which keeps him occupied.' She was aware that she was speaking defensively.

'At least it might keep him out of mischief.'

Kate looked up sharply, wondering what he had meant by that, but it must have been meant as a not-too-funny joke for he was still smiling at her.

'With one novelist in the house already, isn't that rather dangerous?'

'I'm sorry, I don't know what you mean.' Kate could have added 'again' but refrained.

'Well, what if he wasn't as successful as you? What if he became jealous of your success?'

'Stewart isn't petty like that.' *Liar*, her inner voice exclaimed. 'He's very proud of what little success I have had.' She spoke emphatically, hoping to shut it up.

'You're too modest by far. I hear you're very well known.'

'Moderately.' She felt herself blushing at the attentions of this charming man. 'I'm not in the Jilly Cooper or Barbara Taylor Bradford league, you understand.'

'Not yet.' He smiled his charming smile.

'One lives in hope.'

'I do hope you're enjoying the party.'

'Yes, it's great fun.'

'It's an odd mix of people but as we knew no one we

168

decided it would be fun to invite anyone who spoke English and just let them get on with it.'

'It seems to be working well.'

'I hope we get to know each other better when there are not so many people around. Next time we could have dinner perhaps?'

'Just the four of us, how nice.'

When Peter left her, after a few more minutes, she felt disappointed that he had gone. She had only just met him yet she felt she knew him – it was a rare talent to make people feel like that, she thought.

Peter had brought her a jug of Pimm's – she must be careful, it was too moreish for her own good. She watched a group of young people playing in the pool and saw that Steve and Lucy were among them. Where was Dominique? She shaded her eyes to look, and caught sight of him over by a fountain talking earnestly to a young woman. If she was Lucy she wouldn't leave him to talk alone to one so beautiful, Kate thought. But, then, she knew that one of the big differences between her and her daughter was that Kate lacked confidence.

Everyone was having such fun. Fun – that was what her life lacked at the moment. She sat up straight. What a thing to think! Where had such a thought come from? *Me, of course, and you know it's true.* Of course it wasn't, she had a wonderful life – look how often she told herself that.

'You look deep in thought. Would I be in the way if I joined you? Tristram Hargreaves.'

'Kate Howard.' They shook hands, and Kate giggled.

'Something I said?'

'No. It's just the formality of shaking hands when you're in a bathing costume – it strikes me as funny. Help me drink this. I think our host must think me an alcoholic.' She pointed to the Pimm's.

'Great people here, aren't they? I've met a retired general, a journalist, a teacher of English, a plumber, carpenter and electrician, a herbalist, an aromatherapist, a pig farmer, and everyone tells me you're a writer. It's great. You wouldn't get a mix like this back home, would you?'

She watched him as he poured himself a drink. He was tall and fair with that openness of face peculiar to a certain type of Englishman. 'Are you resident or on holiday?' she asked.

'We've got a smallholding over in the Ardèche.'

'You've come a long way.'

'I couldn't keep Mo from a party if it was two hundred miles to drive.'

'You don't look like a smallholder, not that I'm sure what one should look like.' God, she was prattling. 'How long have you been here?' How predictable, she thought. That's what the English always asked each other, as if vying to have been here longest – just like at school one had always claimed to have been someone's friend for longer than anyone else. 'And who's Mo?'

'My girlfriend. She's here somewhere. Ha, yes, there she is. That lovely creature talking to that rather obvious Frenchman – you can see what's on his mind, can't you?'

Kate joined in his laughter. Better not to let him know that Mo was talking to her son-in-law.

3

The party was happening in various places. Kate and the majority of those in her age group spent most of the time in the garden in the shade of umbrellas, their drinks constantly topped up. The younger element were in the outside pool; the elderly had opted for the cool of the sitting room in the house. The small children were being cared for by a nanny and had a large paddling-pool, a trampoline and a bouncy castle; a magician was due after lunch. The teenagers were in the basement where not only was there the indoor pool but computer games, snooker and table tennis. To top it off there was a juke box to which they danced as if they were on Ecstasy, even if they weren't.

'How many people do you think are here?' Kate wondered aloud.

'Everyone's so scattered it's difficult to tell. A hundred or thereabouts? Wonderfully well organised, I must say.' Netta gave it her seal of approval.

'Do you know what Peter Bolland does?'

'Someone told me he's in plastics, toy manufacturing mainly.'

'The idea of returning this hospitality fills me with dread.'

'Give them something simple. Every millionaire I've ever known gets so fed up with rich and elaborate food that they fall on my roast or a simple pie with relish.'

'Do you think he's a millionaire?'

'Undoubtedly. He smells rich.' She threw back her head and inhaled vigorously. 'And who have we here?' she asked, when upright once more.

'This is my family, Lucy my daughter, Steve my son and . . . my son-in law . . .' The pause was not just because she was unused to having one but because, to her horror, she had forgotten his name. No more Pimm's.

'And how long have you been married to this lovely creature, Monsieur?' Netta asked, in her beautiful French.

'Almost a year. You knew I was French?'

'But of course.' She did not explain. 'And where are you from?'

'Paris.'

171

No, you're not, not with an accent like that, Netta thought.

'Mercifully for me, Dominique speaks excellent English,' Kate explained, relieved at remembering his name again.

'Well, then, we shall speak that language. You must forgive an old woman's conceit. I like to show off my French.'

'Madame, how can you possibly call yourself *old*? And it is a pleasure to hear you speak my language.'

Netta graciously accepted his compliments, Lucy glowed with pride, Kate wished he wasn't quite so French, and Steve thought, What a creep.

'Are you intending to stay here?' Kate could have kissed Netta for asking the question she longed but couldn't quite bring herself to ask in case they thought her nosy.

'We'd like to. Dom's found a business we'd like to buy.'

'Really? How interesting,' Netta said, in such a way that she sounded genuinely enthusiastic. Kate could have hugged her.

'Well . . .' Lucy looked at Dominique as if unsure whether to continue.

'It's a pizza business.' Dominique answered for her.

'How nice for you – hard work, though.' Inwardly Netta shuddered at the idea. To her, the proliferation of the pizza was a tragedy that debased the food of this country. And she had noted that all was not well here: she did not like Dominique, and sensed that Kate didn't either. She was unsure of Lucy, and she wondered if Kate realised that she looked at her son with undiluted admiration but warily at her daughter.

'Yes, but Dom's a professional,' Lucy said, with pride.

'Are pizzas difficult to cook?' Netta asked, with disarming sweetness.

'Good ones are.' Dominique looked edgy.

'And, Steve, do you live here?' Netta transferred her attention to him.

'Not yet.'

'Steve?' Kate looked at him questioningly.

'What do you do?' Netta asked.

'I'm a landscape gardener.'

'You should start up a business here, you'd make a fortune.'

'That's just what I've been investigating.'

'Steve?'

'What a clever young man! What a brilliant idea!' Netta clapped her hands with pleasure. 'Gardening is becoming big business – nowadays one is even starting to be able to buy different plants from the ubiquitous pelargonium.'

'You do see rather a lot of them, I must say.' Steve nodded sagely.

'Geraniums,' Kate whispered to Lucy, who looked puzzled.

'You know, when I lived here first there was no such thing as a garden centre but now they're popping up all over the place. And the French need to be shown – they plant everything in serried ranks and the most bizarre colour combinations.'

'I've noticed.'

Kate wished she could get a word in edgeways but Steve and Netta were far too engrossed in talk of gardens to notice her agitation. She was clutching her hands together, afraid she might be dreaming this.

'So, what are your plans?' Netta asked, unconstrained by the curiosity of motherhood, which could be interpreted too easily as interference.

'I'm waiting on some commissions I've got in the pipeline.'

'And when will you know? Forgive me, I'm horrendously nosy.'

Oh, Netta, Kate thought, with glee, I shall have to adopt you!

'I heard this morning before we left that one contract is mine for the asking. I'm waiting to hear about the other.

'You could have told Mum first. You should have thought of her.'

'As you do, of course! If you must know, I didn't want to in case it didn't come off.' Steve was angry.

Was this just sibling rivalry or something else?' Netta wondered.

'It doesn't matter, Lucy, I know now.' Kate was grinning from ear to ear.

'And if you get both contracts, what then?'

'There's a bit of a problem over money. The bank is being a bit sticky.'

'Don't talk to me about banks.' Netta waved her hand in a Gallic gesture of dismissal.

'I'll help you out.'

'That's kind of you, Mum, but I hope to do this on my own.'

'Don't be so selfish, Steve, as to deprive your mother of such pleasure. You can't spoil her fun. You mustn't.' Netta was emphatic.

The call '*à table*' rang out. Everyone ambled towards the terrace – it was too hot for speed. Several long tables had been set up in the shade, under the vine-covered pergola. The children and teenagers were being fed separately.

'I'm sorry, Peter's such a grump where children are concerned,' Wendy was explaining to a couple of disgruntled parents as Netta and Kate arrived. 'I can assure you they will be well cared for. There's a nanny to look after them and a special children's menu.'

'But Sebastian won't eat unless I feed him,' his harassed mother whined.

'Then it's about time he started to learn,' Peter said coolly, looking with marked distaste at the overweight five-year-old who was causing the problem.

'Can't just Sebastian eat with us?' Wendy fluttered.

'No.'

'But why not?' It was Sebastian's father, goaded by his mother, who had not so much asked as demanded to know.

'Because that would be hardly fair on the other parents, would it?'

'The other parents *love* the arrangement. They wouldn't be put out. And he will be so upset.' Sebastian's mother was a pretty woman who, obviously used to getting her way with a flutter of eyelashes and a suggestive pout, performed her act for Peter.

'I'd rather he didn't. If I liked eating with children I would have arranged matters so that I could. I don't like children, I never have and I doubt I ever will.'

'That's insufferable.'

'I've no objection to you going to eat with the children.'

'I think we'd prefer to leave.'

'As you wish.' The situation dealt with, Peter turned his attention to his other guests. 'Sorry, folks, making a scene, but there it is. I don't wish to ruin my lunch by eating with other people's little darlings.'

Netta watched the scene with admiration. 'Isn't he bloody wonderful?' she said, to no one in particular. Now, if only she had met someone like Peter when she was young, how different her life might have been.

The seating had been carefully planned so that no one sat with their own partner. Kate was content to find that

Stewart had been placed on another table altogether: he was far from being her favourite person today. She saw him sitting next to Wendy, while she was beside Peter.

The food was of such excellence that Kate again found herself concerned with what to feed the Bollands when she invited them.

'Catered,' Netta whispered to her, as if she had read her thoughts.

'Are you certain?' She was not sure why this information made her feel better but it did.

Although Peter was entertaining, and appeared to be happy, Kate noticed there was sadness in his face when in repose, which would disappear suddenly as if he was aware of it and was trying to control it. He was an attractive man, although not conventionally good-looking, who was in his fifties, she guessed. A 'well set-up' man, as Kate's mother had been fond of saying. She had never been sure what it meant, but she did now, because Peter exuded confidence, and a prosperity that almost made him handsome. She wondered what on earth could be making him sad: he appeared to have everything, a lovely home, a pretty young wife, money. How strange, she found herself thinking, that she should have put them in that order. She wondered what order others would have used.

From the waitress she accepted a second helping of the perfectly cooked fillet of beef *en croûte* and was glad, once again, that Stewart was not at this table. Not that he'd have said anything about her being piggy but she often thought he might.

'You look as if something funny has crossed your mind.' Peter looked at her enquiringly.

'I was just thinking I'm glad I'm not sitting with my partner.' She was sure she blushed as she spoke.

'As am I, too,' he replied, and then she knew for certain that she *was*.

'You're lucky to have one. I wish I did,' Netta made a mock-tragic expression.

'It's a mystery to me that you haven't, Netta, an attractive woman like you,' Peter said.

'But I'm so old – and look at some of the young here. Is it any wonder I'm alone?'

'To my mind the most attractive women are those of a certain age.' He smiled, and Kate wondered if he meant it or was lying to be polite – his wife had to be a good ten or maybe fifteen years younger than him. What's more, she registered, he'd called her Netta and she hadn't objected.

'Peter, you're a wolf, you really are.' Netta smacked his hand playfully. 'I'm not taken in for one moment.'

Kate watched her play the coquette with fascination. She would never have the confidence to behave like that – she never had. Given Netta's age, it should have been louche but it wasn't, for in flirting Netta seemed to change before her eyes and shed years. Then, to her horror, she found that she didn't like Netta flirting with Peter. It was one of those thoughts that come from nowhere but it hit her like a bullet with its accuracy. *What the hell's got into you?* Yes, what on earth had got into her? She loved Stewart. They were going through a dodgy patch, that was all, they'd soon be over it and truly happy again. She must learn to be more patient with him. Her expression was guilty as she looked around the table, fearing that in some way the others would know what had been in her mind.

'What do you think, Kate?'

'Sorry, Peter, I was miles away. What's the question?'

'It was Jessica's. She's canvassing opinions on a venture she's planning.'

177

'Really?' Kate floundered and smiled apologetically at Jessica, who was sitting opposite.

'I don't want to bore everyone rigid,' Jessica Stone protested.

Kate had seen her in the garden – she was difficult to miss. She was a largish woman who appeared frozen in time – no doubt when she had been at her best. She wore the quasi-peasant clothes she might once have worn to a rock concert way back. Laura Ashley, *circa* seventies, Kate decided, judging by the floral skirt and frilled white petticoat that peeped below it. The peasant-style blouse was slipping off one shoulder, exposing a mite too much flesh, and the ties of the Roman gladiator sandals dug in unattractively as they wound criss-cross up her fat legs. Her eyes were rimmed with kohl and her hair hung loose and long – more befitting a teenager than the mature woman she was. But she laughed a lot, and Kate had thought when she spied her that she would like to talk to her.

'Don't be so modest, Jessica. It's a good idea. Explain it to our daydreaming Kate – she'll give you expert advice.'

'Really?' Jessica looked unsure but took a deep breath. 'I was thinking of setting up an arts centre. You know the sort of thing, painting holidays, music appreciation, writing courses . . . I wondered what people thought of the idea.'

'It sounds brilliant,' Netta volunteered.

'I'd have to find premises – our house is too small for something like that – and people willing to do B and B. But it's something I've always wanted to do – we could do with some extra income.'

'Tell me!' Netta sighed.

'You see, when we moved here my husband's pension seemed adequate.'

'I think too many people just up sticks and rush over without thinking of the consequences,' Joan Oxford said, in her insufferably smug way.

'What? That you might, just might, have to deal with the French!' Netta fired a broadside. 'And how's the video library going? Successful? Or has it gone the way of the Marmite-by-post venture. Your husband was telling me all about your little efforts to raise some cash – so commendable of you.' There were times when Netta was stirring up trouble that Kate felt nothing but admiration. She was one of those people who evidently said what everyone else was thinking. 'You were saying, Jessica?' And she emphasised the name while staring straight at Joan.

'Things aren't too bad at the moment. But, dear God, when we were only getting seven francs to the pound a few years back, I can tell you we felt the wind of discomfort a bit too close – and I don't think we were alone.' She, too, looked pointedly at Joan.

'What a lovely title for a book – *The Wind of Discomfort*,' Kate said hastily. 'And I think it's a great plan. Writing courses are very popular, you know. And I could help . . . We've a large barn.' *Hold on!* Kate's mind was racing.

'Do you really think so, Kate?' Jessica leant forward, her ample breasts resting on the table as if they were not part of her.

'How exciting. I'd be only too happy to help, too,' piped up Petronella who, until now, had been uncharacteristically silent – a little too much wine, everyone had thought.

'You should contact a friend of mine, Jan Johnson in the south-west, near Bordeaux – I'll give you her number. She's been doing this for years. She'd advise you.'

Kate felt more than a little interest in the plans. 'But I'd be in competition.'

'Jan wouldn't see it like that. She's got a big heart – I'm sure there's room for you both.'

'Exactly, that's what I told Jessica,' Peter added.

'And since she's planning to do other things too . . .' Petronella already had a pad and pen open on the table, and was scribbling in it. 'As a writer I have to carry my notebook with me – I'd be lost without it. Little snippets of things you think you'll remember but you never do,' she explained.

'Will you have harpsichords?' chipped in Joan, who, Kate decided, had the hide of an ox.

'I don't understand.' Jessica looked puzzled.

'Petronella here tells me she can't write without playing her harpsichord and communing with nature.'

'Joan! I never did. I said I like *listening*. And, yes, looking at the garden and our view helps me.'

'It hasn't done you much good so far.' Joan looked even more smug.

'Have you nicked that title?' Netta asked, having craned her neck to peer into the notebook.

'I can use it.' Petronella was flicking hair and her scarves in an agitated way.

'How do you know Kate didn't want it?'

'Be my guest.' Kate bowed her head.

'How many books have you had published, Petronella?' It was Joan speaking with an even more unpleasant smirk on her face – she'd been the school bully, Kate was convinced. Petronella began to look flustered and found it imperative to check the contents of her bag with rapt attention. 'How many?' Joan persisted.

'None, but I will,' Petronella said defiantly, flushing to the roots of her hair. Joan's smirk deepened.

'If she's writing she's a writer.' Kate jumped to her defence.

'Well, hardly, Kate.' Joan snorted, which with her porcine features was an unfortunate habit.

Her friends, if she had any, should point it out to her,

Kate thought. 'If someone's learning to be a hairdresser no one thinks less of them if they say that is what they are,' she said reasonably.

'Or a plumber or a motor mechanic,' Peter added.

'Or an actress,' Netta joined in.

'Do you write? You sound very knowledgeable.'

'Yes Joan, I do.'

'You don't!' Petronella looked aghast.

'Didn't you know, Petronella? Kate is our local celebrity.' Peter smiled at her and she almost wished he wouldn't for she found it deeply disarming.

'Hardly a celebrity, Peter.'

'Kate is *Kate Howard*,' Peter said, with such an expansive gesture that she quite expected to hear the roll of drums and the sound of trumpets.

'Should I have heard of you?' Joan asked.

'Evidently not,' Kate replied equably. She was used to that particular put-down.

'Not *the* Kate Howard?' Petronella stood up then sat down and fanned herself agitatedly with her napkin. 'Why didn't you say? I feel such a fool. And there was me showing off. Oh dear! I love your books.'

'How kind.' Kate smiled her author-in-an-embarrassing-situation smile. She only half enjoyed meeting people who had read and liked her books, convinced that they were lying to her out of politeness. And to show she was gratified was often more than she could manage for at her shoulder she could always hear her mother – 'That's enough showing off for today, Kate.'

'Of course, I remember your name now,' Joan exclaimed, evidently feeling left out. 'Weren't you shortlisted for the Red Rose award for best novel? Or did you win?'

'For someone who had never heard of her you seem to be recalling an amazing amount,' Netta said, in a throwaway

181

manner. 'And which of Mrs Howard's books is your favourite, Mrs Oxford?'

'I . . . well . . . I read so little, it's finding the time.'

'I've always thought that if people like Kate Howard find the time to write them then the least we can do is read them. Which is your favourite of Kate's books, Wendy?' Netta asked, as Wendy arrived to speak to her husband.

'Well, I'm so busy, you know. I—'

'Wendy can't read, that's the main problem,' Peter said, in a bantering way – at least, Kate thought he had been joking but there had been a steeliness in his voice too. Maybe he wasn't so nice after all.

'Peter!' Wendy looked close to tears again.

Oh dear, thought Kate, there's something seriously wrong here.

'If you want to know the truth, I hardly read anything myself,' Kate reassured her.

'Yes, but Kate, you're so busy you can't have time. My wife should have plenty of opportunity to read, shouldn't you, *darling*? But you're always rushing hither and thither on your little errands, aren't you?'

'Do you ever get the feeling, Kate, that you might have waltzed into a hornets' nest?' Netta asked, but she smiled in a very self-satisfied way.

4

'Thanks for a memorable lunch. Our turn next.' Stewart shook hands with Peter, planted three kisses on Wendy's cheeks, waved cheerily and swung himself into the driver's seat. While the rest of them were making their farewells, he drummed his fingers on the steering-wheel impatiently before opening the window to chivvy them along.

'Heavens above, Stewart, where's the fire?' Kate asked, as she climbed in.

'You all right to drive, Stewart?' Steve opened the driver's door.

'You think I'm drunk?'

'You've had a couple, yes.'

'And you haven't?'

'I stopped a couple of hours ago.'

'Quite the little Boy Scout, aren't you?' Stewart slammed the door shut.

'You did sink quite a bit,' Kate commented, as she belted herself in.

'Not you too! Listen, everyone, I am perfectly competent to drive this car and anyone who thinks otherwise can get out and walk.'

'Can you manage, Lucy?' Kate twisted round in her seat.

'Of course she can manage. She's hardly an infant.'

'There's a knack to putting that particular seat-belt on.'

'One would hardly need a degree to do it, Kate.'

'You wouldn't know since you never sit in the back.'

'I'm fine, Mum.' Lucy tapped her mother's shoulder and her smile seemed to say, 'Don't have a row over me.'

'Dominique, the air-conditioning doesn't always work effectively in the back but that little window opens. There's a clip—'

'Honestly, woman, he's not retarded. He can open a window. Right, everyone settled? Do I have your permission to begin?' Stewart stabbed in the code to start the car. It was 1815, and Kate had always thought it rather tactless of him to have used the date of the battle of Waterloo, especially when he was at pains to point it out to the French. Kate turned to smile apologetically at her children in time to see Lucy poking her tongue out at him. She shook her head and mouthed, 'Don't be so childish,' then turned back into her seat.

'If you ask me, that was a complete waste of time.' Stewart swung the Peugeot 806 out of the drive as he fiddled with the air-conditioning, indicator and switched on the CD player at the same time.

'I enjoyed myself.' Well insulated with wine, Kate snuggled down in the front seat and tried to ignore the macho flicking of switches.

'You were the one who didn't want to go.'

'I'm glad you insisted, but sorry you didn't enjoy yourself. I met some interesting people.'

'Interesting! Bah! Lot of boring losers, if you ask me.'

'Takes one to know one.'

Kate thought that was what her son said, but it was barely audible. She turned in her seat but he was looking innocently out of the window. Stewart couldn't have heard anything for he did not react.

Perhaps she had imagined it, she thought. There were times when she'd written an incident in a book that she would find herself quoting months later as if it had actually happened. One of the problems with writing was that it wasn't like any other sort of job in that one didn't clock off: she was planning, imagining or plotting in most of her waking hours. It was hardly surprising that the line between her fiction and her life sometimes blurred, as perhaps it had a few moments ago.

They were on the twisting mountain roads, which Stewart hated. He was far too impatient a driver to deal placidly with the lack of overtaking places. They'd have been better off with her driving since she was much more resigned to toddling along behind a slow car or tractor. She wished he wasn't in such a bad mood. What must the children be thinking? She was sure they didn't believe her when she said he wasn't always like this. Over the last day or two she had wondered if he was like this simply because they were here and for some reason he didn't want them to be. Kate felt her eyelids drooping. If she had a snooze she would miss his bad temper when they were held up.

'The problem with living in a foreign country . . .'

'Heavens! You made me jump. I was just nodding off.' Kate shook her head to rouse herself. 'Sorry,' she said – a hangover from her marriage since nothing had annoyed Tony more than a sleeping passenger. 'You were saying?' She sat up straight.

'One of the problems of living here is that you have to meet and socialise with people you would never bother with at home,' Stewart continued.

'Like who?'

'There was an ex-plumber there, and his wife looked as if she'd been on the game.'

'Honestly, Stewart, what a thing to say,' Lucy snapped, from behind them.

'Did any of you talk to that retired policeman? A right Mr Plod if ever I met one.'

'I liked them all – well, I wasn't too sure about that Joan Oxford woman – and I've made some new friends.' Kate could hardly believe they'd been at the same party.

'That creep Chesterton's another example and the dreary, simpering Sybil. We'd never mix with people like that normally.'

'I don't know. There were a lot of couples like them when I lived at Graintry. Harmless types. Sybil is always so sweet. Sim was quiet but that was hardly surprising after you had ranted at him.'

'He's a complete nerd.'

'Why haven't we got these *cartes de séjour* everyone was going on about?'

'Because we don't need them.'

'Sim knows a lot about gardening,' Steve piped up from the back.

'Exactly. Boring!'

'Stewart!' Kate hissed, under her breath and yanked down the vanity mirror to peer at her son in the back. Evidently he had decided to ignore the jibe.

'Why is he called Sim?'

'You might well ask, Dominique,' said Stewart. 'It's a stupid name. Sometimes he's even called Sim-Sim. In my experience when people give themselves stupid names it's a pathetic attempt to make themselves appear interesting.'

'Sybil told me he was christened Simon Simon. He had two uncles with the same name and his mother didn't want to offend either so she named him twice.'

'And you believed her?'

'I thought it was a rather nice story. Gracious, Stew, you're so irritable, what *is* the matter?'

'Lunchtime drinking,' Lucy said accusingly.

Stewart took a deep breath, about to reply, when Kate said quickly, 'What did you all think of Netta? I find her fascinating.' Stew and Lucy sparked each other off at the least thing, she thought. 'She's had an interesting life. So many husbands . . .'

'Mum! You said that in such a dreamy way, as if you envied her,' Lucy teased.

'Well, as Sybil would say, variety is the spice of life.' She laughed.

'Not content with what you've got?'

'Oh, Stewart, don't be so sensitive. It was a joke.'

'A not particularly funny one.'

'Then I'm sorry.' She wished she could stop saying *sorry* all the time. She wasn't in the least – she just didn't want any arguments.

186

'I liked Peter very much. He listens as if he's really interested in what you're saying,' said Steve.

'That's a typical con-man trick, Steve. You should be wary of those coves with the over-firm handshake, who stare you straight in the eye.'

'Con-man? Isn't that a bit harsh?' Kate sat upright.

'No, darling. I reckon there's something very fishy about our Peter Bolland.'

'Like what?' Lucy sat forward.

'He's all charm but cold as ice. You look at his eyes. I bet he's a right bastard to his wife. Poor Wendy.'

They had halted at the slip-road on to the motorway, always a dangerous moment in the French system since it seemed to Kate that it was beyond any French driver to move over and let another car in.

'I don't think she needs our sympathy. She seems to be doing all right to me.' Lucy snorted.

'Do you?' Kate turned in her seat. 'I thought the opposite. I thought she had the air of an unhappy woman. There was something in her face – she seemed to be trying too hard all the time. And I don't think she and her husband are happy.'

'What makes you say that?' The car lurched forward as a gap appeared in the traffic.

'I don't think he likes her, Stewart. It's as if he's having to control himself all the time. I think she's hurt him badly and he doesn't intend to forgive her.'

'You've too much imagination for your own good, Kate.' Stewart blasted his horn as he overtook a car with GB number-plates then confused the occupants by waving cheerily at them.

'She doesn't get my sympathy vote,' said Lucy, from the back. 'All that money and miserable, she needs her head examined.'

'As Sybil would say—'

'Money isn't everything,' they chorused.

Netta sat in the back of the Chestertons' car and for once did not mind the snail-like speed. She was in no hurry to return to her little flat and she closed her eyes, leant back on the upholstery and let herself think of Peter. What a lovely man. What a manly man. What a rich man!

Observing people, she had decided long ago was one of the happier and cheaper pursuits in life. But this party had been exceptional. There was the antagonism she had sensed between Peter and his wife, and she wouldn't be honest if she didn't say it had quite lifted her spirits. As long as she lived she would never understand men like Peter, clever, successful, yet choosing pretty but rather vacuous younger wives. Serves him right for being such a stupid old goat – it was never a good idea to mix autumn and spring. Well, more like late summer in his case. She smiled at this idea.

She had liked that young man Tristram, but not his girlfriend. She was trouble if ever Netta had seen it. She had a theory that you could tell a troublesome young woman from the way she moved her behind. And that one hadn't sat still for a moment, as if she was constantly in need of sex – which, judging by the odd snappy remark, she wasn't getting. Perhaps she frightened the poor young man into impotence. She was that dangerous breed of woman who thought she was more intelligent and cunning then she actually was. In Netta's experience they normally caused upset and havoc wherever they went.

Netta had arranged to meet Tristram on Monday – she hoped the girlfriend wouldn't turn up for coffee at the Palais Brasserie – when he came into town to buy the Sunday papers. Wonderful, she had thought. She'd be able to have a peek at them, which she had not been able to afford to do for some time. She sighed. Being poor was such an exhausting business, always having to be on the lookout for wangles and perks.

'Penny for them.' Sybil peered into the back seat. She had a nice face, Netta thought. She looked so many years younger than she was, but always reminded Netta of a ferret.

'I was just thinking that Mo creature spells trouble.'

'Really, Netta, you'll be sued for slander.'

'Will I, Simon? Why? Are you going to shop me?'

'I didn't mean . . .'

'Of course you didn't, sweetie.' Netta laughed sardonically, which was guaranteed to annoy him.

'I didn't like her at all,' Sybil added. 'She's a sheep in wolf's clothing, if you ask me.'

'Sybil, you're adorable.' Netta laughed again, but genuinely this time. 'And that's the first time I've ever heard you say something . . . well, a little bit catty.'

'Really, old girl, if you must trot out the clichés get them right. It's a wolf in sheep's – silly old thing.' He patted her – just as if she was a dog, Netta thought. I'd swipe him if he did that to me.

'No, I haven't got it wrong. I meant it that way round. She's pretending to be bad and sophisticated. I think she's frightened, and I think she needs him far more than he needs her.'

'Do you?' Netta sounded doubtful. 'Care to bet on it? I'll lay five hundred francs that she'll have caused havoc in some way or another within six months.'

'You're always saying you've no money, Netta, so how can you afford to bet that?'

'Because it's a sure-fire winner,' Netta said confidently.

'You're on.' Sybil turned in her seat to shake her hand. 'If you haven't the money when we know, I'll take those black Louis Jourdain shoes in lieu.'

'Done!'

'Steady on, old girl.'

'If you call her that one more time, Simon, I swear I'll hit you for her.'

'It doesn't bother me.' Sybil grinned at Netta, who raised an eyebrow.

'You obviously didn't like Stewart but what about Kate, Simon?' she asked.

'If I was her son I'd be worried. She's done well for herself, hasn't she? I wouldn't be surprised if he's ripping her off.' Sim spoke round the stem of his pipe, which made him sound as if he had a speech impediment. He did not smoke it when driving – it required far too much attention – but he kept it hanging out of his mouth.

'He obviously likes well-off women,' added Sybil.

'What does that mean?' Netta asked.

'He's having an affair with Wendy.'

'Come on, old girl. You mustn't say things like that. It's not on.'

Netta was so intrigued by this that she didn't even notice that he'd said *old girl*. 'You sound very sure?'

'They fit together. They know each other's bodies. And they go back a long way. Wendy says she's known him for years.'

'From what Kate's said I doubt if she's aware of that.'

The last car had left and Peter strode back into the house. He crossed the terracotta-tiled floor to the back of the hall and made for his study. Wendy's shoes clicked on the stone as she ran after him. 'Peter, we've got to talk.'

'There's nothing to say.'

'But I need to talk with you.'

'There's no need for that. I want you out of this house by the time I return from London.'

'What have I done?' Wendy burst into tears.

'Don't bother to cry. It doesn't work with me. I've little time for you but, by God, I never thought you'd be so tacky as to invite your lover into my house. Get out of my sight!'

The door of his study slammed behind him with such force that an ancient sword fell from the wall with an echoing clatter.

Chapter Five

May–July

1

Netta was in such a state of excitement that she didn't know if she was coming or going. Her godchild was paying her a surprise visit. She only had the one, which was just as well since she could never have managed to give birthday and Christmas presents to an army of them.

In many ways, she supposed, this was the child she had never had and a much more satisfactory arrangement. Over the years she had enjoyed Caroline's company immeasurably, even when she was small, but she had always known she could hand her back to her mother. She had been spared the terrible twos, the teenage angst. Instead she had always had a good relationship with her, hence her tizzy now.

Always punctual, today she was uncharacteristically early. For nearly half an hour she had been pacing up and down the station platform at Le Puy, waiting anxiously for the train from Lyon to arrive.

'Caroline, my darling!' She held her arms wide open for her goddaughter to rush into. 'I was so afraid something would happen and you would have to cancel.'

'What on earth gave you that idea? If I've said I'll come, nothing will stop me.'

'Such a dear you are.' Netta picked up one of her bags. 'Heavens above, what's in this? Bricks?'

'Goodies.'

'Bliss. Edible ones, I do hope,' she exclaimed, as they left the station.

'Aren't we taking a taxi?'

'It's such a lovely day I thought we should walk.'

'With this baggage? Netta, please.'

'It will do us good.' She knew that Caroline understood that economy was the real reason.

'No point in me offering to pay the fare?'

'None whatsoever.' Despite the heavy bag, Netta marched purposefully down the hill from the station.

'I went to Fortnum's before I left.'

'Yummy!'

'Netta, do you think you could walk a little bit slower? I'm not as fit as you.'

'Still smoking?'

'Don't start, or you'll sound like my mother.'

'I would be the last person to lecture you. In my heyday I resembled a factory chimney.'

They stopped at the traffic lights to cross the road, then began the climb up to the top of the town. 'I've been beside myself with excitement,' Netta said, without any hint of puff.

'That's only because you lead such a dull old life.' Caroline would have laughed had she had the breath.

'How true. Sadly. And how are your parents?'

'Dad's making even more money. We can't get him to stop.'

'Bless him. Such a talent he has.'

'I'm to ask you yet again if you'll accept an allowance from him – just a small one.'

'What a dear he is. But I couldn't possibly, he knows that. If I'm in a mess it's of my own making. And your mother?'

'She's gone blonde.'

'Is that wise at her age? Bleached hair can make the face look so hard.'

'No, actually, she looks lovely, it's been beautifully done – vegetable dyes, they're not as harsh. She's had it cut, too, and she looks years younger.'

'Such a beauty and you take after her.'

'Hardly. No one looks as good as her. That's a new handbag shop, isn't it?'

'Quite good, but I prefer the old one. I wish they would come and visit. Each year they say they will but they never do.'

'And each year they invite you and you never come.'

'You know I can't.'

'Netta, I sometimes think you're the most stubborn woman I know. It's silly to be so sensitive. If they offer to help it's not charity, you know, it's because they love you.'

'I was born a stubborn cow and I'll die one. Here we are.'

'Thank God!' Caroline said, with feeling, aware that sweat was trickling down her back, yet Netta still looked bandbox fresh. 'I've *got* to get fit.'

There were still the five flights of stairs to negotiate but once they were in Netta's flat Caroline collapsed into the armchair and fanned herself with a magazine. 'Give me five minutes to get my breath. How do you do it?'

'I'll get us some iced tea, that always helps.'

When Netta returned with the glasses, it was to find Caroline already unpacking her bag.

'There's no need to do that now, have your tea first,' she

said, though she did not really mean it. 'What an assortment. Caviar! Blinis! Vodka! Bombay Sapphire! What a thoughtful child you are.' But that was not all: chocolate digestive biscuits, tea, pâté and Bath Olivers emerged from the bag as if it had no bottom. 'And you remembered! Corned beef!'

'I'd have brought you sausages if it hadn't been so hot.'

'This will keep me going for weeks.' Netta was gleefully putting her goodies away.

'Have you booked a table for tonight?'

'Of course. At the Lantern – they always have such good paintings to look at.'

The strange thing about Netta was that while it was impossible to help her with money or air tickets, she accepted graciously any food or restaurant bookings. Long ago Caroline had decided that in Netta's eyes those didn't count as charity but as normal social intercourse.

Once their meal was ordered they sat with their Kir and a small plate of *amuses-bouche*.

'So, to what do I owe the honour of this visit?'

'I wanted to see you.'

'I'm sure you did. But, my dear Caroline, every time you come there is always another reason. I don't mind. In fact, I take it as a compliment that when you have a problem or a little upheaval in your life you like to confide in me. It's nice to think I can be of use.'

'It's a bit complicated.'

'The best dramas always are.'

'I was in love and he fell for someone else. There's no advice you can give me for that, is there?'

'You say *was*, don't you mean you *are* in love?'

'All right, then, I am.'

'My poor darling, when did this happen?'

195

'November, December time.'

'And?'

'And what?'

'There has to be more to it than that for you to come here. Undoubtedly, even if you are still in love with him, you'd have adjusted to the situation in the intervening six or seven months.'

'I've found out something about the other girl.'

'And you want to know if I think you should tell him?'

'No, I've already told him. I think she's stolen a lot of money and some odd-looking people are after her. They came asking me if I knew where they were.'

'And did you?'

'Fortunately no. They believed me.'

'So what is the problem?'

'Well, he said it was nothing important – you see, I offered to pay off her debts for her. He refused and made it sound as if it was no big deal, but if that was the case why were the heavies moving in so menacingly? It has to be a considerable sum of money.'

'That wasn't very sensible, offering to help her out if you didn't know what you were letting yourself in for, was it?'

'I love him.'

'You might, but that's no reason to be foolhardy. I'm glad he refused. He'd have been entirely in the wrong to accept. And what do you think this money is for?'

'Drugs.'

'Good God. How exciting.'

'Netta, this isn't a game. It might be a nightmare. These people are capable of murder.'

'Were they Yardies? I've read all about them.'

'No, more your Essex Mafia, I'd say. But whoever they are they mean business.'

'Then I should keep well away, if I were you. Otherwise where will you end up? In a ditch?'

'I can't just let him come to harm.'

'He didn't think much of you to run away with this other creature.'

'He doesn't love her, I'm sure of that. He's in lust with her, not love.'

'Heavens, I know that feeling.' A memory or two surfaced briefly. 'And you've forgiven him this aberration?'

'Yes.'

'Woman, where's your *self-esteem*? You see? Even tucked away here I know the right expressions to use. Are you in *denial*? There's another.' She chortled with delight – she'd been dying for an opportunity to use them.

'Netta, I do wish you wouldn't find it so funny. It's not. And I can't help how I behave where he's concerned.'

Netta put on a serious face. 'You seem to know too much about these people. You're not involved in any drugs, are you? Only, you would tell me if you were, wouldn't you?'

'No, I'm not, and yes, I would.'

'I had a nasty expensive cocaine habit once. Such a devil to get rid of. I'd hate you to go down that route.'

'Is there nothing you haven't done?'

'Well, I've never slept three in a bed and I've often wondered what it would be like. I suppose I've left it a bit too late to find out now.'

'Netta, you're such a shocker!'

'But tell me, this man you love so much. What's his name?'

'Tristram Hargreaves – he lives near here. I've come to see if I can find him.'

'Kismet!' Netta declared dramatically. 'I know them – just acquaintances, you understand.'

'Where is he living? He never gave me his address – to

protect her, I suppose. But the bank where I sent the money for him, not her, was in Le Puy. So . . .'

'You see I was right. You always come here for a reason. I was right about that creature Mo, too, though I could wish I'd been wrong. You have a difficult adversary there, my dear, and my advice to you is to get on the next train and forget Tristram.'

'Netta, I wish I could but I know I can't. His destiny is mine.'

'What a load of codswallop!'

2

In the few days since the party Kate had seen less of Stewart. He was forever rushing off at a minute's notice to meet people. Forever shopping. Coming home late. She began to wonder if he was avoiding her but rejected the idea as paranoia on her part, especially when he kissed her enthusiastically when he returned. But what other explanation was there? One thing she tried not to think of, but it kept bobbing up and worrying her. They hadn't made love for weeks. Why not?

When she did see him, he invariably had an idea for a scheme to make money, which he had to go and sort out there and then. As often as not, it wasn't mentioned again. His sudden preoccupation with making money bothered her until she wondered whether he was trying to bolster their income since her problems with the publisher. This made her worry, then she felt guilty. If she had done as Joy and everyone had advised and not written *The Lost Troubador*, she wouldn't be so concerned.

'What are you doing all the time?' she asked one afternoon, seeing him preparing to go out yet again.

'This and that. There's a group of us meet in the English pub in Le Puy. We watch football.'

'Is there football in May?'

'There's always football. Why? Don't you believe me?'

'Don't be daft, of course I do. I was just curious.'

'And we play poker too.'

'Does Sim go?'

'No, thank God. If he did none of the rest of us would. Got to rush.' He grabbed his car keys, planted a kiss on her cheek and was gone.

It couldn't go on like this. They were going to have to talk it through. Kate knew herself: give her one thing to worry about and she turned it into ten. Normally she went to bed when he was late but this night she stayed up to await his return. She had suggested that Steve go out to supper with Lucy and Dominique, and then on to a disco. She hoped that she and Stewart might be able to build some bridges – she hated the distance between them. Her primary reason, though, was that she wanted some time alone with him.

'You're up,' he said, unnecessarily, when he entered the sitting room where she had been half-heartedly watching a film.

'I wanted to talk.'

'Oh, yes, what about? Fancy a beer?'

'Us.'

'I'm all ears.' The can hissed as he pulled back the ring-pull. She accepted a glass, even though she didn't want it. It had crossed her mind that if she refused he might think she was being judgemental.

'Are you avoiding me?' she began.

'No. Why do you ask?'

'You're never here. We hardly ever seem to see each other.'

'I told you, I've been doing things – getting the cricket team together, looking into business possibilities. That can't be done lolling about here.'

'It's not just your physical absence. There seems to be a gulf between us that wasn't there before. And I miss you, Stewart, and how it used to be.'

'Quite honestly, Kate, is it any wonder? OK, I'm forever going off to Le Puy, but do you want to know why? To have some peace. There, I've said it.'

'Peace from what? Me?'

'Don't be silly – your bloody family.'

'But they don't bother you.'

'Yes, they do. You say you want it as it used to be, well, you're not the only one. I liked it when it was just you and me. I never expected to have to live with your family. That wasn't part of the deal.'

'Deal? Did we have one?' She reacted to his use of the word as if their relationship were some business arrangement. She heard her voice rise and forced herself to control it: getting angry wasn't going to help anyone.

'You know what I mean.'

'But Steve goes at the end of this week.'

'That still leaves Lucy and her hubby. Any idea how long they intend to be here?'

'You know I don't know. Once they're settled—'

'Here, no doubt, if you don't watch it.'

'Perhaps they could rent a house in the village.'

'And who'd pay for it?'

'Come on, Stewart, be fair. This started before they came. You've been irritable since way back in March. The least thing sets you off.'

'I wasn't aware I was.'

'Well, you are. And you never were before. In fact, you were one of the most equable people I'd ever met.'

200

'Am I turning into a curmudgeonly old bore?' He grinned at her. 'I'm sorry, Kate, my darling, but we've a lot on our plates at the moment, haven't we? All the worry about your book and things . . .'

'What things?'

'Money – or, rather, the cut in your earnings.'

'Is that really all that's bothering you? Lucy being here and money?'

'What else is there?' He held his arms wide in an expansive gesture.

'We so rarely make love,' she said, in a quiet voice.

'That's soon rectified . . .' And he was laughing as he leapt up, crossed the room and grabbed her.

The days following her talk with Stewart were, Kate thought, some of the best she had spent in France. He had reassured her of his love in the most satisfactory way. He had vowed not to be so bad-tempered. For her part, she promised to ask Lucy how long she intended to stay and vowed never again to comment on his drinking. Peace returned to her life and with it the shadowy fears faded too.

She was getting up at six to work on the editing of *The Lost Troubadour*. If he was worried about money she intended to make this book the best ever to recoup. Editing was a process she enjoyed. She knew writers who loathed it, but she saw it as a final polishing process, making the book the best she could. As the work progressed the doubts she had harboured about her new editor faded. Portia was sympathetic to her aims – though Kate wished she understood when she was being funny. But that apart they made a good team.

In each book she had written there was always one word she overused – 'slid' had been one. Her characters had 'slid' through doors, out of beds, downstairs. Another had been 'fearful' so that everyone in her book had seemed afraid of everything. In *The Lost Troubadour* it was 'perfect' – days, sun, countryside, men, women, language, you name it, she had made it 'perfect'. Once it was pointed out to her, she was always puzzled as to why she hadn't seen the repetitions in the first place. At least with this one she need not worry about them taking too many baths since no one took any!

She worked solidly for four hours – anything over that and she found her work getting slipshod. By ten she had finished, and by then Steve was up and about and Lucy, her housework done, would amble over at eleven for coffee. It was a perfect arrangement, she thought, and long may it continue.

'That's a long face, Steve, what's the matter?' It was half past ten and she was enjoying sitting on the terrace, when it was still pleasant and the sun hadn't yet stoked up to its full ferocity.

'That bastard bank. They won't go higher on their loan.'

'And it's not enough to do what you want to do?'

'If you start a venture like this underfunded you're soon going to get into deep water. Professional gardening equipment doesn't come cheap.'

'I told you I'd help.'

'When I explained all that to you I meant it – I want so much to do this on my own.'

'I realise that, but if you can't, what's wrong in my helping you? Remember what Netta said? You'd be spoiling my fun.'

'But if Dad gets wind of what you've done, can you imagine what he'd have to say? He'd think I wasn't capable of doing anything on my own.'

'You don't *know* he would, do you?' But she thought he

202

was probably right. 'And in any case, why should he find out? I won't tell him.'

'What about Lucy? She won't like it.'

'Why ever not?'

'She might be jealous.'

'She's not like that. She's changed, you know, since she came back.'

'You reckon?' Steve spoke cynically.

'Yes, I do. She's much more considerate and helpful, not nearly so moody. Marriage suits her.'

'I think you're amazing the way you've forgiven her.'

'What would be the point in not doing so?'

'I'll never forgive her for what she put us through – especially you.'

'I've forgiven her but I doubt if I'll ever forget. That's what's so sad. And I'm schooling myself to be wary, just in case she does it again. But you're diverting me. We could be partners. How about that?'

Steve's frown indicated the struggle he was having with himself. 'It's not how I wanted it to be, but thanks, Mum, I'm very grateful.'

'I know, I know.' She suddenly felt very emotional. 'Coffee?' she asked, for something to do. The last thing Steve needed was his mother blubbing all over him.

'And what have you to be grateful about?' It was Lucy, who, barefoot, they had not heard approaching.

'Nothing,' said Kate.

'Mum's lending me some money,' said Steve simultaneously.

'And I was not to be told, Mum?' Lucy looked accusingly at her mother.

'It isn't as it appears. Steve is concerned that your father will find out and he would prefer him not to know. I thought the fewer people who knew the better.'

203

'I'm hardly *people*!'

Lucy looked belligerent, and Kate's heart sank. 'I phrased that badly. Just don't tell your father, that's all. I'll get the coffee.' She could feel her patience with Lucy fading, and the last thing they needed was another mother-and-daughter argument.

Once the coffee was made she returned to a full-blown row between brother and sister.

'It's not bloody fair!' Lucy was saying, as Kate put the tray down on the wrought-iron table.

'What isn't?' Even Kate could hear the weariness in her voice. How stupid of her to think that such a pleasant time could last.

'Why are you helping him and not me?'

'You never asked.'

'I could never be so blatant as to do that.'

'Neither could I. Mum offered.'

'Oh, great! So you just give him a handout without him even asking!'

'Lucy, are you intending to be obstreperous or is it accidental? I am not going to argue with you about money. Is that clear?'

'I'm not arguing. But I told you we'd found the business we wanted. You weren't interested.'

'I was. You weren't very forthcoming. Of course I'm interested. You said at the party it's a pizza business – that was the first I heard of it. And the way you talked I thought it was cut-and-dried.'

'How could it be? We haven't got any money!' Lucy burst into tears.

'If you don't explain to me, how the hell am I supposed to know?'

'It's Dominique, he's got his pride. He didn't want you to know how poor he is.'

'Come on, Lucy. How can you be furious with Mum if Dominique doesn't want it discussed?'

'He wanted Mum to respect him.'

'Just because he hasn't got any money I'm not going to think less of him. I've never heard anything so stupid.'

'He's not stupid.'

'Oh, for heaven's sake, you know what I mean. So, explain this business to me.'

'You really want to hear?' Lucy sniffed and blew on a tissue that Kate had handed her.

'Of course. I'm *always* interested in whatever you're planning.'

'Sure?'

'Yes.' Hold on to your patience, Kate told herself sternly.

Lucy perked up. 'Well, the important thing is that it's already an established business. It's a van that goes round the various villages and it does take-aways and, as you know, that's virtually unheard-of here. The man is selling the van and the goodwill.'

'Why's he selling?' Steve asked.

'I don't know. Why should he tell us?'

'For the simple reason that it's important, stupid.'

'Mum, tell him to stop being so horrible to me,' Lucy whined.

Good God, thought Kate. Nothing changes. They might still be children arguing over jelly babies!

'What Steve means is he has to have a legitimate reason for selling, otherwise he could be selling because it's not working and he's losing money. We have to know. And we have to see his books.'

'He hasn't got any. We knew enough to ask for them – *stupid*! He runs it on the black.'

'Well, you're not going to, if we buy it.'

'But everybody does.'

'Everybody doesn't. And you could get into serious trouble if you try. If I'm going to help you buy this van I need more facts.'

'So, you'll help us? Oh, Mum, you're a brick!' And in a flash the bad temper had gone, the whining had stopped, and she was flying round the table to kiss and hug her mother.

'Hang on a minute, Lucy. Only if it's viable. You'd better get Dominique to come and talk to me.' On the other hand, it probably wouldn't need much money and the sooner they were established the sooner they would be in their own house and out of Stewart's hair. And then it would be just as it had always been.

When Dominique appeared with a very sensible business plan that he had worked out Kate wondered if she had been wrong about him. He was not as naïve as Lucy in relation to the man who was selling the business. 'I have said to him that he cannot expect the full price when he has no books to back it with. That is the penalty for cheating the state.'

'Quite,' she said, most impressed.

Between them they agreed what seemed to be a fair price. Dominique had also worked out a repayment schedule.

'I really don't expect to be paid back.'

'I insist.'

'But I don't mind helping you both.'

'It would not be right.'

'But I never gave you a wedding present. You could regard the business as that.'

'I couldn't possibly, Kate. My honour is at stake.'

'Ah, well, that's a different matter altogether.' She had to turn away from him so that he could not see her smile – living here she knew the importance to a Frenchman of his honour.

Steve had gone to Paris for the day to see his contacts. Since it would be just herself and Stewart Kate planned a special dinner: she'd light the candles, put music on the CD player, change her clothes. They would dine as they had so often before this summer. She had told him not to be late, that it would be just the two of them.

The duck breast which she intended to serve with a *coulis* of summer fruit, was marinating. It was one of his favourites. Kate began to prepare the pudding – an English trifle, which he adored.

He was earlier than she had expected and she called out where she was. He rushed into the kitchen, lifted her high in the air and kissed her enthusiastically as once he had done all the time. He was laughing, and she knew it wasn't because he had been drinking.

'Did you meet Joan and Harry Oxford at the Bollands' party?'

'I met Joan, a bit of a bossy-boots, I thought. I don't think I met anyone called Harry.'

'He's come up with a brilliant idea and I think we should be in on it with him. A newspaper!' He was waving his hands in the air like a conductor.

'An English one? But there's one already.'

'Yes, but it concentrates on the south-west and the Dordogne. We'd aim ours for this region, central and the east.'

'Are there enough English to make it pay?'

'Around Lyon there are loads – a whole community. And there are Germans and Dutch, the place is littered with them – they all speak English. It's getting to the point where I wonder if there are more of us than there are

French, these days. And we mustn't forget *them* – they like to read English papers.'

'Do they?' She couldn't imagine many grabbing at the opportunity in this neck of the woods.

'He wants me to work with him. He hasn't any journalistic experience but he has a lot of business acumen.'

'Weren't they the couple who tried to run a video library? They didn't succeed with that. Nor, Netta told me, with the pine-stripping business they set up, mail-order Marmite or angora rabbits. And she said they had no money.'

'Do you listen to everything that woman says?'

'I forgot – they've done a bit of estate agenting.'

'Kate, just for once, be a sweetie. Don't piss on my fireworks.'

He might just as well have slapped her. 'I'm sorry. I was just trying to be practical. Trying to protect you.'

Suddenly he smiled. 'Kate, my darling, I'm sorry, I shouldn't have snapped. I'm like a kid, over-excited! But I want you to understand how I feel. You see, I want to do this so badly. I've longed for something of my own to do. Can you imagine what it's done to me, having to rely on you for every penny we spend? I want to contribute! It tears me up that I don't. I should be doing my bit.' He held her hands as he spoke, squeezing them as he emphasised each point.

'Stewart, that's so sweet of you.' Tears brimmed in her eyes. 'I don't feel like that, you know I don't. It's no hardship to me. My work is my pleasure, my hobby, everything important to me. Honestly, if they didn't pay me I think I'd still write from the sheer joy of it. You mustn't think this way.'

'All right, then. I'll be totally honest with you. The truth is that the past few months I've been bored out of my head.'

'But you said it was the children and money that were making you such a . . .' Her voice trailed off. Perhaps it would not be politic to say *difficult* or *aggressive* or *argumentative* – or any of the other words that were whirling about in her mind.

'A pain in the arse? You should have said it.' He laughed. 'All of it. Kids, money, boredom. They all combined. And it wasn't fair on you, and I apologise. You've done nothing to deserve the way I've been.'

Kate opened a drawer and began to look for her vegetable knife.

'Leave that and come and talk.'

'I'll just put this—'

'I want to discuss this . . .' There was a distinct edge in his voice that she thought it best not to ignore. She followed him into the sitting room where he was already laying out papers on the coffee table. 'Now, see here. These are the figures, and this is what Harry would expect us to put in.'

She blinked at the enormous sum. 'Have we the money to do that?'

'Yes. I've been squirrelling it away just in case such an opportunity turned up.'

'You never said.'

'Well, I thought a day might come when you wouldn't want to write any more and what then? We need a second string to our bow and this is it.'

'But . . . honestly, Stewart, I don't want . . . I'm not putting you down. But . . . what if it failed? Could we afford to lose all that money?'

'But it won't fail, that's the whole point. Harry says . . .' And he was chattering away about their plans – and his enthusiasm was lovely to see. *But!* Hadn't he listened to a word she had said about the Oxfords' track record? Their endless schemes? She could not share his confidence in them. She only wished she could. Maybe she would if she studied the figures more closely – though what she knew about business could be written on a pinhead. 'There's just one other thing.'

He looked up from his papers, still grinning with excitement.

'I've promised Steve we'll help him set up his gardening venture and—'

'You've *what*?'

She felt nervous and apologetic, and then she told herself not to be so stupid. It was her money and they were her children. 'And Lucy too. She wants to buy a pizza van.'

As if in slow motion he stood upright. He looked at her with a quizzical expression, his head on one side. She was aware that she was holding her breath.

'*How could you?*' he bellowed. He slammed one large fist into another. 'How *dare* you?'

Well, his good mood didn't last long, she heard her inner voice say.

Kate and Stewart had often bickered, occasionally argued. Just recently Stewart had taken to storming off, but never, in the five years they had known each other, had they had a row of anything like the proportions of the one that now erupted.

It was Stewart's explosive 'How *dare* you!' that made the blood pound in Kate's head, then race round her body so fast that she could almost feel it ripping through her arteries and veins. Her heart beat at such a rate she feared it was about to burst from her chest.

'How can you say that to me? I can do what I damn well want! I can help who I bloody well want. I don't need your permission!' She had to get away from him because she felt a red mist of violence welling inside her. This fury, which

210

had taken to rearing its ugly head recently and which was once alien to her, frightened her once more.

For safety's sake, she stormed from the room slamming the door, thinking that the violent act would help her but it didn't. And she might just as well have stayed put for Stewart followed her, whamming the same door shut, the noise reverberating around the old house. Round and round they went, she leading, he following, the two of them shouting, yelling and screaming all the way.

'Don't you damn well not listen to me!' he hollered.

'I'll listen when you've something intelligent to say,' she yelled back.

From the hall back to the kitchen she sped. There she turned on the taps and noisily banged a couple of saucepans about.

'After all I've done for you!'

At that she swung round and faced him. 'I beg your pardon?'

'You know damn well that without me you'd be nothing. Why, you can't even write decent English.'

Out of the corner of her eye she saw the sleek black handles of the kitchen knives in their wooden block. Her hand itched. She turned abruptly. She couldn't trust herself so close to them. She pushed past him. Up the stairs to her bedroom she raced.

'Don't you understand? You can't *afford* to help them.'

'But I can afford what *you* want to do?'

'Because what I want to do will work, be a success. Are you so stupid you can't see that?'

Ignore him, he's drunk. This time she wasn't too sure that he was. *You hurt him, he'll hurt you.* I want to hurt him! *Calm down.* How the hell am I supposed to do that? *Get away from him!* her voice of reason nagged. Once more she was on the move, running down the stairs, heading, blinded by tears of rage, to the safety of her workroom. She wasn't quick enough. As she closed the door he pushed at it from the other side and burst in. 'Get out. This is my room. My space. I don't want you in here,' she gasped.

'I haven't finished.'

'I have!'

'Anything *I* want is vetoed. Anything those ungrateful brats want and you're racing for your bloody cheque book. You might trip and break your neck in your haste!'

'I'm warning you, Stewart. Shut up.' She was aware that she was shaking. She wanted to pick something up and hurl it at him. Anything would do just to shut him up. Anything to stop that mouth of his yawing and wittering and whining.

'Shut up!' she screamed.

'Temper, temper!' On her desk was a pen tidy, a plastic thing, of no weight and little importance. She snatched it up and threw it. He ducked and laughed, and the mist surged, and she yanked at her printer and threw it in his direction. He ducked and the machine crashed on the tiled floor, cracking in two.

The noise and the wanton damage sobered them for a trice. 'Why won't you listen to me? Why didn't you discuss it with me first?' Now he spoke in a reasonable tone – he even put out his hand towards her as if to say, 'Forgive'.

'I didn't think it was necessary. What is more normal than that I should help my kids?'

'Before me?'

'I didn't know about you and your newspaper scheme then, did I?' she snapped.

'But we are a couple. You didn't have the right to do that.'

It was an unfortunate word for him to choose.

'It's *my* money. I earn it. That gives me the right to do whatever I want with it. Even if I haven't consulted you.'

'Ha! I wondered how long it would be before that charming line came up. Before you'd choose to rub my nose in it. You bitch.'

'Well, what do you do to help out? Sit on your arse and get drunk. That's about it.'

He moved so quickly that she didn't even see his fist. The blow knocked her sideways. She stumbled against her desk, papers went flying, her computer wobbled, she lunged for it, slipped, fell under the desk and the computer tower came down on top of her.

'What the hell's going on?' Steve was in the doorway. 'I could hear you outside when I drew up. For Christ's sake!' he exclaimed, as he stepped into the room and saw his mother struggling to get up. 'Mum, what happened?'

'I'm OK, I slipped.'

'Don't give me that crap. He pushed you. How dare you treat my mother in this way?' He took a step towards Stewart.

'Really, Steve, I'm all right. Please, this is between us.' She was on her feet now and tugging at his sleeve.

'What were you arguing about?'

'None of your business.'

'If you attack my mother it is most definitely my business. What is it, Mum?'

'A stupid misunderstanding, that's all, nothing to worry about.' She knew it was a futile statement as she said it, but even in this appalling situation, she found she was still a protective mother.

'I tried to explain to her that she hasn't enough money for yours and Lucy's little schemes. She didn't want to listen.'

'Is that so, Mum?'

'Stewart says I don't have enough to help all three of you. And while I feel my priority is to you two, he sees it differently.' She glared at Stewart as she said this, her anger under control now but still there.

'So you have a scheme too, Stewart. Is that what I'm to understand? And yours should come first? Isn't that my mother's decision to make?'

'Why should she give you two handouts over me? Where have you been the last few years, and Lucy?' At that he gave a cynical snort. 'She disappears for years, turns up all lovey-dovey and expects everything to be just hunky-dory. Well, who, might I ask, has been with your mother, looked after her, cared for, encouraged her? Where were you two then?'

'Don't whine, Stewart. It doesn't suit you,' Steve said quietly.

'You little shit!' Stewart took a menacing step towards him. Steve was not intimidated and stood his ground.

'If there's no money then I for one would be very interested to know where it is.'

'And what is that meant to imply?'

'Nothing. Simply that I want to know, and I think my mother certainly has a right to know.'

'And you think you've a right to your mother's money?'

'No, I don't. I never wanted her help, if you must know. And as it turns out I won't be needing it. I've made other arrangements. You see, I don't want to be seen to be hanging on to her apron strings – which is, no doubt, what you would have said. I suggest, Stewart, that if you have a venture, and you think it's viable, you should go to the banks and find a backer. At least then you'd be left with some pride.'

'You bastard whipper-snapper.' Stewart lunged at him again.

'Stewart, stop this or I call the police,' Kate cried out.

Steve stood firm, his fists at the ready. His youth was intimidating as he moved between his mother and her lover. 'Mum, I've got to go out – it's something important. I can't . . .' He looked anxiously at Stewart, who at least was quiet now, if still menacing. 'Look, I'll get Lucy and Dominique to come over and keep an eye on you.'

'I'll be fine, Steve. I'd rather you didn't mention a word of this to them. I'm so ashamed, I don't want anyone to know – not even family members.'

'What have you got to be ashamed of? What have you done?'

'I shouldn't have lost my temper the way I did.' It was true, she felt mortified by the spectacle she had just made of herself.

'Exactly!'

'You keep your trap shut, Stewart. For all that, I think I will get them.'

'Don't bother, there's no need. I'm going out. Going where I'm appreciated.'

'Good.' Kate would have liked to add, 'And don't come back.' She wasn't sure how she felt, but she hoped he was gone for some time.

'Mum, I'm so sorry. You look wiped out.' Steve was fussing over her in the sitting room.

'I feel as if I've run a marathon.'

'Drink?'

'No, thanks. I'll make myself a cup of tea in a minute.'

'I'll do it.'

'No, honestly, I don't want one yet. God, I feel dreadful. I

215

shouldn't have behaved in that way. What did it achieve? Nothing. I feel so ugly inside.'

'Quite honestly, I think it was good that you did. You bottle things up too much, you always have. Look how you were with Dad.'

'I don't know, I've had my moments.' She managed to smile.

'That's better. Now, are you sure you don't mind me going out, just for a couple of hours?'

'Where are you going?'

'Secret.' He put his finger to his lips. 'I'll tell you when I get back.'

Alone, Kate tried to deal with the ugliness and shame she was feeling. When had all this unpleasantness started? She was sure they'd been happy once, or had she imagined it? The trouble was that when she was working she got so engrossed in the characters she was writing about and what happened to them that perhaps she had neglected to notice what was going on around her.

She had thought him content. Living here was what he had wanted. It was she who had had doubts, and now she couldn't imagine living anywhere else. Had she been neglectful of him? His trips to the English pub, his huge order each week for all the English Sunday papers, his incessant watching of Sky TV, his talk of setting up a cricket club and this paper – were they all symptomatic of a man who was homesick for all he had left behind? It was he who wanted to search out other English exiles, not her. She hadn't even set foot in the pub he adored. She sometimes read the papers but not always. She rarely watched television. And if the cricket ever came to fruition she'd told him, laughing, that he needn't rely on her to make the teas.

Had she been stupid and blind?

And had she been stupid about her money?

Surely it could all be accounted for. Surely.

'It's very kind of you to see me at such short notice, Mr Bolland.'

'Peter, please. I hoped you would be back.'

'I only gave you a sketchy idea of my plans at the party. I've brought all the paperwork with me.'

'Good. There's nothing I like better than a good idea and a business plan.'

'I hope Mrs Bolland won't be cross at my taking up your time.'

'She's not here. I kicked her out.'

'Oh!' Steve said, not knowing what else he could say.

'Have you got a girlfriend?'

'No, unfortunately.'

'Fortunately, if you ask me. I don't understand women. I never have and I doubt I ever will. You give them everything they say they want but it's never enough. There's always something more.'

'Is there?' Steve didn't know what to say since his knowledge of women was restricted. He hoped Peter wasn't drunk. He hoped to God Wendy wouldn't come back and he'd have to mediate in another row. He'd experienced enough this evening already.

'Mark my words, Steve, women are nothing but trouble.'

'All of them?'

'OK, some of them are all right. Your mother for one. What a success story she is.'

'I'm very proud of her.'

'Is she married to that Stewart Dorchester?'

'No.' Steve was beginning to feel uncomfortable. He'd come here to talk about his gardening plans, not his mother's domestic arrangements.

'Does she plan to?'

'Not likely.' At that he grinned. He had been upset for his mother tonight, no son wanted to see what he had witnessed, but if it meant that Stewart got his marching orders, Steve for one would put out the flags.

'I'm glad about that. I hope I'm not treading on your toes, Steve, but I think that man is an out-and-out bastard.'

'You do?' Steve thought it politic to sound as non-committal as possible.

4

'If I'm to stay another week I'm going to hire a car, and that's that, Netta. There's no point in you arguing with me.'

'You can be so bossy, Caroline, it quite shocks my old bones.' She said this lightly, since in effect there wasn't an old bone in her body. 'I can't think of anything nicer than having some proper transport for a few days.'

'You're so contrary, Netta. Whenever I think I know how you're going to react you do the opposite.'

'The secret of my success throughout my life, my darling. Always, but always, keep the buggers guessing. Good morning, Didier, how are the toes?'

'Madame Rawlinson, I shall be indebted to you for the rest of my life. The magnets worked!'

'I'm so glad. Now, two coffees and a minuscule Cognac for me.' Even when she was ordering something as mundane as coffee, Netta made it into a flirtatious act.

'What was wrong with his toes?' Caroline watched the waiter walk away quite normally.

'He was crippled with arthritis so I recommended some magnetic insoles that a friend of mine sells. I hadn't the foggiest if they'd work, but they have and I shall earn a teeny-weeny commission. Very satisfactory.'

'The things you find to cobble a living together, it's amazing.'

'Needs must . . . How awful – I nearly sounded like Sybil again. I must watch it.'

'How *is* Sybil?'

'The same. Nothing changes in her dreary life.' Surreptitiously Netta looked at her watch. She hoped that this wasn't to be a Monday when Tristram decided not to pick up the papers. They were sitting at a table behind the row of bushes that separated the terrace of the bar from the pavement. She had positioned them close to the entrance so that she could keep an eye on who was coming and going.

She saw Stewart, weaving his way through the traffic on the busy road, carrying a bag stuffed full of newspapers. He walked past their table, entered the bar and sat inside. 'That's another ex-pat. Not one of my favourites, I must say. There's something of the bully about him, which he disguises with a great show of bonhomie. Always suspect, too much *joie de vivre*.'

'Doesn't look particularly full of it today, though, does he?'

'His wife, or rather his partner, is a lovely woman. She writes – Kate Howard, you might have heard of her.' Netta said this in the throwaway manner of one adept at dropping names while not appearing to.

'I've read everything she's ever written. And you know her?'

'Yes, as shall you. We're invited to lunch this week and to stay the night.'

'Me too?'

'But of course. I checked if I could bring my delinquent friend along and she was very pleased as her own children

219

are with her at the moment. You won't have to be bored with us old fogeys.'

'Fishing again! I'm not responding.' Caroline smiled at her.

'She wants my advice. I can't imagine why.'

'Because you're a wise old owl.'

'But this is about setting up an arts centre. A mutual friend, Jessica, has it planned and Kate is to help. Now what on earth do I know about that?'

'Perhaps she's not sure of someone and wants your opinion. You're brilliant with people, and about them. I'd always listen to you if you took against someone.'

They sipped at their coffee contentedly and people-watched. A few minutes later Stewart walked out.

'Do you think he saw you?'

'Oh, yes, he saw me, he just didn't want to. I hope he's in a better mood tomorrow when we go for lunch.'

Another look at her watch. He *was* late.

Then Caroline stiffened visibly. 'Oh, God! Oh, no!' she said faintly.

'Netta!' She heard Tristram call from half-way across the road.

'Well, isn't this a surprise?'

'You knew he'd come here,' Caroline said accusingly.

'But of course. Don't get cross with me, you were the one who wanted to see him. I didn't say anything in case he didn't show up. Think how disappointed you'd have been.' She waved at Tristram as he tangoed towards them through the traffic. 'I don't think he realises it's you – it must be the new hairstyle and the dark glasses.' She was pleased with the way everything was panning out.

Tristram was at their table. 'I hoped I'd find you here,' he said to Netta.

'Hello, Tristram.'

'Good God!' Tristram sat down on the wrought-iron chair in surprise, knocking the table so that the umbrella under which they sat swayed dangerously. 'Caroline! What on earth are you doing here?'

'Well, that's not very gallant. Wouldn't "How wonderful to see you here," be better?' Netta tapped his hand with a teaspoon.

'Caroline, I'm sorry. I just didn't expect to see you here, of all places.'

'I've often told you about my godmother and how I knew Le Puy. We swapped notes on the various holidays we'd had here.'

'I'd forgotten.'

'How could anyone forget about *me*?' Netta joked, to lighten the atmosphere: Tristram looked embarrassed and Caroline hurt. 'Coffee?' She waved to the waiter. 'I expect you two have a lot to talk about – perhaps if I could have a peep at the papers, just so that I won't be a bother to you both. I could even sit at another table.'

'No, no. Please. Be my guest.' Tristram handed her his carrier bag. Netta selected the *Sunday Times* and pretended to read it.

'Caroline, I can't tell you how grateful I was for you-know-what.' He looked significantly in Netta's direction.

'I had to come, Tristram. I've been so worried. Those goons looking for Mo, they mean business.'

Tristram frowned and looked pointedly at Netta who seemed genuinely engrossed in the newspaper.

'Netta knows. I tell her everything.'

'Hell!'

'I don't judge. It's against my principles.' Netta's head appeared round the side of the broadsheet.

'It's serious, isn't it, Tristram? I think it's something to do with drugs. And if she's in danger, so are you.'

'What on earth gave you that idea? You always had a vivid imagination.' Tristram tried to laugh but made an odd gurgling noise instead.

'Tristram, you must listen to me. I think you should get right away from here.' Caroline leant across the table, took his hand and squeezed it.

'What on earth for? You said you hadn't told them where we were.'

'It's only a matter of time before they find you. And I think Mo should know that her father has had a heart-attack – probably caused by worry.'

'Mo's father is dead.'

'No, he's not. Whatever gave you that idea? He was as fit as a flea until this blew up. Her poor mother is at her wit's end.'

'She's an alcoholic.' He said this not quite as a question nor as a statement, but rather as a man who was unsure.

'Gracious me, no. She has a jewellery business. She designs and makes the most lovely stuff – Harvey Nicks, Harrods, they all buy it.'

'She's not poor?'

'Not at all. They've a lovely house in the Cotswolds.'

Tristram sat back in his seat looking exhausted. 'Caroline, I've been such a fool.'

'Tristram, don't put yourself down.' She stretched out her hand again and this time covered his. Just touching him made her heart lift.

Behind her newspaper, Netta thought her goddaughter needed her head examined.

'What a pretty picture!'

'Mo!' Tristram was on his feet, with an expression of guilt on his face, and Caroline blushed. Netta lowered her newspaper and gave Mo a long, cool stare.

'Why, Mo, how pleasant to see you.' Netta smiled, the small sly smile she reserved for such occasions.

'What a lovely surprise, Caroline. I didn't know you knew where we were.' Mo slid elegantly into the spare seat, smiling brightly. She clicked her fingers at the waiter.

'You'll have to wait for ever now. If there's one thing Didier can't stand it's people clicking their fingers at him,' Netta advised. Mo took no notice of her. Expert at appraising people's financial worth, she had deduced that Netta had no money and therefore could not be of any use to her.

'I'm visiting my godmother as it happens – Mrs Rawlinson. But you know her, I gather. It was such a surprise when we saw Tristram crossing the road.' Caroline giggled – from nerves Netta surmised.

'Tristram told me he'd called you. Of course, I was as jealous as hell. He still feels such a responsibility towards you.'

Caroline blushed again and Tristram looked edgy.

'I think you're a brick for offering to pay my debts, Caroline. I know Tristram refused but I accept with such a deep gratitude. You have a wonderful godchild, Netta.'

'Mo, stop it. She's not giving you a penny. Leave her alone.'

'Why? This is between us. It's got nothing to do with you.'

'I won't have her exposed to this sort of problem and those sort of people. This is our mess, Mo, you leave her out of it.'

'Oh, yes, and how do *you* intend to help me? You have to go crawling to her with your hand out so why shouldn't I? She's my friend, too, or have you forgotten?'

Tristram stood up. 'I'm warning you, Mo, leave her alone. She's out of her depth with you.'

'How sweet you are, Tristram. Always concerned for little Caroline's welfare. Just as he's so kind to poor dumb animals.' The brilliant smile did little to camouflage the remark. 'You should watch him, Caroline. Never think it's you he's interested in, it's just your cheque book.'

Netta lowered her newspaper, put out her hand as if to pick up her cup of coffee and knocked it flying all down the front of Mo's immaculate white trouser suit. 'Such a mess! I wish I could say I was sorry.'

'You did that on purpose, you old bitch.'

'But of course. And it's Mrs Rawlinson to you. Come, Caroline, we shall go. You, young man, are welcome at my flat any time. This is my card. But please don't bring your vulgar little friend with you.'

Caroline, looking close to tears, trailed along behind Netta.

'You let that old cow speak to me like that?' Mo said angrily, clicking her fingers in yet another vain attempt to attract the waiter's attention.

'You asked for it.'

'You'd have protected Caroline.'

'She wouldn't have been so rude.'

'So the old bitch can hurl her coffee over me and I'm supposed not to retaliate? Sometimes, Tristram, I don't know where you're coming from. Christ, you're such a fool. She'd have coughed up, she can afford it, and all our troubles would be over.'

'I know she would. That's why she has to be protected from the likes of you.'

'Creep!'

'Perhaps it's seeing you together that makes me understand just how stupid I've been. How could I have allowed myself to be taken in like that?'

'You know damn well. Because you have more fun in the sack with me than you ever would with her.'

He let that pass. It was too close for comfort to the truth. 'By the way, I heard all about your parents. How well your mother's doing. Not such good news about your father, I'm afraid. He's ill, but not dead as you told me.'

'He's dead.' As if on cue the tears formed in her eyes.

'How did you learn to cry on demand?' She ignored the question. 'Why, Mo?'

'Why what?' She looked around as if bored with the conversation. 'At last. Order me a gin,' she demanded, as Didier finally came to their table. 'And look at that,' she said, as he put down the bill. 'That old cow left without paying! Can you beat that?'

'Why all the lies?'

'What lies? There are no lies. My father is dead and my mother is an alcoholic and poor. I haven't lied. It's your friend who's doing the lying.'

'I don't believe you.'

'Then don't. But it's the truth. Why is dear little Caroline to be believed and not me?'

'I should think it's obvious.'

'Not to me. Unless, of course, I was right. Poor Caroline, it is the money, isn't it? She can do no wrong. She can't lie simply because of the state of her bank account. It's a good job I warned her.'

'You bitch.' He stood up to leave, throwing coins down on the table.

Mo grabbed at his hand. 'You won't go and see her, will you?'

'I don't know.'

'Please, Tristram, I need you.'

'In case the bad men come?' He laughed cynically.

Kate didn't know what to do. She felt deeply hurt by Stewart's remarks. She despised him for hitting her, and still seethed with rage about it. But she was also troubled by guilt at her own reactions. Worst of all was the ugliness she felt inside her, that she too could have behaved in such an uncontrolled manner. Those furies, which she had only just discovered lurked in her, might erupt again when he reappeared. But he hadn't and therein lay her confusion, for she found she was worried about him, wished they hadn't had such a row. She wondered if she should begin to look for him.

'You all right, Mum?'

'I'm fine, Steve. Couldn't be better.' She smiled but she didn't think he was deceived.

'It's just that if you really are all right, I'd thought of catching the afternoon train tomorrow.'

'Look, Steve, ignore what Stewart said. I still want to help you.'

'No, Mum. I told you, it's not necessary.'

'But I want to – not just for you but for myself. I had a shock over this latest book. What if they offer me even less for the next one? I need another source of income.'

'I'll always help you out when I've made my fortune. But I've got a backer – Peter Bolland. That was where I went last night.'

'And he agreed, just like that?'

'No, I'd discussed part of my plans with him at the party. He was interested and he offered. I didn't have to ask.'

'Oh, I see.' She felt bleak with disappointment.

'Mum, it's better this way, honestly. What if I went belly up and you had money in it? I'd never forgive myself.

Peter's a businessman and he knows there's risk. And it's purely a professional relationship with him – no emotions, not the same sense of responsibility I'd have if it was you. But it doesn't mean I shall stop being grateful to you that you wanted to help me. I just wished I hadn't been the cause of you and Stewart falling out.'

'It wasn't your fault. Don't even think it. It would have happened anyway, sooner or later.'

'Will you take him back?'

'I don't know.'

'Honestly, Mum, if you do I think you need your head examining.'

While Steve had a swim Kate went to her workroom to continue with her book. But she couldn't immerse herself in it to the degree that was required. The row and Stewart kept getting in the way. *Hardly surprising!* 'Don't you start!' she said aloud.

She had told Steve that a row between them had been inevitable. Why had she said that? Perhaps she had just been trying to reassure him he was not to blame.

Would she take him back? Yes. *Prat!*

Since work was out of the question she began to tidy her desk. She was one of those people who always found that activity helped when there were problems. And her desk needed it since Kate, orderly in the rest of her life, only seemed able to write in a muddle.

She knew why she would welcome him – no, welcome was not the right word. Why she needed him. She shivered at herself for choosing that particular word. But it was the truth. It was something about herself she had known and yet not known – or, more correctly, had chosen not to acknowledge. She could not face being alone.

It was fine while Lucy was here, but what if she suddenly upped sticks and disappeared again, and Kate was totally by herself? She was not good without others around her, she knew that. She had left her parents' home, gone to college, married at a ridiculously early age, had the children, separated, met Stewart, and consequently had never lived alone. There had been moments when she had thought that solitude must be paradise – but that had been when it was unlikely to happen to her.

How could she cope? Especially here, not even speaking the language, not understanding the bureaucracy. Not knowing how much money she had or hadn't.

Which reminded her. She hastened along the corridor to Stewart's study. She opened the tall filing cabinet. Where to begin to look. Everything was neatly arranged and in order. It was one of the reasons she was glad that he had offered to keep the books for her: the paperwork would never have looked like this if she had done it. She pulled out a large ledger: every detail of her spending life was tidily listed. Gracious, she thought, as she looked at the figures, he had been right. She did spend a lot, and she hadn't realised it. Had she really got through all that in this past year? She did a quick mental recap of the recent additions to her wardrobe – shamefully the figure came close. Paper! She spent that much on paper? And postage! Things she had never even thought about as expenditure.

Among the files was one for bank statements. She pulled it out and studied the latest. She had less in there than she had hoped but she wasn't overdrawn or anything like that. Well, that was a relief. But how the hell Stewart had expected her to help with the newspaper venture was a mystery. There was not nearly enough for that – or was there another account that she didn't know about? She should have taken more interest. She should have asked him to explain more to her. She had only herself to blame.

Back in her own room she sat wondering about what she

could do now. Money worries were creeping in and she didn't want to think about them, not yet. Why, she could catalogue all her books – she had a program on her computer but had never got round to using it. That would keep her occupied and the misery at bay.

'Mum, are you busy? Only . . .' Lucy stood in the doorway, looking diffident, Dominique behind her, clutching his pack of Marlboro and the ubiquitous lighter.

Hell, thought Kate. That wasn't fair of Steve. 'You were wondering if I was OK? I'm fine. It was a stupid row, but it'll blow over.'

'Well, yes, of course, but actually, what we were thinking was . . . It's a bit difficult . . . what with all the drama . . . The pizza van?' She smiled enquiringly.

'Oh, yes.' Kate smiled. When you thought people had changed of course they never had. Lucy was still the same, putting herself first. How foolish of Kate to think otherwise. But, still, if it meant she would stay longer . . . 'Of course. I said. Get the figures and if it's viable . . .' So, she wondered, who was using whom?

'Stewart hasn't come home, then?'

'No.'

'I hope he's gone for good.'

'I realise.'

'You don't need him. You've got me and Dominique now. We'll look after you.'

'That's kind.' Like hell, she thought. 'I asked Steve not to tell you. I didn't want you worried.'

'He didn't. We heard you both.'

'Good heavens!' And Kate blushed. How dreadful. How shaming!

The following day, Netta and Caroline set out for lunch with Kate.

'I know that one groans when people say, "It's none of my business but . . ." but, my darling Caroline, I would be failing in my duty if I didn't say something.'

'I'm amazed you've kept quiet so long.' They were driving along the gorge road of the Loire towards Vorey. 'It couldn't wait a wee bit longer, could it? This is a pig of a road.'

'But you're such an excellent driver.'

'It's not my driving I'm worried about, it's the French!'

'I didn't say anything yesterday since I thought we both needed to mull everything over. Words said too quickly can be the wrong ones or misinterpreted in the heat of the moment, don't you find? Oh, look, there's a heron.'

Fortunately for Caroline, the bird distracted Netta as she looked for others. 'When you see one you often see several.' It was not until they had passed Château Lavoute-Polignac and were safely out of the narrow road that she began again. Caroline's hands tightened on the wheel. 'I regret to have to say this, my dear, but I fear that your Tristram is a rather weak, ineffectual person and not worthy of you.'

'I expected you to say that.'

'I wish sincerely that I could say otherwise. Why are you stopping?' Netta asked, as Caroline steered the car into a lay-by.

'I have no intention of driving along the road having a casual conversation with you about the man I love.' Caroline stopped the engine and put on the handbrake.

'That you love him is not in dispute. Whether it is wise of you to do so is the question we have to face.'

'It really isn't any of your business, though, is it, Netta?' Caroline's voice was tight and her body rigid with controlled anger.

'That could be said, of course. But, then, I love you, so

should I just sit back and say nothing? You see the quandary I am in?'

'Not really. You could just keep quiet.'

'But you're not listening to me, are you? I wish I could stay mum, but in all honesty I don't see how I can. I wouldn't be able to live with myself.'

'You said yesterday that you were not judgemental, so what's this?'

'What Tristram does is entirely his own affair. If he wishes to live with a drug-dealer then that is his business. When it impinges on someone I care for, well, I don't see it as being judgemental, I regard it as a balancing of the facts.' She took an old-fashioned compact out of her handbag and studied her face momentarily in its mirror. 'And I might point out that yesterday you said you would always listen to my opinions on people. A wise old owl, you called me.'

'I was being polite.'

'Really? How kind.'

'Tristram refused to let me help Mo.'

'How commendable.' She refreshed her lipstick. 'There is one little matter that bothers me. Since he has been here in France, has he been in touch? Or was it only when he got into a muddle and needed financial help?'

'That's cruel.'

'The truth often is.'

'You lecture me but your own track record with men isn't that great, is it?' Caroline sounded defiant.

'Exactly. So what is more reasonable than that I should point out the dangers to you when I see them? Even I have learnt from my own disasters. If Tristram can become infatuated with a woman once, he can do it again. And you will be hurt again. Each time it happens the pain will remain but bitterness will accompany it, and that is an appallingly damaging emotion to have to deal with.'

231

'And how do you know he will?'

'Because a man who is so influenced by his crotch always will be. One of the nastier facts of life.'

'How crude.'

'I often am. It helps drive home the point more forcefully. Now, if it's all right with you I should like to proceed to my luncheon appointment.' She snapped the compact shut. 'If you do not wish to stay I shall quite understand. I can make up some excuse for you. I shall get a train home.'

'Netta, don't be silly! I know you mean well. I just don't like hearing it or you thinking it. I shan't change my mind.'

'That's your privilege. But at least my conscience will be clear.'

Kate had decided not to catalogue the books after all but to rearrange them instead. An hour of this, and she was hot, sweaty and covered in dust.

'Mum, you've got visitors.' Steve stood in her workroom dripping water from the pool on the floor.

'Can't you deal with them?'

'I've put them in the sitting room. I said you'd be along. Sorry, but I didn't have a towel.' He indicated the puddle he had made on the tiles. 'It's—'

Kate didn't give him time to finish before she swept past him, brushing her fingers through her hair. Who the hell could it possibly be at a time like this? She hated people turning up without a call first. She was annoyed at being interrupted: she'd managed to be content for the last hour, her emotions safely kept at bay. She raced along the corridor to the sitting room. 'Netta!' she said, her voice brimming with surprise.

'My goddaughter, Caroline, a great fan of yours . . .'

They shook hands.

'Have you brought a costume with you?' Kate was

flustered. 'What a shame, my daughter is out on business. And my son, Steve here, is leaving.'

'I thought I'd catch the evening train.' Steve was looking at Caroline with undisguised interest.

'Oh dear. You've forgotten, haven't you? That we were invited to lunch?' Netta looked concerned.

'Of course not. I . . .' Her mind was racing through what she might have in the freezer and embarrassment was rapidly building up. 'And . . .' Without warning Kate burst into tears.

6

'I'll look after your mother, Steve. You and Caroline go and have a swim or something . . .' Netta waved her hand vaguely as if dismissing small children and led Kate, who was apologising, sniffing, blowing her nose and generally feeling dreadful, towards a chair. 'People, I suppose, usually offer tea at a time like this, but I always prefer alcohol, don't you?'

'Help yourself, please. Nothing for me.'

'Are you sure?' Netta was overjoyed at the selection of drinks on offer but eventually decided on a Bloody Mary. 'Since it's still morning it can be regarded as a restorative,' she said lightly, hoping to make Kate smile but it didn't work. 'Do you want to talk or shall I just sit here?'

'No, I can't talk . . . I'm so sorry . . . Just . . . Sit . . . It's too soon to talk . . .' Then Kate burst into fresh floods of tears and proceeded to tell Netta everything. She sat and listened patiently, saying nothing, waiting until Kate wanted her to speak.

'This must be so boring for you.' Kate blew into a tissue, which Netta handed her. 'I'm so sorry.'

'Kate, my dear, I've lost count of how many times you've said that to me. You must stop apologising. I'm glad I'm here even if I do feel ineffectual. I wish there was something I could do.'

'You have, just listening to my ramblings.'

'It really does help to talk. Get it off your chest. Clear the air, the decks . . . What else would dear Sybil say?'

Kate laughed, not a very big one but a laugh all the same.

'Fancy a drink now?' Netta asked.

'I think I do. But lunch!' She began to get to her feet.

'I doubt if any of us is going to die of starvation if we miss a meal, do you?'

'But it's so rude.'

'Understandable in the circumstances. Shall I ask Caroline to rustle something up? She's quite competent – she did a Prue Leith course.'

'Would she?'

'She'd be delighted, and your dishy son could give her a hand.'

From the terrace she summoned Steve and Caroline. 'Is she all right?'

'She's worrying about feeding us.'

'Then she's OK.' Steve, who had been looking anxious, managed a grin. 'I'm so glad you came, Mrs Rawlinson.'

'So am I. I wondered . . . ?' She looked at Caroline questioningly.

'Where's the kitchen, Steve?'

Netta returned to her charge. 'There. That's all under control. You know what I think?' She did not wait for Kate to say whether she did or not. 'I think it would be disastrous for you to make any decisions at this time. Something like this, to my mind, is similar to a bereavement. Widows who rush into selling their homes and

234

moving away always live to regret it. It's the same with a broken romance.'

'I hoped it wasn't broken,' Kate said quietly.

'Of course – presumption on my part, but what else would you expect from me?' She smiled fleetingly and then she was serious. 'On the other hand, perhaps it's best to look at the worst scenario and then, should it happen – I'm not saying it would but if it did – it's not such a great shock to you. And if it isn't, then nothing is lost.' The words tumbled out of her. 'Have you heard from him?'

'Not a word.'

'Do you know where he is?'

'I haven't an inkling. And I didn't like to phone people. "Is my husband with you?" We'd both end up looking foolish.'

'And how long's he been gone?'

'Three days.'

'Then he'll probably be home soon, needing clean underpants.'

'But, Netta, what I don't understand is we were so happy. What changed to make him discontented?'

'Are you sure you were happy? Or did you constantly tell yourself you were, in the subconscious hope that if you said it enough times you would be?'

Kate had to work this out. 'Gracious. Were we. . . ? Yes, I think I can honestly say we were . . .'

'Were you constantly telling people how happy you were?'

'I don't think I was.'

'That's good. I've always found that when people are at pains to tell you how deliriously happy they are, how perfect their marriage is, there's invariably something fishy in the woodpile, which they aren't facing. Or else they're lying their heads off.'

'No, it wasn't like that with me. I hadn't been happy for some time before I met him, so I knew when I'd found it.'

'Or had you been so unhappy with your first husband that anything would have made a brilliant contrast? And it wasn't true happiness.' Netta contemplated her glass while Kate took this question on board. 'By the way, if you think I'm being intolerably interfering, stop me, do.'

'No. No. It's good to think these things through in this way. You're saying things I haven't even thought and maybe I should. And, in any case, it's stopped me blubbing.' She sipped slowly at her Bloody Mary. 'What you say about happiness is possible, of course. I'd only had the one experience to compare it to.'

'How amazing. Just two men? How on earth did you manage such self-control, an attractive creature like you?'

'Me? Oh, come on.'

'You are. I don't hand out compliments lightly to women, you know. It's not in my nature. But you strike me in the way that Sybil does. You're almost afraid to be too attractive, as if you're frightened of your own sexuality.'

'Bah! What sexuality? I've not much of that!'

Netta filed away this answer. Thinking she had asked enough for the time being she changed the subject adroitly. 'How's your work going?'

'Don't ask. I can't concentrate. I've lost interest, and that for a writer is dire – you have to feel passionately for the characters you're writing about. I've had to lie to my editor – I told her I'd sprained my right wrist.'

'Did she believe you?'

'I don't think so since she asked me if anything else was wrong. She said my voice sounded different. All that howling, no doubt.'

'Did that nice Jessica woman ever contact you about the arts centre she was planning?'

236

'Netta!' Kate slapped her hand over her mouth. 'Thank God you mentioned it. I'd completely forgotten. She's coming over for drinks this evening so that we can bat ideas around. It's why I invited you to stay the night. I'd planned it so that you would be here too, and you could see what you think of her and her plans.'

'Me? I know nothing about arts centres.'

'Perhaps, but you're a very good judge of people and you're not afraid to say what you think.'

'How awful to be seen in that way. It's the bossy bit of me, isn't it? It's the only part that people remember – and don't like.' She thought of the conversation she had just had with Caroline.

'Not at all! There's much more of you than that to remember. Have you heard from Peter Bolland? He's interested in the arts centre too. Jessica wants us to work out a viability study for him – God, that's when I need Stewart.' She sighed. 'Peter's such a kind man. He's helping my son out.'

'I doubt if it's just kindness. He obviously thinks your son will succeed. I agree that he's a lovely man but I bet he's a businessman first.'

'One shouldn't gossip but . . . he and Wendy have split up.'

'No! When?' At this information Netta's spirits soared.

'After the party. He told Steve.'

'Why?' she asked, even though, thanks to Sybil, she had a shrewd idea.

'He didn't say, but the way he spoke . . . Well, no, it's not right to conjecture, is it?'

'Oh, how boring of you,' Netta said, but did not press the issue. 'Is he coming this evening?' She felt her heart lift at this possibility.

'No, he's in London. He's coming to dinner in a couple of weeks' time.'

Steve appeared to warn them that lunch would be ready in five minutes.

'Are you and Caroline getting on?' Netta asked innocently.

'Like the proverbial house . . .' Steve grinned.

'She's very pretty, isn't she?'

'You could say that!' The grin was even wider before he scooted from the room.

'Wouldn't it be nice if those two got together?'

'Hasn't she got a boyfriend?'

'No,' Netta said emphatically.

'Steve's very young – he's only twenty-one.'

'And so is Caroline. A matching pair. Kate, don't worry, I wasn't thinking matrimony for them but, rather, a little adventure to put in the storehouse of memory for when they're old and there's no love left.'

'Netta, what a sad thing to say. You'll have me crying again.' Kate smiled at her new friend and wondered how much that comment was masking, and how she could use it in her next book. Then, given the drama she was in, she was shocked that she could be thinking that way.

'Do you think Stewart is having an affair?'

The baldness and suddenness of this question made Kate choke on her drink. 'Sorry, it went down the wrong way.' She patted her chest, giving herself time to collect her thoughts. 'I don't think so. It had crossed my mind fleetingly. No, I'm sure not.'

'You do know the signs, don't you? Unusual attention to appearance.'

'You can rule that out. Stewart always looks as if he's been pulled through a hedge backwards. Laid-back casual is his style.' Kate laughed.

238

'Greater attention to personal hygiene.'

'He's always been clean – thank God.'

'Secretive use of the phone? You know, rushing to answer it before you.'

'I never answer it if I can help it – in case I have to speak French.'

'Very personal question this one. Perhaps I shouldn't?'

'Go ahead. Ask away. You're doing me good.'

'Falling off of libido . . . because he's active elsewhere?'

'Not remarkably. The first flush is over and, well, at our age . . .'

'I understand,' Netta said, though she didn't, since it wasn't a phenomenon with which she was familiar. 'Does he go out for long periods without explanation?'

'He's always doing that but always tells me why and where he's been. At the moment he's engrossed in setting up a cricket club.'

'Homesick, is he?'

'No, I don't think so . . . Well, that's not strictly true. I'd wondered myself if he was discontented here, if it hadn't quite lived up to his expectations.'

'I can't tell you how many times I've seen that happen. People expect it all to be like a holiday, but living here permanently is filled with just as much boring nitty-gritty as living in the UK. People like you sail through it but I'm sure that's because you have your work. I'm convinced there's no such thing as a Lotus Land.'

'A psychiatrist friend of mine once told me that most of his patients were late middle-aged and OAPs, that they had all retired to the West Country to the dream cottage, but when they got there, they knew no one and loneliness and depression followed. It might be the same here.'

'Exactly!'

'And it rains there as it can here.'

'Yes, as you say, it does.' Netta paused. 'It looks as if your Stewart is as white as the driven snow,' she said, while thinking the complete opposite, especially with the news about Wendy.

'Are you two coming or not?' Steve yelled from the terrace.

'Bless you, Netta, you've been such a help.' Kate kissed her cheek.

Netta was sure that Kate had not told her everything. She wondered if there was a problem with money somewhere in the background – from her observation of life, it usually featured at some point. But she could not possibly bring up *that* subject. That would be *seriously* presumptuous.

For Kate the meal went reasonably well. Occasionally a great waft of misery would arrive and she felt herself isolated from the laughter and fun the others were having. Then one of them would notice and haul her back, and she'd apologise and laugh with them until the next wave. It was rather like being in labour, she decided, fine until the pain came again. When the others were chatting among themselves she turned over much of what Netta had been saying. Had she imagined being happy? Had she wanted to be happy so badly that she had made it up? What a depressing thought. And Stewart having an affair? She doubted it. When and with whom? No, that was a stupid idea. *Is it?* 'Yes!'

'Did you say something, Mum?'

'No. I don't think so.'

And everyone laughed at her absentmindedness.

'Kate Howard's residence,' Steve said, into the cordless phone, putting on a silly voice, pretending to be a butler. 'Yes, she is, hold on,' he said, in a serious one. He handed the phone to her, pointing at it, 'It's a woman,' he mouthed. Kate had been praying it was Stewart.

'Kate, it's Sybil. I'm sorry to bother you in the middle of your lunch party . . . Oh, I don't know what to say . . .' Sybil's voice was breathless and she sounded as if she had been crying.

'Sybil, what's the problem?'

Neta stopped chattering with the others and listened intently.

'Something awful has happened . . .'

'Yes, but what?'

'It's so awful!'

'Look, Netta's here, would you rather speak to her?' She was relieved to be able to hand over the phone.

Netta listened intently. 'Sybil, my sweetness, if you don't calm down how on earth can I understand what you're saying? That's better. Now again . . .' The others watched as they saw the concern on Netta's face. 'Stay there, I'm coming.'

'What's happened?'

'It's Sim-Sim. He's in hospital.' And Netta was so shocked that she didn't even notice she hadn't called him Simon.

7

'Did she say what had happened?' Kate asked, as she drove them along the gorge road. She had volunteered to drive when it transpired that Netta had lost her licence some time ago – persistent speeding, apparently, nothing to do with alcohol, or so she said.

'No, you heard the state she was in. Probably fell off a ladder, knowing him.'

'A ladder!'

'He's a DIY fanatic, you know. God knows why when they can afford to have work done for them. I've always thought it so selfish, don't you? Depriving a poor artisan of his livelihood.'

'I can't say I've ever given it much thought. But no doubt you're right.'

'When we get there we'll probably find he's sprained an ankle. Sybil does flap.'

'I do hope so. At least Steve and Caroline will look after Jessica until we get back. I do wish people would get mobile phones – on a day like this you see how valuable they are and I could have put her off.'

'And it's not fair on the French workmen when ex-pats bring in English workers. Not fair at all.'

'I'm sorry, you've lost me.'

'And then they wonder why the local community don't take to them. I was discussing it with Peter – they only used local craftsmen on their house. Properly so in my book. And what's more . . .'

Kate let her prattle on for she suddenly realised that Netta was stressed. Talking too much about anything must be her way of dealing with it. She swung the car through the narrow gateway of the Emil Roux Hospital. 'Are they in Emergency?'

'She didn't say. Let's try there first.'

Kate followed the signs and edged down the congested road within the hospital grounds to the block where accident victims were taken. Netta, she saw, was incessantly twining her fingers. When she had finally found a parking space she turned and patted her friend's hand. 'I'm sure it'll be all right, Netta. Don't be so upset.'

'But you don't understand. If something happens to Simon I fear I shall have to move in with Sybil. The idea fills me with dread.'

242

'Why?'

'Because in a mad moment I once suggested it.'

'But she won't keep you to it.'

'Sybil would – she's useless on her own. But I know myself, I'd want to kill her within a week.'

'Well, let's hope it won't come to that.'

They clattered into the department. At the reception desk they left a message for Sybil that they had arrived, and were directed to a small waiting room.

'Why do hospitals so often have that awful institutional green paintwork? Would a decent, cheerful colour cost more? And no pictures – nothing to distract one,' Netta fretted.

'Would you like a coffee or a Coca-Cola?'

'Neither, thank you. Of course, if the worst came to the worst she might go back to England, mightn't she?'

'Yes. But is there any point in thinking any of this until we know what's happened?'

Each time the door opened, they both looked up. There didn't seem to be much bustle and few people were about, so where was Sybil?

'I suppose we should thank our lucky stars he's hurt himself at a quiet time of day. These places get so busy. I hate hospitals. Do you think we'll be here long? I wish there was something to read.' She was jabbering again, thought Kate, best to let her.

The minutes dragged into half an hour and then three-quarters. Finally Netta went to see the receptionist to check that Sybil had been told they were there.

A minute later the door burst open. 'They didn't tell me you were here!' Sybil flung herself at Netta. 'I've been so lonely!'

'We're here now. It's all right.' She patted Sybil's shoulder. 'What's happened?'

Sybil sat down on one of the plastic chairs. 'It's my fault. It was me who hurt him.' Infuriatingly she burst into tears.

The other two waited patiently for her to stop crying.

'Sybil dear, if you don't stop we can't help you. Now, what has happened? What did the doctor say? Stop it!' Netta's firmness had the right effect: Sybil stopped crying immediately, just like an obedient child, thought Kate.

'It's his pipe.'

'Yes?'

'His pipe, it's . . .'

'Yes?' Kate could hear the mounting impatience in Netta's voice.

'It's gone into his brain.' At that she began to howl again.

'His brain?' There was, Kate was sure, a hint of suppressed laughter in Netta's voice. And she, too, had to wipe a sudden smile off her face.

'Right in!'

'Yes,' said Netta, unsurely. She looked across at Kate, who shrugged her shoulders indicating that she didn't understand either. There was nothing for it but to wait for the storm of weeping to subside.

A young doctor swept into the tiny room. He had the longest eyelashes Kate had ever seen, she thought, and was horrified that she could think such a stupid thing at a time like this. She understood when he asked if they were just friends of Sybil or relatives. She was surprised when she heard Netta say she was her sister – but perhaps that was expediency since the doctor sat down and began to talk seriously to her. The rest of the conversation was too fast and too technical for Kate to understand more than a few words, so she left Netta with the doctor, who was explaining the problem with a multitude of expressive hand movements, and comforted Sybil instead.

'Thank you so much, Doctor, you've been most helpful.'

Netta bent to pick up her bag. 'I suggest we get Sybil out of here, don't you, Kate? Simon's in the theatre being operated on. The doctor said there was no point in coming back for another three hours.'

'Shall we go home?'

'No, my flat – it's nearer. Come, Sybil, we shall go and have a drink at my place.'

During the drive to Netta's, Sybil sat in the back of the car and stared unseeingly into space. 'Shock,' Netta mouthed at Kate.

'So what happened?'

'It would seem that Simon fell down the stairs – apparently he's a mass of bruises. As always he had his pipe in his mouth and they think he must have fallen directly on to it and somehow it pierced his hard palate and, as Sybil said, quite accurately, it's lodged in his brain. He has had a scan and they are hoping to remove it with no further damage, but of course they can't or won't guarantee anything.'

'Good God!'

'My thoughts entirely.'

'But you don't understand!' Sybil wailed from the back. 'It's my fault!'

'Yes, dear. The doctor said you were blaming yourself but you mustn't. Anyone can fall down the stairs.'

'But he didn't. I did it.'

'Did what?'

'The pipe,' she sobbed. 'I beat him. So badly. My old hockey stick. But it wasn't enough for me. I'm so wicked. I was so angry with him that I rammed the pipe into his mouth while he was lying on the floor. It was me.'

Kate almost knocked a cyclist off his bicycle and swerved into the kerb on the other side of the road. She righted the car.

'It's just along here on the left, you can park right outside.' In the circumstances Netta's voice was cool and collected. 'Let's get upstairs, Sybil, and then you can explain everything to us.' She bustled Sybil out of the car.

'Would you prefer it if I left now?'

'No, Kate. I think you should be here too. I think Sybil is going to need a lot of support and advice if this is true.'

If was the operative word, thought Kate, as she began to follow them up the steep staircase. Looking at Sybil it was difficult to imagine that it was. It took them a long time to ascend for Sybil kept losing the use of her legs and stumbling. They took it in turns to support her: slight as she was, she seemed suddenly to weigh a ton.

'Perhaps it's still the shock, making her imagine such things,' Kate suggested, when they were finally in the apartment.

'No, I'm not saying this because I'm in shock. It's the truth.' Sybil thumped the arm of the chair in frustration. 'I tried to tell the doctors but they wouldn't listen to me. And now you don't believe me either.'

'If it *is* true I think it's just as well the doctors didn't take any notice of you. You could be in serious trouble with the police.'

'But I want to be, don't you see? I need to be punished. I'm so wicked. I'm so violent that I don't deserve to go unpunished.'

This information was too much for Netta and Kate, who both had to sit down to assimilate it.

'But I always thought . . .'

'That I was the battered one? I know you did, and I told you constantly he was a good man, but you never listened to me. Maybe you will now. Sim has never laid a hand on me. He's been so patient with me. Even when I've been so awful to him and hurt him. Because you see, the dreadful thing is, I wanted to hurt him. If he annoyed me there were times I wanted to *kill* him.'

'I understand that, Sybil.'

'You can't, Kate.'

'But I can. Once or twice I've had flashes like that.' And she remembered the knives in the kitchen the night she and Stewart had had their awful row. She shuddered. She'd been close to something like this then. She had got to learn to control those wayward emotions.

'Because you had an argument with Stewart?' Sybil spoke through a new cascade of tears.

'Well, yes.'

'But we weren't arguing. I just did it. Something clicks in my head and I'm like a beast.'

'Yes, dear,' said Netta, in the tone of one who still could not believe what she was hearing.

'He's given up so much for me. Sim loved to hunt but he had to give it up because of me. Guns, you see. I just knew if there was a gun in the house that sooner or later I would shoot him with it.'

'I just can't believe what I'm hearing. You're such a sweet, docile person. Is it the menopause? My mother went quite peculiar – well, more peculiar – for a while.' Netta laughed nervously.

'No, it's not. I'm too young for that. I've been like this for ages. Dear God, Netta, I think I'm mad.'

'But a tiny little creature like you! How could you possibly . . . ? Sim isn't a large man but for all that . . .'

'When it happens I've the strength of a man. But when I get one of these turns, there's nothing I can do. It happens, I can't stop it. I need help, Netta. Sim thought he could deal with it but no one can.'

'Now, we have to be practical. You've got to stop crying, Sybil, it isn't getting us anywhere. We have to decide what

247

we are to do. Now, do you think Sim is going to report you to the police? Or has he already?'

'No, he won't. It was he who gave them the cock-and-bull story of falling down the stairs. No one would listen to the truth. I'm going to have to go to see them myself and explain what happened.'

'No,' Netta said, in a tone that brooked no argument. 'That would not be a good idea. Have you any idea what a French prison is like? You wouldn't last a month. The decision has to be Sim's, and we should wait until he's better before we do anything.'

'But what if he doesn't get better? What if he's brain-damaged?'

'He will get better. You must think that. And the doctor was fairly confident that it hadn't penetrated far enough to do damage – close, but they were hoping he would be fine.' She was lying: they'd said no such thing. 'What do you say, Kate?'

'I'd go along with that. If what you say is true, Sybil, then I think you need medical help, not punishment.'

'It *is* true!' Sybil virtually screamed at Kate and they both saw the anger of which she was capable.'

'I phrased that badly.'

'You need a rest, Sybil. You're exhausted. Lie on my bed and I'll call you when it's time to go back to the hospital.'

Netta settled her in her bedroom. When she returned, she said to Kate, 'I don't think she'll sleep but at least she's not flapping and crying.'

'Poor soul. Who would have believed it?'

'I'm shell-shocked, I must say. I was so convinced it was the other way round. And there you were a couple of hours ago telling me what a good judge of people I was. You got that wrong, Kate.'

'No one would have realised this. And we were wrong about Sim too, it would seem.'

'That's the hard part, Kate. I mean how, in the space of a couple of hours, am I to change my opinion of Simon and regard him not as a prat but as a victim, a martyr – a saint? Impossible!'

'But why? Do you think it's something from her past?'

'Presumably. But, you know, the awful thing is, Kate, there have been times without number when I would have loved to ram his flaming pipe down his throat. I hate that pipe.'

'Yes, but you didn't. And she did. That's the problem.'

'The other thing is . . .' Netta began to laugh but stopped herself. 'Oh, I shouldn't, it's no laughing matter, is it? You see . . .' But she couldn't control herself. 'I always said that pipe would be the death of him!'

Kate had to smile.

Chapter Six

July

1

'This infernal shutting of banks, offices and shops for two hours at lunchtime is crazy!' Tristram had missed the bank by five minutes and was now faced with either going home or cooling his heels until two. He had opted for the latter and was now in the Palais consuming a bowl of mussels and chips. 'Don't you think that *moules frites* sounds much more appetising?'

'Undoubtedly,' said Stewart, who had just joined him. 'And don't let the banks get you down, I promise you'll get used to it.' He ordered a ham sandwich. 'I'll risk my crowns.' He grinned.

'You certainly need a big mouth to get round a French ham sandwich.' The plate of chips had beaten Tristram; he pushed them away and took a large gulp of his ice-cold beer. 'It's a mystery to me how they run an economy with everything shutting in the middle of the day.'

'They don't seem to be doing too badly.' Stewart smiled the knowing smile of an old hand at Tristram's impatience. 'And don't forget the parking is free between noon and two. Don't you find that so French and endearing? Only madmen and tourists would want to break the sanctity of the lunch-break.'

As he spoke he was looking around him and assessing the other customers. His glance faltered when it happened upon an attractive woman, whom he appraised coolly, almost arrogantly, Tristram thought. He was an attractive old cove, he concluded, and he hoped he would look as good when he got to Stewart's age – if he ever did.

'My advice to you, old boy, is to forget you ever lived in England,' Stewart went on. 'You'll be better able to deal with the odd idiosyncrasy and you'll settle down more easily.'

'I'll try but I don't know if I have the patience.' Tristram had noticed, in his short time here, that there seemed to be a pecking order in the ex-pat community: advice, unasked, was often handed out by those who had been here longer. They found it necessary somehow to make recommendations even if they were of scant interest. No matter what Tristram had decided to do there was invariably an Englishman to tell him he'd chosen badly or wrongly. In any gathering he could guarantee a list of conversation topics. How long had one been here? How had one managed to get a Sky TV card and what was one doing about digital TV? The advisability of getting the *carte de séjour*. Registering one's British car – yes or no. The advantages of an Isle of Man bank account. The unfairness of the French inheritance laws – that was the women, who, on the death of their husbands, faced seeing their houses pass to their children and not to themselves. It was the first time Tristram had lived anywhere where the cheapness of one's house, rather than how expensive it had been, was reason to boast. Septic tanks, French plumbing and electricity excited many. But most important to them was how much better informed they were than you. 'Sorry, what were you saying? I was miles away.'

'You worked in the City, didn't you? How do you deal with the national disease of unpunctuality here?'

'It drives me mad! Only last week I wasted a whole morning waiting for a plumber. Did he come when he said he would? Oh dear me, no. Two hours late and no apology!'

'I've yet to meet an English plumber who comes when he says he will. But don't forget, the plus side of that is that no one gets in a sweat when you're late. And they're not going to change for you, now, are they?'

'I suppose when we first arrived I found it rather charming.'

'It's only when other things are going wrong that it becomes annoying.' Stewart waved to the waitress indicating he wanted another beer. Tristram looked at him, frowning. How did Stewart know that he and Mo hadn't stopped rowing for days? 'Been here in August yet?' Stewart asked, and Tristram wondered if he wasn't being a bit paranoid. Perhaps he was referring to himself.

'No, we came in February.'

'Would you believe the local swimming-pool supplier closes for his annual holiday in August?'

'You're joking!'

'No, I'm not. When *le grand départ* comes I've seen restaurants and hotels close – tourists mill about wondering what the hell is going on. Don't have a legal problem then and, whatever you do, don't die in August, will you? Gets a bit dodgy.'

'That's incredible.'

'You've got to hand it to them, though. We were too obsessed with time back in the rat-race. This is the place.'

'Do you think you'll ever go back to England?'

'Looks like I'm going to have to.' Stewart stood up and picked up his magazine. He didn't look particularly put out by the prospect for one who had declared how much better was life here, Tristram thought.

'But only the other day Kate was saying how much she loved it here and never wanted to move.'

'She isn't.' He checked his bill and placed some coins on the table. 'See you around, Tristram.'

So, what had he meant by that? Tristram wondered, as he finished his lunch. He looked at his watch – still an hour to kill. He ordered another lager.

Of course Stewart had been right, Tristram thought, as he crossed the main boulevard, dodging the traffic, and made his way to the car park. There was no point in working oneself into a state over things that were not going to change. However, it had surprised him that Stewart, of all people, should think in that way. He wouldn't ever have labelled him as a placid, accepting type of person. Quick off the mark, more like – they'd all seen that at the Bolland party. What that conversation had shown Tristram was that he could never be certain he understood anyone.

He unlocked the car door and threw the carrier bag on to the back seat. Certainly he didn't want to turn into the sort of ex-pat who was always going on about how things were so much better in England. There'd been a couple of those at the Bollands' party, wittering on about their Sky TV, their bacon and eggs, their tea. Only Kate Howard had been totally honest. 'I don't live in France,' she'd explained to him. 'I've borrowed a corner of it and there I carry on much as I did at home.'

'Then why did you come?' he'd asked.

'Actually, I didn't want to. It was Stewart who so wanted to live here. And as a writer it doesn't much matter where I work. Please, don't get me wrong. I'm very happy here. I certainly don't want to be back in England, but I don't think I would enjoy being too French – they have such uncomfortable chairs for starters. But it's there if I *want* it, do you understand? Meanwhile, I'm like a lodger who keeps very much to themselves and in their room.'

'Don't you have any French friends?'

'Acquaintances, yes. I don't speak the language well enough. But I do wonder if those who can ever really make true friends. One is always the outsider looking in, isn't one?'

He'd agreed with her there. 'And I'd love to know what they think of us,' she continued. 'We buy up the houses they never wanted to live in – at inflated prices, to their way of thinking. We then add loads more plugs and use more electricity than they would ever dream of doing. Then some, and I do think they're foolish, import British labour to do the conversions – now that really goes down like a lead balloon. Then we go on about tea and bacon, adopt stray dogs and studiously avoid mentioning the battle of Waterloo!' They had laughed at that.

Tristram sat in his car mulling over that conversation. Had she been right? He'd hoped that, living here, he'd easily make friends, carrying on much as he had in the UK. But if he thought about it, who did he know? There was Martin, his neighbour, but was he a friend? Was he just courteous because, living as isolated as they did, neighbours needed each other in the way they never did in cities?

Tristram had helped out. He'd assisted with stone shifting – an annual event in these parts since the tractors couldn't go on the land for fear of the machinery blades being broken unless the stones were moved first. A bit like painting the Forth Bridge – he didn't know if the French had a similar expression, perhaps they referred to the Eiffel Tower.

He'd helped with the planting and the lambing – neither of which he'd particularly enjoyed, but he had wanted to feel part of the community. But had he been? Mo had told him he was daft, that of course they'd welcome another pair of hands, especially since they were free. And Netta had inadvertently thrown cold water on his scheme when she told him *everyone* did that when they first came – and he'd the harvest to look forward to but that *everyone* eventually got bored with it. And then, presumably seeing his hurt expression, she had said, 'But no doubt you're the exception to the rule.' Was he?

He felt he'd been appreciated. Martin and his wife had invited them to lunch. The meal had been simple and he'd enjoyed the staple diet of these parts – sausages and lentils. He'd have preferred the wine to have been less rough – it had seared the back of his throat as it went down – and the home-made plum liqueur, *gniole*, nearly blew off the top of his head. But poor Mo had thrown up all night long. He had thought it was more likely the sight of a mouse scuttling along a beam in the kitchen that affected her rather than the food, but she'd declared she wasn't ever going to eat there again.

Poor, lying, deceitful, beautiful Mo. What were they going to do?

Now Tristram didn't want to go home to her. He didn't want to go back to their rowing and to the obvious hopelessness of their situation. He didn't want the awful mess he'd made of his life highlighted by their high-octane arguments. He knew he was a prat – she didn't need to tell him so.

Instead he got out of the car, recrossed the car park and the main street, then plunged into the labyrinth of narrow lanes in the old part of town. 'Tristram Hargreaves,' he said, into the mouthpiece of the intercom. 'Is it an inconvenient time?'

'Come up. Fifth floor.' The door buzzed like an angry

wasp. He pushed it open and proceeded to climb the steep stairs, wondering how on earth a woman of Netta's age could possibly manage them.

Netta was standing in the doorway of her flat. She put her finger to her lips. 'If you wouldn't mind being quiet as a mouse, but Sybil is here and asleep – she's had a bit of a trauma.'

They tiptoed into the tiny hall, which was dominated by a huge cupboard, sidled past it and into the equally small sitting room.

'I'm afraid I've nothing to offer you but tea or coffee. We finished the last of my wine last night. It's probably why Sybil is sleeping so soundly.'

'Easily remedied.' From the bag he was holding he took a bottle of wine.

'Bliss! How dear of you. If you'd do the honours?' Netta touched his hand, squeezed it, then skittered across the room to return with a corkscrew. It was the first time he'd ever been asked like that to open a bottle of wine. Had he not known better, he'd have taken it as a come-on!

'I hope it's nothing serious with Sybil?'

'It is and it isn't. Simon had to have an operation yesterday.' Tristram couldn't understand why this was cause for the wide grin that appeared on Netta's face. 'But he's fine and is expected to make a full recovery.' He was even more confused that this should make Netta laugh. 'He swallowed his pipe, you see. Such a careless thing to do.' She couldn't control the laugh this time, though she kept apologising and saying it was no laughing matter, which only seemed to make things worse. 'Poor Sybil, as you can appreciate, was in a bit of a state. She blames herself but we've reassured her, I hope,' she finally managed, when she had more control.

'Why? Did she ram it down his throat?' Tristram laughed this time.

'What a thing to say!' She looked theatrically arch. 'No, silly Simon fell down the stairs. Now, glasses. There's nothing I like more than a Chablis, don't you agree?' There was more sweeping and swooping, glasses were produced and wine was poured. 'I'm afraid she's not here.'

'Sorry?'

'Caroline.'

'I didn't expect her to be. I dropped in on the off-chance of seeing you.' He was glad he'd got over blushing years ago.

'Don't fib, Tristram,' she said teasingly. 'She's staying with a friend – that's how I could keep Sybil here with me. She says she can stay there until the dust settles.'

'I see.'

'I don't want her hurt, Tristram.'

'I don't understand.'

'Yes, you do. You've done it once, I don't want you doing it again.'

'But I never would – hurt her, I mean.'

'And if you returned to Caroline, what would you do about Mo in these uncertain times you find yourself in?'

'I wasn't planning to do any such thing.'

'Weren't you? I think you were. If you managed not to harm her I would still have serious reservations about your present companion. I'm afraid Mo is the type of woman who would have no compunction about hurting Caroline.'

'Caroline is a woman. She can make her own decisions.' He felt himself bridle.

'I agree. It's her life, and she can take any path she wants. But, as you know I'm sure, she is naïve and vulnerable, and if I can alter the direction of any of the signposts along the way she has chosen, then I promise you I will.' She spoke in such a charming manner, and with such a wonderful smile, that it was difficult to believe this was a warning.

'Such as?' Tristram thought that attack might be his best weapon.

'Mo. Don't tell me you're naïve too! She, for Caroline, is the most dangerous but she is also the easiest to defuse. In the years I have lived here I have made many useful contacts.'

'You wouldn't!' He couldn't be a hundred per cent sure of what she meant, but he had a nasty idea that he knew.

'Tell on her? You don't think so? Well, of course, you must believe what you want, that is your privilege.'

'But if Mo was arrested because you welshed on her, you'd be doing me a favour since I'd be free. Then there would be no one to stop us getting back together.'

'You believe so? How could someone capable of thinking like that be a suitable person for Caroline? I really thought even you would have more honour. Perhaps we should put it to the test, see which one of us is right.' Still the smile, which now seemed ominous to Tristram.

'No, don't do that.'

'Then we understand each other. Good. More wine?'

Tristram hadn't even got out of the car before Mo came rushing down the path towards him. 'Tristram, I'm sorry about this morning. I was a bitch.'

'Doesn't matter. We're both under intolerable stress.'

'I should never have called you the things I did.'

'Don't worry, I'm getting used to it.' He hauled the gas cylinder from the boot of the car.

'Let me help you.' She took a couple of carrier bags from the back seat. 'Didn't you go to Soleil?'

'I didn't have time,' he lied.

'But they have a better selection of veg than Géant.' She pouted.

'For Christ's sake, don't let's argue about a few vegetables, please.'

He followed her into the house, removed the empty gas cylinder and replaced it with the new one, then lifted the remaining shopping bags on to the table.

'You're right. A spud's a spud, isn't it? Bless you, you remembered my shampoo. Anything interesting happen? Any gossip?'

'Incredible amounts.' He was packing the shopping in the kitchen cupboard. 'Sim swallowed his pipe and has had surgery to get it out. Sybil has had the vapours but Netta is coping.'

'Netta?' Her voice took on a shrillness. 'You mean . . .' And then she stopped herself, went over to him and stroked his jumper. 'Tristram, don't be cross, but I've got to ask you.' There was no shrillness now. 'Did you see her?'

'Netta, yes.'

'And Caroline?'

'No. She's not in Le Puy.'

'Where's she gone?'

'I don't know, I didn't ask.' At that she flung her arms around his neck and kissed him full on the mouth. 'Mo, I don't think I'll ever understand you. You act as if you really care about me, yet this morning you wished me dead and out of your life.'

'That was this morning. Now is important.'

'But we can't go on like this. I can't take many more of the rows, the insults.'

'You called me a bitch.'

'I shouldn't have, I'm sorry.' He sighed with weariness at it all.

'But you were right. I was. I do love you, Tristram.'

'You don't, Mo. You just say it when you think you've gone too far.'

'I *do* mean it. I'm going to change.'

'I don't think I've enough years left to wait for the metamorphosis.' He grinned. Joking was better than battling. She hit him playfully. He continued to see to the shopping. He wasn't going to row any more. On the way back he'd made his mind up. He'd stay with Mo until somehow he'd sorted out the mess she was in. He was going to approach his father, ask for a loan – against his inheritance or something, he'd yet to work the details out. Then . . . then he'd find Caroline.

'Why are you smiling?'

'I wasn't aware that I was. Sim and his pipe, I suppose. There is a funny side. There was another monumental bit of gossip. I think Stewart and Kate might have split up.'

'You're joking! Never.'

'I think so.' And he relayed Stewart's conversation with him.

'Sounds odd. But I'd have thought that an old has-been like Kate wouldn't let him slip through her fingers. She won't get anyone else at her age, will she?'

He smiled again. That was more like Mo. Then he glanced out of the window. 'You fucking bastard!' he roared, as he saw Martin opposite mercilessly beating his dog. '*Arrête!*' he was shouting, as he raced out of the door. So he didn't see the calculating expression on Mo's face.

2

Every time the phone rang Kate prayed it was Stewart. Yet again she was disappointed. It was his wine merchant, asking about an unpaid bill. She thought, from the tone of his voice, that he was being understanding. But when she replaced the receiver, she had something else to worry about. Had Stewart simply forgotten to pay it or was a whole stack of bills waiting for her? And what was she to do if he didn't come home? How could she deal with people when she could barely understand them?

'If you want my opinion he's behaving like an inconsiderate oaf.'

'I don't need your opinion, Lucy.'

'It's unfair. He's been gone over a week. He should contact you. It's not on.'

'I really don't need you to tell me that.' She busied herself with her papers, Lucy was staring vacantly out of the window. What was wrong with the girl? She was always mooning about instead of doing. Several times it had crossed Kate's mind that Stewart was punishing her. She reacted to this idea in several ways. On the one hand it was awful to think he could be cruel and petty, but on the other there was relief that if she was right he would be back. And the third thought, which she tried to squash since it was so uncharitable, was that if Lucy and Dominique hadn't turned up he would never have disappeared in the first place.

'Now, what is it you wanted? Anything I can do?' Guiltily she made her voice sound warm and caring. She'd been checking the pages of alterations she had done for Portia, for *Troubadour*, and slotting them into the typescript. It was a bit of a mess, and she would have liked it to be immaculate as usual – but in the circumstances it would have to do. 'Sod it!' She cursed as she dropped a pile of papers on the floor.

'See what he's done to you? You never used to swear.'

'Lucy, when the mood's taken me I've always been perfectly capable of it. And if you don't tell me quickly what it is you want then you will hear the rest of my quite extensive vocabulary.' Her patience was wearing thin this morning. Lucy turned from the window. She looked ill. Pale and tense. A nasty cold sore at the corner of her mouth. 'Are you all right, Lucy? You don't look well.'

'I'm fine.'

'Are you eating? You look even thinner than when you came.'

'Mum, don't fuss!'

'I won't. Promise. So what is it?'

'It's a bit difficult.'

'Darling, do come to the point, I've masses to do.'

'Well, it's the van. There were a couple of things in the MOT, or whatever it's called here, that needed fixing.'

'Like what?'

'The brake linings for one, and the clutch needs something but I can't remember what it is.'

'But I thought that Mr da Costa had said it was fine.'

'We didn't take it to him. A friend of Dominique's looked at it for us and said it was OK.' She was looking around the room, not at Kate. 'We weren't to know,' she said, in her old belligerent way.

'Really, Lucy! You didn't listen. I insisted on Mr da Costa checking it because he's excellent with cars and I trust his opinion. That was part of the bargain we had. If he found things wrong with it, we agreed the deal was off.'

'I don't remember.' Sulkiness had taken over from belligerence. 'In any case, Dom was only trying to save you money.'

'Well, he's failed miserably on that score, hasn't he? You really can be so infuriating.' She burrowed in the chaos of her desk for her cheque book.

'While you're writing a cheque, Dominique thinks we would do well to have a real coffee machine. He reckons it would double our turnover – especially with young people.'

'Does he now?'

'And then there's the signwriter.'

'Can't it stay as it is for the moment? After all, it only says "Pizza". It's not as if you're selling something else.'

'Dom thinks it should be personalised. We want to call it Dom's Pizzas.'

'Why not Lucy's?'

'I think Dom is better, don't you?'

'And how much is the signwriter going to charge?'

'I don't know.'

'Then tell Dominique to find out.'

'He doesn't like to be told what to do, Mum.'

'Then I suggest he begins to learn.' Briskly she folded away her cheque book. 'Come back to me with estimates for all these things, right? Written ones.'

'Dom isn't going to like this.'

'Then Dom can go and whistle,' she said, though it wasn't what she was thinking. She had something far more anatomically complicated in mind. It was inevitable that Lucy would flounce out of the room just as she had in the past. Hard luck! If she let them walk all over her now, at the beginning of this venture, then she'd be lost. As it was, the bills were mounting in an alarming way – in a matter of days they had racked up a pile, none of which had been allowed for in their earlier calculations. The excuse was always the same – some tax she'd never heard of but which, apparently, made it impossible for them to trade unless they paid it.

She wished Steve was still here. She'd been lucky, he'd stayed two days longer than he had intended – Caroline had been the attraction. But since he'd gone the problems kept mounting. Kate liked Caroline. She was kind and thoughtful, and wonderfully helpful, but all the same she worried for Steve. With a new business to start up the last thing he needed was a heavy romance. And with Peter

Bolland as a backer! He would not put up with Steve having distractions that took him away from the business.

Netta seemed overly keen that the two should get together – which Kate found odd. She adored her son but at the moment he could hardly be regarded as a cast-iron catch – one day, perhaps. And such matters, she was sure, would be of great concern to Netta, who was forever alert to money, as she was the first to admit. From odd things Netta had said, Kate had deduced that Caroline was a wealthy young lady, so Netta's enthusiasm for them to be together seemed strange. Curiouser and curiouser, she told herself as, for the second time that day, she checked the numbering of her typescript.

The whole lot went flying again when the phone rang and she dived for it, sending up her now customary prayer, but it was Netta. 'Kate, forgive me, but would it be possible for you to drive over to Sybil's? You know where she lives – up the hill from Lavoute. We're picking up Sim and I think it would be a good idea if you were there. Sybil is in a state of hysteria.'

'Can't Caroline go with you?'

'She's popped back to England. Something to do with a young man called Steve!'

'But I hardly know Sim.'

'What's important is that he respects you. There's more chance he'll listen to you about what's best for Sybil.'

'Honestly, Netta, it's hardly our business.'

'Of course it is, Sybil's our friend.'

'And he won't listen to you?'

'He knows how I feel about him. I've been rude once too often, regrettably. No, I'm the last person to be handing out advice to him.'

'Surely there's someone else who knows him well?'

'Of course, but the fewer people who know the truth the

264

better. I wouldn't ask you, Kate, but I'm at my wit's end. The silly woman has gone catatonic on me.'

'I thought you said she was hysterical?'

'I did. Hysteria-induced catatonia.'

Getting ready to drive to Lavoute, Kate was muttering to herself as she collected her handbag and keys, left a note for Lucy and one for Stewart – just in case. And then she heard herself and was so appalled that she might be becoming like her mother that she clammed up immediately. But, for all that, it wasn't fair. Didn't people realise she had to work for a living?

It was a lovely drive to the Chestertons' and one that she normally enjoyed since the road wound up a high hill that was densely forested with deciduous trees. Once, driving this way, she'd even seen a wild boar.

At the top, in a lovely clearing with breathtaking views of the valley below and the mountains beyond, was Sim and Sybil's house. Given their modest way of dressing and their rather mundane appearance, the modern, expensive house they lived in never failed to surprise Kate. It was all steel and glass and looked as if it had flown in from outer space rather than anything so commonplace as being built.

The front door was wide open, but although she rang the bell and called no one came. She ventured in. Still calling that she was there she crossed the stark hall – white walls and stunning modern art – towards the back of the house where she knew a large verandah was poised over the ravine. Since it was so hot they were probably there.

'Ha! Here she is, at last.' Netta sprang to her feet from the stainless-steel and white-cushioned lounger she'd been sitting on. Sybil was curled up in a matching chair, looking smaller than ever and very wan. Her eyes were even pinker than usual. Sim was sitting opposite, bolt upright on a chair, with what Kate took to be a wary expression on his face and no pipe in his mouth. As he turned to greet her she saw there was a large plaster on the side of his head and that his hair had been shaved, which made his head look vulnerable and unprotected, like an egg coloured with cochineal for Easter.

'How kind of you to come, Kate. Sybil has needed her friends. She needs support.' His voice was thick, as if he had a bad cold.

'It sounds as if you could do with some too.'

'It's my mouth, sorry, it's the swelling. The old vocal cords took a bit of a whammy.'

'That's not exactly what I meant.' She smiled at him as encouragingly as she could. She really didn't know what possible use she could be to them.

'I've been trying to tell Sim that he and Sybil need help.'

Kate wondered if she was the only one who registered that Netta had called him by his nickname.

'What nonsense you do talk, Netta.' His laugh emerged more like a gurgle.

'I think she's right, Sim,' Kate plunged in, thinking she might as well now that she was here. 'What if it happened again?'

'If what happened?'

'Well, it's a bit difficult to say delicately but . . . if Sybil attacked you again.' She looked nervously across at the silent woman, but either she hadn't heard or had gone off into her own world for she did not respond.

The gurgle was louder this time. 'You mustn't take any notice of what Sybil says, Kate. I'm always telling her she should have been a writer, like you, with her imagination.'

'But she said—'

'That cock-and-bull story about attacking me. It didn't happen.' He looked straight at Kate with such a determined expression that she knew he was lying. 'I fell down the stairs.'

'But she told us . . . She needs help, Sim.'

'What about some tea, old girl? Do you feel up to making some?'

Without a word Sybil got to her feet.

'I'll help her.' Netta jumped up too.

'No, I'd rather you both stayed with me,' Sim said pointedly. He waited until Sybil had left the room. 'Dear ladies, I know you both mean well but, I promise you, if you pursue this line you're not helping either of us.'

'But, Sim—' Netta began.

'She's my responsibility. I know her, and I understand her. That's all there is to be said.'

'But she needs a doctor.'

'That's the last thing she needs. You haven't seen, you can't possibly . . . Just drop it!' he said sharply. In anyone else it might have been interpreted as the beginnings of anger, but with Sim it heralded agitation.

'You were lucky – this time.'

'Netta, did you not hear me? I do not wish to talk about this. I'll say only one thing and I hope you will respect my better knowledge. It isn't the first time and I would not presume to say it's the last. But I have to keep her out of the doctors' hands. They will sedate her and put her away, they will institutionalise her, and she will come out a sadder person and less the Sybil I adore.'

'I just don't understand. How can this be?'

'No more, Netta. IIa, my darling, the tea . . .'

'Sim, I'm sorry. I didn't understand you. I apologise for all my rudeness in the past,' Netta said.

'No matter. It's been worth it just to hear you call me Sim.'

Netta and Kate were subdued in the car on the way back down the hill. It was almost as if, by mutual consent, they had decided not to talk until they got to Netta's flat.

'I read him all wrong. He was so dignified. Wasn't he humbling?' Netta said, as she opened the bottle of wine Kate had thoughtfully brought with her.

'Completely.'

'I'd even thought him a gold-digger and it's him with the money all along, I gathered.'

'One could never have guessed.'

Netta paused in opening the bottle. 'You know, in my years here I have discovered that people come for different reasons. Some because they are just in love with France and everything French, others because they think they can live cheaper here. There are those who think they can catch a dream that doesn't exist. And those who are running away from something – the law, unhappiness, money or emotional problems – and, you know, the more I see, the more I think that for most people it's the latter.'

'Is she mad as she says? Is that why they came here?'

'Running away from people knowing? Probably. She's not mad, though. Rather, she suffers periodically from severe depression. When Sim was in hospital she told me things – maybe I shouldn't tell you but you know so much already. You see, her first husband was killed in a car crash and she was driving. Worse, she was pregnant at the time and lost the child. Her son won't forgive her and doesn't speak to her.'

'How old is he?'

'Twenty-five.'

'Then he should grow up.'

'My sentiments exactly. Poor Sybil. Laden with all that guilt, is it any wonder she's had a number of nervous breakdowns? Several times she was hospitalised for her own protection. Everything looked good when she met Sim. Imagine me, calling him that!' She smiled. 'Anyhow, it wasn't. She had medication which – understandably, I suppose – she stopped taking. That was when she first attacked him.'

'Why?'

'She said if she doesn't take her drugs she gets agitated, severely so. She feels in danger all the time. She said she felt as if the world tipped.' Netta shuddered. 'She "flipped", was how she put it. That time Sim saw what hospital did to her. It turned her into a zombie, he said, and he vowed never again. So he managed, checking her drugs every day.'

'So what happened this time?'

'She'd been so good he felt it was safe for him to go away on a business trip. But you know how scatty she is, she forgot her medication. She spiralled down so fast this time – I gather they don't know why. And wham! When he came home she thought he was going to kill her so she got in first.'

'What a nightmare.'

'Isn't it? Poor darlings.'

'And I thought I had problems!'

Kate felt incredibly weary as she parked outside her house, pushed the gate open and walked across the terrace.

'You missed him,' Lucy called, from her side of the orchard.

'Who?'

'Stewart. He came to pack.'

Kate let herself into the empty house. Her hand was shaking and she had difficulty putting the key into the lock. Once inside, with the door firmly shut, she let out a wail like that of an animal in pain. She flung herself on the floor and beat a tattoo with her fists on the tiles. And then she wept as if there was nothing inside her but tears.

'My poor darling. Does it hurt dreadfully?' Mo was straightening the bed on which a very bruised Tristram lay. Twice he'd tried to get up and both times he had collapsed back on the bed. It was as if there was not one part of him that wasn't sore and damaged. 'I really think we should call the doctor. That's a nasty gash on your head – it's weeping.' She kissed him gently. He was finding her ministrations nerve-racking. For Mo to be so sweet for a whole evening and this morning was a lot. Surely it couldn't last? 'I don't like the look of that bruise on your stomach. What the hell was he wearing? Hob-nailed boots?'

'What do you think?' He smiled wryly.

'You shouldn't have interfered.'

'I know, I know. Spare me the lecture. At least I rescued the mutt.' He put his hand limply over the side of the bed to where Max, the dog, lay cowering, unsure of his surroundings. He had never been allowed inside a house in his life.

'And for what? He'll only get another one and mistreat that. He must have thought you mad when you gave him money for the creature, after he'd beaten the living daylights out of you.'

'Here, do you mind? Martin doesn't look too pretty himself. I know for sure I knocked a tooth out.' He would have laughed, had it not hurt him too much to do so.

Mo bent and stroked the dog too. He licked her hand. 'I don't even like dogs. I prefer cats.'

'He's a nice dog. He's so gentle – it's only sheep he's horrible to. You'll grow to love him.'

'You reckon?'

'I know so. Especially when I can bath him. He needs de-fleaing and worming, that's for sure.'

'And you let him up here in our bedroom!'

'I couldn't leave him downstairs – he was shivering so. Dog fleas don't like humans,' he said, in reassurance, as he saw her begin to scratch.

'You always said you wanted a dog. Now you've got one.'

He smiled at her. Did she care? In an odd way he felt everything was changing but for the life of him he couldn't think why.

'I'll go into town for you, get the flea powder, see if there are any magazines, buy you a steak,' Mo said.

'You needn't bother. You hate driving here.'

'I'm getting better at it. No, I'd like to go.' Mo, who had walked across to the window, turned and faced him from the bottom of the bed. 'You do realise we can't stay here,' she said abruptly, as if she needed to say it before she lost the courage to do so.

'Why not?'

'With a neighbour who tried to kill you? Who'll put all the locals against you?'

'He's none too popular in these parts. You should hear what people say about him in the bar.'

'Like they say about everyone else and you, too, when you're not there, no doubt. Don't be so naïve, Tristram. Everyone around here is related to each other. You can't say a thing to anyone about anyone because it's their aunt or cousin. And you think they'd take your side against one of their own? I know for sure they wouldn't.'

'We can't go. We're stuck here. This place had been on the market for eight years before we moseyed along. How could we go? It's all we've got.'

'We can let it. Move further south.'

'Prices down there are through the roof. Whatever we got in rental for this wouldn't get us a shed down there.' This was a pointless conversation to be having. Even if he did borrow from his father he'd have to go back to work, if not to repay him – he had a fairly futile hope that his father would tell him not to bother – then to show the old bastard he wasn't the waster he thought he was.

'But at least we'd be poor in the sun.' Mo knelt on the floor beside Max and took Tristram's hand in hers. He winced, but tried to hide it. 'Oh, Tristram, I'm so sorry – that you're in pain, that I've caused so many problems. That I've been such a bitch. Forgive me about Caroline. You'd be happier with her. You're free to go, you know, I'd understand.'

'Mo, what's happened? Why are you like this?' At the drop of a hat she could turn on the charm and sweet-talk him into doing what she wanted. But this time it was different, it was as if she really meant it, as if she had changed.

'Being nice, you mean?' She gave a sad little laugh. He felt wary. 'Last night, when I saw you fighting with Martin, I was sure he was about to kill you and I knew then what I'd been too blind to see, that I must love you, after all, and I didn't want you to die.' At which point Mo began to cry and Tristram would have bet the very little they had that the tears were genuine. He lifted his hand and stroked her hair, feeling confused. This wasn't how the scenario should be playing out. She mustn't mean it, it would complicate everything. And yet it was so nice having her like this, caring for him, saying she loved him.

'There, there, Mo, it'll be all right. You can rely on me, I'll always be there for you.' And as he said the words he didn't want to say, didn't understand why he was saying them, he

knew with certainty that everything had changed and that
he spoke the truth.

'Stewart, I hoped I'd find you here.'

'Mo, what a lovely surprise. It isn't every day that I look
up and see such a beauty wanting to find me.' He gestured
for her to sit down.

'Just coffee,' she answered his query. 'If you've got a
minute, I need some advice for a friend of mine.'

'If I can be of service.'

'This friend, I've known her for years, well, she's been a
bit stupid and she got involved with a group of drug-
dealers.'

'Nasty.'

'Very! Anyhow, she owes them a lot of money for drugs
she didn't pay for.'

'Which she sold?'

'Yes.'

'Nastier!'

'The point is, could she sell her story?'

'What angle? The drugs? Old hat. I doubt if anyone
would be interested.' He shrugged his shoulders dismissively.

'I saw it more along the lines of showing how easy it is to
get sucked into that sort of problem in London. She worked
in the modelling world. Everyone's always fascinated with
that business.'

'Been done. Old hat.'

'But what if she told *all*? You know, like who she sold the
drugs to.'

'It would depend who it was.' He tried to sound
noncommittal, willing himself not to sit up straight and
show too much interest, for his journalistic instincts told
him she was about to tell him something extraordinary.

'Well, like . . . strictly in confidence?'

'You have my word of honour.'

'Like . . .' And there in the Palais bar, in the quiet town of Le Puy she rattled off a list of names. A couple of politicians, TV personalities, minor royalty, even a cleric. 'That's just for starters.'

It was difficult not to show his excitement. 'You sold to all these people?'

'Don't be silly, Stewart, I am asking you for my friend.'

'Of course, I'm sorry.' He didn't dare smile in case she flounced off and took her story to someone else.

'What's more, she knows the names of a lot of others who friends sold to. She knows who the big boys are, where the skeletons lie, everything.'

'Have you told anyone else this story?'

'No. She didn't want me to. She had this stupid idea that if she ran away she could get away. Well, you can't, can you? I told her that,' she added hurriedly. 'The heavies are sniffing around and they want their money. She'd be happier if they were paid.'

'I can understand that.' This time he allowed himself to smile. 'What about her . . . How would you describe them? Customers? Victims?'

'Clients, I think. What about them?'

'They're not going to be too happy if she spills the beans on them. What if they came gunning for her? Could be nasty too.'

'She wants to move away, get a new identity. She wants to buy a house down in the south and have enough to keep her for the rest of her life. She couldn't possibly do all of that unless she received a lot of money for it.'

'I see that. But there is one problem – a little matter of libel. You can't just name names without proof.'

274

'She's got that.' Mo unzipped a large black leather bag and brought out a couple of small red leatherbound books.

'I thought they were always little black books?'

'Sorry?'

'Nothing.'

'And these.' She produced a pile of audiotapes and a small packet of photographs. 'It's all there. She never did a deal without being wired up. Smart, wasn't she?'

'Very.' He flicked through one of the notebooks. He smiled broadly. 'Your friend has a valuable story here. As it stands you could do a deal with a Sunday paper. But you'd be throwing away a golden opportunity. There's a book here, serial rights, a film. This woman could be sitting on a small fortune. What sort of background does she come from?'

'I don't think she'd want her family involved. I could ask, of course. She was adopted, you see. Her real mother is an alcoholic and her father is dead – not that she ever knew him. Her adopted mother is a jeweller and her father well, he's . . .' She leant across and whispered in Stewart's ear.

'Christ!' The name of one of the country's leading Shakespearean actors was not one he had expected to hear. 'Then she's sitting on a gold mine. No doubt about it. I'd be only too happy to help. You know, talk to publishers, set up meetings.'

'But you can't do that from here.'

'No, I've had my fill of France. I'm planning to go back home once I've sorted out one or two things here.' In fact he had no such plans. But having burnt his boats with Kate, and with Peter having sneakily squirrelled away most of his fortune offshore so that Wendy was going to come out with little, he hadn't the foggiest idea what he was going to do. This girl and her story were like manna. 'You might as well

275

know, because it'll soon be common knowledge, that Kate and I have split up.'

'I am sorry.'

Stewart shrugged. 'When the fires go out there's not much you can do but face reality, is there?' He looked at her in a soulful, meaningful sort of way, which he knew from experience often worked as a come-hither. He was disappointed when she didn't seem to react – she was a lovely creature. In for a penny . . . he'd been thinking. Still, maybe it would be better to keep it on a business footing.

'I'm the opposite, I think I've just put a match to my own particular fire. Though it might be a flash in the pan. You know, a sympathy vote.' She giggled, but realising she had not reacted to his flirting as she normally would pulled her up short. Maybe she wasn't imagining how she felt about Tristram.

'Any chance of me looking and listening to those?' He nodded towards the tapes and red notebooks. He needed to get her back on track, not start gossiping.

'I couldn't let you have them, but you can study them while I'm with you – that's only fair. You see, I promised my friend I'd never let them out of my sight.'

'Let's have some lunch.' He waved to the waiter. 'Then we can go to my place. It's just out along the road to Mende.'

Stewart's Alfa Spider sped up the steep hill out of Le Puy. He felt good. The possible coup of a journalistic lifetime was almost in the bag. Kate and Wendy could both go hang. He'd a good lunch in his belly, a fine bottle of claret too. The top was down and the warm breeze was ruffling their hair. Madonna was playing on the tape deck – he had thought of suggesting they listen to Mo's tapes straight away but decided to leave it. He had the joy of a stunning-looking woman sitting beside him. He felt as if he was back in his thirties. With this young lady all his problems would be solved.

Just past a large furniture store, approaching a trading zone, a slow-moving car impeded them. 'Get out of the way, you decrepit Frog!' he shouted, at the aged driver. They both laughed at the annoyance on the man's face. They waved at him as Stewart gunned the car, which leapt forward overtaking him. Neither was looking when the large articulated lorry swung out of a side road and they rammed straight into its side.

In the silence that followed the screeching of torn metal, Madonna continued playing. In the road, coated with blood, lay a packet of flea powder.

4

The following morning when Kate awoke she felt dreadful, as if she had consumed a huge amount of alcohol even though she hadn't. Sleep had not come easily for she had lain a long time tossing and turning, worrying about why Stewart was behaving in this way. Back in time she went, trying to discover a hint of when and why things had gone wrong. Surely it wasn't over her wanting to help her children. He hadn't given her a chance to explain, and of course she would have helped him in his venture – all she wanted was for him to be happy. And yet ... She shuddered at the memory of their ugly fight ... and to think that Steve had walked in on them ... The shame of that would always haunt her ...

What had started as a tiny doubt was beginning to grow, as if her anxiety and misery were fertilising it. Had he wanted them to row? Had he engineered the situation? Had he wanted to be free of her? She put her head under her pillow – not that it did any good: her thoughts followed her in the suffocating heat induced by the feathers.

She had put the light on, sat up and drunk a glass of water. If that was the case then she had to pull herself together, she had to plan, she had to know what she was going to do, how she was going to handle it. She was determined, if he had really gone for good, that no one, not even her children, was to know of her unhappiness. For one thing crying was not going to help.

The problem was that her tears didn't know that, and she shed them into her pillow until it, her cheek, her hair were sodden. She knew she would never sleep, doubted that she would ever sleep again . . . But she did.

In the morning, however, she felt as if she had been awake all night, as if she had cried all night. She felt an enormous lethargy and had, literally, to haul herself out of bed. In her bathroom she looked with longing at the bath but stepped purposefully into the shower. What was the point in soaking and going over in her mind everything that had preoccupied her during the night? She would get nowhere.

She made herself tea – the thought of food made her feel nauseous. She toyed with the idea of taking it down to the pool but that was what they had done together on so many mornings. Memories should be avoided. Instead she went straight into her workroom.

The last thing she wanted to do was work but she wondered if she could perhaps escape into her imaginary world where she was in control and where she could make happen whatever she wanted. She switched on Alice but this morning skipped the chat – that too was part of the recent past. She clicked on the *Bitter Memories* file. She read the first sentence of the first chapter and closed it. No, that was wrong for now – it was too painful for her to write; it would only feed her present predicament. Instead she created a new document. She paused, looking into space, thinking. *Jokers Wild*, she wrote, and then, underneath it, *A comedy*.

By lunchtime she had finished the first chapter. The words had poured out so that her fingers could barely keep up with them. That's how she had worked at the very beginning. When it was like a game, before the responsibilities had set in and mounted. Then her writing had slowed, become more laboured since she was conscious that she had to succeed. Now when she wrote, although she still loved it, there was always the thought of the bills that never stopped coming in and which were her obligation alone.

Quickly she read through this morning's work. The next time Portia asked her what her work plans were she had her reply all ready: 'A tale of middle-aged angst, cock-ups and the search for happiness.' She had been right: while she was working she was forgetting. And, more, this book had made her laugh.

She knew herself and she knew she could do no more for today; now she would think. It was what she always described as 'the marinating process' when she gave a lecture on writing, the time when she did nothing but let her mind create, imagine and plan for her, so that next time she came to the computer the following chapter would be ready and waiting to be put down on paper. Lectures! That was a possibility, and one that she must not let slip through her fingers. She pulled the telephone directory towards her. 'Jessica, what must you think of me?'

'Don't worry, Kate. Your son explained. I hope Sim is all right. I didn't know whether to telephone Sybil or not. It's always difficult in such circumstances, isn't it?'

'He's home now. He was talking about taking a long holiday. I think they both need it. But that drama was no excuse for my not coming back to you sooner.'

'It's a difficult time for you, I quite understand.'

Kate looked at the receiver with a puzzled expression. How could Jessica know that she was going through a 'difficult' time? Maybe she'd imagined it. 'I started a new book today,' she said. 'A new venture for me – a comedy. Something to keep me occupied.' How would she respond to that?

'Work is always the best palliative.'

She knew. She bloody well knew! But how? Well, she wasn't going to discuss it, she hardly knew the woman, but in any case she wasn't ready to do so. She might sound in control but in fact she felt as if all of her nerve endings were visible, covered by a sheet of glass, which at any moment might shatter and leave them raw and screaming in the air.

'How is Stewart?'

'He's fine.' She was quite proud of the control in her voice.

'Dreadful business!' Jessica tutted.

'*To* business,' Kate said briskly, not wanting sympathy, mindful of the tears she was holding back with effort.

'I've been thinking about your proposed venture, which was why I invited you over to dinner, so that we could discuss it in depth. I wanted you to see our barn – we have three and I've converted one, but the other two aren't done yet. I wondered if we could make one into a study-seminar sort of place. That is, if you don't think I'm being too pushy.'

'You're really interested?'

'Oh, yes. If you want me I'm here for you. I love to teach. You did say you'd have to look for premises, and it is lovely here, and we've the pool. I wouldn't have accommodation,

280

though. We'd have to put them into B-and-Bs as you suggested.' She knew she was talking too much, too fast, and committing herself too soon. She had not thought this through but she felt that if she didn't keep busy . . . Well, she didn't know what she would do.

'As partners do you mean?'

'Well, I hadn't really thought. We'd have to sort out the nitty-gritty. I'd be no use to you other than to lecture and do workshops. I wouldn't have the time, you see, for any administration. And I've no idea how businesses are run. Perhaps you could come over – say, lunch on Sunday?'

When the call was finished she congratulated herself: she really was coping remarkably well. If Stewart insisted on playing these silly games – Heavens, what would he think of all this? He'd be livid at not being consulted again. But if he was still being stupid by Sunday that was his problem. She'd invite Peter too – he'd be back by then. Come to think of it, she'd invited him anyway.

What if she'd invited him to dinner rather than lunch? What if they were having a *diner à deux* and Stewart walked in? How wonderful that would be, how jealous *he* would be! Or would he? She didn't know . . . She felt a lump rise in her throat, knew the tears would follow. *Keep moving, keep doing!* For once she listened to her inner voice.

'Lucy, I've got to go into Le Puy, to Bricolage. Anything you need?' She could see Lucy sunbathing in the orchard, Dominique at her side, tickling her bare stomach with a long blade of grass. Seeing them, their happiness, made her feel desperately sad. 'Shouldn't you two be working?' She hated herself for wanting to break up this moment for them, for speaking so sharply. But she couldn't stop herself.

'On a day like this?' Lucy propped herself up on one elbow, sounding drunk.

'There's a festival over near Rosières, perhaps you could do some business there.'

'The van's not working.'

'What the hell's wrong with it now?'

'Something to do with the camshaft, I think.' Lucy had stood up and was walking towards her through the long grass.

'Well, then, maybe Dominique could get the mower out and cut the grass.

'He's not your gardener.'

'I realise that, but in the circumstances I'd have thought he would want to help.'

'What circumstances?' Lucy was climbing the steps from the pool. Kate frowned. She had such a vacant look in her eyes again . . . Was she on . . . ? Not again! Surely not!

'Why should Dominique do it? Just because Stewart isn't here?' Her irritation reassured Kate, if she looked vague she wasn't sounding it.

'No, because of all the things I'm doing for you both.'

'I thought you were doing them because you wanted to help. No one forced you. No one tied you down and made you.' She giggled. 'Honestly, I do want to help.' If she offered then undoubtedly she *was* drunk, not high! But if it was simply alcohol, why were her eyes so pink, like a ferret's, just like Sybil's.

'Then cut the grass.'

'Today? It's too hot.'

'I would remind you, Lucy, that you asked for help. But I'm beginning to wonder if I might just as well have torn the money up.'

'Just because Stewart's pissed off you needn't take it out on us.'

'I'm not. I would just like someone to cut the bloody grass. Is that too much to ask?' She turned on her heel.

'Temper, temper!' she heard Lucy say, as she got to the gate. But she decided it would be politic to ignore her – this time.

As she parked her car outside Bricolage she hoped there would be no English inside, not if the news about Stewart was out. She could not bear the idea of all the sympathetic, curious looks she might meet.

From her bag she took out her list – all garden maintenance stuff. The house repairs were Stewart's responsibility, but the garden was down to her. She quickly found the anti-aphid spray, and a fork – her favourite had snapped only last week. She was sure they didn't make garden instruments to last as they had in her father's day. Finally she selected long-poled secateurs – she was going to have to do something with the buddleia this year.

'Madame Howard!'

It was the manager. Her heart sank. Not more new English people to be introduced to? She couldn't face that today.

'Hello.' She congratulated herself on the normality of her response and smile.

'We, all the staff, were desolated by the dreadful news.' Even though he spoke slowly she had to get him to repeat it before she understood what he meant.

Christ, she thought, even the shopkeepers know! She'd love to get her hands on all those who were spreading this gossip – though could it be gossip when it was undoubtedly true?

'That's very kind of you.' Again she switched on a successful smile.

'If there is anything we can do?'

'Thank you, but I can't think of anything.'

'Could I get him some books, magazines?'

'No, thanks, I write my own.' She laughed at that – a mite hysterical, it had to be said.

'Madame Howard, are you all right?' The manager looked shocked.

'Never felt better,' she lied.

'Only with Mr Dorchester in the hospital . . .'

The floor of the shop zoomed up as if to hit her in the face. 'You said?'

'The accident. Why? Did you not know?'

She did not stop to answer but fled from the shop, pushing through the other customers in panic. She could hear the screeching of terror in her head. *So that's why he didn't call you!* And she heard *that* with a sense of joyous release.

5

Having driven twice around the hospital grounds, unable to find a parking place, Kate abandoned her car in the middle of one of the roads that criss-crossed the site. She ran blindly until she found herself outside the maternity block, then she retraced her steps and hurtled down a road where she had seen a sign indicating *Urgence*. Presuming that meant Accident and Emergency, and remembering where she had come with Netta, she had just set off again when she heard someone shouting.

The man's French was too fast and voluble but from his gesticulations it was obvious that her car was the problem so she threw her keys at him and raced on. Eventually she was in the same room where she had been with Netta when they had come to find Sim. What little French she had deserted her as she tried to make the receptionist understand her.

After a lot of enunciating, pointing and finally writing down his name it was evident that Stewart was not here, but for the life of her she couldn't understand when the woman explained where he was. As she ran out of the door she wondered if he was even in this hospital – she hadn't asked the man in Bricolage, she had simply panicked and fled. At this point she cannoned into a young doctor – from his long white coat she assumed that that was what he was. Not thinking she said, 'Sorry.'

'May I help you?' he asked in English.

'Oh, please.' She clutched hold of his sleeve. 'I'm looking for my husband who might have been admitted . . . An accident.'

'And he is not in the casualty department?' The young man's English was grammatically perfect but heavily accented. She had become used to this in the French: it was as if they knew the language well but spoke it rarely and were uncomfortable with it when they did.

'No, he wasn't on their list.'

'Then we shall go to the admissions office.'

He held open the door of the *Bureau des Entrées*. Once inside he took control and spoke to a receptionist.

'He's in intensive care,' he said kindly to Kate. 'I'll show you.'

Kate followed him on legs that felt as if they were made of cotton wool. There was a strange ringing in her ears and she saw to neither right nor left. She could not focus straight ahead either – it was as if she were looking through a pair of binoculars. Her stomach had changed its position and her heart felt as if it was fighting to be free. She puffed as she raced to keep up with the doctor, who rang the bell of the ward and explained that Stewart Dorchester's wife was outside. When the automatic door buzzed he held it open for her. 'If you wait, a nurse will come to see you.'

She sat on one of the steel chairs and forced herself to take deep breaths, but it was a losing task. *Dear God, if you let him be all right, I'll do anything, anything* . . . She felt sick now, and she was sweating, she could feel it running down her back beneath her T-shirt. And she realised she hadn't thanked the young doctor – she hadn't even registered his name.

She looked up expectantly as the door swung open, and slumped back on the chair when she saw that it was not a nurse.

'Kate? It is Kate Howard, isn't it?'

'Yes.' The young man was standing over her but, given the swelling and dreadful bruising on his face, she did not recognise him.

'Tristram Hargreaves,' he said. 'Sorry about the face.'

'You were in the accident?'

'No, I had a row with my neighbour about a dog. So predictably English of me, wasn't it?' His attempt at a smile reminded him of the extent of his bruising and he grimaced. 'May I?' He indicated the chair beside her and sat down, placing a large black leather bag between his feet. She wished she had the courage to tell him to go away and leave her, that she didn't want to talk to anyone. 'I'm sorry to impose but this has all been one hell of a shock.'

Courtesy momentarily overtook her soaring fear. 'Were you here because of . . . ?' She gestured to her face.

'God, no. It's Mo. She's been in a crash.'

'Mo too?'

'Why? Who else is here?'

'Stewart.'

'When?'

'I'm not sure, today, I suppose. You see, I've only just heard.' And in some inexplicable way she felt ashamed at having to say those words as if she should have known exactly when and how.

'It happened to Mo yesterday. But I only found out today. She didn't come home, you see . . . And, well . . .' He laughed self-consciously. 'At first I thought she might have left me. Then I got worried and then this morning I got on the blower . . . I haven't even seen my car yet or what state it's in.'

'Where did it happen?'

'I don't know. Mo's out like a light. She was with someone but I don't know who. She must have given someone a lift. I've warned her never to do that. But tell Mo not to do something and she does it straight away! She's that sort . . .' The words were tumbling out of him. Kate felt sorry for him and the state he was in. Instinctively she put out her hand and covered his, giving it a small squeeze. He looked at her and his eyes, surrounded by bruised and swollen flesh, mirrored his fear. 'They only let me see her for a moment. She's got so many tubes and bandages it's hard to know it's her, but this bag is Mo's, so I have to accept that it is.' At which he began to make a rasping noise. It took Kate a little while to realise that he was crying. 'They say she won't ever walk again.' The ugly noise intensified.

'Poor Tristram.' Kate patted his hand. 'She'll be all right. She's in the right place. I hear this hospital is excellent.' She trotted out the right words to comfort him when she didn't want to, when she wanted to wrap herself in her own fear and worry, when she wished he would get up and go.

The door to the small waiting room swished open and a male nurse appeared. 'I'm sorry to have kept you waiting,' he said, in passable English to Tristram. 'Here – I think you'll find it's all there.' He handed over an envelope from which Tristram tipped Mo's rings and her gold chains, one with a St Christopher medallion. At the sight of them he made the strange noise again, but louder. 'Are you a relative of his?' The nurse turned to Kate.

'No. Just a friend. I've come to see my husband.'

'Your name?'

'Kate Dorchester.'

'You're Madame Dorchester?'

'Well, strictly speaking, I . . . Yes, I am,' she decided to say instead. If she said they weren't married maybe they wouldn't let her see him – hospitals could be funny about visitors.

'If you wouldn't mind waiting a moment.'

The nurse left them and Kate was left to comfort Tristram as best she could. 'I'm sure she'll be OK.' What stupid things people came out with in situations like this, she thought. How the hell did she know one way or the other what would happen to Mo? But Tristram didn't query her assessment, he just seemed grateful for her words.

'It's hard when it's someone you love, isn't it?' There she went again, tired old cliché after cliché.

'But you see, Kate, I don't love her and yet . . . I think I should. Especially now . . . with this.'

'You can't make yourself love someone, can you?'

'Not when you love someone else.'

'I see.' There she was again! She didn't *see* a damn thing. 'Who?' she asked, more out of politeness than anything else.

'Caroline.'

She felt the skin on her face stiffen. 'Caroline?' she said inanely.

'We go back a long way.'

'Does she feel the same about you?'

'I hope so.'

Well, I don't, she thought. Poor Steve, he'd been so

excited at meeting Caroline, convinced, she was sure, that he had found real love. From not wanting her son to get too involved with the girl she suddenly felt protective towards him and his new relationship. 'I doubt that Mo will be too happy about that,' she began, shocked by how spiteful she felt towards Tristram. She was unsure how to continue but was sidetracked by the reappearance of the male nurse with an older, female one.

'This is the senior nurse in this department, but she doesn't speak English.'

They shook hands formally. The new nurse launched into French, while the first one translated. 'If you wouldn't mind repeating that you are Madame Dorchester.'

'Of course.' Kate looked straight at the rather steely-eyed woman. 'I am the wife of Stewart Dorchester.'

More French followed. 'My colleague wants to know if you have any identification.'

'What on earth for?'

'We have to make certain.'

'Not on me, no.'

This was translated back and another voluble sentence followed.

'She wants to know why not.'

'Because I didn't know I was going to end up here when I left home.'

'Passport?'

'At home,' Kate lied. She had to – it had the wrong name on it.

'*Carte de séjour*?'

'No, at home.' She was certainly not about to admit that she hadn't got one.

'Driving licence?'

'Look, I understand that you French never go anywhere without a dossier of identification, but I am English and I

289

don't feel the need to. I want to see my husband. And I want to see him now, this instant.' Her cheeks felt wet as she put her hand up to them, she hadn't even been aware that she was crying.

'You see, Madame Dorchester, we find ourselves in a very delicate position. We have the other patients to consider – we cannot possibly have a scene.'

'A scene? What are you going on about?'

'Madame Dorchester is already at his bedside. There can't be two of you, now, can there?'

6

'So, did you ask this other person for identification?' Kate stood her ground. In the space of a few seconds she had gone from shock to anger. No one answered. 'Did you?' Her voice was rising and the 'Shush' from the male nurse fuelled her fury. 'Well, did you? Answer me that.'

The translation took place and from the sheepish expressions on their faces she knew that they hadn't and her confidence grew.

'You do realise you have an impostor in there? Someone saying that she is his wife when I am. She's lying. Ask Mr Hargreaves here.' This was better, she thought, as sense took over from rage.

'Yes. This is Stewart's wife,' Tristram assured them. 'I know them both. There must have been a mistake. I suggest you are much more careful in future. Look how you've upset poor Madame Dorchester.'

Kate could have kissed Tristram for his stalwart support. She waited impatiently as the interminable translation between the nurses took place.

Immediately there was a pause, Tristram jumped in:

'You've only her word for it, after all, haven't you?' The bruises, Kate decided, made him look even more fierce.

'Not so.' The male nurse wore an insufferably smug smile. 'Monsieur Dorchester himself says that the woman beside his bed is his wife.'

Just as it had in Bricolage, the floor of the waiting room seemed to fly up and hit her in the face and she swayed where she stood.

'He *what*?' Tristram asked for her. 'He's delirious.'

Both nurses went into a huddle, urgently whispering to each other.

'I am not at liberty to discuss Monsieur Dorchester's condition with those who are not his relatives.' The male nurse looked pointedly at Kate. 'However, my colleague and I are in agreement that it is not breaking a confidence to tell you that Monsieur Dorchester has regained consciousness and is lucid and has assured us that the woman is his wife. Since visiting is restricted to close family members, Madame, we suggest it would be better if you left.'

'I'm not going anywhere.'

'Please, Madame, co-operate. If Monsieur Dorchester wishes to see you he can tell us, and if you leave your telephone number . . .' Kate didn't give him the chance to finish his instructions before, with a strength which obviously took him by surprise, she pushed the male nurse out of the way and swept past him. She was through the door before anyone was aware of what she was doing.

She sped along the corridor with its subdued lighting. On either side were the brightly lit rooms where the patients lay. Most were lying flat, with so many tubes and, in some cases, bandages concealing their faces it was impossible to identify them. Down one side and up the other she ran but seeing the nurses bearing down on her she turned tail and went back the way she had come. This time she concentrated on any women sitting or standing by the beds.

It was the shoes that gave her away. She had her back to the corridor, and her hunched shoulders indicated that she was afraid of something or someone coming up behind her. But on her feet were sandals of such thin leather they looked like laces. The vertiginously high heels were multi-coloured and at the back of her ankle the buckle was decorated with a pretty daisy.

'Wendy!' Kate said the name quite quietly, no hysteria, no screaming, no anger, just surprise. The nurses had caught up with her and had grabbed her by the arms. She tried to shake them off but their hold was too tight. 'Wendy!' she repeated, as if she wasn't sure she had said it the first time.

Slowly the woman turned. She smiled graciously as if still at her own party. 'Kate, how nice to see you.' The calmness of her voice made the nurses ease their hold on Kate's upper arms. 'I thought you would come.'

'Of course I bloody well came. *Once* I'd heard the news.' She peered past Wendy. At the sight of a battered Stewart, linked to a series of monitors with not only blood but two plastic cartons of a clear fluid dripping into his arm, she clapped her hand over her mouth to stop herself calling out to him. The machines clicked and hummed. She stood stunned, not knowing what she wanted, what she needed to do. Stewart's eyes were closed. How would he have reacted if he had seen her there? Would he have been embarrassed? Would he have bluffed his way out of this situation? Would he have been pleased to see her?

Wendy had taken up a position between Kate and the bed. There was a proprietorial air about her as if she was protecting him from her. How dare she. But . . .

'Will he be all right?' Her concern for him dealt a blow to

all the other emotions scudding about her mind. 'Is he sleeping or has he . . .' She couldn't form the words 'lapsed into a coma'. If she said it then it would be so. 'Is he badly hurt? What happened to him?'

'He's sleeping. The doctors expect him to make a full recovery. He had a collapsed lung and some internal bleeding, which they were able to stem. Not like the poor bitch with him. He'll be fine, Kate. Promise.' Wendy put her hand on Kate's arm, which galvanised her. She shook it away as if it were a snake.

'Perhaps you would have the courtesy to explain yourself to me. Outside, I don't want him disturbed,' Kate said pointedly. She swung round, sure that Wendy would follow her. As she strode back up the corridor on her practical, soft-soled Clark's sandals, she could hear the click-clack of Wendy's heels behind her.

Tristram was still in the waiting room, looking even more lost than when Kate had left him. He jumped to his feet as she entered. 'Are you all right, Kate? You don't look well,' he fussed. 'Wendy!' he said, his voice brimming with surprise as she joined them. 'You!'

'Yes, little old me.' She giggled.

'The nurses tell me you claimed to be his wife. Why?' Kate asked, without preamble.

'Because I almost am.'

'I beg your pardon?'

'You heard.'

'I want to know what you mean by "almost".'

'Do you want me to go?' Tristram looked as if he longed to be anywhere but here.

'Stay.' Wendy pointed at the chair he had been sitting on. 'I don't want to be left with Kate, she's bigger than me. It might get physical and I wouldn't stand a chance.' She smiled unpleasantly.

293

'You didn't answer my question.' Kate decided not to give her the satisfaction of rising to the insult.

'You don't want to know.'

'But I do.'

'It's a long story and goes back a long way.'

'I've nowhere to go. I'm all ears.'

'Well, you asked. Stewart and I have been lovers for years – nine, at least, I've never kept count. Of course he had other women, but I didn't mind. After all, I was married, and in any case he always came back to me.'

At this Kate's hand itched to slap the smug expression from the other woman's face, but she controlled herself. For the first time in years she was longing for a cigarette.

'He'd been nagging me to go to France with him for ages. He'd always longed to do it – as, no doubt, you know, Kate. I wasn't prepared to leave my husband for the peasant life – I liked my standard of living too much. I suggested we compromise. If he persuaded you to move then I'd get my husband to buy us a holiday home. Which he did. Men are so easy to manipulate, aren't they, Kate? Oh, sorry – of course, you wouldn't know how to, would you?' Again the supercilious smile.

Kate took a deep breath. Wendy's gratuitous unpleasantness was meant to annoy her, to make her lose control. She was not about to give her that satisfaction. 'So why did you change your mind? Why did you leave your husband?' She congratulated herself on the steadiness of her voice.

'Stewart begged me to. He said he couldn't live without me. And then, silly me, after all these years, well, I gave in. You know what he can be like, Kate.'

'Funny. Your husband says he threw you out.' She bent down and picked up her bag from the floor. She wanted to get out, breathe some fresh air, get away from this bitch. 'Coming, Tristram?'

Tristram leapt from the chair as if it were electrified, then winced at the pain that shot through his chest.

At the door Kate turned. 'Who was with him?'

'Why, Mo, of course. Didn't you know?'

Tristram dropped Mo's heavy bag on the floor with a thud. 'Mo? She was with him?'

'Quite the little mystery, isn't it?' Wendy patted her hair, straightened her skirt. 'But, then, she's an attractive woman, and you know Stewart, he never could resist. Excuse me.' She made an exaggerated show of moving past Kate. In doing so, she brushed against Kate's breasts. 'You know what Stewart once said? He finds large breasts quite disgusting.' And, with a giggle, she skipped down the corridor back to his bedside.

'What a cow!'

'Don't insult the cows, Tristram.' Purposefully Kate swung the strap of her handbag over her shoulder. 'If I can find my car, do you fancy a drink?'

7

Kate felt quite odd as she sat in the Palais. There was bustle about her as the high-school children clattered in at the end of their day for their Coke, a smoke and a flirt. She saw them but she could only hear them as if their noise was filtered through thick cloth. It was a hot day, but she felt ice cold. She waited for Tristram, who had gone to the loo, and wished she hadn't suggested this drink. It had seemed a good idea at the time, a way of exiting with dignity, she supposed. Now she knew she would have been better off alone.

'Christ! What a day!' Tristram sat down heavily on the chair opposite her.

'You can say that again.' She smiled at him to make up for wishing him not here. She felt mean – after all, he had had his share of shocks too.

'Ha, Madame. Monsieur Stewart, he is well?' The proprietress asked.

'He's doing fine, Madame, thank you.' She smiled again and marvelled at how she could carry on with the social niceties while reeling inside. They ordered a carafe of wine.

'I'm so sorry, Kate.'

'Me too. I mean for you, not me.' She managed a small laugh. 'You have far more on your plate, and at your age too. Are the doctors sure Mo is paralysed? Isn't it early days for such a prognosis?'

'They seem certain enough.'

'I've heard of cases where, after a time, the feeling comes back. Perhaps Mo will be one of the lucky ones.'

'Perhaps. I've decided it's best to look at the worst scenario, then there are no shocks to come. If the doctors are wrong it will be a lovely surprise. *Merci*.' He thanked the waiter for the wine. 'But what will you do? You think I'm worse off? Hell, what a bummer! What a four-ace bitch! He can't love her, it must be a physical thing – I know about those sorts of relationships.' In his turn he managed to laugh.

'And that would make it all right? Not in my book, Tristram. If you really love someone you don't need anyone else – or you shouldn't. He might not love her but he wanted her, and over me. So that's that.' She was surprised that she felt able to talk to this young man about her problems – when he was young enough to be her son. The last weeks, it would seem, had seen many changes in her.

'Are you just going to let her win? Just like that?'

'It's not a competition, Tristram. And if I look at it as dispassionately as I can, he's not much of a prize, is he?'

Had she said that? *Wonders will never cease!* But was that how she really felt? *Don't let it slip away!* 'Will you manage? What about the hospital expenses? Don't you have to pay twenty-five per cent of all treatment in the French system? Even that's going to amount to a pretty penny.'

'That's been occupying my mind, as you can imagine. We're not in the system here. We're OK for the time being. We've got our E111 forms, so the NHS will cough up for her treatment now. But long term . . . I suppose the ideal is to go home.'

'What would stop you?'

'Things.' He felt himself become flustered. 'Money, mainly.' Well, that was the truth. He grinned inwardly.

'Is there anything I can do to help *pro tem*?'

'You're very kind.' She was more than that: she was behaving brilliantly. He had nearly not taken her up on the offer of a drink for fear she might cry all over him and he wouldn't know what to say. Instead she was thinking of him. Suddenly he thought of his own mother and home-sickness hit him like a tidal wave. He stood up. 'I've got to get back to the hospital. I think I should be there when she wakes up.'

'Yes, you must.'

'Will you be all right?'

'Of course I will.'

He swung Mo's heavy bag over his shoulder. 'It feels like she's got bricks in here.'

'You know young women and their makeup.'

He turned to go. And then, as if changing his mind, turned back. 'You don't know why Mo was with Stewart, do you? I didn't realise until Wendy said. I assumed the wrecked car they talked about was mine.'

'Sorry, Tristram. I haven't the foggiest idea.'

'They said it happened on the road to Mende. What were they doing there?'

'I can't help you Tristram, I'm afraid.'

Left alone she wondered if she would be all right or if this strange calm she was feeling would leave her. Then what would she be like? And Tristram had a point: why had the two of them been together and on that road? And then she found herself wondering if perhaps there had been something between them, as Wendy had implied, or had that just been bitchiness on her part? Evidently she did not know Stewart as well as she thought she did. After all, if he had been having an affair with Mo, Kate would have been the last to know. *Don't feel sorry for yourself. You've had doubts long enough.* 'I never did!' She looked around her, aghast at having said that aloud. But, then, so often – too often for comfort – her intrusive thoughts told her a truth she did not want to hear. She poured herself another glass of wine. At least now she was alone to think.

'Kate, my darling! I've just seen Tristram. He told me you were here.' It was Netta, peering anxiously at her. 'Now, if you want me to bugger off, just say so. If not, I'm a good listener.'

'Sit down. Join me.' She waved to the waitress. '*Encore une,*' she said, which was just about all the French she could muster today.

'No, not that stuff. This calls for a proper drink. I've always found in an emotional crisis that champagne invariably helps. It's something to do with the bubbles. My treat.'

'Netta, you can't afford to buy me champagne.'

'I've always got some loot put by for emergencies and this, from what I hear, fits the bill.' Taking control, Netta recalled the waitress and reordered. 'Now, are we nursing a broken heart? Planning how to get someone to do a hit job

298

for you? I hear the Russians are very reasonably priced. Or resigned?'

'Numb, Netta. I don't know what I feel.'

'What an arsehole he is. And what a nasty little tart Wendy is. Tristram told me what she said – I think you have perfectly lovely boobs. She's just jealous, with those tired manilla-envelope things she's got.'

'I don't think they are, Netta. But nice try.' Kate smiled. 'And poor Tristram.'

'Poor Tristram indeed. Now he really is stuck with Mo.'

'What? You mean he could never leave her now? Guilt and all that?'

'Exactly. It's almost Greek tragedy, isn't it? But maybe he'll persuade himself he loves her. His sort often do.'

'What does that mean? He's always struck me as rather a nice boy.'

'Oh, he is. But weak, you see. Easily led. I'm rather pleased. At least my Caroline will be safe from him now.'

'Netta! You can't say that! Poor Mo!'

'But I can. I didn't take to her at all, you know. It would be total hypocrisy for me to say otherwise.'

'But she's paralysed.'

'Oh, yes, that bit's unfortunate. I mean I wouldn't wish that on her, but on the other hand . . .' She smiled slyly but suddenly became serious. 'I think I should tell you before anyone gossips to you. I knew about Stewart and Wendy.'

'You didn't say.'

'I've made it a rule never to divulge gossip of infidelity. Either your friend doesn't believe you or hates you for telling her, or goes back to the sod. Whichever, the messenger always ends up in the wrong.'

'Who told you?'

'Sybil was the first. Instinct with her, bless her. They're

going on a cruise, you know. I do hope she doesn't throw Sim overboard.' She laughed.

'Netta!'

'And Peter told me in the most discreet and roundabout way.'

'You've seen Peter?'

'He took me to dinner the other night. I think he was lonely and needed someone to talk to. Lovely meal! I'll be anyone's agony aunt for good grub.'

'Poor Peter.' She found, to her discomfort, that she didn't like to hear that Netta had been dining with him, which shocked her. *So much for being the deceived one.* She shook her head to shut out the unpleasant truth. But from the way Netta spoke of it, it had not been a romantic meal.

'I think he's quite pleased. I gather it was a fairly disastrous marriage. Men are so odd, the muddles they get themselves into. Look at Tristram. But, and this is in strict confidence, Kate . . .' she leant forward with a conspiratorial air '. . . if Stewart thinks he's landed in a feather bed with Wendy, he's in for a shock. Peter won't pay out happily.'

'Why can women marry for money and men not?'

'Don't be reasonable, Kate. This is not the time. A good dollop of healthy loathing will stand you in good stead.'

'You know, I think a part of me deep down already knew about Stewart. I just wasn't prepared to acknowledge it.'

'And hence the need to keep telling yourself how happy you were?'

'Yes, just as you said.'

'What now?'

'How do you decide? How long does one give oneself? I know one thing. I'm not leaving here. I like it here. If they stay, so be it. It might be embarrassing but I'm not selling up for them.'

'Darling! I just knew you were a gutsy doll!'

It was night by the time Tristram got home. He had sat holding Mo's hand, talking to her – just as he'd seen people do in films – until his bottom ached from sitting and his hand from gripping hers.

In the dark he nearly fell over a basket on the doorstep. He picked it up and carried it inside. Max whimpered with joy at his return, rolling on the floor, paws up in happy submission. He patted the dog. 'Sorry, old mate, leaving you so long,' he said, as he filled Max's water bowl and ripped open the bag of dog food he'd remembered, in all the drama, to buy for him.

As the dog ate hungrily he inspected the basket. It was from Martin and his wife – a jar of what looked like cassoulet, and an apple pie, with an almost illegible note that said they were both sorry to hear about Mo. Funny bugger, he thought. He tries to kill me one day and gives me friendship the next. He'd go and see them in the morning and make things up.

He heated the cassoulet on the stove. It looked grim but smelt wonderful. Presentation of food obviously did not feature large in Martin and Giselle's kitchen. He opened a bottle of good wine he'd been saving, rather than drink the cheap, acidic stuff he'd bought in bulk and to which he had never quite taken. He ate in his armchair, watching Sky News but not really taking it in.

If Mo didn't recover he was trapped. He poured another glass of the wine, as if to console himself. How could he leave her now? How could he ever return to Caroline? Would he begin to hate Mo? Would she hate him? And what about the drug people looking for her? Would they hurt her now or would they turn their anger on him? 'There are so many imponderables, Max, old boy.' The dog looked at him solemnly. Perhaps they could let this house and move as she had suggested. But who, other than a lunatic such as himself, would want to live in such an isolated spot. And in any case the heavies would find them – it was only a matter of time. He was almost resigned to that. He should have stayed in London, where he knew the people, the ropes. He'd pandered to a silly dream that the grass was going to be greener. Instead? He felt he had landed in a mire.

Once the news was over he pulled Mo's heavy bag towards him. What had mystified him was that no one had got in touch with him when the accident had happened. She must have had something in there to identify her. Within the big black leather bag was a small pouch in which she normally kept her passport, her credit cards – that was, when she could still use them. It was empty. There was a large bag of makeup – typically Mo – some chewing-gum, two hundred francs and a book. The hospital had been right. There was nothing in there to identify her.

How odd. Had her passport been stolen? He stood up and crossed to the small desk in the corner of the room. In the top drawer he found the passport, her credit and blood-transfusion cards. She'd removed them on purpose. What the hell for?

He went back to the easy chair, picked up the bag and began to remove the rest of the contents. There were some audiotapes, two small red-leather books and a folder of photos.

The list of figures and names in the books puzzled him at first. 'Good God!' He opened the second, and was pulled up short by two names. The cunning creature, he thought. The photos were all of Mo with the well-known people whose names were in the small ledgers. Someone had taken these pictures as the punters had accepted the drugs from Mo. And the tapes?

Two at a time he went up the stairs. In their bedroom he grabbed the tape recorder she kept there. Back in the sitting room he listened to a few, not all. On some the quality was bad, on others the conversations were damagingly distinct. Clever girl, he found himself thinking.

So what had she been doing with Stewart, carrying these?

Journalism! That was it. Was she selling them to him? Was he going to use them in some way? Would Kate have known and kept mum about them?

And why no identification? For once Mo had thought ahead – in case there was an accident, just as had happened.

There was an angle here that he had to work out. To help him he fetched another bottle of his precious wine and, Max at his side, sat down to think.

Chapter Seven

August

1

Kate wondered how other women, with problems such as hers, managed if they didn't have the advantage of work as she did. For days now she had got up at six, made her tea and begun to write. The words poured out on to the machine, and the characters she was creating took over her life. They infused her mind so that there was no room for anything else.

The minute she stopped working, when hunger came, when her hands ached, when her body was stiff, then the worry, the grief and the anger rushed back like a tidal wave. Worst of all were the nights when, though she was exhausted, the moment her head touched her pillow the fury and bitterness returned elbowing sleep out of the way. She would think of the past and long for it, and at times weep for it. She mourned for the love she had thought was to be for ever. Then she would think of what was to be, and her mind would shy away from the emptiness of her future. She would rage, holding whole conversations of what she would say to him when she saw him, how she would tell him in no uncertain terms what she thought of him. And time and again she practised the smart, cutting remarks with which she would destroy Wendy.

Revenge, that's what she needed. She couldn't destroy his clothes, he had already taken them. Instead she made outlandish plans, which ranged from sending him unpleasant things in the post, except she didn't know where he was living, to tampering with his car brakes, not that she had the least idea of how to achieve that.

The idea of that woman in her car, in her seat made her seethe with fury. She'd demand the insurance payout – it was hers, after all . . . or was it? When she'd bought it she'd said, 'See, I've registered it in your name so it's really yours.' And he'd argued but she wouldn't relent. Bloody fool she'd been!

At least the house was secure. She broke out in a sweat at how nearly she had put it in joint ownership. She'd planned to, had asked for it to be done, but the *notaire* hadn't understood and the deeds were drawn up in her name only. Rather than delay the purchase, she had signed intending to change things later. But when she tried to, it became so complicated that they'd decided not to bother. They were content, it wasn't that much of a problem. What was hers was his, it was that simple.

Now she could kiss the lawyer for having been thick. What would she have done if Stewart had been able to insist on his half of the house? She'd only wanted to do it to make him feel secure. At that memory a tear slid down her cheek and plopped on to the pillow. Many followed.

Everything hurt, but perhaps the cruellest blow was that at the same time as she had been so deliriously happy to have found him, he and Wendy were already planning their deception of Peter and herself.

Of course! She sat up in the bed. Her sunglasses! He'd said he'd lent them to a woman he'd met in Bricolage when she'd been in London. Was that Wendy? More than likely. And the scarf he'd said was Netta's. He'd slipped up there, he was lucky she hadn't twigged. How pleased he must have been that she was away. Had he taken the opportunity and brought her here? Had they slept in this very bed? She switched on the light and pushed back the covers as if the sheets could tell her. She *had* to find out. She would have to ask him. She couldn't continue to sleep here if they had been in it together, made – No! She wouldn't even think of what they did as *making love*. It would have been sex, lust, not what Kate and Stewart had had. How could she ask him? How would she form the words? How humiliating to ask. Better if she presumed they had and have the bed and the linen burnt.

Quickly she got out, wrapped herself in her robe, padded into her bathroom and looked at her soaps, the oils, the lotions she indulged herself with. Had Wendy used them too? She grabbed at some and noisily threw them into the bin, then more until the shelves were empty.

Towels!

Get a grip of yourself. Don't be so stupid! You don't know! Stop it!

Despondently she sat on the lid of the loo. It was true. She didn't know. Surely he wouldn't have. Surely he had more taste than that. *Taste? He's not showing much of that choosing Wendy.*

'And over me!'

That's better.

She might have been a fool not to suspect but he was a fool to be with Wendy. Why, Peter had said she never read but shopped. Stewart would be bored rigid with her in a week or two.

They go back a long way.

Yes, but an illicit affair had an excitement and an edge to

it, which would disappear once they were settled into domesticity – everyone knew that. No, it wouldn't, couldn't last.

Surely you won't have him back!

I don't know.

After the way he's treated you?

How can I cope on my own? How do I deal with the loneliness?

You do. That's all there is to it. Thousands do. What makes you so special? I'm so unhappy! And I didn't get my sunglasses back!

She spent hours arguing with herself, back and forth. Finally she would give up and return to her writing – the one place she felt safe.

The book grew apace. At this rate it would soon be finished. And then what would she do? How would she keep the monstrous fears at bay? How would she fill the hours? She began to think of taking a holiday to get right away from here.

Each morning she phoned the hospital to check on his progress. Invariably she was asked if there was a message to give him, but she always said no. Who was calling? She always answered, 'A friend.' The afternoon she went to the travel agent to get brochures for the holiday she couldn't get excited about, she even drove to the hospital. She sat in her car for some time, watching the comings and goings. Eventually she drove through the gates but turned round and went back out again.

Oddly, it was as if the rest of her world knew that she wanted to be alone for the telephone rarely rang, and it was several days before she registered that she hadn't seen Lucy, and that there was no sign of life in the house tucked away across the orchard. She feared Lucy had run away again. But this time she found she could not think about it, as if she had to reserve all her mental energies for herself. Then, when she finally remembered that she hadn't checked her post for ages, she found a note from her daughter in the box to say they had gone away to friends for a week and she would phone, but she hadn't. She didn't even fret that they should have been working with the pizza van. And then she was glad Lucy was not there. It was not in Kate's nature to agonise about her problems with others, she needed to work them out for herself.

With her writing going as well as it was, and with energy only for that, she now regretted the lunch party she had planned. But she couldn't put Jessica off again: it wouldn't be fair, and far too rude. And in any case, if money was going to become a problem, she needed to see her to try to work something out. She'd invited Peter, out of courtesy for all he was doing for Steve in his business, she could hardly put him off either. And no doubt he'd already arranged to give Netta a lift and she couldn't disappoint her.

However, when it came to it, she found the preparation of the meal as cathartic as her writing was. She had decided on an avocado mousse with giant prawns. Then they would have barbecued lamb, with the special sauce she'd invented, and different salads – she loved preparing salads even more than eating them. She'd do individual summer puddings and then cheese. As for wine, she'd no idea. In Stewart's cellar she looked at the rows and rows of bottles and hadn't the foggiest what went with what. She'd ask Peter to choose.

On the Sunday morning she was up early. She showered only when she had prepared all she could before the guests came. She had changed into a white cotton Indian trouser suit she'd bought ages ago by mail order, but which Stewart disliked. She'd loved it and, as she inspected herself in the mirror, she felt that wearing it was a gesture of independence – at least, that was what she told herself.

The setting of her dining-table had always been important to her, and the table under the pergola was to be no exception. She scattered small branches of rosemary over the stone surface and arranged Canterbury bells, larkspur and poppies in a large azure-coloured bowl. She admired the plates, gaudy with their bright blue and yellow flowers, which she had purchased for outside eating but which she often used in winter for they reminded her of fun and summer. She collected the blue-stemmed glasses and the blue-tinted water jugs, the blue-handled cutlery and the sky blue napkins. When she stood back and studied it she decided it looked perfect.

'You found me. Not too difficult, I hope?' she asked Jessica and Geoffrey, her husband, as they clambered out of a British-registered car that had seen better days.

'Easy as pie. And it's no distance – we're on this side of St Paulien, you see.'

'So if we can work something out it wouldn't be too far for you to travel.'

'Exactly!' Jessica had brought with her a box of canapés, lovingly prepared, and Geoffrey had a *vrac*, the plastic container in which cheap wine was sold in bulk.

'Since it's so hot it'll go down a treat.' Geoffrey handed her the *vrac* with as much loving respect as if he was giving her a crate of Puligny Montrachet. At the sight of it her tastebuds winced and she berated herself for being such an ungrateful snob.

'How thoughtful of you,' she said. 'I'll put it in the cellar so it will stay cool.' She carried it through as they oohed and aahed over her sitting room. Now, how did she handle this problem? Cheap white wine, she thought, was a worse abomination than cheap red. But it was kind of them, when they were short of money.

Somewhere – she searched at the back of the cellar – she'd a box of small carafes. She'd decant her own white into them for everyone but Jessica and Geoffrey. That way honour would be saved. There'd be no problem with the red, or would Peter choose rosé?

At the thought of him she stopped her search. Kate didn't understand herself, but that was nothing new. She had to acknowledge that she was excited at the prospect of seeing him again. Yet how could she be, when she was stacked with misery over Stewart? How could she be heartbroken yet look forward to seeing another man? It didn't make sense. It was so shallow of her. *But then he is rather* . . . Shut up!

She rinsed out the carafes as she heard the expensive purring of Peter's car. She knew how flustered she seemed from the quizzical look Netta gave her as she stepped out of Peter's silver Mercedes. Was it silly and uncharitable of Kate now to find herself wishing she hadn't invited her?

'Might we ask how Stewart is – or is that tactless of me?' Netta kissed Kate on both cheeks and one over, French style.

'I'm glad you asked. I haven't any idea.'

Netta insisted on accompanying her and Peter to the cellar to select the wine. In the circumstances Kate felt she couldn't blame her – Netta must be picking up on her thought waves. At this rate they risked looking ridiculous, competing for a man at their age. Was that what she was doing? Of course she wasn't! *You know damn well it is.* As they left Peter paused. 'Would you excuse us, Netta. I need to have a word with Kate.'

They waited for Netta to leave.

'Kate, I just had to tell you how sorry I am at the

behaviour of our spouses. I had known for some time but felt there was no point in warning you. Why make you miserable for longer than necessary?'

'How long have you known about them?'

'I found out five, maybe six years ago, but I know now it had been going on for longer than that.'

At that Kate's heart sank. So what Wendy had said was true.

'And you forgave her?'

'I suppose I didn't care enough to make a fuss. And whenever I thought it was over and decided to let sleeping dogs lie, it would start up again. It's very rude of me, Kate, but quite honestly I was more furious about the man she had chosen – I never liked Stewart, you see.'

'I don't understand how you could live with her, knowing what was going on.'

'It was greed. Pure and simple. I didn't want to frighten the tigress in her lair – moneywise. But now I've made suitable arrangements.'

Then Netta had been right – he was avoiding paying Wendy off. Part of her was shocked and thought him diabolical – she was his wife after all. But another part of her listened to the information with glee.

'So why now?'

'She invited him to our house. And you too. And I loathed her for that. In a way I'm relieved. Our marriage has been mortally ill for some time. At least now the pain is over. I should never have married Wendy – it wasn't fair on either of us. But one does these inexplicable things, doesn't one?'

'Yes, I did.' She laughed. 'I should never have married my first husband. We were totally incompatible.'

'It seemed a good idea at the time?'

'Actually, no. Looking back, I think I just slid into it

somehow, that it would have caused too much kerfuffle not to have married him. Aren't we careless with our love when young?'

'Sadly so, but no doubt we'll fall in love and do it all again.'

'Not me!' But her voice lacked conviction.

The lunch was a success, although Netta had sat in the wrong place and got Jessica's carafe of acidic wine rather than Kate's. Her face was a picture as she took the first sip then pointedly drank no more while Jessica looked gratifyingly puzzled at the excellence of hers and finished the lot.

Having rashly committed herself to Jessica's plan Kate watched her carefully throughout the meal and found that she liked her more as it progressed. She was full of plans and ideas, and she had the sort of optimistic enthusiasm that Kate often lacked. She'd brought a business plan with her, projections, and a mapped-out advertising campaign.

'You have been busy, Jessica.'

'I think Kate should be paid rent for the facilities she's providing.' Peter looked up from the figures he'd been poring over.

'I offered Jessica the use of them.'

'Kate, you should always start a venture like this with the parameters firmly set in case you fall out later. You never know what's going to happen in life, do you?'

'That's true.' And Kate realised she was laughing again, had done so several times that day.

Jessica was keen to start advertising immediately so that, hopefully, they would have the first students the following year. She had found an artist to do painting courses, a poet, someone willing to teach the guitar and she was keen to add cookery classes when she found a tutor. They agreed that the courses should go in fortnightly blocks with a fortnight's gap, and take place in the summer. 'Otherwise

Kate might find sharing her property becomes irksome,'
Peter advised. Kate didn't say that, without Stewart, and
Lucy hardly there, she would welcome the company. And
she had thought that she might well get on with the sort of
person who went on such a holiday.

As she was seeing them off with much kissing and plans
to meet up again she felt more relaxed and happier than
she had for days. And she found that she did not resent
Netta being with Peter, which puzzled her. How could she
swing from one feeling to another with such speed?

The pizza van drove up the hill, far too fast, wobbling
dangerously, and screeched to a halt inches from Peter's
car. Lucy was driving – Kate hadn't known that she had a
licence. She and Dominique piled out, giggling senselessly.
Two others, cold pizza in their hands, tumbled out of the
back. Their hair was long, tangled and dirty. The man was
heavily tattooed, and the girl could have done with more of
her flesh covered.

Kate stepped forward, expecting to be introduced, but
Lucy flapped her hands impotently in the air, laughing
helplessly at a joke she could not share. Dominique
shrugged his shoulders in what she took to be an apology.
Then they waved, giggled more and sauntered cockily
across Kate's garden.

'Who's that?' Peter asked, with unmasked concern.

'My daughter and her husband. I don't know the other
two.' Kate's face was equally concerned.

'Call me any time if you need assistance.'

'Don't be so middle-aged, Peter. They're young and
having fun,' Netta admonished.

And drunk or, worse, stoned, thought Kate.

2

Early the following morning the phone rang.

'Kate, it's me. I need to see you.'

'What for?'

'I have to explain myself to you.'

'That might be courteous.'

'Kate, are you very cross with me?'

'Not so much now, Stewart. Not nearly as much.' She was pleased with the way she had said that and, what was more, it was true.

He needed to see her he'd said. Kate sat for a long time over her coffee, debating with herself. She was unsure if she wanted to see him. One moment she did, the next she didn't. That she was afraid to see him was probably closer to the truth. What if it was just to sort out matters between them? How devastated she would be. What if he was going to ask to come back? How confounded she would be. *Would be? You're doing pretty well as it is!* She was happy he 'needed' to see her but at the same time fearful to meet him. She imagined a reconciliation, then rejected it out of hand. She would forgive him and yet felt she never could. She would not go. Yes, she would. She was confused, and being aware that she was only added to her bewilderment.

Finally she decided that she should go: if she didn't face him, and presumably *her*, she would probably regret it for the rest of her life.

She took time over getting ready. She washed her hair and took extra care with her eye makeup – she went for the subtle look since Wendy was always plastered with the stuff. There was no need for foundation with her tan, which always made her look more attractive. She tried on several outfits before settling on a white skirt teamed with a navy and white striped top and her navy blazer – despite the heat. It had cost her a small fortune and consequently gave her much-needed confidence. Still not satisfied she chose a scarlet silk scarf, which she decided set off the outfit perfectly. Her patent leather pumps were the final touch – a conscious opposite to the clickety-clack shoes that *she* always wore.

No one answered the telephone in Lucy's house and, looking out of the window, Kate saw that all the blinds were still closed although the front door was wide open. She had spent the evening hoping Lucy would come over and talk, tell her news, but she had simply popped in to borrow some milk and left again. There was a barrier between them which, if invisible, was there just as it had been years ago when Lucy had been a difficult teenager. Kate hadn't surmounted it then, she doubted if she would this time either.

They had been noisy in the night, skinny-dipping in the pool, playing music far too loud. She had refrained from telling them to be quiet since it was the first time Lucy had done anything like that, but she hoped she didn't do it too often or the neighbours in the village would soon be complaining. Instead Kate left her a note, explaining that she had gone shopping – she had no intention of letting anyone know she was seeing Stewart until she knew which way the wind was blowing.

To say that she was nervous as she parked her car in the hospital grounds was an understatement. She felt as if she would throw up at any minute. It was only as she walked towards the building to which Stewart had been moved that she noticed the red statue of the Madonna, which guarded the town, looked down on the patients here. She hoped Stewart couldn't see it – he would be enraged by it.

She found his floor. As she stood outside the door of

room eighteen, she found her hand wavering before it, much as it did every morning before she pulled the shutters back. Then she tapped.

'*Entrez.*'

There was no Wendy, she saw immediately with relief. And Stewart was not in his bed but in a chair, a rug over his knees and a drip still in his arm. He wasn't having to share his room with another patient. And, yes, the Red Lady was visible from his window.

'You look well.' He put out his hand towards her, not to shake hers but to touch her. She ignored the gesture.

'And the Red Lady is looking after you.' She said this with an amused look as she put the fruit she had brought him into a bowl – what a predictable thing to have done.

'Actually, I seem to be getting rather fond of her. She grows on one.'

'Especially in the circumstances.'

'What circumstances?'

'Being hurt, of course.' What else could he have thought she meant? 'I was very sorry to hear of the accident. Is there any news about Mo?'

'I'd rather not talk about her.'

'It must be hard for you knowing how badly she's—'

'I don't feel guilty, if that's what you mean.'

'Oh, I thought you would have.' Should she have said that? *Why not? It's true.*

'Accidents happen. I've seen her – they wheeled me over. She doesn't hold it against me. She said exactly the same. And I want to talk to you, but not about her. Please sit down and stop fiddling.'

She took a seat opposite him. It was strange to see him again after all the thinking and hating and longing she had done. In an odd way it was as if she were watching someone else sitting here, that it wasn't her. She waited.

316

'Kate, I've been an idiot.'

She could have agreed with him but didn't.

'I should never have hurt you the way I did. You didn't deserve that.'

She looked at her hands neatly arranged in her lap.

'I don't know what got into me. Male menopause, I suppose.'

A bit late for that, she thought.

'Only . . . I want you to forgive me. Kate, I want to come home.'

She looked up at him now. He was saying the words she had wanted to hear and yet dreaded. He had such a pleading expression. Most definitely she wished he hadn't said them and she didn't like him begging.

'Wendy tells me that you and she go back a long way. That your meeting up here was a long-term plan. She implied that you don't like my breasts.'

'She what?' He laughed. 'Cheeky bitch! I said no such thing. She's jealous, more like. She hasn't got real ones, just silicone implants.'

'That's not very worthy of you, Stewart.'

'Probably not. On the other hand . . .'

'You didn't comment on the other things she said.'

'Because it wasn't true. Oh, I've known her for years. We had a thing about eight years ago – long before I met you. Even then I was talking about wanting to live in France. You know me, it's been my life's dream.'

'Why did you end your affair with her then?'

'She met and married Peter. His bank balance was a greater attraction to her than mine and there was no ex-wife bleeding him dry in the background.' He smiled, she didn't know what at. 'We never saw each other again, not until we met in Bricolage – I promise you.'

'That's strange. Both she and her husband say different-ly.'

'Wendy lies when it suits her, and he would. He's paranoid. Big businessmen often are. Don't tell me you've been seeing him? I told you, he's a cold bastard.'

'I find him completely the opposite. He came to lunch. I needed some advice about a business I'm involved with.'

'What business?'

'Really, Stewart, when you barged out of the house I think you gave up the right to ask me such questions.'

'You are angry, aren't you?'

'What did you expect?'

'That's what I'm trying to put right.'

'Is the fact that Peter has arranged his affairs so that his money is away from his wife's grasping hands anything to do with this change of heart?'

'Kate, now it's my turn to say that's unworthy of you. Of course it isn't. I was in the wrong. When I came to and found out how close a shave I'd had, it made me sit and think things through. I was risking so much, and for what?'

'It didn't stop you telling the hospital staff that she was your wife, leaving me to make a complete fool of myself.'

'That was her, not me.' What a lie, she thought.

'Look, Kate, let me try to explain. I know I've behaved abominably, I said that.'

'Before you go on there's one question. I need to know if you slept with her in my house, in our bed.'

'Sweetheart, no! I wouldn't be so tawdry.'

Could she believe that?

'But you're at fault too,' he added.

'Me?'

'You were always so engrossed in your work that you never seemed to notice that I had nothing.'

'You could have written *your* novel.'

318

'Not when it came to it, I couldn't. I lack your discipline, your talent.'

'That's not what you said the other day.'

'That was jealousy speaking. I was eaten up with jealousy at your success. I wanted it to be me earning the money, not you. It cut my balls off every time you wrote a cheque, every time you bought me a present, got me new clothes.'

'That's silly. You knew how I felt about money. That we had one honey-pot and we shared it. I don't think I ever made things difficult for you.'

'You didn't. But don't you see? The situation hurt me. It made me feel less of a man. And then when the kids came and you . . . Well, there's no point in going down that road. I was hurt that you'd help them and not me. That you didn't confide your plans to me. Call me childish, I know I am, and stupid. There isn't a word I haven't thought of to describe how despicable I am. How much you must loathe me when all I want to do is to love you.' At which and to Kate's horror he burst into tears.

Momentarily she froze, unsure what to do or say. And then she was on the floor kneeling by his chair. 'Stewart, don't cry, please. Love, don't take on so . . .'

'I love you, Kate . . .'

At which point the door opened. Noisily a nurse pushed a wheelchair into the room. 'Sod it! I have to have an X-ray. Promise me you'll be here when I come back.' He looked at her with such pain and longing in his eyes.

As the door shut behind him Kate collected her bag, waited to be sure that he had been wheeled out of the corridor and fled, afraid at how close she'd been to forgiving him.

3

Contacting Caroline wasn't easy. Tristram had phoned Netta several times but she was always evasive: she didn't say outright that her goddaughter wasn't there but whenever he mentioned Caroline's name she changed the subject adroitly. He had called Caroline's number in London but each time he had got the answerphone. It upset him more than he had expected to hear her voice on the tape. As yet she hadn't responded to his messages. At this rate, he was going to have to fly to London and find her – he'd scrape the fare together somehow.

His days were full. He had the animals to see to, the house to straighten – it was a mystery to him how muddled it got with just himself in it. Only then, after doing bits and bobs of shopping, could he go to see Mo.

'At least you're picking up the lingo at a rate of knots,' he said, putting the books that Jessica had sent for her on to the bedside table.

'How the hell do you expect me to read them lying flat on my back?'

'I'll read them to you if you like.'

'You don't want to do that.'

'I've just offered to.'

'Only because you're a gent, not because you want to. Why should you? It's a lovely day, why should you spend it in here with me?'

'Mo, I want to. And that's all there is to say. And, by the way, Martin and Giselle sent these in.' He unpacked the box of biscuits that Giselle had made for her. From the tone of Mo's voice it was going to be a difficult day.

'They're obviously trying to make amends for beating

you up. I'm not eating anything from *that* kitchen with its rats.'

'Mice. Fine, then I will. They're scrummy. I'll lie for you and say they were wonderful.'

'You don't have to lie for me. I can fight my own battles.'

'I know.' He laughed.

'Were you given my bag – the big black one?' she asked abruptly.

'Yes.'

'Where is it?'

'At home.'

'Is it safe?'

'Perfectly. I hid it when I saw what it contained.'

'You looked inside? You had no right to do that.'

'I apologise, but you must admit the circumstances were a bit odd. Why did you have something as incriminating as that with you? What if the bag had been stolen?'

'It's none of your business. And I'd appreciate you forgetting you ever saw them.'

'That's where you're wrong. It's very much my business. And I think I have a right to know what you were doing with them, and with Stewart of all people.'

She looked at him long and hard, as if making up her mind. 'He was going to help me write a book and sell it to get us out of the mess I got us into. He reckoned I could make masses. It's all right – I wasn't going to make a fortune and piss off, if that's what you're thinking.'

'I wasn't. And I appreciate that you were trying to do something. But, hell, Mo, not this. I know some of the people on those lists in your little red books. You could ruin them, fuck up their lives big-time.'

'They should have thought about that before getting involved with me.'

'Is he still going ahead with it?'

'I called him, and I asked what we were to do now we were stuck in here. He said he wanted no further involvement, that in the circumstances it would upset Kate, that it might hurt her career, and in any case, she wouldn't want him involved in anything like that. So I'm back on my own, it would appear. When it rains it pours, as Sybil would say.'

'But I thought they'd split up?'

'Apparently Kate has forgiven him and is taking him back, once he's out of here.'

'Odd. Well, we can discuss later what to do. Not now. All we have to do now is get you better.'

'Don't talk such crap, Tristram. I'm not going to get better. You know that and I know that, so don't talk rubbish. I'm not an idiot.'

'You are in a grump.'

'So would you be in a fucking grump if you were stuck here like me.'

'I fancy reading to you. When was the last time anyone read to you?' He ignored her ill-temper and opened one of the books.

'I shan't listen.'

'Then don't.'

'Right, here we go. *The Happy Prisoner*, by Monica Dickens . . .' He hadn't got far into it before he found out that it was about a cripple. 'Bad choice, I'll try another.' He slammed it shut.

'No, it's fine. Actually, I was enjoying it. Carry on, it's very kind of you.' Her mood had changed.

Even when she fell asleep he continued to read for fear that if he stopped she might wake. He watched her as she slept. She'd a bruise on her forehead and that was all to show she had been in the crash. Had her face been scarred, her spirit would have been broken, for sure. As it was, the damage was invisible – to her spine. Nearly two weeks later the doctors were still pessimistic about her chances of walking again. But Tristram had been to see Jessica, who had a computer and a link to the web. He'd searched for hope and had found it. He was sure that Mo's body was in shock and in time movement would return; he had to keep that thought foremost in his mind.

She had no pain, which was a blessing. However, had she felt pain she wouldn't have been paralysed. He hugged himself and the book slipped to the floor. He didn't want to think about that, not yet: he wasn't ready either.

Her moods were the biggest problem. Each day he came in with trepidation at what he would find. She switched from courage that humbled him to desperate self-pity, which, while understandable, was hard to deal with. Then there were the days when she was bad-tempered, the nurses scurried from her room and Tristram wished he was anywhere but there. On others, she was so sweet he wanted to hold her tight, weep for her, and make her legs work again. Which of these would be Mo in the future was anybody's guess.

What they were to do and how he was to care for her kept him awake at night. Capitalise on the lists was the obvious course. But that was a road he didn't particularly want to go down. It stank. And it would damage Mo and himself, he was sure. He spent hours tossing and turning, making up schemes, getting nowhere.

One solution came to him in the night. His grand-mother! He should have thought of her before now. She was in an old people's home and ga-ga so there was no way he could ask her direct, but he knew she'd left him a legacy in her will – enough to get Mo off the hook. He phoned his father and asked diffidently if he could have a loan against it. He might just as well have saved the money on the call.

'If you've got yourself into a mess, Tristram, then you're going to have to get yourself out of it. The answer's no.' Before his father hung up he hadn't actually said Tristram was a tosser but he came perilously close to it.

Oh, Dad, don't do this, his mind had screeched. *Don't make me!*

What else could he do? Sell his house, which would probably take years. And did he want to? In selling up he would also be selling his dream, and what would he have left then? Broken dreams could lead to bitterness, he'd seen it in others. And if he was forced to look after Mo properly he could not afford such an emotion. She would notice, and it would, in turn, damage her.

The bottom line was that they would have to return home so that the NHS could take over. But what if *they* were still searching for her? Pity was unlikely to be high on their agenda. He'd a plan worked out, but he needed to talk to Caroline and time was running out . . .

He woke with a start. Mo was watching him, her brown eyes full of tears.

'Mo, what is it?' He sprang from the chair, sat on the edge of her bed and took her hand. 'Mo, are you in pain?'

'You looked so beautiful, asleep.'

'Hang on, that's my line.' He smiled.

'And the strain had gone from your face. You've looked so worried these last days. And it's my fault.'

'Hardly. It was that clod Stewart who smashed you up.'

'Tristram, you don't have to stay with me.'

'Go on, I've nothing else to do today. The animals are fed, and I'm going to buy Max a kennel for when I'm not there.'

'That's not what I meant. I'm trying to tell you to get out of my life. I would understand. It's not fair to you.'

'And what's happened is hardly fair to you either, is it?'

324

'I know you don't love me, Tristram. I know you just used to say it, no doubt hoping that you might one day.'

'Oh, come on . . .'

'No. We have to be honest with each other, Tristram. No more games. I didn't love you, and you knew that too. So why, just because this has happened to me, should you be stuck with me?'

She was trying to control her tears, but as she spoke they trickled down her cheeks, leaving a sheen in their wake. She was the only woman he had ever met who could cry and still look beautiful. 'Look, Mo, now is not the time to make any decisions. I'm staying, so you're stuck with me.' Christ, why couldn't he have taken her up on her offer and scarpered? 'Let's look at the situation a long time in the future.'

'I don't deserve you.'

'I haven't been a saint, Mo. I used you. We both used each other. If the tables were reversed . . . What then?'

'I'd run like hell, Tristram. I know that for sure.'

When he returned to Max it was to find a message on his answer-machine. It wasn't from Caroline but it was the next best thing: it was from her flatmate, telling him that Caroline was staying with a Kate Howard but she had no number.

Kate was not listed in the directory but Stewart was. He had picked up the phone and was about to dial when he stopped. What if Netta had warned Kate that he might phone and told her to deny that Caroline was there? He had liked Netta in the past but he had gone off her rapidly. He saw her now as an interfering old bitch. Instead he got Max's lead. The dog did not know about leads so there was much pulling and cajoling to get him into the car – another new experience for him, and one that was too exciting: a dozen miles down the road he threw up all over the back seat. Tristram had never been to Kate's house but he knew where her village was. An hour later he was driving up the hill towards the large house from whose garden came raucous laughter.

There was a bell on the gate but when no one answered it he opened it and, dragging Max behind him, walked in. A group of young people were crashing about by the pool and loud music was playing. They looked like zombies. Caroline was not among them. He called, but they either didn't hear him or didn't want to – he thought the latter.

The front door was shut although it was a warm evening. He knocked and saw a movement in the hallway. He peered through the glass door and knocked again.

'I told you, go away!' he heard Kate call.

'Please, Kate. I need to talk to you.'

'Piss off!'

'Kate!'

The shadow moved closer. He saw Kate's worried face peering out at him. 'Tristram.' He was glad to hear the relief in her voice. She unbolted the door. 'Sorry, I thought you were someone else.'

Tristram entered the house. 'Do you mind the dog?'

'Not at all, bring him in.'

'Are you all right, Kate?' He hadn't seen her since the day at the hospital and was shocked by how tired she looked and how nervous she appeared.

'Am I glad to see you.' Kate ushered him into her lovely sitting room.

'My, this is civilised. You should see my shack—' He didn't get any further for they both jumped at a particularly loud noise. 'What was that?'

'They never stop.' She nodded towards the window. 'They sleep all day and make that noise half the night.'

'I recognised your daughter and son-in-law when I came in. Who are the other two?'

'I don't know. They've been here several days but I haven't met them. Usually I can ignore them but tonight – oh, I don't know. I just got so fed up that I shouted at Lucy and it developed into a full-scale row. Now they're being even noisier. I'm not sure if they're on drink or drugs.'

'They're certainly making a racket.'

'I hate that awful thump-thump music they play. I try to be tolerant but I find it hard. It's so raucous. No tune to it.' At which she suddenly laughed. 'God help me, I sound like my parents. It must be an age thing.'

'I can't stand it either, so age doesn't come into it.'

'There's a relief. I'd loathe to become like my mother!'

'Do you want me to speak to them?'

'Bless you, Tristram, but you're still bruised from the last altercation you had. Better not. I feel much better with company here.'

'I'm looking for Caroline. Netta won't tell me where she is.' He had decided to be up-front with her.

'She was here but that was some time ago.'

'Do you know where she is?'

'Yes.'

'Will you tell me?'

'She's with my son. They're in Italy for a few days looking at gardens. It's all Steve does.' Her laugh this time was not so sure, as if she was wary of him.

'Please, Kate, I wouldn't ask if it wasn't important. Can I have a phone number? It's very urgent.'

'I think I would have to know why.'

Tristram's mind raced at what to do, what to say. But he had no choice. 'Could you keep this to yourself?' When she nodded, he went on, 'Mo is in trouble with a gang of drug-dealers. I don't know how to contact them but Caroline does.'

'Caroline? Involved with drugs? I don't believe it!'

'No, *she* isn't. Don't get me wrong,' he said hurriedly. 'No, she was approached by them when they were looking for Mo. She and Mo are old friends. You see, I have to pay them off. Mo's got enough on her plate. I've got to sort this for her.'

'Well, in that case . . .'

Kate took Tristram into her workroom and switched on her computer to access her address file.

'Are you working at the moment?'

'Yes, I've almost finished a new book. Luckily, with the noise that lot make, I prefer to work in the mornings when they're asleep. It's taken my mind off so many things – you know . . .' She looked embarrassed.

'I'm glad you've resolved it, and that you and Stewart are getting back together again.' He wasn't particularly, but it seemed polite to say it.

'We're not.'

'Aren't you? That's odd. Stewart thinks you are.'

4

Tristram expected Kate to question him about Stewart and steeled himself.

'Would you like to stay for supper?' she asked instead.

'That would be great. Come to think of it, I haven't eaten since breakfast.'

'You shouldn't ignore your own health, you know. Listen to me pontificating! I haven't eaten all day either.' She paused. 'But it's difficult when someone's in hospital, isn't it? The visits seem to dominate the day.'

'You can say that again. I've had to give up on my garden – it's just weeds now.'

'There's the phone. Call Caroline, then come into the kitchen. Come on, Max, you come with me, and I'll find you something to eat.' As Kate and the dog left the room, Tristram picked up the telephone. He'd assumed he'd been given the number of a hotel so was not expecting an uncomprehending Italian to answer the phone. It took time to make the woman understand he wanted to speak to Caroline.

'I fell into the typical Englishman's trap and was shouting at the poor woman hoping that would make her understand better.'

'Sorry, I wasn't expecting any calls. I'm visiting my aunt, she has a lovely garden.'

'With Steve,' he said bleakly.

'Yes, with Steve. I wanted them to meet him.'

'I see.'

'How did you get this number?'

'Steve's mother gave it to me. I'm here with her now.'

'Has Stewart come home?'

'He's in hospital . . .' There then followed a long explanation about the accident. He didn't mention Mo – he didn't think it was fair: he knew Caroline, she'd feel she had to help in some way and, no doubt, come rushing back posthaste.

'Is Kate all right?'

'She appears fine. Stewart seems to think they're back together but Kate doesn't. Although . . .' He clammed up. Maybe it was none of his business, perhaps he shouldn't say.

'Although what?'

'I don't know if I should tell you.'

'You can't start and then stop, Tristram. I'll worry if you don't.'

'In a way it would be handy if Stewart came back. Lucy has got a couple of weirdos here. They all look high as kites to me. They ignore Kate. I think she's frightened of them.'

'Do you think we should come back?'

'No. Don't worry, I'll have a word with them.' He had no intention of doing any such thing: the strange man was a big bugger and he didn't want to get beaten up again. And he shouldn't have said anything – Kate would be furious if she knew. But, then, at least he'd let them know that all was not well so he need not have that on his conscience.

'So what else are you calling about?'

That was so unlike Caroline, he thought. She sounded quite cool and businesslike with him.

'I need to know how to get in touch with the heavies who are looking for Mo.'

'Oh, Tristram, no!'

'I have to, Caroline. Look, I don't intend to go crashing in and see them. I need to contact them, that's all. I have to solve it once and for all.'

There was silence at the other end of the phone. 'You there, Caroline?'

'Yes. It's against my better judgement but hang on a minute . . .'

He sat on a high stool and watched Kate as she began to prepare their meal. Another of his great whooshes of homesickness hit him hard: she reminded him of his mother as she pottered about her kitchen. Even the kitchen was similar to theirs.

'You look wistful.'

'Seeing you cooking made me think about my mum. You know, it's odd how I go for ages not thinking about her and

330

then, just recently, I often have and I'll even admit to being homesick.'

'Troubled times. It does that to you. It makes you think of happier days. Just recently I've found myself thinking of my home in Graintry. Do you know it? A lovely village. The children were happy then.' She, too, looked wistful. And then she smiled. 'One thing, though, I might think of my old home but never with my ex-husband in it.' She put the bowl of scraps she'd been collecting together on the floor for Max. 'He's a friendly-looking soul. What is he?'

'God knows. I rescued him. My next-door neighbour beat him and I interfered. That's how I got my bruises.'

'I hope you beat the living daylights out of him too.'

'I did.' He grinned. 'At least he let me buy him. It's their way I suppose.'

'I've always wanted a dog.' She began to rinse a lettuce.

'Why haven't you got one, then?'

'The men in my life never approved of dogs. Said they were too much of a tie. I suppose they were right.'

'I think the disadvantages are outweighed by the advantages.'

'Anything you can't eat?'

'I eat everything.'

'Good. I thought we'd have some pasta with chicken livers in Marsala and a salad.' She stopped moving around for a moment and looked at him, smiling. 'I can't tell you how nice it is to have someone to cook for.'

'I assure you the feeling is mutual.'

As she chopped the other salad ingredients he asked her about her writing and what it felt like to see her books on sale. She answered his questions good-naturedly. She could do so while cooking as if she was on autopilot – the questions people asked were always the same, how she worked, when she worked, where the ideas came from, how many words she wrote a day. She wished she had a pound for every time she'd answered them.

Over the meal they were relaxed with each other. Both were grateful for as they chatted they could forget their problems.

'You should stay the night, Tristram. It's late and you've had too much wine to drive.'

'You needn't repeat the offer. Thank you.'

It was hot in the room that Kate had shown him to: the noise of heavy-metal music from beside the pool was deafening so he had closed the windows. What inconsiderate sods, he thought. He couldn't sleep, not only because of the racket but because of the heat. He was going over and over his plan: what he needed, what to say, how to approach the subject.

At two in the morning he heard Kate's voice from the terrace. Max, lying on the floor, began to growl. He lay awhile listening as Kate and Lucy shouted at each other. With the window shut he could not make out what they were saying but the tone sounded unfriendly.

'It's OK, boy. Dad's in control.'

He opened the window.

'Lucy, how many times do I have to ask you! Turn that bloody music off!' There was an hysterical edge to Kate's voice. Tristram thought she might be crying. He put on his jeans and T-shirt, reassured Max and told him to stay, then ran out of the room and down the stairs.

He was right. Kate was crying. Lucy was laughing and the others were lolling about, finding the scene highly amusing.

'Lucy, I have to sleep!' In her nightdress, Kate was leaning on the wall as she yelled down to the poolside. 'This noise is too much.'

'Well, who's adding to it?'

'Lucy!'

'Get lost!'

'How dare you speak to me like that?'

'Well, get off my back!'

Tristram ran swiftly down the steps to the pool. 'Look, you lot, cool it,' he said calmly.

'Mind your own fucking business,' Dominique joined in.

'Can't you see your mother's distressed, Lucy? It's not fair.'

'We're not making that much noise.'

'But you are.'

'Let's throw him in the pool.' The other girl laughed.

'Look, I've been polite to you and I think it's time you were polite with Lucy's mother. She's asked you to turn it down, so do as she says. If not then I'll get the *gendarmes* up here. Understand?'

'Oh, yes. Go on, then, do it.' Dominique stood his ground, hands on hips, aggression pouring out of him.

'With pleasure. *Immédiatement.*' From his pocket Tristram took a miniature spanner kit, a present from Mo. In its black leather case it looked remarkably like a mobile phone.

Lucy's guests disappeared into the shadows. Dominique spat at him then told him to do unspeakable and virtually impossible things with his own anatomy. But, for all that, he turned away.

'You'll regret this,' Lucy shouted at him, and muttering ran after the others as they stumbled off across the orchard towards the little house, whose lights were all burning. Neither Lucy nor Dominique could resist a last shout of abuse before they slammed into the house.

'Thank you so much, Tristram. They went like lambs.'

'Fairly voluble ones.'

'Just because you said you'd call the police.'

'It was one of the first things I learnt from living here. The French are terrified of them. It works every time.'

'Perhaps now we can get some sleep.' Kate turned towards the house. 'They were high on drugs, weren't they?'

'I'm not sure.'

'Tristram?'

'I'm no expert but, yes, I guess they were.'

'What do you think?'

'Who knows? Coke, Ecstasy, maybe a cocktail.'

'We've had trouble before with Lucy. I really hoped it was going to be all right this time. Maybe it never will be.'

'What will you do?'

'I don't know. I can hardly turn her out, can I, my own daughter? As for Dominique . . .' She sighed.

'Has he been involved with drugs before?'

'Tristram, the sad thing is I don't know. Oh, he's always polite to me on the rare times I see him. But, you see, I know nothing about him. He could be a mass murderer for all I know.'

'Kate, they obviously worry you. I have to go to London tomorrow for a couple of days. Would you like to hang on to Max to look after you?'

'That would be lovely. I shall enjoy having him to care for – he'll be company.'

'See? They don't have to be a tie. Get yourself a dog, and if you want to go away I'll always look after it for you!'

'Deal. After that little scene, I reckon a brandy is called for, don't you?'

5

'Did you have a lovely holiday?' Netta was trying not to fuss over Sybil as if she were an invalid, but it was hard not to when all her instincts made her want to look after her.

'Wonderful. Did you get my cards?'

'It was kind of you to remember me apart. I love getting postcards.' This was an out-and-out lie: she hated them. It was so long since Netta had been able to afford a holiday that she was certain she wouldn't have the faintest idea how to amuse herself on one now. But this didn't stop her longing to take one even though she told everyone that holidays were boring and she'd much rather stay here. So when friends sent her cards from exotic locations, she found it as difficult to control her jealousy as it was to stop herself fluttering over Sybil. 'I know I'm being a bloody nuisance but I can't seem to stop making sure you're fine.'

'As I am. Don't fret, Netta. I took my pills today like a good little girl. I won't do anything odd. I've been having anger-control counselling.'

'Good gracious, how modern! Sim sounded fine on the phone. I gather he's not worrying about leaving you with me?'

'Not a scrap. He knows that for the few days I'm here in your care I wouldn't dare to forget my medication. As I told him, I'm terrified of you!' She laughed to show that she wasn't, but Netta was not so sure. Often, she had found, things said as jokes had a grain of truth in them, just like gossip.

'At least he came back safe and sound. You didn't ditch the poor sod in the briny!'

'Bless you, Netta. I think you're the only person who can

joke about it. Dear Sim, I think he's half afraid even to mention my nasty little problem.'

'Perhaps he thinks if he doesn't it will go away.'

'He doesn't want to hurt my feelings, more like.'

'You're a lucky woman, Sybil. You've a good man there, one who really loves you.'

'Just as I told you.'

'I know, I admit I was wrong. But rest assured, I'm not going to spend the rest of my life apologising for being so.'

'So what happened while I was away?'

'You should go away more often. There was mayhem . . .' Like so many people Netta was not averse to being first with the news.

'Poor Kate.' Sybil looked shocked, when told that she and Stewart had split up.

'Rubbish! Best thing for her. There's something brutal about that man.'

'I think he's gorgeous.'

'But, then, good-looking men often are the least sensitive, haven't you found? They've less need not to upset the women in their lives because there'll always be another silly bitch for them to charm.'

'Wendy, you say? So I was right.' But Sybil said this with no hint of satisfaction.

'Best thing for Peter.'

'Netta, you can't keep saying that. It's as if you were taking pleasure in another's misfortune.'

'I mean it. They'll be a lot happier and can get on with their lives.'

'You don't mean Kate and Peter have got together?'

Netta pressed her finger to her lips. 'My mouth is sealed. Divorce can be a tricky thing.'

'But Kate wasn't married to Stewart.'

'I didn't mean him.'

'Oh dear. And are Stewart and Wendy living together?'

'No. Wendy's scarpered – though not many people know that. Peter told me. Stewart's still in hospital.'

'Poor Stewart.'

'He got away lightly. It's Mo you should feel sorry for. It's doubtful that she'll walk again.'

'Oh, no!' Sybil's hand was clamped over her mouth.

'Mind you, from my experience French doctors have a tendency to exaggerate. I think they do it to oblige their patients and make them feel important – you know, so they can go home and say they nearly croaked it and how their doctor had never seen aught like it.'

'Netta, you are a shocker. And poor Tristram?'

'Still being a nuisance. Still trying to get on the right side of my Caroline. Well, he'll do that over my dead body.'

'Poor Mo! . . . You seem to be seeing a lot of Peter. Is there something you're not telling me?' She smiled slyly.

'Sybil, would I keep it from you of all people if there was?'

'Probably.' Sybil grinned.

Netta went to answer the telephone and was gone for a good five minutes. Sybil idled away the time by looking at Netta's few books and wishing she had brought more for her. She wished Netta would let Sim help her out with money. She had so little and . . .

'Talk of the devil. That was Tristram. He's at Kate's. He says she's in a spot of trouble and would we go over and keep her company?'

'With pleasure. But I'll have to tell Sim.'

Netta shuddered at the cost of a call to Bahrain.

'Any news on the writing courses that Kate was going to do with Jessica?' Sybil asked, as they drove, far too fast, along the Loire gorge road.

'Jessica is a born organiser. She's beavering away. They hope to start at Easter.'

'Do you think they could find a little job for little old me?'

'Don't lay it on, Sybil, it doesn't suit you! Sorry! I vowed not to be horrid to you.'

'I'd think I'd done something wrong if you stopped being rude to me. Well, what about my prospects?'

'Not really, my dear. The way it's going there will be more people organising the courses than attending them, if Kate doesn't watch out. That Petronella Thunder, or whatever she called herself . . .'

'Storm, it was Petronella Storm. The pretty girl who so wants to write.'

'That's the one. Kate has roped her in to help. She says that writing has been good to her and she must give something back. So she's going to martyr herself with Storm.'

'I thought she was rather sweet. And I admired the way she pretended to be a successful author. That took courage.'

'Some people might have called it lying. Dodgy, if you ask me. You always see the good in people, don't you? That's dodgy too.'

'I suppose you've been given a job. But, then, you need it.'

'Gracious me, who's being sharp now?' She smiled to show she didn't care, but she did, really. 'No, I am not helping in any capacity.' She didn't add that she was disappointed in this – she felt it was better never to show it when one felt let down or left out. Which wasn't fair on Kate since she hadn't promised her any role. Still, it would have been nice. 'I was in on the first meeting with Jessica – Kate wanted me there as a good judge of people.'

'I'd better tell Sim that one.' Sybil laughed loudly as they bowled along.

'It's left here . . . Here!' Netta held on to the dashboard as Sybil braked, the tyres complaining bitterly as she did so. 'Why you have to treat the public roads like a racetrack beats me.'

'You're getting staid in your old age, Netta.'

'Not at all. I just want to stay alive.'

It was with considerable relief that Netta saw Kate's village appear. 'It's the last house at the top of the hill. She's got the most stunning views imaginable.'

They rang the bell on the gate and waited. 'I still think we should have telephoned first.'

'No, Tristram was adamant we should just turn up. Ha, here she comes. Kate, my dear, do forgive us but we just happened to be passing and, trusting to friendship, hoped it was all right to drop in.' Netta's smile usually worked wonders in such circumstances but not this time.

'Normally it would be fine but I'm working,' Kate managed to say. She always found it difficult to do so as if one day someone would turn round and say, 'Work! You call what you do work?'

'See? What did I say?'

With one glance Netta shut Sybil up. 'The truth, Kate, is that Tristram asked us to come. He said he was worried about you. Some druggies on your land causing problems, he said.'

'He had no right to tell you that.'

'Probably not, but he did all the same – he was concerned for you. Why, what a delightful dog!' She diverted Kate's attention by greeting Max, who was himself greeting Netta with the exuberant enthusiasm of a dog who knew he was on safe ground and that she wouldn't object.

'We should go.' Sybil was tugging at Netta's sleeve.

'Well, now you're here . . .' Kate held the gate open wide. The two women stepped in looking anxiously from side to side as if they expected assailants to pop out at any moment. 'Don't worry, they're all asleep. They only cause havoc at night.'

'You poor dear.'

'Did you enjoy your holiday, Sybil?'

'Thank you, Kate, I did, but there's no place like home sweet home, is there?'

Netta rolled her eyes with exasperation and then, remembering her promise to be nicer, stopped.

'Don't be cross with Tristram, Kate,' she said. 'He meant well. If you want to work you carry on, we'll just be here in case you need us. Like the Praetorian guard. What about if we made lunch for you? We'll pop into Vorey, get something.'

'No need for that. I've got plenty here. Would you mind looking after yourselves? It would be such a luxury and, you see, I've almost finished. Another couple of hours should do it.'

Kate left the two women deciding what to prepare for lunch – twittering at each other like birds, she decided – and returned to her desk and computer. Her initial reaction to being interrupted had passed. It was nice to know they were here, though what on earth she had been frightened of she couldn't imagine – Lucy was all mouth and she couldn't see Dominique getting violent, it might upset the creases in his trousers. Still, there were the other two, she'd no idea who they were.

She was going to have to talk to Lucy, calmly and rationally. Though how? *Just ask her. Are you back on drugs?* That's a sure way to send her into a tantrum and accuse me of interfering. *Coward!*

There were moments when Kate wished she could simply

shut Lucy out of her life and slam the lid on the box marked Problem Daughter. She'd often said to Stewart that she'd had enough of her daughter, that she'd hurt her once too often, that she could stew for all she cared. But it had all been a pretence. She could no more turn her back on Lucy than stop breathing. Years ago a friend had told her that it was possible to not like your child but you could never stop loving them. She'd been shocked at the time, but she understood it fully now.

If Lucy was back on drugs she did not know what she would do or which way she would turn. Just as she hadn't the last time. The child-rearing manuals didn't have a section on this. What had happened to make Lucy so self-destructive?

A chat-show Kate had watched said addictions such as this were caused by lack of self-esteem – though of course it had been an American show, which might have made a difference. She wouldn't have thought that Lucy was lacking in that department – she'd have said that in the past she had had an abundance of it. If anything, she herself should be an addict of something if that was the case. But, then, perhaps she was – writing!

Apart from the worry she felt hurt by Lucy. Her daughter was most certainly taking advantage of her. She took everything for granted and showed not a modicum of appreciation for what she had been given, as if the only thing Kate was here for was to support her. She wouldn't have done any of this if Stewart had been here.

Stewart. She had called the hospital this morning as usual to be told that his progress was so rapid that he would be discharged next week. Then she would have to make a decision.

Decisions, how she hated them. She sighed as she returned to her writing, and within minutes she was back in the imaginary world of her characters, a much safer and happier place to be.

6

'THE END.' Triumphantly Kate tapped out the final words in large bold print. She sat back in her chair with that strange muddle of emotions she always felt when a book was finished. Relief that it was over, sadness that it was. Elation that she'd achieved it – and fear that it was rubbish! What a career to choose.

In normal circumstances, before thinking of posting the manuscript to her agent, she would get Stewart to read it and tell her what he thought. Now she had no one, just her own judgement which, where her work was concerned, was always pessimistic. There was a moment, a scant time, when she loved what she had done. Then all the doubts crept in and she began to doubt its quality, and invariably regret that she hadn't handled it differently, told the story from another angle. And the fear! That bloody awful fear of failure that she had never had when she was a novice but which was now always at her shoulder.

Just as she was about to join the others the phone rang.

'Kate? Portia here. Many thanks for doing that work for us so quickly. It's looking and reading well.'

'I'm glad.'

'You know, I've got this feeling that *The Lost Troubadour* is going to be hot.'

'Really?' Kate presumed that being *hot* was a good thing.

'I'm talking it up already and I have high hopes for it at Frankfurt.'

'That's great!' It really was. She'd read of other books being hyped up and sold at the largest book fair in the world, but never her own. If something good came out of that, a lot of her worries and problems would be over. Still, no point in thinking along those lines in case nothing happened.

'And we simply have to enter it for the Red Rose Book of the Year award. That's getting big, you know.'

'I'd love to win that more than anything else, I think.' Since she had once been shortlisted for the award, it had ever since proved elusive.

'So, what's next?'

'Your call came just as I finished the new one.' She hadn't meant to tell her that.

'Finished?' Portia shrieked down the phone. 'Kate, you're a star! Why, with the editing of *Troubadour* only just finished I thought I had months to wait. Tell me, tell me!'

'Well . . .' She hadn't wanted to discuss the new book with anyone until she had reread it. What if it wasn't as funny as she thought? What if it was total crap? 'It's different,' she said diffidently.

'How different?' Her editor sounded cagey and she knew why: the ideal writer for a publisher was one who produced variations on the same theme for book after book. 'Reader identification,' Joy had called it. Look what had happened when she had insisted on writing her historical novel rather than the contemporary one they had wanted and expected. Sacked, that's what she'd been. She wished she could unsay everything.

'It's short, compared with the others.'

'We can always make it look longer than it is. What's the subject?'

'It's a comedy. At least I think it is.'

'A comedy?' The doubt in Portia's voice dripped down the phone.

'Yes.'

'What sort of comedy?'

'Well . . .' She wished she could stop saying, 'Well', it sounded so spiritless. 'Well . . . you know all those thirty-something angst books – diets, calories, booze, knickers and fellows? I've done it for the middle-aged.'

'Ha, interesting.'

'Not a navel-watching mid-life crisis book, all doom and gloom but a fun look at it. I think it shows that there isn't much difference, really, just the ages,' she finished limply. At least, that's what she thought it showed.

'Does it have a happy ending?'

'I suppose it depends on how you regard it. I think it's happy.'

'Does the heroine get her man?'

'No. She decides that men are a waste of space – in a funny way,' she added hurriedly.

'When can you get it to me?'

The day was hot and Netta and Sybil had laid the table under the pergola. In the two hours they'd been there they had knocked up a feast. There were several different salads. Large vol-au-vent cases oozed with chicken in a white wine sauce. Giant prawns and pork sausages were sizzling on the barbecue. Stuffed mushrooms had been put under the grill. Bowls of tabbouleh, taramasalata, hummus, a fresh fruit salad and a cheeseboard completed the spread.

'Are you sure you've done enough?' Kate asked, laughing.

'I know, it's a habit of mine. I always cook for a cast of thousands.'

'Still, waste not want not.' Sybil chipped in, although, looking at the amount, it would seem there was going to be a lot of waste.

'I'm not complaining, it all looks wonderful. I didn't know I had any taramasalata.'

'You didn't. I found some fish roe in the freezer.'

'You're both so clever.'

'It's all Netta's doing. I was just the washer-up and general dogsbody.'

'I didn't know you liked to cook.'

'I so rarely do. There seems no point just for me. Mike and I used to have wonderful feasts – he loved his grub, dear man.'

'What about doing cookery courses here, add them to the list on offer?'

'Me?'

'Well, not me! I'd never fit it in.'

'What would Jessica say?'

'We've already discussed it. The problem was finding a cook.'

'In France?' Netta looked dubious.

'We need someone who speaks English.'

'I shall be honoured.' Netta was smiling broadly, Sybil looked downcast. 'And Sybil could be my assistant.'

'But of course.' At which Sybil perked up immediately.

'How very satisfactory. And champagne too.' Netta pointed to the tray Kate had added to the feast. 'I'm so glad Tristram called. Such treats. I can feel that my eyes have gone all piggy!'

'I finished my new book and I always celebrate when I manage that.'

'We saw all the empty champagne bottles in the kitchen with the occasion and the date written on the labels. I thought it a lovely idea.'

'Stewart started it.'

'Like a filing system of happy memories.'

'Yes, Sybil, it is.' Kate was overwhelmed by a feeling of sadness and loneliness.

'But there's no reason why you shouldn't continue the custom. Build new happy moments.'

'Exactly, Netta.' And Kate smiled at her, knowing she understood the emptiness she felt.

Just as she had enjoyed her first lunch with them so Kate was happy at this one. Sybil appeared her old self, and it was difficult now to remember the sad, withdrawn creature she had been just a few weeks ago. And there was something about Netta that was different too, though she couldn't put her finger on it. Halfway through the meal she realised that her friend had shed a good ten years in looks. Always attractive, today she looked stunning. She couldn't afford plastic surgery so . . . ?

'May one be indiscreet?' Netta said.

'You're going to ask me about Stewart.'

'Not in a nosy way, a concerned way.'

'He wants to come back.'

'Will you have him?'

'I don't know. I'm not much good on my own.'

'Kate, it *is* possible to live alone. I thought I'd never manage it but I have. And I had the added complication of no money.'

'It's surely better by far to be alone than miserable with someone.' Sybil paused. 'That must be the greatest loneliness of all. Love so near and yet so far . . .'

'My problem was that I didn't know I was – miserable, I mean. Netta was the first to put her finger on it, weren't you? She said I'd kept saying how happy I was so that I'd begin believing it.'

'Still, you have your daughter here.'

'Yes, Sybil, I do. But, then, she might just as well not be, the little I see her. I think I lost her years ago, if you want to know the truth.'

Netta and Sybil had stayed until quite late and went off loaded down with leftover food, or at least Netta did. They had hardly been gone an hour when the noise erupted from Lucy's house. Loud banging and shouting carried through the darkness of the garden. It sounded to Kate as if a wild animal was roaring in there. Then there was a sound of crashing, of breaking glass. Hysterical laughter followed and tears.

It's none of your business. But it was, that was the problem. *She's a grown woman.* But Lucy was still her child; the years couldn't erase that. Tomorrow she would talk to her. *You keep saying that.* In her bedroom Kate closed the shutters against the night. Even if she couldn't sleep, her bed seemed the best place to be.

Through the night she read her new book. She laughed. That was amazing – she could still laugh at it. Was she being self-indulgent or was it really funny? In the small hours she finished it. Incredibly, she still liked it.

Come the morning, as always, her hand hesitated before she opened the shutters to the day. Once the fears she felt had been abstract, amorphous, unspecified. Now when she dithered the fear was real. What would she see? Would the house still be there? Would Lucy?

Once breakfast was over she packed her new book into a padded envelope, drove to the post office and sent it by Chronopost. She wanted Portia to receive it as soon as possible for she was anxious to hear what she thought. She did a little shopping and returned home.

The day was lovely and, having decided she liked her book, she felt positive and confident for once. Not giving herself time to think what she was doing she walked purposefully across the grass to the little house. The door, as always, was unlocked. She pushed it open and entered. Within two steps she wished she hadn't. The place was in chaos. The floors were unswept, the coffee table was littered with unwashed plates and mugs. Ashtrays were overflowing with cigarette stubs. Flies buzzed incessantly over the debris. The heavy smell of incense failed to mask the underlying stench of filth and God only knew what. She did not go into the kitchen – she couldn't face it once she had peered in at the door and seen the piles of dishes and unwashed clothes. How on earth had all this happened? The mirror that she and Lucy had bought together in Le Puy was smashed, as were the figurines Kate had put here. The place was a shambolic wreck. This wasn't normal. Lucy wasn't used to living like this. Or was she? What did she now know about her daughter?

'Kate! I thought I heard someone.'

She swung round to find Dominique standing in the doorway.

'What is all this?' With her hand she indicated the debris that had once been such a pretty room.

'I fear your daughter doesn't like housework much.'

'Evidently you don't either,' she snapped back.

Infuriatingly he smiled. 'I have suggested to her many times . . .' He, too, looked about the room, not sadly but in a detached way as if it had nothing to do with him.

'Couldn't you have done something? Couldn't you have told me things were like this?'

'You never came here so I thought you didn't care. At least, that's what Lucy said.'

'That's rubbish and you know it. I left you alone. I didn't want to interfere.'

'Then perhaps you should have explained that to her. She's hurt.'

'*She*'s hurt! How do you think *I* feel?' She braved the kitchen, and under the sink, which was piled high with dishes, she found a large black plastic bag and returned to the sitting room. She moved quickly, almost frantically, as if by clearing the room she could make everything better, make her daughter better. *Get rid of the mess and then pretend all is well, typical.*

'What the hell?' Lucy erupted into the room, shouting. Kate had been so busy she had not even noticed that Dominique had left, presumably to fetch her. 'What are you doing?' She sprang across the room and wrenched the bag from her mother's hand. 'Get out.'

'You can't live like this.'

'I can live how I want.'

'Not in my house you don't. Just look at this. It's disgusting. It looks like a squat!' She snatched back the bag.

'Oh, I see. It's your house.'

'Of course it's my house.'

'I thought you had given it to me.'

'What on earth gave you that idea? I certainly didn't.'

'You said I could stay.'

'Until you got back on your feet. Which I've tried to help you do. But what use was that? Have you sold one bloody pizza?'

'There have been problems. You know that.'

'I should have saved my money.'

'Money! That's what it always comes down to with you, isn't it? You're money-obsessed, you are.'

'Someone has to earn it to feed us – and if that's being obsessed then I am. And with reason. You evidently have no intention of getting off your arse and pulling your weight.'

'No wonder Stewart left you. No wonder he stole from

you. You're so bloody mean.' Lucy was screaming at her, her face contorted with fury.

'Stewart may have done many things but stealing from me wasn't one of them. How dare you? And to say that I . . . Thank you, Lucy, for thinking me mean. How sweet of you. What a dutiful and grateful daughter you are.' Kate turned away from her in disgust.

The two friends were now lurking in the doorway, looking bleary-eyed and as dirty as the day they had arrived. There was much more Kate wanted to say but not in front of them with their smirking, superior – yes, that was it, that was what was so infuriating. They appeared to be sneering at her, as if they knew something she didn't. 'And you can take that insolent grin off your faces, this is none of your business!' she shouted at them.

'Don't you speak to my friends like that. You've no right to be here. I resent you being here, bossing me about. Interfering in my life!'

All through this scene Kate had been seeing red, her blood pounding noisily through her veins. Now the red became magenta and the blood sounded like a waterfall in her ears. She had done everything she could not to interfere yet was still accused of doing so. 'Maybe if I had interfered then you wouldn't be in this wretched mess. I want your friends out of here.' She pointed at them. 'I'm fed up with your inconsideration and with subsidising you. They go.'

'You can't tell me to do that.'

'I pay for the house, the electricity, the hot water – not that it looks as if they've used much of that. All the time I'm paying out then I call the tune. Understood?'

'Money again!'

'Yes, Lucy, that's right.'

'If they go then I go.'

'You must suit yourself, Lucy. Do what you want. What

you think you should. Now, if you'll excuse me.' The hippies moved to one side and let her pass.

Kate stumbled over the grass to her own home. She would have liked to cry, it might be a balm to soothe her, but she'd gone past crying. She had to get this rage out of the way first.

'Mum, what the hell?'

'Steve!'

7

'What's going on, Sis?' Steve, standing at the top of the steps to the swimming-pool, asked his sister equably. Lucy, looking a fright, had followed Kate through the orchard. Caroline stepped back, taking a great interest in a climbing rose, but obviously feeling in the way.

'I don't think Mum has the right to tell me what I can and can't do in my own house.' Lucy stood, hands on hips, belligerence in stance and voice. Her face was still crumpled from sleep. Her hair was lank and unwashed, her T-shirt dirty, her feet grimy. 'She invites me to stay, then interferes with how I live. Barges in without a by-your-leave. It's not on!' Although she had started with a reasonably modulated voice, as she listed her complaints Lucy's voice rose with her anger.

'You look a mess. When did you last wash?' Steve said, with brotherly lack of tact.

'I was yanked out of my bed at this ungodly hour – I haven't had time.'

'It's ten, for Christ's sake.'

'I woke her, maybe I shouldn't have—' Kate started.

'Too right you shouldn't have!'

'But I was angry. I'd had enough.'

'You've had enough, what about *me*?'

In these few seconds Kate had decided not to burden Caroline and Steve with her problems, but her daughter's continued intransigence put paid to that. 'I'm sick to death of the inconsideration, Steve. I don't know what's got into her. Lucy and her friends keep me awake at night with their incessant racket. I didn't invite them to stay. I wanted the noise to stop or them to leave.'

'That's not what you said. You ordered me to get rid of them. And I wasn't aware that I had to ask permission to have friends stay.'

'If Mum is paying the bills, which I guess she is, then she has every right. It's her house, remember.'

'I knew you'd take her side.' Suddenly Lucy began to shake and wrapped her thin arms around her emaciated torso, trying to find warmth. And yet she was visibly perspiring. She swayed and looked as if she was about to fall over. Kate ran down the steps to her.

'Lucy, are you all right? Lucy, what is it?'

'You wake me up, you scream abuse at me, you upset my husband and then you ask me what's the matter. You're the matter, Mum. Why can't you just leave me alone? Why don't you get out of my life?' She was screeching at Kate, who found herself moving back as if to get away from the hatred in her daughter's eyes.

Dominique ambled across the grass towards the group. He was deeply tanned and sleek in a crisp white T-shirt and shorts. Not a hair out of place. He was carrying the ubiquitous packet of cigarettes and gold lighter.

'Steve, hello.'

'What do you mean by upsetting my mother in this way? Have you no consideration?'

'Don't blame me, Steve. I've tried everything to get your

sister to behave differently. You know how strong-willed she is. It's not my fault. I'm sorry, Kate. I regret all this.'

'You creep! Whose side are you on?' Lucy shouted at her husband.

'There are no sides. We have a problem – correction, *you* have a problem – and we should be discussing it rationally and sensibly. It's not my fault if you're not capable.'

Kate looked at Dominique with disbelief. How could he be blaming Lucy for everything when he'd been part of it too? 'Hang on a minute, Dominique. Why should she do everything? Why can't you help? I see you've energy enough to iron your own T-shirt.' *Oops, watch it, you shouldn't have said that.* 'After all . . .' Kate tried to make herself sound reasonable '. . . you've been living there too, you can't have enjoyed the mess.' Yes, she sounded very balanced while all the time she longed to slap his face.

'The domestic arrangements are Lucy's. I take care of the business side.'

'What business!' Kate snorted with derision. *You're losing it again!*

'These friends of yours that my mother has taken against, can't you do something about them?' Steve asked.

'They're not my friends.'

'But I gathered they were.'

'I can't think where you got that idea, Kate. Lucy knew them in London, not me, when she was squatting. If she told you they were my friends she was lying – but, then, perhaps you don't know about Lucy and her lying. I fear, Kate . . . I didn't want to tell you this . . . but I fear that Lucy is back to her old ways.'

'Drugs, you mean?' Kate's hand flew protectively to her throat. She might have thought so but having someone else confirm it! 'But where's she getting them?' Kate felt hysteria

353

rising in her. Not that path again. Dominique bowed his head in commiseration, as mutes do at funerals.

'And what were you doing? Why didn't you stop her?'

'Obviously, Steve, you know nothing about addicts. There was nothing I could do. I've felt so helpless. Believe me, Kate, this has torn me apart. I love her so much.'

Kate looked long and hard at him and found she didn't believe him. There was something odd going on here that she didn't understand.

'Perhaps if you'd worked, run the pizza business as you planned, it would have given her an interest. A sense of pride in achieving something.' Kate had her arm round her daughter, whose shaking now was almost uncontrollable.

'But Lucy didn't want to. I tried. I really tried.'

Sensing someone behind her Kate turned around to see that Caroline had joined them. 'I know you,' she said, pointing at Dominique. 'You're a friend of Mo's.'

'Mo? I don't know anyone of that name.' Dominique looked innocent. 'Oh, yes, I remember. I met her at the Bollands' party. You must have seen me with her there.'

'I wasn't there to see you. You were one of those who hung around Mo in London. You were part of that scene.'

'What scene?'

'You know damn well what I mean.'

'Am I to take it that you were involved too?'

'Me? Never. I've too much respect for myself. I've learnt a lot recently – since I got inadvertently involved with the people looking for Mo, the big boys who never get their hands dirty and use little people like Mo to distribute the drugs. And she in turn uses others to sell them on. People like you, people who never touch the stuff themselves but enjoy playing God with those who do.'

'For someone who claims to be clean you know a lot.'

'I made it my business to find out. I learnt about your sort. It's a power thing, isn't it? Sick!'

'I repeat, I don't know you and I have no idea what you're talking about.'

'But *I* know *you*. You came to her flat on several occasions when I was there. She was always a bit odd with callers like you, taking you into another room, saying you were placing bets for her on the horses and she didn't want Tristram to know. Only you weren't, were you? You were buying drugs from her to sell on . . . Or to make people dependent on you . . .'

Kate could listen to no more. She let go of Lucy, who slumped to the ground. With a scream of pain she leapt at Dominique and slapped him sharply across his face. 'You loathsome scum. You gave them to my daughter!' she cried, her voice full of anguish. And then she began to pummel him, the red mist blanking out everything as she hit and hit him wanting him dead.

'Mum. Don't.' She heard Steve's voice vaguely, and fought him, too, as he tried to pull her away. Finally, with Caroline's help, he succeeded.

Dominique straightened his T-shirt, which she had yanked to one side, patted his hair back into place and bent to pick up his precious cigarette lighter from the flagstones where it had fallen. 'She looks to me as if she could do with a fix.' He pointed at Lucy, curled up in the foetus position, moaning quietly. 'Shall I do the honours?'

With a strength she didn't know she possessed, Kate wrenched herself free of her son, rushed at Dominique and sent him flying backwards into the swimming-pool.

'That'll have ruined his cigs,' she said, brushing her hands together as if removing any speck of him that might have adhered to her.

*

Steve and Caroline were both towers of strength. Without them Kate knew she could not have coped. The nightmare had begun for Lucy and for them. And none of them knew what best to do.

They held her and comforted her but her distress, as the need for her drugs flooded her brain, was hard to deal with. She had become a stranger, a wild creature whose body, whose whole being and energy, was concentrated on one thing – the one thing they could not and would not give her. They could see her agony, listen to her cries of pain yet not comprehend what it was like for her, what it was doing to her.

'Mum. Help me!' she cried out, time after time. And all Kate could do was hold her and try to comfort her. But each time her daughter cried out to her, her inadequacy crucified her.

'Should we call a doctor?' Steve asked, his anxiety at the state of his sister making him look suddenly years older.

'I've thought of that but I don't know the consequences. Perhaps under the law here we would have to tell the authorities. I thought of Netta but it's not fair to embroil her either.'

'A friend of mine's mother called the police. They were very understanding. It's called tough love.'

'Yes, Caroline, perhaps they were, but that was at home and we don't know the attitude here. What if they locked her up? My Lucy in prison!'

'Another thing, Caroline, what if Mum was arrested for having drugs on the premises? We just don't know.'

It seemed there was no one she could ask for help. She wished Stewart was here. But she had no guarantee that he would be sympathetic to the situation. It made her long for the one thing that nothing else had in her time in France: to be back in England. She and Lucy would be safe there. It would be so simple to get hold of advice. To find help for Lucy. She knew her doctor, he'd delivered Lucy, he would have been as anguished as she.

But here? There had been odd disadvantages to living here but this was the worst, the insurmountable one. She was a foreigner in a foreign land, and her ignorance of that country blared at her from every solution she could come up with. This was the outcome of being an exile.

'Tony? It's Kate. We've a problem . . .'

Five minutes later she put down the phone and found that she, too, was shaking. How could the man allow his loathing of her to get in the way of his love for his child?

'So-called love,' was Steve's opinion when she told him of how his father had reacted.

'He just didn't want to know. Told me it was my problem.'

'Wouldn't go down well at the golf-club, would it? A drug-addict daughter doesn't fit the image of a pillar of society.'

'You think so, Steve?'

'I know so, Mum.'

'But why does he always blame me? If Lucy was damaged by us we should both take the responsibility.'

'I don't see why either of you is to blame. I had the same upbringing and I'm all right – well, sort of.' He grinned and Kate tried to respond, but nothing was funny at the moment.

'Do you know what Netta says about people who blame others? She says it's because they lack the courage to look at themselves and see their own faults,' Caroline said. 'She said she always blamed her husbands for her broken marriages until one day she took a close look at herself – she said it was the hardest thing she had ever done.'

'Dear Netta. I wish she was here.'

'Let me call her?'

'No, Caroline, it wouldn't be fair.'

They were very English in this crisis for the teapot never seemed to be empty. 'At least I haven't rushed to the gin,' Kate said, as she took the mug of tea Caroline offered her. Stewart would have been legless by now, she told herself.

'Is Steve all right with her? They were taking it in turns to be with Lucy. Initially Kate had wanted to stay with her all the time but she had finally accepted that a shift system would be necessary, since all of them needed breaks and sleep.

'He's fine. He loves her very much, doesn't he?'

'They've always fought but I hoped they did love each other and now we're seeing that they do.' She sipped her tea, her feet up on the sofa, feeling a dreadful weariness not just of her body but of her soul.

'He's gone.' Caroline turned from the window. 'He's taken the van.'

'I don't care about that, especially if it takes him as far away from us as possible. Though how Lucy will react when she comes out of this I shudder to think.'

'Did she love him?'

'Yes, Caroline, I think she did. Poor Lucy.'

'Let me get you a duvet, try and rest.'

She doubted she would sleep because she needed to keep alert for Lucy. It was a warm evening, yet she needed the cover. She felt icy cold.

'Netta! Hello,' she said, her voice thick with sleep. It was dark outside. One table lamp was on in her large sitting room. The windows were open and she could hear the familiar sounds of the crickets starting up their night-time opera. She sat up with a start as reality flooded in. 'What are you doing here?'

'The children called me.'

'I told them they shouldn't. I told them I didn't want you bothered.'

'Kate, how could you? I thought I was your friend!'

'Netta, I'm at my wit's end. I don't know what to do.'

'It's all right. We're arranging everything.'

'We?'

'Peter's here. He's arranging a plane to get Lucy back to England.'

'But I can't afford that!'

'It's a friend of his, owes him a favour and he's calling it in. He's been on the blower for ages. He's booked her into a clinic there. Isn't he just marvellous?' Her eyes shone and through her own despair Kate saw her expression, and knew for sure why she thought Netta looked so different.

'Oh, Netta. I'm so happy for you.' She took Netta's hand.

'You don't mind? I always had this idea that we might be rivals for him.'

'No.' Kate managed to laugh. 'I find him very attractive and I suppose I might have, well, had the odd thought or two . . . or three! But I think it was more that I was unhappy and . . .'

'Needed the comfort of a dream.'

'Yes, that's it exactly.'

She put up her arms and Netta sank on to the sofa beside her and they hugged each other tight.

'Will you marry him?'

'Doll, give me a chance. It's early days.'

'You'd be much more suitable.'

'I'm nearly ten years older.'

'So what? It doesn't matter these days, and you look fab.'

'I don't know. I'm such a failure at marriage.'

'Join the club! But I think you will.'

'It would be nice. But he'd have to sell that house.'

'It's a lovely one.'

'I agree. But Wendy lived there. I want her expunged from his life.'

'Ha, then you are in love.' Kate laughed because for one minute, from Netta's expression, she realised that she'd made her cool, sophisticated friend blush.

'Caroline tells me that, most commendably, you've been quaffing gallons of tea. Does it have to go on like that? Or could we perhaps have a teeny-weeny little drink of something?' Netta recovered herself quickly.

'Anything, Netta. Anything for you.'

8

Tristram looked out of the aeroplane window at the chequered pattern of France below, a sight that would normally have fascinated him. Today he looked but didn't see. His mind was far away, back in England. He felt depressed. Deeply so. It wasn't every day that he distanced himself from his family to the point where he knew that he would be ostracised for life. And for what?

He had been prepared for his father to disown him but not his mother too. That had come as a big shock. He should have been happy on this flight, with everything sorted out, not feeling suicidal.

When he had arrived at his family home he had felt sick with nerves. His mother was pleased to see him, that was obvious, but it was not the effusive welcome he had expected. He had felt a distance that had never been there before. His father was not yet back from his constituency office, which was a relief: it gave him time to be alone with his mother. Tristram and Plantagenet Hargreaves, MP, had never got on. He had sat in the kitchen, his chair pushed up tight to the Aga – it was a cold English summer day and he was now used to higher temperatures than this.

While his mother made him tea and cut him a slice of cake – oh the comforts of home! – they chatted about France, about Max, about the smallholding and how he was doing. About everything except Mo.

'She's been in an accident.'

'Who has?'

'Oh, Ma, you know damn well who. Mo.'

'Really?' His pretty mother busied herself with folding a tea-towel that looked perfectly neat to Tristram.

'She's paralysed.'

'How unfortunate.'

It puzzled and shocked him that someone as sweet as his mother normally was could be so cold about Mo, especially at that news.

'No chance of you changing your mind about her?'

'None whatsoever. I didn't like her the first time I met her and it would be hypocritical of me to change simply because she's hurt.' Abruptly she changed the subject. 'We'll have roast beef for dinner – I bet you don't get that in France.'

'Why did you never say you didn't like her?'

'It wasn't my business. And would you have listened?'

'Probably not.' He fiddled with the label on a jar of mustard. 'I've seen Caroline. She's visiting her godmother.'

'Netta Rawlinson? She was already a legend when I was a deb.'

'I didn't know you knew her.'

'She's just an acquaintance. I do hope you don't intend to try to get Caroline back.'

'I thought you'd want me to.'

'You've hurt her badly once. I'd prefer you not to do it again.'

At that point he'd gone into the garden. He and his mother had always been so easy with each other, but that was before Mo came into his life. Now, it would appear, a barrier was firmly in place between them. He'd hoped that, given time, she'd forgive him for Mo.

'You're back,' his father said, somewhat unnecessarily, when he returned from his office. 'What do you want this time?'

'We can talk now or after dinner, it's all the same to me.' He tried to sound as nonchalant as he could, while his stomach was churning and his heart was racing.

His father had been generous with the pre-dinner whisky he poured his son when they were alone in his study. 'So?'

'I'll ask you one more time, Dad. Will you lend me £30,000 against my inheritance from Gran?'

'And what if your grandmother changes her mind and leaves you nothing?'

'I explained on the phone. I'm prepared to come back to London and work and pay you back. Either way you can't lose.'

'You reckon?' His father laughed. 'I'll answer you one more time. No.'

'Dad, please.'

'You won't even tell me what the money is for. So why should I help?'

'I told you it was a confidential and personal matter. I need to help out a friend, that's all I'm prepared to say.'

'Mo? Honestly, Tristram! You're a fool. If you get involved with a scrubber like that you must take the consequences. Mind you, given that poncy actor father of hers! It always amazed me he could conceive a child, batting the wrong way as he does.'

'He isn't her father, she's adopted.'

'Really? Now that is interesting.' He busied himself

pouring them further drinks. No doubt he was filing away this snippet of information, as he did most things – just in case they came in handy one day.

'So you won't help?'

'No.'

His father's back was to him as Tristram unzipped his document case and produced one of Mo's little red books. 'Is this why you hate her so much?' He had flipped open the pages and stabbed at one name – Plantagenet Hargreaves. 'If that got out it wouldn't do your political career much good, now, would it?'

His father snatched the book. 'What the hell?'

'Mo isn't stupid. That's the list of some of her customers. I have others. Tape-recordings, photographs too. So there's no point in you denying it.'

'Are you blackmailing me? Your own father? You little creep! You bastard,' his father shouted, as he lunged at him. Tristram sidestepped him. He hated what he was doing and loathed himself for doing it, and to compound it by hitting his father would be unthinkable.

What happened next happened so quickly that he was still reeling from it. His mother had appeared. Somehow, he hadn't quite worked out how, he'd been branded an evil, unnatural son, an ingrate, yet his father emerged whiter than white. And Tristram never got a word in edgeways. But what could he have said? He'd never intended to ditch his father to his mother – he wanted to protect her. But in so doing he found himself ordered out of the house, told he was never to return, and no roast beef.

'You are not my son!' his mother had declared, and that had hurt the most. But in a way it had made it possible for him to go without more fuss.

Now he sat on the plane, his relationship with his parents disintegrated for all time. No doubt his father would have told Tristram's sister by now and she wouldn't want to know him either.

He'd never liked his father, and now he found he loathed him for the hypocrite he was.

The one good thing to come out of the whole fiasco was that the cheque his father had slipped into his pocket on the driveway, unseen by his wife, had been banked, the cash removed and the dealers paid off. That had been a scary scene, and he never wanted to do anything like that ever again. The hairs on the back of his neck had bristled, and he'd expected the crack of a pistol shot at any moment – but it was done. Once and for all.

When he entered the hospital room Mo burst into tears, and when he told her it was all over, she cried long and hard. He laughed as he held her close. 'There, there, Mo, it's over. We're free. No more worries and fears.'

'But how?'

'I borrowed the money.'

'Who from?'

'My secret.'

'How much?'

'I paid them off, I just told you.'

'So we can still do the book deal. Brilliant.'

'No, we can't.'

'Don't be silly, of course we can. Stewart thought we'd lost the books in the crash and his relief when I told him you had them was quite funny. I think that crap about not working with me because of Kate was a smokescreen – he'd lost the chance of any loot with Wendy, and he was pretty confident that Kate would have him back. I'd have shared fifty–fifty with him but he's so obviously desperate for money that he'll take less I'm sure—'

'I burnt them,' he interrupted.

'You what?' She looked at him in disbelief. 'Don't tell me!' she shrieked. 'You fool! You bloody cretin!' She was beating him. He leaped off the bed but she, trapped in it, was reduced to lambasting the coverlet.

He waited for the storm to calm. He sat there, the invective she hurled at him making him wince as if the words were stones. And then she began to cry again, sobbing loudly, pitifully. He sat in silence waiting, biding his time. This was the Mo he knew. He'd been stupid to think she had changed, that a life with her, if only for a short time, was a possibility. No one could be expected to put up with the abuse she hurled at him. Finally there was silence, just the occasional sob from Mo.

'Finished? We couldn't have kept them, Mo. It was wrong. It was a filthy idea you had. This way you've come out relatively clean.'

'It would have given me a decent life. What right had you? They were mine, not yours.'

'But the people. My father . . .'

Mo laughed at this. 'That was such a joke for me, knowing that when you didn't.'

'But Kate's daughter and son-in-law. Would you have wanted to destroy them? What has Kate ever done to you?'

'I didn't know it was her bloody daughter, did I? I thought Lucy was just a fool. Anyone involved with a slimeball like that gets what they deserve. How was I to know her mother was well known? I only learnt that here. Don't you see?'

'Mo, I've paid off the heavies. I've been to see your parents.'

'You what?'

'They had every right to know.'

'That's my decision, not yours.'

'I said I would stick by you and I meant it, but now . . .

After that little scene, I don't think you and I stand a hope in hell. Your parents are prepared to have you back and look after you, so I'll take you home, but after that, Mo, I'm sorry but I've had enough. I'm tired. I can't deal with you any more.'

'Going to creep to that milksop Caroline, are you? Shit, Tristram, you're so predictable. She's welcome to you!' She was shouting again. He stood up and made wearily for the door. As he walked down the corridor he could hear her screaming, shouting his name.

9

Peter Bolland was at Netta's.

'I'm sorry to butt in,' Tristram apologised.

'Not at all. Would you care to join us?' Netta asked, in a distant sort of voice, which made him aware that that was the last thing she wanted him to do.

'No thanks, I've had lunch,' he lied. 'You won't like it, Netta but I'm looking for Caroline. I looked her up in London but her flatmate said she was back here.'

'She's at Kate Howard's,' Netta answered, to his surprise. He tried to leave politely but his need to see Caroline overtook all niceties. He raced down the stairs, almost whooping with joy.

'Why did he say you wouldn't like him looking for Caroline?' Peter looked up from the plate of quail's eggs in aspic with salad that she had prepared for them.

'Because he isn't suitable.'

'That was your judgement, not Caroline's?'

'Too right. Caroline is sweet but, sadly, can also be very thick where men are concerned.'

'But you don't mind him going now?'

'No, she's in love with Steve. She's safe.'

'Poor Tristram. He seemed nice enough to me, if in a bit of a hurry.'

'He is. But he was unfaithful. A serious flaw.'

'You believe in fidelity?'

'Totally.'

'Were your husbands faithful to you?'

'I told them I'd cut their balls off if they strayed.'

'So they were?' He laughed.

'One wasn't. And, no, I didn't take the kitchen knife to him, but I think by the time it had happened I'd fallen out of love with him so it didn't matter so much. I should never have married him. We were a disaster waiting to happen.'

'It's still a mystery to me why I married Wendy.'

'She must have been a pretty woman.' She purposely didn't say beautiful since she had always felt that pretty was never good enough.

'She was, and she was fun at first. I don't know what happened. But I didn't mind Wendy playing the field. Was that wrong of me?'

'It merely shows you didn't care.'

'But you think that one act of adultery is enough to terminate a relationship?'

'I do. I've never been unfaithful to any man in my life – I always told him first.'

'You're priceless.' He laughed loudly. 'Why didn't I meet you years ago?'

'I wish you had.' Netta looked suddenly serious.

'Netta, when this mess with Wendy is over, will you marry me?'

'I'd rather the "mess", as you describe it, was over before we discuss it.'

'So you're saying no?'

'I'm saying maybe.' She smiled at him, that wonderful

smile that had made so many hearts race. She helped him to another spoonful of salad. Netta was far too canny to say yes at the first time of asking.

In his haste to get to Kate's, Tristram had acquired a speeding ticket, and was literally hopping from one foot to the other as he waited for someone to come to the gate, which was locked.

'Sorry, I have to lock it because of the puppies,' Kate explained. She was accompanied by a hysterically happy Max who threw himself at Tristram the minute the gate was open.

'Puppies?'

'I got so attached to Max in the week you were away that I dreaded him going. So I took your advice and decided to get a dog – only I ended up with two.'

'Oh, my God, they're wonderful.' He bent down as two tiny dogs, with wide-spaced eyes in square-shaped faces, staggered towards him, their fat tummies slowing their progress, one falling over in her haste to reach him. 'What are they?' He laughed as they jumped up at him, trying to lick any exposed area of his skin.

'Bulldogs. Gertie and Gussie. As I said, I only meant to get one but when I got to the breeder's and saw them I had to have them both. They've kept me occupied – you know, with . . . Thank you, Tristram, for helping me out, letting Steve know the muddle I was in.'

'I was afraid you might be cross.'

'I was at first but eventually I was glad.'

'Is Lucy here?'

'No. She's in England, at a clinic. Peter Bolland sorted it all out for me. He was a brick. I wanted to go with her but I was advised not to be there, not until they say. It's hard but she's in good hands. I suppose the last thing they need is an

368

anxious mother hovering about. We're down by the pool. Fancy some lunch?'

'No, thanks.'

'Then join us for a glass of wine. You go down, I'll get you a glass.'

Tristram's heart was in his mouth as he approached the pergola where Caroline was sitting. To his disappointment he saw Steve too. 'Hi. Back again?' he said, and immediately regretted it since it sounded like a criticism. But he couldn't think of anything else to say to change it.

'Yes. Mum can't get rid of me.' Steve grinned good-naturedly. 'I took the weekend off. I've been rushing about like a demented bat these last few weeks.'

'Setting up the business? How's it going?'

'Fine. I've got premises lined up.'

'In Paris?'

'No, in Le Puy. Peter advised that we start up in a smaller city.'

'He'll be all over the place with his landscaping, though, won't you, Steve?' Tristram didn't like the proud look Caroline gave Steve as she said this.

'I should think that will take time. Thank you,' he said to Kate, as she appeared with a glass.

'Are you sure you don't want any food? There's plenty.'

'No thanks, really.' He hadn't felt hungry before, and he felt even less so at finding Steve here.

A swallow swooped down and skimmed over the water of the pool. The talk stopped as they admired it.

'They'll be gone soon. Their leaving always makes me sad.' Kate poured the wine.

'When do they come back? April?'

'Yes. They herald summer and then winter.'

'Don't you like the winters here, Kate?' Caroline asked.

'I love them. The snows come and sometimes I can't get

369

down the hill for a week. The world is silent and so beautiful and there's a serenity here that I've never found anywhere else. Which season it is doesn't matter. I love them all.'

'That's a sign of a contented person.'

'Do you think so, Caroline? You know, I think I am.' Of course she was. At that moment she knew she was all right, that she was going to survive.

Tristram coughed and they all looked at him. 'I wondered if I might have a word with you, Caroline? If you don't mind.' He looked at Kate, he couldn't bring himself to look at Steve.

Kate stood up.

'No, no, Kate, you stay put. What do you want, Tristram?' Caroline pushed her chair back.

'It's a bit difficult.'

'Come into the orchard – if you'll excuse us.' She smiled at the other two.

Kate and Steve watched the two of them walk past the pool and into the orchard.

'Mum!'

'Don't worry, Steve.'

'He's come to try and get her back.'

'Yes, I think he might have.'

'What do I do?'

'There's nothing you can do, darling. She'll either send him packing or not.'

'I couldn't bear that. I love her.'

'I know you do, Steve, and I think she feels the same way about you. But if I'm wrong, better to find out now rather than later.'

'Mum, I hate it when you're being logical.' Steve managed to grin. 'What are they doing? I can't look.'

Across the orchard, Caroline and Tristram had sat down on an old wooden bench. 'You know why I'm here, Caroline?'

'Yes,' she said calmly. 'And I wish you weren't. There's no point.'

'But I love you.'

'Yes, I think you do, but not enough, you see.'

'Because of Mo?'

'I don't know if there were any others. But it would be irrelevant.'

'There weren't any. I promise. And I've finished with Mo.'

'At this time?'

'She doesn't need me. I've made arrangements. I've paid off her debts. We don't get on. Not as you and I did. We were so good together.' He knew he was saying this all wrong, that it wasn't coming out as he had planned it. Where had those words gone, that fine speech he'd honed?

'You hurt me dreadfully.'

'I'd never hurt you again.'

'But I got over it, you see. So I couldn't have loved you as much as I thought I did. Otherwise I'd still be hurting, wouldn't I? I can look at you and love you as a friend, but that's all.'

'Steve?'

'Yes.'

'But he's so young.'

'So am I! And we really do love each other.'

'Is there any point in arguing?'

'No.' She leant over and kissed his cheek.

Back under the pergola, Steve groaned. 'Did you see that, Mum?'

'It was only his cheek.'

'Shit, they're coming over.'

They both watched them approach.

'Thank you for the wine, Kate.' Tristram's voice sounded strained. 'Good luck with the business, Steve.'

'Why, thanks . . .'

'I'll see you to the gate.' Caroline went with him up the steps.

'Mum, I don't think she's going with him.'

'So I see.' Kate was grinning.

'What do you think he'll do now?'

'Go back to Mo. He's the sort that will be useless on his own.'

They watched Caroline, such a lovely creature, thought Kate. When she returned she sat down beside Steve and took his hand. The expression of sheer joy on his face made Kate want to cry out. There was no point in Kate excusing herself to them, they were oblivious to her presence.

It was not a peaceful afternoon. From the village green, called the Grande Place, which always made Kate smile, came the noise of banging, shouting and the testing of the sound system as her neighbours erected the dance floor for the annual Bread Festival. Kate had paid for her ticket but she had decided not to go: better to leave that to the young.

When a book was finished there was always the most amazing amount of wastepaper and general debris to get rid of. She was collecting her papers together, sorting which were rubbish, which to keep, when she sensed someone in the room. She swung round. Her stomach lurched as she saw Stewart standing in her workroom.

'They let me out.' He was grinning. The puppies woke up, and slithered and slipped over to investigate. 'What have we here?'

'Company,' she said shortly.

'Lucy still here?'

'No. She's in England.'

'Steve?'

'In the garden.' At least he wouldn't try to hit her this time with Steve here.

'Have you forgiven me?'

'No.'

'Are you going to?'

'No.'

'Oh, Kate, come on. What do you want me to say or do? I love you, Kate.' He was smiling at her as if he hadn't a care in the world. She could look at him quite dispassionately and see that he was oozing confidence. Evidently he thought it was only a matter of time before he was back here and with her.

'Stewart, there's no point in going over all that again. I don't want to know. Don't you understand?'

'But how will you manage without me? You need a man in your life.'

'I'll be fine.'

'There's someone else? Peter? I'd heard he'd been sniffing around.'

'There's no one. Why do you have to think that? Are you so conceited that you can't grasp that I would prefer to be on my own than with you?'

'You could never live on your own.'

'I haven't done so badly these past weeks. I didn't think I could – I thought I needed someone. But I find I'm enjoying it. It's the first time for me, really. There's always been family around.' She said this in a pleasant conversational tone. No bitterness, no anger.

'But your accounts?'

'I have an accountant. I'll rely on him.'

'I never stole from you, Kate, although the kids think I did.'

'I know. But I didn't think that.'

'Then this is it?' She was surprised he didn't argue further, bluster and bully. He must have seen that she meant what she had said.

'Yes, Stewart. Thanks for the good days – there's nothing else to say.'

Kate went to the Bread Festival after all. She sat under an awning at one of the trestle tables, Gertie and Gussie on leads at her feet. She was surrounded on all sides by her neighbours, who fussed over her, filling her glass, making sure she had enough to eat. She watched the dancers, fascinated by the way they moved, round and round, as if on wheels. A couple, slim as reeds, unlike Kate's more portly well-upholstered companions, took to the dance floor. They swooped and pivoted across the floor, the others standing back to give them room. At times the man bent the woman backwards to the floor like an arched bow. They held their heads high, superiority leaching out of them, as they danced what seemed to be a *paso doble*. '*Maison secondaire*,' a woman, sitting beside Kate confided disparagingly. It lifted her heart: obviously she was regarded almost as one of them, not a second-home owner. She would always be the English woman on the hill, but she was accepted.

The accordionist played with a passion, caressing the instrument as if it were his lover. Everyone but Kate joined in the songs, jigged to the beat, applauded enthusiastically.

Children were playing under the tables, dancing in their own way, in their own little worlds. Everyone watched and guarded them. Lovers disappeared into the shadows, women gossiped, men argued amiably. The wine and pastis flowed. The night was warm, the air pungent from the

374

smell of the bread baking in the recently restored bread oven.

Kate watched them. What kind and considerate people these were. How wise was their way of life. How much the people at home had lost. She'd been so afraid of being alone and now it had happened she had no fear. And she wasn't alone. She belonged in this community now. Tomorrow she would unpack her language course, and this winter she would learn French out of respect to her new friends. She owed it to them. This was where she would stay.

The next morning, Kate overslept, and it was the dogs, hungry for their breakfast, who woke her. 'Hang on, hang on,' she said to the fussing puppies, as she climbed out of bed. Her head wasn't too good, she thought as she crossed the room and briskly opened the shutters. The late summer sun streamed in.

It was then she realised what she had done. She had pushed the shutters open without hesitating. She leant on the windowsill and looked at the view. She felt contented. All those unnamed amorphous fears had gone.

She resented the telephone ringing, interrupting the peacefulness.

'Kate? Am I calling too early? It's Portia.'

'Good morning.' She looked at her watch, surprised that Portia should be calling. She wasn't normally in the office until ten and yet it was only eight English time.

'I know it's the crack of dawn but I simply couldn't wait another moment to tell you, I love *Jokers Wild*. Love it!' She laughed as she emphasised the words. 'It's so pacy, so real, so true. I think you've created a genre of your own.' Her excitement was bubbling in her voice. 'There's some-thing about the writing – it's . . . Well, I never said before since I didn't want to upset you, but your writing had become a little inhibited. You seemed to have mislaid some of the easiness, the fluidity – how shall I put it? The freedom of your writing – yes, that's it . . . It's as if you've been liberated . . .'

Kate was in a daze of happiness when they finally stopped talking. She went back to the window and gazed at the view. Of the six books she had written, Stewart had been involved with four. The first and the last she had written without consultation with anyone. She was better alone, without the opinions of others blocking her.

The fears had gone, a weight of constraint had been lifted. She was free to be herself. Free to write as she wanted.

available from
THE ORION PUBLISHING GROUP

All Orion/Phoenix titles are available at your local bookshop or from the following address:

Mail Order Department
Littlehampton Book Services
FREEPOST BR535
Worthing, West Sussex, BN13 3BR
telephone 01903 828503, *facsimile* 01903 828802
e-mail MailOrders@lbsltd.co.uk
(Please ensure that you include full postal address details)

Payment can be made either by credit/debit card (Visa, Mastercard, Access and Switch accepted) or by sending a £ Sterling cheque or postal order made payable to *Littlehampton Book Services*.
DO NOT SEND CASH OR CURRENCY

Please add the following to cover postage and packing

UK and BFPO:
£1.50 for the first book, and 50p for each additional book to a maximum of £3.50

Overseas and Eire:
£2.50 for the first book plus £1.00 for the second book and 50p for each additional book ordered

---

BLOCK CAPITALS PLEASE

name of cardholder ....   *delivery address*
....   *(if different from cardholder)*
address of cardholder ....
....
....
....
postcode ....   *postcode* ....

☐ I enclose my remittance for £ ....

☐ please debit my Mastercard/Visa/Access/Switch (delete as appropriate)

card number ☐☐☐☐ ☐☐☐☐ ☐☐☐☐ ☐☐☐☐

expiry date ☐☐☐☐   Switch issue no. ☐☐

signature ....

prices and availability are subject to change without notice